PAUL JOHN ADAMS

To Fail with Flying Colors

OPTIONAL BOOKS

To Fail with Flying Colors

INTRODUCTION, BY DR. EUGENE BLOOD-WORTH

The psychiatric profession is quite different from what it once was. The typical goal of treatment today is very modest: managing, maintaining, medicating. Gone are the days when patients viewed certain psychiatrists as charismatic sages with deep insight who could pull off a miracle cure through a combination of talk-therapy and innovative technique. The death of the medicine-man image, with its good and bad associations, can largely be attributed to the fall from grace of Dr. Percival Shieling upon the closure of his institute just over twenty years ago.

Though he has long been out of the public eye, since the release of a new sensationalist film about his institute, there has been an explosion of interest in Dr. Shieling. He has been called, by various voices, "revolutionary," "egotistical," "innovative," and even "criminal." Dr. Karl Dorsey, the American Psychiatric Association president, has tried to distance his organization from Shieling, stating, "... his theories, his method, his research... should be regarded as aberrations not representative of mainstream practice."

Now the history of our profession is undergoing renewed scrutiny. The layperson would remain mostly ignorant of the changes in psychiatric practice—and the causes for these changes—if it were not for the curiosity that the film *Madman, Madhouse* has inspired. This film was produced without Shieling's participation or approval; no attempt was made to interview him during its development. Those of us who knew him most intimately were not consulted. The film is thus inaccurate and perhaps intentionally deceptive, but it has prompted many questions.

Some questions have had a hostile tone such as, "Was he really a doctor?" "Why did people trust him?" "Did he even understand psychiatric theory or medicine?" Surprisingly, the other side has started to speak up: "Was Shieling entirely mistaken in his approach, or was he merely misunderstood?" This question has lingered in my mind for a long time, though I never dared to vocalize it. But the underlying question has continued to be, "What is the true story of Dr. Shieling and his Institute?" It is in answer to this question that *To Fail With Flying Colors* will now be presented.

Because I was a fellow at the Shieling Institute, the editors at H.J. and Sons asked me to track the doctor down and see whether he would like to give his own perspective. But when I went to see him, he surprised me at once by handing me an already completed manuscript. He told me he had shopped this book around, and it had been categorically rejected, time and again, until all publishers had forgotten its—and his—existence. When I read the contents of the book, I was startled. Though the time may not have been right for this book to be published seventeen years ago, it is certainly right now.

This book does not describe Shieling's more successful treatments. Those cases are detailed instead in earlier, out-of-print publications, which can sometimes be seen passing from hand to hand between students at university—students who treat his books almost like a contraband substance. But I believe the reader will be pleased to find—even within this more cynical text—how generous, warm, and sympathetic the doctor was, and to understand the nurturing relationship he had with patients—a relationship which often achieved results that are unthinkable in the current sterile environment of our psychiatric hospitals.

I requested that the author write an up-to-date preface, but he has declined. Instead, he told me to present his book with its original, unedited preface. "This is the only way to tell the true story," he said. "I can no longer attempt to spin or justify my life and career. Let it be seen for what it truly was."

Thus I thank the publishers for accommodating the author's request and including the original preface in this edition. Please welcome the doctor into your heart, and you will discover much of man's inherent beauty in the stories of his most notable patients.

AUTHOR'S PREFACE

On September 14, 2026, while newspapers across America were reporting the death of Leland Holbrook, the *New York Post* published a two-word banner-headline across the front page, reading "Not Cured." This headline succinctly summed up the public sentiment regarding Mr. Holbrook's death; the headline was picked up and echoed by other papers and news outlets across the country, and it signaled a major turn in my career. It ruined my public image and destroyed my reputation within the field of psychiatric medicine.

My name is Dr. Percival Shieling, and I thank the reader for his indulgence. I was recently a prominent figure in American psychiatry, mainly due to my treatment of Mr. Holbrook. Before his death I received a great deal of positive attention from the press. I made several appearances on television talk shows, viewed by millions. To me, the attention was not an end in itself, but served a valuable purpose as publicity, as it helped me raise an enormous amount of money for psychological research. A point which may have escaped the awareness of most is that the publicity was a crucial aspect of Leland's treatment, as his psychosis did not allow him to believe anything was real unless it happened on television. Yet, the events of the world are much bigger than me and even my most notorious patients. Today's news is tomorrow's fish wrap, and the world is well on its way to forgetting all about me. So, for those readers who may be unfamiliar with my work and its social impact, I will briefly supply a few details.

The media's interest was mainly due to my successful cure of Leland, a psychotic. He was a very wealthy man who, after I cured him, contributed a large sum to fund a research center which I headed. He donated $240 million. This money constituted about a third of his inherited wealth, his share of a family empire.

Before I met Leland, the word "cure" had almost vanished from the world of psychiatry. The notion that a severely psychotic patient could even be effectively treated (let alone cured) without the use of drugs was considered dubious. The rather unorthodox way that I concluded Leland's treatment inspired a great deal of controversy and skepticism. Nevertheless, as soon as his cure was effected, the public poured additional funds, through charitable contributions, into my research.

The "unorthodox" cure I refer to was broadcast on September 18th, 2017, on the Chasey Williams show. On this program, I served Mr. Holbrook a large bowl of chicken noodle soup prepared according to a popular recipe that was circulating on the Internet, but with three times the normal amount of salt. After he had consumed the soup, he was entirely and permanently cured of his mental illness. I was well aware that some people would regard this as a kind of carnival act or medicine show, and many of my professional colleagues would scoff. Yet, the fact was quite apparent that Mr. Holbrook went from a state of total mental incapacity, which had crippled him for his entire adult life, to being a fully functional human being with obvious intelligence, charm, and wit.

The Shieling Institute of Psychiatric Research was thus born, and our new hospital was constructed on its campus in Kansas City, Missouri. It seemed an opportunity had arisen to bring some help to patients previously considered incurable and untreatable. I brought together a team of some of the world's best and brightest clinical psychiatrists, and launched a program which combined treatment with further research into some of the most challenging cases in psychiatry.

Little attention was given by the public to my research itself. They were mainly interested in spectacle. Though I had performed an apparent miracle, I lapsed into obscurity for a few years, while Leland Holbrook rose to some degree of public prominence as a Liberal political activist. He also got some gossip column coverage for his involvement in the sometimes scandalous Los Angeles celebrity social scene. He drank a bit too much alcohol, and stirred up a little trouble at a couple of parties and film premiers, but when he was sober he devoted a lot of effort and attention to anti-war and anti-globalization efforts. Eventually he was married to Hollywood actress Melissa Reyes.

Then a sad and surprising turn of events brought an end to Leland's life and resulted in a great deal of negative publicity for me and my research center. Mr. Holbrook publicly assaulted his wife in a popular restaurant, beating her with his shoe. An hour and a half later he committed suicide by self-immolation. Specifically, he wrapped the upper half of his body tightly with many rolls of surgical gauze, soaked himself with gasoline, and lit himself on fire while sitting in the woods behind his house. The flames soon caught the attention of his neighbors, but none were able to save him.

Those who had labeled me "quack" and "charlatan" then seemed confirmed in their opinion. I was harshly and publicly condemned for having falsely claimed to have cured a man who was obviously very ill, a mortal danger to himself and society, an ultimate suicide. A series of law suits, along with the withdrawal of many patients from my program, resulted in the closure of the center. Many who had pledged support for my research suddenly cut off my funding, and I was advised not to attempt to legally force them to meet their obligations. My situation was regarded as untenable.

Now, there is little hope in trying to convince the public that one need not be psychotic to commit suicide. The fact that Leland never showed any sign of a relapse is regarded as irrelevant. I say it now, though it will certainly make no difference: Leland was cured. His suicide was not the result of psychosis. Neither was his alcohol abuse, nor even his occasional anti-social outbursts. The fact is, he simply had difficulty adjusting to the new life he found himself in. He had not yet learned the skills he needed to handle the power and independence which he received. He also, unfortunately, removed himself from any support network that could have helped him cope better. Regardless of how it all played out though, the news media's refrain has been properly summarized by the *Post's* "Not Cured." I have been branded a failure. This has, for now, brought my research to an end.

So, why has this book been written? Because my research was not fruitless. My personal career, leaping from obscurity, to fame, back to obscurity, and on to infamy, is actually an irrelevant footnote to the research which was conducted outside of the public eye, over a span of nine years. That is the subject to which I will devote the remainder of this book.

Here I will reveal to you the true stories of six of my most interesting patients. I will not conceal any names, and I will be quite open in discussing their treatment. I held a remarkable, privileged position in my research. Patients in my program, or those who served as their legal proxies, all willingly gave their consent to full disclosure of the details of their lives, their illnesses, our conversations, and their treatment.

It must be confessed, though, that several patients came to the program more out of necessity than choice. For some, enrollment in my program was the preferred alternative to jail time, abandonment by family, homeless wanderings, or continued futile imprisonment in a mental health facility. The personality disorder cases in particular found themselves in my program mostly through a lack of other options. In all of these cases, however, the need for help was real, and their participation in my research was immensely valuable.

Besides the intractable cases whom I mention here, there were many dozens more, many of whom were brought to successful improvement, sometimes a full cure. Some example cases can be found in my previous publications *Breaking the Surface* and *Rising From the Waves*. As a whole, our program was remarkably beneficial to patients. We achieved truly great results, which are a source of pride to me and my fellow doctors. Yet, as the program was specifically targeted towards the "incurables," this book gives attention principally to those most mysterious and frustrating cases which resisted even my best efforts and most advanced techniques.

That I was not ultimately able to cure the patients described in this book does not diminish the value of the program, and the personal stories revealed in this text should be very helpful in moving forward our understanding of the state of mental health, as a witness to the troubles that exist on the very fringe.

My principal impression, though, is that these most extreme cases, with all the variety of forms their mental illness takes, are united mainly by their audacity. The obstacle to their treatment lies in their unshakable commitment to their delusions, their obsessions, their characters, and their quirks. Success sometimes comes to daring people in our world, but those who leap willingly into the jaws of death, who steadfastly hold to a lifestyle that admits no compromise, are usually deemed spectacular failures in the judgment of the sane.

Olga Lukin

1.
Self-Sufficient

Olga Seeks Outpatient Treatment

Unlike most of the patients in my program, Olga Lukin was able to maintain a mostly stable and secure life. She was well integrated into society, and she was largely self-sufficient. As the wealthy founder and C.E.O. of her own company, "Lukin," Olga travelled frequently, and she could have enjoyed a lavish and luxurious lifestyle if not for her natural frugality. Her business talent was enviable, and she was notably intelligent—intelligence being a quality that several of my most troubled patients tended to share. When I met her, she exhibited a manageable degree of anxiety, accompanied by a few peculiar symptoms that were curious in their own way, but she didn't appear to require urgent care.

She lived in Glastonbury, Connecticut, near the headquarters of her company in Hartford, but she more-than-willingly flew the twelve-hundred miles to see me for two separate interviews, and she proposed that we meet on a weekly or biweekly basis thereafter. At the first of our interviews, she told me she was most troubled by a condition that she called "dry water," from which she claimed to be suffering greatly. She gave a few details:

First Meeting

"If you need me to take any prolonged time away from my work, I'm willing to do that," she said. "I have a deputy and a team of vice-presidents who will simply have to manage in my absence. I'm afraid that lately I've not been up to the job anyway, and I may soon have to retire from running my own company if I can't get relief.

"The problem that's just torturing me is that I can't taste or really even feel the water that I drink, and I'm constantly thirsty. I mean, I've been to psychiatrists, they've been treating my anxiety for years, but this is a new symptom and no one seems to take it seriously. They say it's manageable, but who other than me has to live with this on a daily… no, a *constant* basis?"

"That sounds really unpleasant," I said. "But you know, some of the medications you've been taking could have thirst as a side effect…"

"This is unrelated."

"And the truth is, you have your life pretty much well in order. There are people with so many afflictions—chronic physical pain for instance—which cause terrible psychological distress as well, but there are ways of managing such things…"

"I don't want to manage it, I want to get rid of it."

"That's exactly my philosophy, but in your particular case I'm not sure there's anything special I can do that another good psychiatrist couldn't do just as well. I mean, we haven't even gotten into your history and condition, but I have indigent patients; I have patients that every institution has given up on; I have patients who can't… do what you do. If you see what I mean."

"No one will help me. No one. It is impossible. Do you see what *I* mean?"

"I really do want to help you. I know you came here especially because you've heard of some of the successful treatments…, but some things can be a very involved process. I'm not saying you can't be treated or even cured. Just the opposite. I think it can be done without my help. You can afford the best doctors, and I'd like you to put me in contact with the doctor who has been treating you most recently… Dr. Glick."

"Didn't you speak to him on the phone?"

"Yes, but I want you to encourage him to speak with me again so he can share what he recommends. He struck me as a very good doctor with a professional attitude, so he would be the best judge of whether you need treatment in a program such as I offer."

"I'm through with him. You're not going to get a referral from him, because we're through. He's been very *nice*, he's helped me through some troubled times, and his pills are wonderful, but he does not hold out any hope that I will be cured any time in the near future. Not this year, not… could you imagine not drinking water for a year?"

"I understand that you drink a lot of water. Actually, Dr. Glick told me you have experienced some bouts of confusion because of overhydration, and your work performance is suffering."

"The experience of water is gone. My body may suffer from too much water, but my sanity is suffering from no water at all."

"And it seems your unsatisfied desire for water is a psychological manifestation of your stress over your mother's death."

"Yeah. There's no secret there. My mother drowned. So isn't it poetic that I'm now slowly drowning myself while feeling desperate for one taste of water?"

"You're not drowning. You're not dying. You're mildly overhydrated… a dangerous condition but again manageable because you *have been* managing it. You're not out of control here. You're distressed. Glick has suggested that conditions in your workplace may also be significant stress factors, so delegating more of your responsibility could be a good move for you now."

"But talking about my mother and the psychological root of my condition has done no good. Even my guru has told me that awareness is a cure.'Awareness and attention lead to the dissolution of every crisis.' But I know the root of my suffering, and nothing is dissolving here… except my brain and a few internal organs."

"That's a clear exaggeration. But… I didn't know you had a guru. Tell me about him."

"Yeah, I've been a regular practitioner of yoga ever since I was a university design student. But at first it was just a physical exercise. You know my company got started with yoga towels and mats."

"No, I didn't know that either."

"Well do your homework! Douglas Wright, my business mentor, was very insistent on the power of being well informed."

"So you've had a psychiatrist…"

"Several!"

"…and a mentor, and now you have a guru. And you're looking for help from me."

"Yeah, but our company… we do all sorts of stuff now, mainly related to pigments—imported from India—and pre-colored metal products. But it started with yoga mats. 'Color Harmony,' you know the slogan?"

"No."

"It was very successful, people liked the color arrangements, and we advertised with images of Indian women in traditional saris throwing powdered pigment as part of the Holi pigment festival. It was very attractive and attention-getting, but our company's image has always been one of *harmony*, which could also be expressed as *correctness*. Anyway, I got my seed money from the mini-fad that grew up around my yoga mats, and we even had an innovative campaign where we sold dyes, surveys, and instructions for customers to create and dye their own custom mats—we called them 'craft mats'—and towels based on a personality assessment that would determine their *personal harmony colors*. I felt it was… well, attractive and philosophically intriguing at same time that I can admit it was a little bit of hokum too. I mean, color harmony is about what is beautiful. There's no magic in it, but some people developed a kind of spiritual association with it and… well I still have and use my own custom mat that I made fourteen years ago."

"Okay. Well it's obvious you're passionate about ideas and get creative satisfaction from your job."

"And money, I get a lot of that too. But I'm really not a materialist. People don't understand that because I strive to accumulate, I'm building a mini-empire, nothing to be noticed by the big movers in the world, but something beyond what my family ever imagined possible. But I'm aiming every day to become detached. Because I went from a Hatha-yoga based exercise program, to my current sincere devotion to the teachings of Fanishwar Atlan. You've probably never heard of him either, though."

"Oh! I have! Wait. Maybe. He's famous, right?"

"In his way."

"Does he do lecture tours, I may have met him."

"No. He's not that type of popular guru. He's an enlightened being, and very detached. You probably have him confused with someone."

"Okay."

"So, are you going to help me?"

"I need to think about it. It comes down to exactly what I told you. Can I meaningfully help you, and can I offer the kind of help that you wouldn't easily get elsewhere?"

"And also, can you afford to take a break from the serious lunatics to help a spoiled and whiny eccentric millionaire?"

"I would never even think such a thing."

"Okay, but don't be prejudiced. You know, I've been misjudged and I've confronted more negative judgment since getting rich—by supposedly open-minded people—than I ever experienced when I was lower-middle class. Then people thought I was a weird and brainy half-Russian chick without an accent, whose best option would probably be to marry money. And they weren't very wrong about that. But now they think I'm a spoiled princess who somehow just got a free pass, an easy life, and I'm always leaning on someone, seeking vague answers somewhere, when the fact is I'm mentally tougher than I get credit for, I'm calculating, I'm self-made—and still there's that endless suffering, in here."

She struck her fist against her chest, over her heart. I saw a reflection of her intelligence in the fact that she correctly placed the heart in the center.

Second Meeting

Shortly after our first meeting, Olga sent in a check for $80,000 as a contribution to our center "with no strings attached." The message she followed up with told me, "I sincerely want to help your institute, and I respect that you must make a professional decision about whether or not to take me on as a patient. Whatever you decide is acceptable to me. However, I think you owe it to me to at least meet me one more time before making a decision." We scheduled her next visit, and she flew out to see me.

At this second meeting, she again attempted to elicit sympathy for her symptom of constant thirst.

"It started with dreams. I often dreamed that I was thirsty—when my body *was* thirsty—but in my dream I'd find water fountains, glasses of juice, all kinds of things to drink… but when I drank them, it was like drinking air. There was no way to be refreshed. I'd even resort to sucking on a wet frog, or a spot of glue that spilled on a countertop. When I awoke, I brushed off the dream and got a glass of water. Just before drinking, I'd sometimes feel a bit of panic in anticipation that I might discover I was still dreaming. But the water fulfilled me and then I could sleep peacefully.

"That's how it was until recently. But the terrible night finally arrived when I awoke, drank from a glass of water and… nothing! It's just like the nightmare has never ended."

"Do you believe that you're still in the dream world?"

"No, I can easily tell that I'm awake, except when I try to drink something… it's hopeless! Air! On my burning tongue, with my thirst constantly plaguing me. And Fanishwar has tried to persuade me that this is a good thing! That it might indicate a new awareness of *Self* that transcends this body and this place."

"What event in your life do you think precipitated this sudden change?"

"Nothing. I just had a normal day… a normal week even… before my new symptom arrived. I tried to carry on after, too; I have a lot of business concerns to deal with. We've been working on a deal to provide painted metal cladding for a hospital construction project in Gothenburg, Sweden."

"I thought you did yoga mats."

"No, that's just where we got started. Once we got involved in pigments, related to the mats, we wound up expanding into all kinds of pigment products. We sold paints for hobbyists, then colored metal components for skateboards—trucks and hubs—hobby karts, pre-painted and custom-molded steel and aluminum bodies for go-kart parks… now we've gotten into construction metals for roofing and wall cladding, all metals outsourced to the highest quality manufacturers in Indonesia, with pigments from three suppliers in India."

"Okay, I'm getting a better sense of the scale of your business."

"Yeah, and we broke into the Swedish market with skateboard wheel-hubs, which have established our name in the Euromarket. It's all about attention to specific needs. Customization. The Swedes had a fad for what they called 'stålaktig' or 'steely.' It's a color like a silver-metallic with just a tinge of cool color like violet-indigo, a bit of a tang, which they use on the hubs, while the boards are a kind of gray-on-white or white-on-white. It's its own look, and we were a part of developing it based on interviews, interactions, and just awareness of what was going on in the subculture. It takes a lot of involvement, hiring locals with the right connections to assist in research, all to break into what looks like a niche market, but it can grow into a phenomenon and establish the right image for our company. We provide top quality color harmony with an awareness of what suits the customer's needs. This of course leads to poster ads and TV spots, and we're bringing out oils, poster-paints, acrylics, all kinds of pigments for fine-artists…"

"Olga? I think I'm going to need to take some time to think about your symptoms and what you've told me, but right now it looks as though I will not be able to take you on as a patient."

REJECTION REJECTED

I followed through on our conversation with a final decision to reject Olga, which I communicated politely and diplomatically through a phone call. I also referred her to a psychiatrist closer to her home whom I knew personally.

This doctor, Dr. Leonard Youngberg, called me up after a month with Olga.

"Percy," he said, "you've got to take Olga into your program."

"But why? She's exaggerating the urgency. I mean, her family history is interesting, but I've heard you're getting along well with her."

"I'm getting nowhere. Not that I'd expect to get far with such a delusional patient in a month, a year, or a decade."

"What are you talking about?"

"I mean her insistence that her father murdered her mother, which just about defines her life."

"What? Murder? There's nothing…"

"It's all in the case history."

"No it isn't…"

I brought up my files. There was nothing there.

"No it isn't," I again insisted. "Is she just making this up now to make an impression?"

"No, Percy, come on. Are you telling me you didn't know about her delusions when you pushed her onto me?"

"Well…"

Just then I noticed that the case history file I'd received was incomplete. It ended in the middle of a sentence, and whole pages of data that I would have expected were absent.

"Okay… I think I need you to resend me her files, with whatever new material you've written up on her…"

2.
The Drowning

THE DEATH OF DIANA LUKIN—AS DESCRIBED BY OLGA

When I was six years old and my brother Max was nine, we travelled with our parents to Boracay in the Philippines. We stayed in a rather luxurious resort, the *Hotel Karingalan*, which was a little remote from the more popular beaches. We travelled in the off-season when the hotel was only partially occupied. This resort has since been demolished. On the second day of our vacation, we spent some time at the pool in the mid-afternoon when most of the guests were either out of the hotel or resting. After some time spent playing and swimming, Max and I got tired, and I fell asleep on a poolside lounge. My father—everyone calls him Tommy— brought us up to the hotel room on the third floor so we could nap. I suppose he carried me. Meanwhile, our mother stayed down at the pool. She had been wading with us in the shallow end of the pool, but she was not able to swim. She had been drinking beer with Tommy.

My dad got me out of my swimsuit while I was pretty much still asleep—got me into my pajamas—and put me to bed. Max had, by this time, climbed into the second bed and fallen asleep. He has told me several times that he has a vague memory of the walk up the stairs, dressing, and lying down, but he's sure he was asleep before anything notable happened.

My dad, Tommy… he then went to the window, looked down, and saw my mom floating face down in the deep end of the pool. He shouted something; no one remembers the words he shouted, or whether he merely shouted without language. In a statement to the police, he reported that in the moment he looked down, just after seeing my mom's body, he had seen the back of someone running away from the scene, through an archway, towards the front of the resort that opens out onto the ocean. He saw very

11

little of the man, only enough to report that he had short-cropped dark hair, he wore shorts or swimming trunks with no shirt, and he had a medium-dark tan. He seemed physically fit. However, Tommy hasn't been willing to talk to me about this mystery witness. When I get up the nerve to ask him, he always dismisses the subject angrily. Wordlessly.

Tommy raced down the stairs to the poolside. His shout had brought the attention of other guests, and there were a few screams of women who—looking down from their balconies—had now discovered the body in the pool. Tommy dragged my mom out of the water, and tried to revive her, but was unsuccessful. No member of the hotel staff had any special medical training. By the time Mom was transported to a medical clinic, she was dead.

You can imagine the chaos of me and my brother screaming and crying and not knowing what was going on… actually, I can only barely imagine it too, because I can remember the fear and sadness, and some of the events leading up to when I had woken up in bed, but I don't remember much else of where I was or what I saw and heard after that. It seemed like a very long day, and we kids were alone for the first time ever. There were authority figures offering us candy. Again, and again, more candy. My dad, Tommy, he just forgot about us in his grief… or his supposed grief. Can you imagine? In all his weeping and wailing, at the end of the day he had nothing to say, no words of comfort? The family pretty much went to Hell after that.

A Collage of Images, Half-remembered

We had a funeral.

In the days that followed, Tommy just turned into a kind of brute. It's not that he was very violent much, but he was more pathetic and sullen than he had been before my mom's death. Not that he was such a great dad in the beginning either, but he got worse. And then he would get into a kind of false-elated mood and try to act cheerful and optimistic for a while. But he had no tolerance for *our* moods, though we were children, and he acted martyred sometimes, like we were ruining everything and burdening him more if we couldn't keep up with him the way he expected us to. Though Max, actually, was better able to appease my dad, so then it started to seem like I was the troubled one.

My dad reminded us frequently about the importance of school for developing us and giving us opportunities in the future. Here I was in sync with his message because when I started first grade I liked it, because school got me out of the house. At school, especially as I got older, I was a mostly normal kid, not that I ever forgot about my mom's death and the feelings of loss that could just… catch me at any moment… but still I wasn't fully oppressed like I felt at home. And as time went by, my blame of my dad— my suspicion—went further and further. It wasn't just that he was inadequate as a father and a poor substitute for my mother. I started to think of him as a literal murderer.

My mom's folks visited us often, and we visited them. That was Grandma and Grandpa to me. And my aunts and cousins. I didn't know my father's family; they were strangers. When I saw *them* at the funeral, I didn't know what to say. They seemed nice, just not like members of my family. Awkward, really. But my mom's family was my family, and I felt really happy when I saw them. I think they could easily sense how miserable I was with Tommy. They mostly tried to relate to us kids without stirring up trouble. But Tommy just went nuts on them one day and started screaming at them. It should have been the other way around, he was the one that killed their daughter, but he just went into a rage. I don't know why. Tension.

One of the most suspicious events that really got me thinking was when my brother Max came into the living room one day with an air rifle and shot my dad in the chest. My dad was reading the Russian language newspaper, *The Russian Bazaar*. He's always been in denial about being Russian, but then he gets in these moods where he wants to remember his "roots" and maintain his language. These moods are temporary. So, while I was laying out some clothing and thinking about what I was going to wear the next day, my dad called out to me to come to the living room because he wanted to tell me something. He was always telling me about some trivia facts or jokes he read in the paper, even though I just hated even the sound of his voice. But when I came in… I don't remember what he was telling me, but Max came in right behind me and shot a BB into Tommy's chest. It gave him a nasty, painful bruise (he showed us later), and my dad leapt up and grabbed the gun, knocked Max to the floor… and then Dad started whining and simpering pathetically, worse than I ever did, and I was maybe nine at the time. He used some bad language, but mainly whined about how he was friendless and worked hard—he was a shop clerk—and nobody ever gave him a break until *Diana*, and she was gone, but… well you get the picture, he was doing so much for us but we were going to throw away our lives because we couldn't get over, like we were the only people to suffer, etcetera… it was a heavy trip to lay on kids.

That incident really made me think. There had been no fight between Max and Tommy leading up to that. There was no reason for Max to suddenly act out in violence against our dad, unless he just hated him from his gut. But Max had never expressed that kind of serious hatred. I was the only one to do that. But it seemed to me after that that Max must have had a reason to hate Tommy. More than the fact that he was a horrible dad and a pathetic role model. Max must have known more about our mom's death than he ever let on.

I have tried to talk to Max about this many times. He says he knows *nothing* about mom's drowning except that it was accidental, and he absolutely denies that the BB-gun incident ever happened. He says he never had a BB gun, Tommy wouldn't let him have one, and he doesn't even remember having *one* big conflict. He says the worst he ever did was to shout at Tommy, and that was reasonable considering his age and his own depression he had been coping with, mostly alone.

In my psychiatric treatment, the doctors have told me that there's a significant chance that I misremembered the details of the event, and they suggest that maybe Max is right. Maybe he never shot a BB at my dad. But that's... nonsense, because I clearly remember it. It's not like a recovered memory of some suppressed image, it's something I've remembered in detail my whole life. It's as vivid as the memory of my mother's smile on the plane to the Philippines, when I gave her a picture I had been coloring. It's the last clear image I have of her face from before she died.

3.
Yoga

Yoga

"Tell me about Fanishwar Atlan," I asked.

Olga said, "Fanishwar has really helped me a lot. I think if I hadn't met him, my business would have turned me into a strict materialist, and I'd be trapped with all the suffering that that world-view entails. It's hard to explain Fanishwar and his philosophy to someone who hasn't practiced meditation… do you…?"

"No."

"No, I thought not. But it's basically a philosophy of monism. You know, there is only one phenomenon, the now is eternal… And there are times… many times actually… that all this that I've told you becomes an array of non-troubling facts, details remote and without personal consequence, but this is a brief experience. Fanishwar doesn't like the way I talk about this either; he doesn't believe in 'troubling facts,' or 'non-troubling facts'; it all gets complicated when it comes down to words.

"When I'm supposed to be meditating and focusing only on *being*, eliminating the mind, I sometimes imagine things and get distracted by these imaginings. For instance, while thinking of my mother, I conjured up a strange sort of image… not a dream, and nothing that is proper to the practice of yoga, just a kind of image or conscious thought experiment. I imagined that I looked into a sort of two-sided round makeup mirror, with a magnifying mirror on one side, and a flat mirror on the reverse. By looking into the magnifying side, I could see distorted and intense details of my mother's face, without getting a complete image. This was like having her with me, in life. But when I rotated the mirror, I saw her whole image, crystalline, whole, and perfect, though she was absent. In death, she was a perfected memory image that was eternally with me. I felt I'd had an insight…

"I don't know why, but this... sort of vision... led me to believe that the physical death of my mother was somehow a part of the creation of a new memory-mother, a more perfect and lasting phenomenon. I tried to express this in a conversation with Fanishwar. I said to him 'I wonder. Could my mother's death have been a kind of creative act? Can we say, in some sense, that destruction and creation are two sides of the same coin?'

"'What you say is a half-truth,' he said—his wisdom is greater than mine—'and a half truth is worse than an untruth. There is no coin and there are no sides. Destruction *is* creation. That is the complete truth.'

"He also explained how my mother has never been anything but that whole, crystalline memory. I'd touched on a true insight, but I'd overintellectualized it.

"'The diversity of phenomena is a falsehood. It exists only in the mind. Your identity is a falsehood. You are not the identity, and you are not the one who identifies. Your memories of the actions of others are memories. You are not the memories, and you are not the one who remembers. The *Self* is that which witnesses the identification, and witnesses the remembering. When you recognize that which the Self is *not*, then the rest falls away.'

"My own meditation shows the truth of what he says. Fanishwar does not tell me what to think. Rather, he gives word to the things that I wordlessly think.

"I have experienced a sort of tentative realization. I know the elation of perceiving that my troubles are not mine, and I have felt the enjoyment of a depersonalized experience of Self. But this does not persist. I get dragged back down into it, I identify with *Olga's* experience and *Olga's* childhood too much, and this is a sort of pettiness that I can't escape right now. The trauma of orphanhood is too much for someone in our weak and modern times... Still, I get occasional short-term relief. There are even times when I can almost forgive my father. There are even times when I *am* my father. But that's when frightening things happen."

4.
Through the Eyes of a Killer

IDENTITY WITH THE FATHER

It's so easy to see how I killed her, especially when I imagine that I am he. The kids are asleep. My wife is in the pool, perhaps sitting on the steps, pretending everything is all right. She's forgotten for a moment how cold and distant I've been, how our marriage has been a sham for years, just a show we put on for the benefit of the kids. She's relaxing. It's easy enough to go back down and join her. Let's splash about in the pool a bit, let's flirt with the edge between shallow and deep. How funny! And then, no fighting, just a release. Leave her in the deep. Drowners don't scream; they don't get attention. They just die silently, inches from the air that could save them, every instant becoming an eternity of terror.

By the time I get back up the stairs, she's as good as dead. Anyway, she's not breathing. Her lungs, her sinuses, her stomach are filled. Maybe she's buoyant enough to float, maybe not, but she won't be revived. Now look out the window and shout.

LEARNING HER OWN FEAR, AND BEATING IT

It's not hard to imagine how our mother suffered and how she died.

My brother was a decent swimmer. He'd had a few lessons. And I could at least dog-paddle a little. But it wasn't so nice when, only a few months after he killed our mother, Tommy forced Max and me to take up swimming. It was madness! Why would you do that to your children? But he told us it was for our own good. We weren't going to be allowed to be afraid for our whole lives.

Max remembers our forced swimming lessons better than I. He has complained about them many times. But he never believed my father was a killer. But I still remember clearly enough. Just a snort of water up the nostrils, a trickle down the throat, and tears flowing from my eyes while I struggle are enough to give me a taste of a drowning death. I'm sure I've gotten that sensation many times, just for a moment here or there. But when I found I could tread water by restraining my fear, focusing only on my hands, my feet, the water as a medium, and then I could float on my back, breathing shallowly, I knew I would never die *that* death. My dad, sick bastard that he was, may have had a point when he forced us back in the water. I'm a good swimmer now. I don't like swimming, but I can do it, and I practice at least a couple of times a year. Fear is not my master.

5.
The Self and Others

"What do you believe, Olga?"

"I'm explaining that. It can be simple or complex. For you to understand depends on your sincerity and effort."

"Are you Hindu?"

Olga laughed. "What is Hinduism? It doesn't exist. Neither does Christianity. Neither does heterosexuality. You may think this is typical Eastern obscurantism, but it is not. What if I told you that what I've said is not mystical, not metaphorical, but is a literal fact?"

She elaborated. "You speak to me; I understand. Another person speaks to me; I understand. I speak to both of you, and both of you understand me. Yet none of us speaks the same, and none of us understands the same.

"In any language, religion, or complex phenomenon, a spectrum exists, but how broad is this spectrum, and how many hues does it contain? There are no defined limits. No rules can be defined which cannot find exception.

"I can tell you what I believe, but I can't tell you what to label it."

"Why do you have a guru? Why do you need a guru?"

"I don't need a guru."

"Then why do you have one?"

"You're a psychiatrist. Did you go to university?"

"Of course I did."

"Why? Why didn't you become a psychiatrist without going to university?"

"Psychiatry is a science. It requires learning, training. I'm a doctor. It's not something you can just make up as you go along."

"Neither is understanding the nature of the universe, or the truth of the *Self*. Do you think that's simple? Why should I not benefit from learning from someone more knowledgeable, experienced and wise? If you spend a decade studying your science formally, and your lifetime practicing it, shouldn't I be equally devoted, or more so?"

"But who is Fanishwar Atlan to you? If you have less knowledge and experience than he, then are you even fit to judge his expertise? There is no qualification process."

"When I first met him, you could have fairly accused me of surrendering unknowingly to the teachings of a charismatic stranger. You could call that foolish. Fanishwar's own realization came to him quite quickly, mainly because he possessed a simple-minded trust in his own teacher. But there can be no learning in the absence of trust, at least at first."

"What is that trust based on?"

"It starts from nothing. It's like opening your eyes, not knowing what you will see, but trusting that you will see *something*."

"But do you ever question what you've been taught?"

"Here's where it may seem complicated to you. I *always* question what I've been taught, even while trusting it. There is light. There is the one who sees the light. Then there is the one who witnesses the observer and observes how she is transformed by the observation. You might want to think of it as a believing entity and a skeptical self. People can resolve this difference in various ways. One way would be the error: the observer excludes the critical witness. This observer mistakes the illusion for reality. The other way is for the observer and witness to become one; the observer resolves all of the witness' doubts, and the witness reforms the observer's perception."

"If this is the way that Fanishwar Atlan teaches you to believe, then do you even believe that he is a person outside of yourself?"

"That doesn't matter. Whether he is inside or outside... ultimately there is no outside. But there is a voice that communicates with me, and it is wise, and it knows, and it shows me the way. Even if that voice really is the Self, and not a separate entity. The realization that comes is the same."

I became frustrated by what seemed to be a very convoluted

logic. "To hear you speak," I said, "It's easy to imagine that you believe everything, or nothing, or that your belief is too nebulous. In other words, it's all confusion."

"Is it confusion, or are you confused? What puts people off and prevents them from understanding is the honesty and truthfulness of what I say, which includes a recognition of what is not known and an admission of what is not necessary to know because it is outside the question. But you, who regard your thinking as scientific, build your beliefs on clouds that are far more nebulous. Fanishwar's teaching disperses the clouds. You are certain about details which I cannot know about, not being the type of scientist you recognize as such. But there is no certainty without faith. *You* are a practitioner of faith, *I* am a practitioner of knowledge and awareness. That includes an awareness of what is unknown and unknowable. But I'm not stupid. I know how people perceive me, and what people think of a westerner who unashamedly declares she follows the teachings of a guru. That's an appearance I won't apologize for."

"I don't ask that you apologize. But I must still ask questions. Now, with the honesty you claim to have about what is unknown, how is it that you believe so strongly that your father killed your mother, particularly in the absence of evidence?"

"I perceived it directly."

"You mean by being your father?"

"No. That's more of a thought exercise."

"Then, do you mean that you actually remember it?"

"No, not consciously."

"But if you remember it unconsciously, then it's unconscious… you can't know."

"I have another sense besides seeing and hearing."

You mean taste? I thought. But for once I restrained myself from saying it. People don't always appreciate a psychiatrist with a sense of humor, and I've made more than my share of errors by speaking my mind too readily. "Do you mean you have a sixth sense then?"

I asked. *Wait, what about humor… is it a seventh sense? Balance? Hmmm… Stop, doctor, stop and listen to the patient.*

"Call it what you want, but I know that he killed my mother."

"For how long have you known it?"

"I've always known it."

"Even before it happened?"

She hesitated. Then: "I must have."

And does this mean she was complicit in the murder of her own mother then, I thought. And if she identifies with all parties, what does she think of her brother's attack on her father? Does she want to destroy herself in revenge for her having destroyed herself? What is this process of recursive self-destruction? And can there be an unaffected witness outside the act? Stop! Some patients should not be identified with.

"Now," I said, "I want you to ponder something. The idea that your father could be a murderer is terrible. But what is more frightening to you? The idea that your father killed your mother, or the thought that your mother may have died by accident, for no reason at all?"

Olga did ponder for a moment before replying.

"There's no inherent contradiction. Since there is no fate, my father's act of murder could be regarded as a kind of 'accident' too. It does not mean that there is a 'reason.'"

"Okay, but I want you to stop talking about what you've been taught, or your 'beliefs' as such. I'll ask again. What frightens you more: that your father may have killed your mother, or that she may have died by accidental drowning?"

"You're implying that I may have invented the murder as a way of escaping the greater fear of living in a senseless universe."

"I'm not suggesting anything. I'm just asking. Please…"

"Well… I don't know. I've never asked myself that question. I think… I need time to answer."

"Never mind. Tell me your first thought now. I'll give you the chance to revise your answer later."

"I… I just don't want my mother to be dead."

Though we were not scheduled to meet again for another two weeks, Olga returned five days later. In the meantime she had met with Fanishwar twice. When she saw me, she seemed relieved.

"You've already helped me so much, I can't tell you. After speaking with you, I felt a lot of sadness for several days. I talked with Fanishwar, and he helped me too. I've been holding myself back by my constant thinking about the *hows* and *whys* of my mother's death. Beneath it all, I've been concealing my pain at the fact of her loss. Fanishwar compares this to the existential grief at the loss of *everything*, as one comes to terms with the illusory nature of the world of perceptions. But you really lead me on the first very big step to seeing and resolving this inner conflict."

"Well, all right, that sounds very good."

"But what really surprised me, what I've been dying to tell you, is that for three days, in my suffering, reliving a lot of the unexpressed horror of my loss in childhood, I *completely* didn't think of my thirst—or its absence. I didn't even think about it until Sunday evening, when I was sitting alone at a table in my kitchen, with a three-quarters-full glass of water before me. I had absent-mindedly drunk from it. Then I thought, *What is this?* I felt… normal. And I picked up the glass to take one more sip… it was wonderful! Absolutely tactile, refreshing… normal. I'm cured!"

"That's… what we hope for, obviously. And what did your guru say about that?"

"He approved. 'This is a joy, like that of the vivid dreamer who takes pleasure in the dream. It is a more direct perception of the Self and its role in creation.' Well, he had more to say, and he related it to events that are as much of the Self though not perceived, but the point is he was supportive… but this elation may be a danger too, because for a moment I lost track of what he was trying to teach me. We meditated, and soon I experienced an inner bliss that refocused me on the experience of Self and obliterated the unnecessary details of memory and sensation. So progress is being made all around."

6.
Transition Years

College, Mentoring, and Entrepreneurship

My high-school years were tough because when Max left home it basically ended our close sibling relationship. Even though we had gotten along very well recently and, without sentimentality, we supported each other and felt a kind of best-friends-who-won't-admit-it love for each other, Max had gradually developed an emotional distancing strategy towards Tommy which he would soon apply to the household in general, i.e. me. He just wouldn't let himself get affected too much by Dad's little cruelties, or any other little troubles that came along. And then, when he went away to school, he immersed himself in his own private life to the degree that he could easily forget what he'd left behind. When it was my own turn to leave home and go to college, I adopted the same basic strategy.

It was a thrill, and real liberating, to get out of that dreadful house at last. I could leave Tommy to rot and fester in his own miserable life. But he did help pay for my school, he was never negligent financially though he could only barely afford it. I focused on my studies and got very busy. I wrote reports and did my design projects—I was an industrial design major.

Along the way, I dated several guys, but it was never very serious. One guy somehow stuck with me longer than the others. That was Nicholas, whom I eventually married.

In my senior year I took part in a program that helped place design students in an unpaid six-month internship with companies that were run by—or that employed—alumni from our school. Not everyone got a placement, and not all placements were good, but I was a good student and I got lucky (though I didn't recognize it at first).

I interviewed with Douglas Wright, the alumnus who would be my mentor. He was brilliant—a better teacher than my professors though they were quite talented too—and I was fortunate to make the right impression on him in the interview. He was very frank, and I was somewhat scandalized, actually, to hear him use a lot of filthy language even in our interview. In my own company, I maintain a very professional atmosphere where open dialogue, expression of ideas, opposition and even well-reasoned dispute are encouraged, but using crude language to express oneself in the office is not acceptable. But Douglas was very blunt. He was in his early forties, not a designer, but an administrator, and he was now director of the design department of a large corporation that manufactures kitchen appliances. You've heard of Stoneworth?

I was expecting to work as a designer, but Douglas was determined to "take me under his wing" and teach me administration—an idea I didn't really like at first. So, I was wary, and I wasn't all that obsequious in the interview. He told me he liked my "sass." I didn't think I was being sassy, just not a pushover.

One thing I learned from working with him is that you *can* learn from someone who's a total sexist pig and somewhat of a social idiot. I mean, if you look at a person's strengths, and not his or her weaknesses, especially if that person has exceptional talents in some area, then there's a lot to learn if you are unprejudiced in your own mind. I mean, a guy like him is not going to teach me anything meaningful about gender relations or feminism, except by setting a *negative example*, but he could and did teach me a heck of a lot about how to isolate the important factors that lead to good business decisions and good ways to maximize the advantages that come from the individual talents of members of a team. Also how to determine when diplomacy doesn't apply and a strong head and determination are required. In fact, what I was saying earlier, that was one of the lessons he wanted to teach me: you can learn from anyone, and the best approach to staff, coworkers, teammates, anyone you have to interact with, is to emphasize strengths, not weaknesses. Really, he taught me a big meta-lesson about how to learn, beyond the specific skills related to management.

I parlayed my internship into a year of regular employment,

this time as a junior member of the design team, and I continued to learn… I was out of school then and ready for full employment. I saved money diligently while paying down some of my debt, and I got feelers out seeking some investment money from among some of the wealthy ladies I met in my twice-weekly yoga sessions. I was selling mats that I'd hand-manufactured, and I wanted to get started on putting together my own venture. I actually did find some interested parties, interested enough to get together a small seed of capital—really pathetically small to tell the truth—but enough to get started. So I left my design job at Stoneworth, hired a staff of two, and managed to get some of my mats into athletic shops, and with the first profits I generated, I bought out the investors who had financed me so I could maintain full ownership.

Within two years, the faddish quality attached itself to my product, we got out some advertisements, and slow initial growth suddenly—with a bang—turned into a huge and rapid success that I couldn't have anticipated. I almost failed for not being able to ramp up and expand quickly enough. I attracted new venture capital from some more serious investment groups, got some loans, started diversifying into new products, and it wasn't until several years later that I was able to buy myself back up to 85% ownership of my own company. We did manage to meet demand and grow as necessary. And I've never taken the company public. I don't think I ever will.

I've maintained a relationship with Douglas all along. I mean a platonic relationship. There was a point when I got the impression he was more than just physically attracted to me, but we kept it professional. Nicholas—we were married by then—was foolishly jealous of Douglas, but I just had to laugh that off. It would be ridiculous to get involved with Douglas in that way, I mean he's a pig, like I said. But he's a real business talent, and I've paid him good money as a consultant when I needed to make some structural changes in my company—he's out of the appliance business. But one thing that's for sure: I'll happily call on him for advice, but I would never hire him as permanent staff. We've got a lot of female managers, and experience has shown that he has a real habit of driving talented female staff away. They just leave because he offends them. So, I guess I'm guilty in a way of not quite learning my lesson, because when looking at him now, I emphasize his weakness, not his strength. But that's just how it is.

Divorce (Where was the marriage?)

I don't know how to explain why I married Nicholas. It just kind of happened, I guess. I mean, we had our giddy little thrills. The wedding was beautiful. Not a big, elaborate, or expensive affair, but just beautiful. I was carried away in an emotional way that's a bit uncharacteristic of me. I'm not the sentimental type. But marrying was a thrill, the honeymoon was wonderful. Nick and I went to Istanbul for something a little exotic and something cultural, and I avoided swimming. My anxiety was pretty well under control at the time, but I didn't want to spoil anything by going to some Pacific island surrounded by water.

We didn't spend a lot of money on the whole thing because my business was just getting underway at this time, it was the early years, and my net worth wasn't much more than a million dollars yet. A million and a half maybe. Nick wasn't making much money, and he never did, but that wasn't an issue.

Then work took over. I *rarely* saw my dad. Sometimes my grandparents, they're great people, but I didn't see them much; I didn't like being reminded of things. Some nights were hard, hard, hard. A murderer in the family! I tried a couple of times to reopen relations with my brother, we were always cordial. Where was the love? We're closer now, but there were cold years in there. And where did my marriage go? It was nice, it really was. Everything was fine, it was good. And then it was worthless. Nick and I just had to get out, there was something painful and oppressive there that I neglected while my nose was buried in business matters, you know?

Nicholas did hurt me.

I can't ever prove he cheated on me. Maybe he never did. He says he never did. But I know there was a huge element of fraud in that relationship, and he said some unkind words.

Ha! You know what? I'd like to tickle his ribs today—with a feather glued to a baseball bat!

For three and a half years I was Mrs. Kopala. I guess I didn't tell you his name before.

Anyway, I'm with Chris now. It's a lot better than it was with Nicholas. It's beautiful in its own way, with no pressure, and no expectation. He's not expecting me to marry him or anything, and there's no pressure to have a baby. That would just get in the way, and he knows the importance of my business. I'm not good with *family*, you know, I mean it's quite reasonable.

A lot of people look at trends in divorce and worry about what it means for the future, but it's meaningless. Marriages don't fail because of social trends, it's all about the individuals involved, it's up to you. Marriage depends on you and your partner. The reason most marriages fail is because most people suck at life. There's random factors too, but you both have to contribute something. But maybe I just suck at marriage.

Anyway, my boyfriend's name is Christopher Easter. We live together, and he mostly stays out of the way, but he treats me nice when I need it. And I'm never going to be "Olga Easter," that's just a pathetic name. Speaking of names, he once tried to give me a "cute" nickname. You know what he called me? "Ga." I'm serious, I nearly slapped his face, I really did.

There's only time in life for so many complications, and my plate is full.

7.
Signs of Greater Trouble

Business has had its ups and downs, and my life has had its smooth times and its rough times. I'm glad to say that it has all mostly gone well. I don't always feel that way, though. Sometimes I'm just terrified, and sometimes I make the most idiotic mistakes. Sometimes at night, when I'm alone, or when Chris is nearby but asleep, thoughts and feelings push their way to the forefront of my mind, and I can't get them out. I've sometimes talked about this with my various psychiatrists, and I know that a lot of this comes from a sense of guilt. I feel guilty for being successful, and I feel even guiltier when I stumble and fall on my face. Squandering my opportunities for success can just drive me mad. I don't know *why* I have to feel this, when there's already enough external pressure on me, and enough demands.

Sometimes I don't know what I'm thinking, or how long I've been lost in unfocused thoughts. Yeah, part of it is that my mom never had a chance to experience what I'm experiencing, or to stand by my side and witness my success. The unreal nature of this life I'm living, and all that's in it... the mundane stupidity of having to repeat myself at work... I have to repeat myself so often, and nobody seems to learn. Anyway, how can it be real when it's just me to experience it, when she's not here?

I sometimes have bad dreams. Weird dreams. But I don't want to talk about that.

And Tommy is still out there in the world, still stocking shelves and setting roach traps. What does he do for sex? Is he celibate now? What contemptible creature would let herself be his woman, even for a night? But from when I was a teenager until today, he has never admitted to having an interest in another woman besides my mom, yet I'm sure his mind has been consumed by *only* that:

other women. His secret, shameful life that he keeps hidden in shadows. It's like he's some kind of conjurer… how has it always been invisible to me, even when I've looked for it?

Does he have any remorse at all? He's not the type. He worries about getting the carpet shampooed or… being alone. But he doesn't think about *what he did* unless I remind him. And I just don't come around to remind him all that often. There's no use in it anyway, he alternates between rage and false pity, as though it were so wearying for him to endure my criticism and so sad to see that grief has broken me down, inspired mad fantasies. Would it not be suitable for me to surrender to my grief, knowing what I know? I see him a couple of times a year at most. Max visits less often than that. And Tommy… listen, he's educated but he's not smart. He's smart, but he doesn't think the things he needs to think. I'm sure he never even took seriously the idea that one day *he'd get caught*.

When I first started learning from Fanishwar, it helped me quite a lot. Today too, it helps me, but while I wasn't very wise or quite so aware of my relationship to the Self—the Self was lost in a cloud then—Yoga was a distraction from *the dread*, and that distraction was good. Like in business… in my marriage too, come to think of it… the early days were days of forgetting. Not in the literal sense. The thoughts were present, but I became numb to their sting.

Yoga has been the most consistent good in my life, and my relationship to it has been transformed. It isn't escapism, it's new-aware-ism. But the troubles return, and the thoughts still seize me from time to time.

ABSTRACTION

One day I had a very important business meeting in the morning. Well, that's not unusual, I have a lot of meetings, and they are all important to a greater or lesser degree. But I don't golf, I don't drink, and as a woman I don't feel just right about sending out sales staff to go drinking and partying with buyers, taking them to strip clubs and prostitutes and that kind of thing. So I have some disadvantages. Plus I'm... honest. Scrupulously so. Satya: non-lying. That has its good side with regards to reputation and establishing trustful relationships. But buyers who don't get the royal treatment, don't get flattery, don't feel "chumminess" ... I'm kind of an ice-bitch to them... well, they expect at least an extreme of professionalism. In such circumstances, missing a meeting with no excuse just doesn't fly. Good quality at a good price doesn't sell itself, and even senior sales staff can't compensate for a bad impression given by the company C.E.O.

So, I had this appointment for a meeting with a buyer from a pretty big construction firm that was shopping for roof-cladding for a housing development. But I missed our appointment. Why? Where was I? At home, just standing there. Doing nothing.

I knew I had somewhere to go. It was important. The meeting, of course! But I couldn't go yet; I wasn't ready. Why? I was looking for something. And thinking. I was fully dressed, and anyone objective would have said I was ready to go. But... thinking. My mind was ajumble. Just like the feeling I had that day, I have the feeling now that somewhere in time—the future, the past—maybe both—there is a woman in trouble and she's living my life, and I'm living hers. We're interconnected. I'm moving for her, but I can't see through her eyes. She's acting in ways that affect me in every detail of every life-event. But I don't know how she affects me, and neither does she know the effects she has on me.

There were lights and shadows projected up, from outside my window, reflections of the outside world, streaking and moving, flowing and dancing on the ceiling. It was like the room and I were moving together and the world was still. I was traveling somewhere, to an important event. And I needed some item. I shuffled around, looked through drawers. I may have looked in the same drawers repeatedly. I had a meeting to go to, and time was passing, there was no point anyway anymore. Who could move fast enough to get there now? I was standing there. And what I was looking for was a white lace glove. I don't have any such glove. I've never had one. What was I thinking?

I showed up at work three hours late, and I didn't call anyone before my arrival. I didn't answer my phone when it rang. Then, at the office, I called up the buyer and explained I had had a personal crisis. I'd like to meet him another day. "What kind of crisis?" "I can't explain it. It's nothing to do with business. Stress from my private life just got in the way for once. It won't affect our business going forward." Needless to say, we didn't make that sale. More painful still, the sales staff who had worked on that job, I think, must have gotten a pretty bad impression of me that day, and I had always maintained the image of perfection and self-mastery. I demanded a lot, and most of all I demanded perfection from myself. But I was a total disaster on the inside.

ABOUT CHRIS EASTER—IN RESPONSE TO THE QUESTION, "WHAT IS CHRIS TO YOU?"

Chris is a good guy, and someone I feel comfortable with. Things are easy between us. I don't unburden my troubles on him. Sometimes he tells me about some of the things that bother him. Sometimes he tells me about his feelings, his thoughts, his opinions. He's not demanding, he's just a bit talkative. It mostly goes smoothly. We're lovers, not friends.

MAX'S FAMILY

Then there are the problems in Max's family. Though there was a lot of distance between us for several years, we made our occasional efforts to reconnect, and more recently we have gotten closer again. Max has been married for a decade, and because he and his wife Carissa have invited me over for dinner pretty often, I've gradually gotten to know her too. We've come to be friends. They have two kids, Heather and Myles.

Anyway, my friendship with Carissa is kind of strange because I'm just not the sort to keep friends, especially female friends. I've got the people I work with, but that's always a strained kind of relationship when we socialize outside of the office, for obvious reasons, plus Chris has his circle of friends—when I'm not too busy he sometimes persuades me to join them, and I've gotten to know some of the ladies. We can joke a bit, and I've got a cordial relationship with them, but... it's not real friendship, is it? They see me as different, I see them as different. Chris has time for friends, I basically have time for acquaintances, and that only sometimes.

But with Carissa it's different. It's like, having a sister-in-law is like having a real sister in a sense, but at the same time it's not as demanding as real family. The kids are like that too. I'm an aunt, which is pretty much perfect. I love the kids, I can see them when I want, but I don't have to be responsible for them twenty-four hours a day. Strangely that makes the relationship closer, or at least more positive in a sense because of its simplicity. There's not much at risk, nothing to resent, we don't get on each other's nerves, we're not too intimate. I don't have to go crazy and have my own kids, which I don't want, but here I get to be a big playmate and semi-serious mom-substitute (I've babysat twice when Max and Carissa needed a spousal date night).

The kids, they're growing up beautifully, I can sympathize with them, I can see some of the weird struggles they go through with their parents, the rivalry. Myles is a totally uninhibited kid most of the time. Kind of a ham. But then he can get really dark and moody, and then suddenly he shouts and locks himself in a room, and then gets real quiet and brooding for an hour or more. It seems like there's no cause at all, but I've figured him out. It usually happens right after his big sister has said something funny or otherwise gotten some positive attention from the adults and he can't handle it.

The best thing about Carissa is that I can talk to her about all sorts of things, and it's casual enough that she refrains from judging, she just listens and speaks to me like... like I'm normal. I know she patronizes me a bit, but she's nice. I can even talk to her about my dad. Whereas, with Max, whenever the topic comes up, he has one of two postures. He sometimes "humors" me, but his humoring isn't as sympathetic as Carissa's, it's got an ironic and hurtful edge to it. While his other posture is an expression of outrage—and this is most common when he's drunk.

Once I went to visit their house in Madison on a Sunday—I was invited—and Max was out. He's a real working stiff—a finance actuary consultant, and he commutes to New York a lot. But he's got his family obligations, and he's almost always home on weekends. To be out on a Sunday is very unusual, or I thought that was the case.

Carissa said to me, "We're having problems lately."

"What kind of problems?" She didn't usually make serious complaints about Max to me, so I wasn't expecting this.

Carissa said, "He stays away from home a lot. And he's just edgy. If I ignore it, he's edgy, if I try to talk to him about it he just gets really cold. I don't want to scream in front of the kids, sometimes I do. But someone's got to wake him up. He's not… Go play!"

Heather had wandered into the kitchen, where we were chatting, to look in the fridge. She gave her mom a look, and walked out resentful.

"Sorry, darling, sorry!" Carissa told her. "We're having a talk is all." Then she turned back to me and made a kind of pouty face but hesitated to say more.

"Well, what's he doing?" I asked.

"I don't know. How can I know?"

I understand Max is getting drunk more frequently lately. He's not an alcoholic, but he's just… depressive on some days, and just plain inconsiderate on other days. The truth is Carissa is just a lovely sweet person, she works hard too. And they've got such wonderful kids. And Max is the kind of fool who will just lose all that. I know he feels worthless sometimes, he's not accomplishing anything. I've helped his family out financially at times, and he resents it. You know, he's candid sometimes with me, but only halfway so, then he gets angry, then there's no talking to him.

I tried to open things up with him a bit when he came home later that night and Carissa had the kids in the other room watching a movie. Not to say they didn't run in and out and all over, running to the bathroom, the bedroom, grabbing snacks… it's like that most of the time. But Max and I had a sit down.

"Max, come on, what are you doing staying out all day?"

"What are you talking about? Are you going to chastise me?"

"Hey, don't dodge. I know it's not for me to judge other people's relationships, but I'm just suggesting you look out for what's best for you. You've got something good here."

"What has Carissa been telling you?"

"That's a stupid thing to say. Seriously."

"Oh, get off it! You've just walked in on a family dispute that's complicated. Carissa doesn't want me here, the kids eye me strange. If I try to live my life a little, just decompress a little… because the stress and the expectations are just unbearable at times…."

"Don't act like it's so hard. No one says you can't relax. Speak your mind if you have to, even argue sometimes if you have to, but it's spooky when everyone's in the house just wondering 'Where the Hell is he?'"

"Shut up, what do you know?"

"The tension level gets pretty high sometimes, but when you're out of the house… it's not your wife's style to show her frustration to me, but when she shows it, it's obvious. What kind of stress do you think it produces for the kids, huh? And all I asked was, 'Where were you?'"

"Again, you'd better just keep quiet. I don't put my fist in anyone's face around here. No one gets whipped and no one gets humiliated."

"And no one gets murdered, right?"

"Oh hell, you had to say that! What's wrong with you?"

"Being not as bad as Tommy doesn't make you a saint. To be better than him is merely human."

"I'm not going to get into this. I have problems here that are more serious for me right now than your nonsense, your damned accusations that are based on nothing."

"Not based on nothing. I read a letter once, part of a letter. Dad was writing it, it wasn't finished. And it was almost a confession. I picked it up, in the living room, I was reading it and he snatched it out of my hands."

"Stop."

"He snatched it out of my hands and ripped it up."

"That never happened."

"Yes it did."

"No! That was me, you idiot. You don't even remember... everything gets distorted. I told you, I was writing a fiction, a story, I had to write something for school..."

"Liar. You're covering for Dad again."

"Why would I do that? Look, this tension in the house is more about you than about me."

"To hell with you. Why'd you invite me then?"

"Carissa invited you. If she said I wanted you here, she's lying."

"That doesn't mean anything. If she invited me, it's because of you, because you're not here and she needed to talk. I don't want to see you mess up this family."

"Shut up! And for your information, this nonsense of yours about 'Tommy...' he's Dad, right, don't you respect him enough..."

"Respect!"

"I wrote a story, right. You picked it up. I was embarrassed, and I ripped it up right in front of you. A childish dispute you'd expect from teenagers. You never forgot, you argued with me about it just five or six months ago, right? Don't you remember? And now, what? How does this become about Dad?"

I really got confused when he started telling me this. I remember seeing my dad rip up a letter... maybe another incident... but what Max was saying made sense, and I was starting to doubt those shadowy images...

"You always find something new to back up your theory," he said. "But it's not new. It just comes out of your own head. There's nothing to find, all right? I'm sorry. I try to talk you down from this kind of nonsense, but you never listen, and now's not the time. I've got my life to deal with."

"Your life is a product of what our dad did to our mom, all right? Just as much as my…"

Tommy picked up a stool and smashed it against the wall, leaving a big gash. He ran out through the living room. I heard him stomping, and the kids had gasped then fallen quiet, Carissa too. I heard his voice with a really pathetic tone in it, obviously crying.

"I'm sorry kids, I love you…"

And he went out and slammed the door.

I didn't dare come out of the kitchen. I just sat there. I heard Carissa comforting her kids however she could, but I didn't really listen to the words. Then, in a few minutes, Carissa came into the kitchen suddenly. I thought she'd blame me for everything.

"I'm sorry!" I said.

"Come in, come in," she replied. I went into the living room with her. The kids were crying, sitting on the carpet, but mostly silently.

"Let's be patient, kids, it'll be all right. Daddy's sad sometimes too. Why don't we play some cards, then go to bed."

She negotiated it somehow so the kids calmed down enough, and we all played a few rounds of hearts together. She persuaded me to stay the night, even though I wanted to get out of there. I, weirdly, felt trapped by the situation, and almost understood why Max had to run out the door. But my marriage had failed, and I didn't want to see that happen to him.

Mundane Details of Life Become Everyday Anxieties

Little things have been setting me off lately. Like, for instance, I went into a bakery to buy a little bread. It was a pathetic little bakery, with no customers. Tons of bread, and cakes, and cookies were destined to be wasted. And the woman who worked there looked miserable. I'm sure she was running her own store, and the business was fighting for its life.

She looked at me, and in her expression I felt I could almost read her mind. *Why are you here*, she thought. *What do you want from me? Bread? Why do you come in here to buy bread? Just go away!* Which seemed like a strange attitude to take when her livelihood comes from selling bread.

But then I thought, *maybe it's like she's just tired of anyone giving her any hope, she just wants the business to finally fail and be bankrupt, and be done with it, rather than having to go on and on and just keep selling bread and pretending that the business will be a success when she knows it never will be. A customer is sort of like an unwanted doctor who comes in and keeps a dying loved one alive for just one more day, or maybe two more days, until it reaches the point when the family just wants to say "give up, and let it die already!"*

For the next couple of days, I felt a mix of contempt and hatred for this poor woman, mingled with a sort of terror that she was I, and that my business was going to collapse from under me.

Then I had Chinese food for dinner with Chris one night, at a local Szechuan place we like to go to. After dinner, I opened my fortune cookie, and the fortune read "Your luck is about to change!" I had to laugh at the absurdity of this. The fortune cookie was obviously written with the idea that most people would be thrilled by a change of luck. But what about me? This fortune was a *ring of Solomon* for me. *This too shall pass.* For those of us who are most fortunate, a change of fortune is like a death sentence.

At work, there's been a conflict between two members of the staff. Ronald, chief of sales for hobby paints, keeps running into trouble because the design staff doesn't respond quickly to his requests for information. Late-stage changes to the design of some of our literature does not always agree with the stated goals of the sales team; they have to cross-check and give feedback. Stephanie, chief designer on our sales brochures, who also has a lot of information about what goes on in design in general, has been complaining about him in meetings lately, saying that he doesn't understand the process by which they revise publications nor does he seem sufficiently knowledgeable about the products, and he always makes untimely requests for a revision to one of our brochures when the design process is nearly complete without any consideration of the time constraints… anyway, there are a lot of complications in it, and Ronald and Stephanie have a history of conflict.

Ronald seems rather timid and polite, at least in these kinds of in-company exchanges, but actually he's really an ace when it comes to sales. Whenever I speak to him, I get the impression he does his research and he knows how to sell. He's made a couple of mistakes, but they have only occurred when he was misinformed about new products, or once about a product that was being discontinued.

Stephanie seems to depend a little too much on the fact that I was once a designer, so I can understand the particular challenges that the design team faces. Well, I think she's being a prima donna, actually.

I tried to smooth things over. I guess I just wasn't in the mood for a headache. Which is uncharacteristic for me… headaches are my pride and joy! Anyway, I told Stephanie to be proactive in bringing Ronald into the process, to keep him informed of any developments that come to her attention, and to let him familiarize himself with the contents of new brochures well before they go to press, while I asked Ronald to write memos requesting information with a cc: to Mel, our VP of Administration, to be sure nothing slips between the cracks.

When I consulted with Mel about this ongoing friction, and I asked her to try to keep an eye on things and advise me, she confronted me with the fact that I hadn't taken a strong enough hand in the situation. I encourage candor in our private meetings, but I didn't expect her to throw my own philosophy back in my face. "If you haven't offended anyone, you probably haven't spoken the truth," she said.

I got her point. I was being a coward, or being irresponsible, in expecting this conflict to resolve itself. I was being diplomatic when I needed to be blunt. The fact is, just a little reflection revealed the truth to me. Sales and design never respect each other, and I needed to make Stephanie answerable to this problem.

I know Ronald, I know he's smart, and I know he doesn't fail to ask questions. If he wasn't getting informed, it must have been because of a total lack of respect from Stephanie and her team. The designers need to be told the plain truth: they think *they're* the experts, but they could never do what Ronald does. Sure, he could never be a designer, but until I meet a designer who knows how to sell, I'm not going to let them play this game of contempt where they act proud of their ignorance of everything relating to business and sales. They're snubbing him.

So, I don't need to say any more about the topic, I took the bull by the horns and let Stephanie know my perspective on it, the point is that I should have seen this from the start. I've been letting this kind of thing slip by because my mental confusion and stress over *non-business-related* problems are getting in the way. I mean seriously, can a fortune cookie lead to corporate bankruptcy?

8.
Shifting Perspective

"If you could change one thing, what would you change?"

Olga didn't hesitate: "I'd want my mother to live again."

"But you don't think you can live her life for her?"

"No. Mmmm, obviously not. But I guess that's what I'm trying to do, right? It's motivating me."

"We've talked about this. It's obviously a big factor for you."

"Yeah."

"But it can't work. You don't believe it can actually work, do you?"

"No. No, my mom's dead. She's staying dead."

"So why the self-doubt, the self-torture?"

"It's not that. I have to live, don't I? I mean, no matter what, I have to do something. I can't… just… die."

"Do you want to die?"

"Never."

"Never? What does your guru tell you about immortality?"

"It doesn't exist as you might conventionally think of it. Everyone, everything dies."

"Well, you won't hear anything different from me. So… where's the enjoyment? When do you reward yourself?"

"I don't."

"Why not? Do you really think you'll lose everything if you relax a bit and treat yourself?"

"To what? What do I even want? I'm fine."

"Fine?"

"No! But what do you want me to say? There's nothing but hell and misery in every moment of life? There's nothing but the never-ending threat?"

"What threat?"

"Don't play coy. We're talking about my dad again. You know that."

"Tell me about your dad."

"I've already told you everything about him."

I had to laugh at this, but I kept it to an ironic chuckle. "You can't have told me everything," I said, "because every time the topic comes up, you tell me something new."

"Even though that's true, it's a technicality. The core facts don't change. My dad is a killer, on the loose, justice has failed. Our whole family has been victimized."

"But you, principally."

"No. My mom, first and foremost."

"Do you feel guilty about her death?"

"Why should I?"

"You shouldn't. But do you?"

"No. Yes. I mean, I was only a child, what could I have done? But what *have* I done? Since then? It's only words."

"But let's just imagine a scenario for a moment. Just imagine, what if your father didn't kill your mother? Now answer your own question: what have you done?"

Olga was stunned. My direct challenges came rarely in our sessions, and they always seemed to catch her off guard, as though she'd forgotten the purpose of our meetings.

"I have unfairly accused my father."

"Forget him. Okay? That's not the point right now. What else have you done?"

"I don't know. Nothing else."

"Think. If you just assume for a moment that your mother died by chance…"

"Then I've wasted my life."

"Why? Why a waste? You've achieved a lot."

"Maybe. But… It's so damned empty."

"Do you always feel that way?"

"No. Only if I think that my mom's death was chance do I suddenly feel like a failure."

"Why do you think that is?"

"Because..." She trailed off.

A couple of minutes of silence passed. Then she spoke again, agitated, with energy:

"Fanishwar too denies the existence of cause and effect. Philosophically, within the mind, I comprehend this, but that's not enough. I must let go of this mental struggle. When I direct my meditation towards the Self, there is sometimes, miraculously, a flowering where I find relief from this terrible cause-and-effect delusion. But I can't stay in that place. I'm pulled down by my attachments. I can't find the cloud that will separate me from the troubles and thoughts that assail me from below. Yet, here, talking with you, that same thought of a world with no cause and effect is not blissful. It's a nightmare. Why is this?"

"Perhaps you give too much of a grand meaning to your understanding of 'cause.' Cause does not have to be human, and it does not have to be intentional. What if big things happen without such a grand cause... but they *really* happen. No *Self* outside the self. Just you. A child who's lost her mother, for no reason at all?"

"Do you want to drive me to suicide?" She was weeping now.

"Never."

"Why ask me to confront such a thing?"

"Remember something. If there's no cause, there's *no cause*. Your intent cannot be a cause."

"What intent?" She was angry now. Her eyes glared. Her lips were taut. Her face was a mask of horror. "My father... my father laughed at my mother's funeral. He laughed at her, and he laughed at me."

I just looked at her. Her conviction was cracking, but she spoke with more vehemence.

"He keeps one of her bones in the closet. A wishbone."

She had roughly the same expression, except that a trembling between frown and laugh within her lip showed that she wished she could disclaim this ridiculous thought. She was ashamed of her foolishness, but it was too late to call this a "joke." She was spiritually naked in this moment.

Rapid Progress

Over the next few months, Olga made rapid progress in her recovery. She was willing to entertain the possibility that her father may not have killed her mother. She reexamined all of her accusations and considered how she could have, somehow, become irrational. Exaggerated. Fabricated a false history within her mind. She still had anxiety, still suffered a great deal, but she talked more and more about how much her *delusions* had cost her. And then she entered a period of introspection, to examine her profound inner feelings. Between denying herself and externalizing her emotions, she had too long avoided a necessary inner-confrontation.

As per my advice, she delegated most of the responsibility for the management of her business, so she could take a long-needed break. I didn't discourage her from meditating or meeting her guru, but she took a break from that too, on her own initiative. And then she spent a week and a half at my center as an in-patient. She was released, and she continued to visit me on a weekly basis, while bringing herself back into her role as chief executive.

Without my prompting, she told me she had also opened up to speaking much more seriously about her troubles to her boyfriend Chris. She trusted him, and he was extremely sympathetic and helpful. Glad too. Because he told her he had suffered a lot from feeling pushed out of her life. He loved her deeply, but felt that she was too guarded and kept him too emotionally distant.

Max's Guilt and Envy

In this period, Olga also had some frank discussions with her brother. Max finally broke down and told her something he had never dared tell her before:

"At the funeral, or just after it, Dad had a heart-to-heart talk with me," Max said. "What he told me was intended to be a valuable lesson, but it just killed me to hear him say it. 'Maksim,' he said, 'you now know the true meaning of death in a way that no one else around you understands. Make this a point of strength, not a point of weakness. Some people will call it a trauma. Some people will not understand how you can overcome such a thing, but you know life is very fleeting. Take the opportunity to become supreme, to become something greater than most people can ever accomplish in their lives.'

"I never told you this because… well, because you blamed our dad for killing mom, and I thought hearing these words… you'd just spin them in a way to further convince you that you were right. But you were not right. Dad's just a terrible, weak, pathetic man. He abused us, you more than me, mainly because you were more vulnerable. But that doesn't make him a killer.

"But the bigger reason why I couldn't tell you was because he had no such advice for you, and I hated him for that. When he gave me this encouraging message, I saw how he just walked out, grim look on his face, and gave you a patronizing pat on the head. 'I'm sorry,' he said. 'I'm sorry'? He was going to make our mom's death a lesson for me to guide my life to great success, but for you… Ah… what an imbecile.

"I'm sorry our dad was no good to you."

This was all very affecting for Olga, and she told me more about the emotional turbulence it stirred in her. But Max had more to say.

"Of course, I knew how rotten it all was, but I internalized dad's advice anyway. I figured I'd go right ahead and make myself a real success in life, rise up, make a ton of money, and leave him in the dirt. He'd get nothing. That would be my triumph. And, by any reasonable means of evaluating, I did it. I've made it in life. Except, you totally outdid me. You are such a stunning success in life, and you have so thoroughly shamed our dad, you've won the triumph that I was after. I've envied you so much I couldn't bear it. It doesn't matter… I can tell you I love you, and that I wish you all the luck in the world, it's true, but still there's this feeling of resentment I have to fight against."

They kidded each other a lot after this. They trivialized. But I believe they both profited from this candid exchange.

Further Developments

The healing process went on, there were hitches, she had some setbacks, but progress was made. Anxiety diminished. I'll share one secret with you now. Just as in the treatment of a physical ailment, oftentimes the most successful cases are those where the patient cures herself.

I encouraged Olga to bring me news items each week. She was to direct her critical scrutiny at uncovering the falsehoods and distortions in the news and entertainment media. As a substitute for routinely reanalyzing her past, she was to use her skepticism to uncover the lies that are published daily. "Who edits this garbage?" became Olga's new refrain.

Olga continued her yoga too, and it seemed to do her good. Why not? I encouraged it.

Spoil Yourself

I played one little trick on her, perhaps it was a cruel one, but it had its point. I told her one day that she needed to go out and buy some expensive gifts for herself, pretending that she could send them back in time to her *young* self, roughly to the time when she was just finishing high school. "Spoil yourself with the luxury that a typical young lady would value. You've never done this for yourself, so do it now."

She followed my advice, and bought herself some diamond earrings, expensive cosmetics, a luxury brand handbag, and so forth.

I then insisted she wear them every day. To work. On dates.

At first she said she felt "joyful." Then she called me two days later and said it was a stupid experiment. "It's not for me to tell you how to be a psychiatrist, but this is dumb," she said.

"Don't make a fight of it," I countered. "Just do it."

"For how long?"

"A week. Until our next session."

"But I never wanted this kind of stuff in the first place. And I'm not sixteen or eighteen years old. It's embarrassing. Every compliment I get has a secret mockery hidden within it, like they can't wait to laugh at what a fool I'm making of myself."

"Do it. It's my prescription."

She came out to our next session. I met her in a different office than usual, and I lied about my own office being renovated. I asked her to show me her jewelry and cosmetics.

"Are you going to analyze my choices?" she asked.

"Just show them to me."

"Here."

"No, don't lean over and show me them in your ears. Give me the earrings, the cosmetics, the bag, I want to examine them closely."

"Well, all right, but I've found this whole exercise childish and annoying. Not to mention expensive."

I looked at the items briefly, then placed the diamond earrings and cosmetic items in the purse, and I threw the whole package out the window (my own office had no window, which is why it had been necessary for me to swap offices).

"Now get out! Now! Get out of my sight, and don't come back!" I screamed at her and chased her as she flew to escape me. "You're never getting your toys back, now go!"

She was stupefied for the next three days, and she had to deal with her feelings mostly alone.

After that she became less frugal. She wasn't profligate, she just relaxed a little. Mainly she learned what she had lost, because she'd cheated herself her whole life.

I never asked her to reconcile with her father. I thought that would be impossible. But she was doing much better for herself, and when she resumed her sessions with me, it seemed the progress was sure to continue.

9.
Blessed Relief

"All is going well," Olga said. "Business is going well. Lukin products have been selling well in Sweden, and the brand is gaining respectability. Once again we've found success by giving full attention to the demands of the market. We're looking for new inroads into Swedish building construction. The hospital project is still in development. Nothing's settled, but we've got a name in the market, and people are coming to trust us.

"I think Max is really lucky. Despite his ridiculous childishness, his wife accepts him, and I've visited them. The kids seemed happy. There was a warmth in the home-life there that I haven't seen in ages. I really give all the credit to his wife, Carissa; she just has to be an angel to put up with and forgive him. But she must see deeply. She knows how hard it's been for Max. You know, the kind of sensitivity that men aren't supposed to have, but, well... we're all just wounded kids, aren't we."

I told Olga, "The fact that you can say that is really a good sign for your recovery." I was very encouraged to see that she was depersonalizing a bit and could see her own emotional wounds as an outsider would, by looking at their counterpart in Max. But I didn't say so explicitly because it might trigger her self-consciousness again. "Now, what are things like in your relationship to your father?"

"Cold. As always. But I'm willing to accept that. When you get down to it, it's too much for me to try to take on responsibility for my relationship to my father. Parents have that responsibility, or else we can just leave it broken. You'd probably recommend that I apologize..."

"I'm sure you've discussed this with Fanishwar."

"Yeah. And he has me working on the *Self* again. The 'I' beyond my consciousness, beyond the world. He probably wants me to find out that my father is a part of that eternal 'I' as well. Maybe… maybe I have seen and felt that too. But Fanishwar isn't pushing for any reconciliation. To him, it's trivial."

"Ok. Olga? You know what you have?"

"No, what?"

I laughed as I said it. "Normal problems."

She laughed too. And tears came to her eyes.

"I have an important question now. Are you ready?"

"Yes," she said.

"How are you?"

"I still have nightmares sometimes, and sometimes I feel some familiar anxiety… not much, but it's a daily hurdle of sorts."

"Yeah, I know. But bigger picture. How are you, generally speaking?"

"I'm… cured?"

"Do you think so?"

"Yes."

"Well I agree. Go back to work, and enjoy your seeking of the Self or whatever your guru's turning you on to. You can probably do seven- to nine-hour days at work, but don't push too hard; you have a competent management team; let them do their jobs."

"Does that mean I shouldn't come back here anymore?" This worried her.

"No, you can come around to chat and we'll work on the daily hurdles. After a month, I don't think you'll even want my help with that anymore. But I'm not kicking you out."

She rose and shook my hand like a real C.E.O. Then emotion got the better of her and she hugged me for a moment before thanking me for all I'd done.

10.
Bad Dream

Olga wrote me to say that she had had a nightmare:

"I'm in a rush to arrive at the scene of a spectacle. I'm being transported in some kind of carriage that pitches a bit from side to side as we ride, and I look out at a bright but featureless landscape with hints of snowflakes and mist in the air. As I'm arriving at my destination, I realize that I have known all along what to expect. My father is about to executed.

"I climb up a crudely built and wobbly staircase made of bare, untreated wood, very pale like slabs of rough-hewn pine. I'm climbing to get atop an enormous execution scaffold… very big, and very high… the platform is big enough for dozens of people, and it is crowded with spectators… for some reason all of the spectators are *on the platform* rather than watching from below. They are all dressed in black, grey, or otherwise drab clothing… olive, brown… in an ambiguously nineteenth-century style, including some women with bustles, but some men are wearing something more like a twenty-first-century synthetic windbreaker… One kid is wearing roller skates with hubs similar to the ones we manufacture for skateboards—we've never done roller-skates—it's breezy and the platform is wobbling and shaking with the movement of people. There are no executioners, and my father is seated in the center of the platform on a chair that is bolted to the wooden surface. He's tied into the chair, with a black bag over his face (but I know it's him), and there is a noose around his neck. A long, thick, and scratchy hempen cable runs up to a crossbeam overhead. The beam is supported by two sturdy columns which are firmly rooted in the ground, unlike the tenuous platform which supports us. I soon realize that there is no trap door beneath my father's chair.

"Then I found myself fading into consciousness with a kind

of buzzing in my head, while the scene that had been so visceral receded from me. There was no resolution.

"I awoke and felt that life had become more dreadful in an undefined way.

"Other than having another bad dream... well, other things are okay. I'm feeling anxious again, but it's manageable. I just want to see you and talk things over. I'm hoping this dream is a kind of step towards letting go or... well..."

Olga and I made an appointment to meet again later that week.

11.
Not Finished

As optimistic as I had been feeling about Olga's treatment and the positive changes in her life, it did not come as a complete surprise when—the next time I saw her—she told me she had discovered new reasons to investigate her suspicions "a little bit more." I knew this was a dangerous game for her to play, and by revisiting her doubts she risked undoing all of the progress she had made. But I was unable to stop her.

Olga told me that she needed to find a way to experience real "closure," "for now and forever," to come to terms with the tragic, chance, meaningless accident which had killed her mother.

"After my latest nightmare, I've stopped dreaming completely," she said. "Every night is blank, but sleep does not refresh me. It's a new kind of restlessness. As a consequence, I've had difficulty in my meditations again. I've struggled to find any calm space within. I can't let go of a strong sense of attachment to details and sensations. When I told Fanishwar on Wednesday, he agreed that I had probably left something undone; maybe I had left a lot undone. Yet he advised—as you would have advised, I'm sure—that it is *better* left undone. It is my commitment to *doing*, my *rajas*, he said, which is my problem. Nonetheless, after an hour of observing me and speaking with me, when he saw how much I was struggling, he offered me a compromise.

"'The best thing would be for you to do nothing,' he said, 'but second best would be to do something. You will not find closure by looking outside of yourself. But, as your awareness is clouded by the dust and noise of your overactive mind, you may only be able to look inside after discovering the futility of effort. In that way, great effort may yield the profit you had better earned through no effort.'"

"But Olga," I objected, "what further effort can you make? I have to agree with your guru's first instinct. To do nothing is best. You have closure already except that you keep insisting on reopening the same questions. Let it lie now."

"But you haven't heard what I've already discovered. It will surprise you, I'm sure. I started browsing through old news stories, but not so old, something closer to our own time…"

"Why…?"

"I read this, I read that, and soon by chance I stumbled on a four-year-old news story from the Philippines about a conflict on Boracay. *Two Killed in Struggle over Squatter's Rights.* You see, it turns out that the old *Hotel Karingalan* that I stayed in with my family—the same place where my mother drowned—was not completely demolished. There are people living in it."

"How is that possible?"

"It's been complicated and controversial from the beginning. The hotel was shut down and condemned because the builders violated environmental and zoning codes, but the owner of the hotel wanted to fight it out in court, and he wouldn't pay to demolish it. Then the government started demolishing, but they used public money. Amid taxpayer protests over misuse of funds, they gave up the demolition project halfway through."

"Huh. But that was still thirty years ago."

"True, but after a couple of years, some local families were discovered living in the ruins. To them, it was free real estate, rent-free homes. Then they got pushed out, but some other locals took possession… they couldn't get pushed out for long, neither by the property owner nor the government, which progressively lost interest. Long story short, some new 'owners' took control and started charging a nominal rent. Some families lived there for decades. Then a new local government effort led to the police raiding the place, there was a shootout, two residents died, and public sentiment supported the squatters. There were rumblings, then silence. No one's talked about it in the media since."

"Ultimately, this sounds like a tragic mess for the Filipinos, but it's irrelevant to you and your life. Why does any of this matter to you?"

"You're such a close-minded fool. Don't pretend you can't guess what I'm hinting at."

"Well…" I was taken aback by this challenge to my credentials as a psychoanalyst. "Well, okay, I know you want to go there. But you're conveniently ignoring my point. You *shouldn't* go there."

"I'm going there. It's already arranged. I had to pay a private agent to go figure a way; he ran into some trouble, but he found a way to contact the new 'manager' of the place, named Paolo Dacumos. The residents came back, they're still living there, the buildings are still standing, or some of them. I'm going to pay him a ton of money to get me in, guarantee my safety, he's arranging everything, air tickets, a driver… Paolo's arranging it… for twenty-thousand dollars, if any problem arises he can afford to walk away and let someone else manage it."

I'm sure I looked completely dumbfounded when she finished speaking.

"This is exciting, really," she insisted. "Until this week it didn't seem possible, but now it's happening. I'm going to see the place where my mother died."

And so she followed through on her plan. When she returned, she told me the following story about her adventure.

12.
Boracay

I arrived at Kalibo airport, having gone without sleep for forty-six hours—eighteen hours in the air, and the rest, well.... The airport was very crowded and chaotic, and it had a very third-world feel. People were packed in everywhere. I maneuvered my way through the masses, and emerged into the hot night, where I was confronted by the looks of anticipation of dozens of people waiting or looking for... something. The sky was black as ink, but I had bright lights shining in my eyes from somewhere above, so that I felt as if I were on a stage, and all the people staring out of the *dark behind the light* were like a barely visible crowd of spectators.

My driver found me and politely took my bag. I barely comprehended what he had said to me, and quickly forgot it, but as soon as the bag was out of my hand I suspected I was being robbed. But no, he led me to the car, I got into the back seat as he loaded my luggage into the trunk, and then the long drive through the jungle began.

Everything on the road seemed more ominous to me than it would have to a casual tourist, but I did my best to calmly observe without reacting to or interpreting anything. Everything was infinitely unfamiliar. I couldn't remember a single thing from my childhood trip. Maybe I had driven over this road only in the daytime? At night, the jungle seemed like the primordial presence, a threatening, mysterious, and eternal force that swallowed up humans along with their habitations. There were few structures visible along the way, and many of them were in a state of partial or complete collapse. *And yet*, I thought, *so many tourists pass through here with their money.* Yes, they pass through, but they don't stop. No wonder the jungle was swallowing up all roadside enterprise.

After the long drive, there was a long wait for a ferryboat, and then a ride on the boat. That stage wasn't quite so long...just... slow. A sudden and intense downpour of rain fell. The boat itself had a pleasantly reassuring, iron solidity. It seemed the most concrete item I had yet encountered, while everything else seemed ethereal and fictive. Then, after the boat stopped, the man who had been my driver introduced me to "Paolo's man," who would guide me from there. He led me out under a large umbrella—then folded it again as the rain ceased—across a dark dock, and we hiked a short distance through the mud to a truck that delivered us, along with several other passengers, north along the spine of the island.

The road was flooded, and I saw many motor-tricycles transporting passengers slowly, as the ankle-deep water and the ruts caused traffic to crawl. I saw some laughing girls in short pants and bikini tops—illuminated by the surprisingly bright nighttime street lighting in this section of the island—riding in the sidecar of a tricycle behind us. That is what triggered my first memory.

A Fragment of Memory

I remembered riding in one of those tricycles. I remembered both of my parents shouting at me repeatedly to "hold on" because they were afraid I might be shaken out of the sidecar when going over a bump. I didn't really think it was serious, but then I felt a bump, got scared, and held on tight. Then I noticed that my dad wasn't looking at me. He was looking past me. I looked forward and saw a young and dark-skinned Filipina with long hair and somewhat scandalously revealing clothing. I turned back to look at my dad once more, but he was looking away, obliquely, and I knew he had been looking at that girl. I didn't understand why it upset me, but knowing he had been looking at that girl made me feel a little afraid, and a little disgusted.

What Remains to Be Discovered

I put this memory aside and quietly observed the mix of tourists and locals milling about along the way, still active despite the darkness and the flood. After our truck dropped off several people at various places, I was finally delivered to the hotel where I would spend the night.

I relaxed a bit, and had a meal in the hotel restaurant: Sushi. For some reason they didn't have anything particularly Filipino in style, but rather offered a mix of Japanese and Korean options. Eighty percent of the diners were members of a large Korean tour group. After dinner, I did yoga in my room and then lay on the bed.

How was the night so blank? In the midst of what I had expected to be an anxious time, the night before visiting the place where my mother had died, I was focused on little details that buzzed in my mind until my *small-s self* fell away. The little details, too, fell away. And this little night seemed only a gesture made in the midst of a void. At some point, sleep came.

I went the following day to the condemned hotel. Paolo Dacumos met me at the place where I was staying and delivered me by motorboat to the ruins. There was very little to see from the water except for a large concrete platform that had been cleared of structures. The jungle had overgrown much of the rest, and some of the grounds of the former resort were set too far back to view from the low angle at the surface of the water. But when we jumped out of the boat into shallow water and scrabbled over some rough stones and fine sticky sand—and Paolo was actually stung on the foot by a sea urchin but tried his very best to make little of it—we came upon the shore, and I could see the white of some of the buildings at the back which peeked out from within the vegetation.

"You'll see some people living in the old hotel buildings, where the government gave up on demolition. No one would even pay to tear it down. Please excuse me...," Paolo said, as he hobbled over to sit on one of the old plastic beach chairs someone had tossed onto the rocks. He waved with a backhand gesture to indicate I should go on without him, and he winced but resisted any further display of pain.

Hesitantly, I did proceed with a weakly expressed, "Are you going to be all right?" which he didn't respond to.

But as I was walking and he started pulling out a couple of sea-urchin spines from his flesh, he called out: "I told them to clear out of your room for a day, so you can look at it in peace."

I came around some concrete rubble and saw that there was still a sizable section of the hotel largely intact, and in the midst of a u-shaped arrangement of buildings I could see a courtyard with a small empty swimming pool, which was about eight feet deep at the far end, but most of it was wading depth. Some women and children looked out of windows of the buildings, down at me, as though they had been expecting my arrival. A teenage boy stood in the empty colonnaded space that had once been a lobby, under the building at my right, and he greeted me.

"Hi, are you Ms. Lukin?"

"Yes. Have you been waiting for me?"

"Paolo called me. He told me to show you up."

The boy led me up some wide concrete stairs to the third floor, then handed me a key and told me where to find room 303. I noticed that despite the decrepit state of most of the site, these few buildings had been painted and kept relatively clean. Someone was maintaining this place pretty well.

"This place doesn't look so old," I said.

"Nah, we don't respect the poor and dirty. We're poor and clean!"

"I guess it doesn't cost much money to wash."

"Exactly. But don't go to Manila. Those people are no good."

"I'll keep that in mind."

I walked towards the room, along a sort of half-covered back passage which had a roof to protect from the elements, but it opened out at the side to give a view of the wilderness. I felt a breeze blow in from the ocean that fluttered the jungle leaves, and it made me anxious once again. I opened the door to room 303, and entered the long narrow room within.

The tenants had cleared out most of their belongings. The

room smelled of cooking and the ceiling was smoky. One of the two bedsteads that had once adorned the room was still there, but the bottom had dropped out. They'd filled the space within the frame with a mattress on the floor. A few crumpled blankets with Disney characters lay on the mattress. The rest of the floor was bare, but when I approached the window I saw that some other bedding had been rolled up and placed outside on the balcony.

This room I remembered. I remembered there had been two queen- or king-sized beds, and I remembered I had been sleeping on one of them when I woke up to hear someone screaming. I also remembered there had been a TV on a stand against the wall, which was now absent. But one thing I couldn't remember was looking out the window.

Whoever was currently keeping up the place had installed a hinged shutter made of bars which could lock over the window. I was sure this shutter had not been there before. But it was now open…

It shocked me when I looked out now through the window glass and discovered *I couldn't see the pool!* From the third floor, it was impossible to see past the floor of the balcony, which had a low wall around the edge of the balcony's lip but no rail. I couldn't look down at an angle acute enough to see the pool.

The widow was only open about seven or eight inches, and it was hard to slide it up any further. Then I noticed a kind of screw-bolt I had to undo by hand in order to get the window fully open.

By sticking my head out as far as I could, I now saw a mere strip of the pool's edge. If there had been a safety rail similar to the ones that adorned all the other balconies, it would have been difficult even to see a person standing across the courtyard, but rail or no rail, it was impossible to imagine my father had spotted my mother in the pool from within the hotel room. Had he gone onto the balcony to see her?

I pulled my head back in and went to the balcony door. Not only was it locked, it was welded shut. Only by climbing through the narrow window could one access the balcony. I kicked aside some of the rolled up blankets so I could plant my foot securely on the platform. It felt a bit shaky, and it sloped forward, away from the building's face. I climbed all the way out to the edge, and below me I saw the teen who had guided me, now waiting in the courtyard. He looked up.

"What are you doing!?" he shouted. "Don't go there."

"I just have to see…"

There was then a thunderous snap and the balcony collapsed under me; it fell crashing upon the second-floor balcony, which cracked and lurched but didn't come loose. In the shock I was tossed down over the edge—hardly aware of what was what and which direction was up or down—I thought only *"he lied!"*—and I struck the concrete of the patio below, where I shattered my left shoulder and banged up my head pretty good.

I had seen the pool as I came tumbling down. But I had gone to where no six-foot-four 320-pound man would have gone merely to get a casual look around. And if the balcony had once been secure and accessible, why had it decayed so dramatically over the years while the residents had maintained the rest of the building so well?

13.
New Insight

"Max flew out to see me in Iloilo," said Olga, "where I had my surgery and spent a week recovering. I also corresponded with Paolo Dacumos a few more times and got all the information I needed."

"What did you discover?" I asked.

"I offered him $2000 if he could get together all of the pictures available that might show what the hotel looked like thirty years ago, when it was still operating, but he had to decline my offer. 'There's no pictures' he said. 'I mean, you can see the hotel, but not your section.' But he had access to old records he'd pilfered from an abandoned office, and I paid him for information and copies. He went on to tell me how the third-floor balcony across the courtyard, in the 320 to 328 section, had fallen shortly after the hotel opened. They closed up the whole place for two months to do repairs and reconstruct the facade on that end, but money pressure forced them to open without fixing the upper-level balconies on one side... our side. They rented those out at a very steep discount, with *no balcony access*. The doors out to the balcony were welded shut before my family stayed there, and they had been for over a year. So there you have it. My dad's alibi was a lie. He killed my mom. It's all proven."

"Well..." I stammered a bit. "To tell the truth, it sounds as if... Well, if he couldn't see the pool then your father surely lied about his alibi, which is very suspicious. I really hate to say this, but I'd have to conclude that you're probably right; your father *did* kill your mother."

When I said this, Olga's eyes sparkled. She showed such a bright look of relief I thought she might burst out laughing, but she merely smiled with some satisfaction. I had to backpedal, quick.

"Now, wait a minute Olga. There's no way you're going to prove anything here. I mean, all you have... and you don't even have that much, is something to suggest that your father's report wasn't factual. I mean, we know psychologically that his lie reveals a lot, but no police are going to investigate this, and no one is going to go to jail over this. You have no hope of putting your dad in prison. This is a tragedy really."

"I know all of that. I'm not stupid."

"But what are you going to do now, now that you know that your father is a killer who can't be caught?"

"I already knew that. That's nothing new to me. That's been my whole life. But now it has been proven. I was right."

"Wait, wait, wait. No. This… This is going to be very challenging for you to work through and to really grasp, I'm sorry. But you've been delusional your whole life, we've been over this, and you are now almost recovered. Really, astoundingly, you've made great progress, so you can't go leaping backwards now."

"What are you talking about? I was right. I was right all along."

"No. You're going to have to trust me here more than ever and not go back and reverse the progress we've made. No. You weren't *right*, exactly. You believed a lot of strange stuff, things you've recently come to see as mistakes—hindrances—which is exactly what they were."

"I haven't been hindered. My life has been on course most of the time, and hell, you'd expect the survivor of a murdered mom to have some anxiety issues."

"But listen, seriously. Your case is perhaps more surprising and extreme than other cases I've heard of, but it sometimes happens that a delusion, by coincidence, happens to be true. That doesn't mean the patient hasn't been suffering delusions."

"The only problem," said Olga, "is that no one would ever listen to me."

Abrupt Consequences

Right after she left my office, I fell to thinking about Olga's brother Max. I panicked and called her.

"Olga! Listen, you've got to set up an appointment to see me again, and we'll proceed with your therapy. But I've got something else on my mind. Could you put me in contact with your brother?"

"Why?"

"Well, obviously he's going to be extremely distressed now that he knows. I mean, after what you told him in the hospital, now that he's not responsible for taking care of you and he's putting the pieces together, he's going to start really getting distressed... He hasn't had a lifetime to process this, you understand..."

"Oh my God!" Olga dropped her phone, then picked it up again. "Oh my God! You... I just had plans to go meet him for dinner with his wife and kids, but Carissa sent a message to say he hasn't been... What..."

She hyperventilated a bit, then hung up and wouldn't respond to further calls.

Our worst fears were soon realized. The police called Olga, and she called me. Max had murdered his father with a gunshot to the chest. He had fled and was hiding somewhere.

It took them eight days to find him and put him in prison.

In childhood, he had never shot his father with a pellet gun as Olga's false memory had told her, but now he had acted out this same symbolic act with a forty-caliber bullet, and the *symbol* was deadly.

The Dust, the Mind... Gone

The Gothenburg hospital project didn't pan out. No longer wanting any responsibility for the company she built, Olga not only resigned, but also sold out her interest at a significant loss compared to what her shares had been worth a few years prior. But she remained very wealthy regardless, in her new condition of early retirement.

The coincidences between her experiences and her imaginings were too much for poor Olga to handle rationally. Her delusions became worse, and they became stubbornly resistant to all treatment efforts.

Olga came to the radical conclusion that none of her memories had ever happened; they were visions of her future-to-be. Time was reversed; all her hopes for the future were now memories of a shadowed past. She stopped associating with Fanishwar after she declared she had achieved "the falling away of the mind." Fanishwar did not agree that she was "realised," but she told him that by striving, *he* would one day be enlightened as she was.

The worst outcome, though, was that Olga formed a stronger bond with her boyfriend Christopher, and they decided to have a child together. Olga, by far, is not in any reasonable condition to be a parent. She wasn't, and she isn't suitable to the role of mother. But she told me, shortly before her daughter was born, that she believed her own mother had not lived yet—that her *daughter* would soon become her *mother*, the loved one she had always desired.

Considering what Olga believes about the inevitable death of her mother by drowning, I can't stand to think of what future this child might really face.

What motivates a murder? Very often we have to be content with never knowing the answer to such a question. But Maksim Artemevich Lukin told the jury at his trial that before going to confront his father he had spoken to him on the phone and demanded to know why "the old man" had murdered his mother, the beautiful and innocent Diana. At first, Max's father denied his crime, but he crassly concluded the phonecall with the statement that got him killed. It was a virtual confession:

"To tell the truth," he said, "I just couldn't stand that bitch."

Olga continued treatment with me until the closure of my center, and I did my very best to help her, with no appreciable results. Then she started therapy with a new doctor in another experimental program—a program which, as far as I know, has never shown any real promise for the recovery of any of the participating patients.

Ino Zhikbi

1.
Meeting Randall/Zhikbi

A SELF-STYLED KING

One of my most fascinating patients was a psychotic named Randall Glasper. He was maladjusted to the point of violent criminality, yet there was a remarkable structure and consistency to his delusion. His mind was, in a sense, a work of art, and it's a tragedy that he has been lost. This is not to diminish the great harm he did to his victims and their families.

Randall first came to public attention when he attacked a police station in Kansas City, Missouri. In the bizarre and seemingly unmotivated assault, Randall charged into the station armed only with a primitive homemade spear and wounded three officers whom he encountered. They ended his assault by gunning him down, expending thirty-two bullets, seven of which struck him in various parts of his body. The shooting caused critical injuries to several of Randall's internal organs and major blood vessels, and he was injured in the nerve beneath the fourth lumbar vertebra.

After a long period of treatment in intensive care, he underwent rehabilitation therapy. The state declined to prosecute, having judged him incompetent to stand trial, so he was confined for nearly three years at the Northwest Missouri Psychiatric Rehabilitation Center (NMPRC) as an involuntary commission by order of the department of criminal justice.

The public resumed its interest in his case when media reports claimed a link to an earlier unsolved crime: "The Gentleman's Club Fire," an arson attack that killed seventeen. When this news broke, and there were hints that the private source of the information was a member of the psychiatric team assigned to his case, there was immense pressure to remove Randall from NMPRC into a new program. Suspicion and anger were fierce, while police investigators denied he had ever been categorized as a suspect. It was at the height of this controversy that I took over Randall's treatment.

By the time I got to know him, Randall had transformed himself, in his own mind, into King of the Wawli people, residents of a fictional universe that he insisted was his true home. His name for himself was Zhikbi, and he sometimes employed the style "Ino," meaning "King."

FIRST INTERVIEW

Zhikbi entered my office and I waited for him to speak.

"*Igemno gwam*," he said in greeting.

I replied with the traditional salutation, "*Li wamkol otono olali.*" Zhikbi broke out laughing at my first attempt to speak his language. But his laughter died in an instant.

Randall was now thirty-one years old, and he was angry. His naturally long eyelashes were enhanced by the use of mascara. Meanwhile, he was incapable of communicating in English, or in any other language but the one he had created for himself: Wawli.

I must now ask the reader's forgiveness if I fall into the habit, acquired from many sessions with this man, of referring to Zhikbi primarily by his adopted name, rather than the name given to him at birth. It was on such terms that I was first able to establish communication with my patient.

Every time I met Zhikbi, starting with our first encounter, Ned Lincoln attended. His assistance as translator was immeasurably valuable. Ned had learned Zhikbi's language by studying him for two and a half years and speaking with him on an almost daily basis. I will say more about Ned and his relationship to Zhikbi when I find the time to relate a few of our private conversations.

After Ned and I had a brief discussion on the practicalities of our interview, Zhikbi began a more formal self-introduction.

"*Li wawlituhldosuhn ino Zhikbi'uht ne'i*," Zhikbi said. "*Lison zawldino Wibawwe abeshno bozuht nebi. Way uhk.wa.swi donaapkol ponbikat geshno woedutuht weson indwonno lembasis hebi. Li abeshast gwoezhkol lupgan pwibishal wiknano le.zmuhksis li lison misis zuhmkwikol nibi. Kawnbish kate holdawwe lison emawkol daashno nawinlo ohizlikol pwimishas. Tung.uhdiwe honkol go'an.ololkeshishas.u kwiskishas. Tokon holdawgan embaluno tuhldowe in.gedentno tung-uhdikol pwim."*

Ned translated: "I am Zhikbi, king of the Wawli people. My father, Wibaw, was a great hero. He established a just monarchy, and punished the priestly class for their corrupt morality. I too was bound for greatness, but by political intrigue I was driven out of my land. My exile and dishonor have put my life on a tragic course. I do not know what the future holds for me. Those of your people who act in dishonor have an uncertain future."

With this as a start to our dialogue, I wanted to get a quick impression of how well he understood his current circumstances. Here I present all that we said, translated except for a few conversational asides. I am depending on recordings of our meetings.

"Which of these facts do you acknowledge, which do you reject, and which are you unaware of? First, you reside in the United States."

"I am aware of this. I am in a foreign land. The people are known as United States of Americans. I accept this fact."

"You are in a wheelchair because you are unable to walk."

"I am aware of this."

"You have been accused of several killings. You are a criminal."

"I am aware of this."

"You are a black man."

After a puzzled response, and a brief attempt at an explanation, Ned said, "He doesn't understand."

I restated my comment literally. "You have black skin."

"I am aware of this."

"Ummm… do you prefer the term 'dark skin,' or 'brown skin'?"

"I don't care."

Preliminaries aside, I tried to get more to the point.

"Do you understand that you're in a mental hospital? This is a hospital for people who have psychological problems… problems of the mind."

Zhikbi leaned forward and became more animated.

"Among my people it is said that I have *clu*. This is *strangeness*. It is a natural property of a king. It is a divine blessing, but also a curse. I am not really of the mortal world. I am like a bear, or a spirit, or the wind."

"That's not really to the point. I want to help you understand that this…" I gestured around at the walls of the office, and at the wheelchair he was sitting in. "This is your world," I continued. "This is all of it."

"I understand that I am a hostage, that my captivity is real. I know that I am imprisoned here because of my attack on your warriors, because I had the courage to strike with my spear against your men with their *body-rippers*. It is a shame that I was taken alive. My strength was overcome by force, but I never surrendered."

"But why did you want to attack the police officers? They were strangers to you, and you were under no threat."

"They were treacherous. I don't know what will happen to them."

"They have recovered well."

Ned interrupted. "I think I have to explain. Zhikbi is not expressing concern for their wellbeing. Zhikbi is not permitted to make threats, or oaths regarding future action…"

"*Honkol ton wazu nomi?*"

"…it's a cultural taboo."

"*Slel^naa. Li tonsis keumkwikol nilest aameumi.*"

"*Li sukapkol daylkeugan mutslin emba'i.*"

"*Ukicluwe tonson benapkol aamne'ishas.*"

"Wait," I said, "I want to know what Zhikbi is saying."

Ned said, "It would be indiscrete to ask."

"But it's important that he be direct."

"*Otonsis li ginkol nomsi aamitoni'u kwiskishas.*"

"I'm sorry, I can't be explicit without offending him," Ned explained.

I was agitating Zhikbi, and I could tell he had little tolerance for any conversation that went untranslated. His lower lip jutted out on one side and he set his jaw a little forward as he seemed to suppress an urge to grind his teeth together. He darted a couple of angry looks at Ned, each time quickly looking away again, as though to hold his rage in check by redirecting the focus of his eyes.

I tried to avoid offending his cultural beliefs, though it was difficult and frustrating to negotiate around the taboos of a "culture" which was simply a fiction. But Zhikbi's delusion was constant and unyielding. He very convincingly represented himself as an exiled king of a foreign nation with its own foreign etiquette. If taken at face value his whole concocted background story seemed almost seductively persuasive.

"Zhikbi attacked a police station," I said, "completely out of the blue, with no apparent motive. The men he attacked had never seen him before. If we can't discuss the future, then let's start with what we know of recent events."

Against my expectation, Zhikbi seemed to get angrier, and this time he directed his anger at me.

"You want me to understand you, but you don't want to understand me," he insisted.

"You're mistaken. I'm trying to help you, and I very much want to understand you. It's most important to me."

"If you want to understand, don't speak. Listen."

2.
Zhikbi's Tale: Early Years

MEMORIES OF YOUTH

When I was a child, my father, Wibaw, was a powerful local chieftain, not yet a king. Our settlement, which stood in one place for many years, was named Wibawdaw in his honor. Our family was wealthy, and our status was so great that we lived in a house with wooden floors. My father was a loving man to his family and a terror to his enemies. He knew no fear, and no one who dared to defy him ever kept his honor for long. Some were cast out. Others lost their lives, or they surrendered their wealth to buy their skins.

Even in my infancy, my father was very kind to me. Most children were handled exclusively by their mothers, and a father typically kept a distance from his child until he could stand and speak. But my father often rocked me and slept by my side. I have a very early memory of him carrying me in a clearing just outside of our house. He produced a hypnotic sound with his voice, both humming and whistling at the same time in two different pitches. It wasn't a complex piece of music, but rather a drone which cycled through a few notes and repeated. I remember it mainly because I once heard him intoning the same melody for my infant brother Anbi. It triggered a deeply buried memory from before I could speak. It reminded me of the stars on a chill autumn night. I still think of it at times to help me sleep when I'm troubled.

When I was eight years old, one of our envious neighbors, a man named Sipi, attempted to murder my father while they were out on a boat fishing together. It was his bad luck that my father turned to speak just as Sipi came behind him with his knife. My father trusted his ability to swim, and leapt into the water as the blade-thrust caught him in the back of the thigh and cut deeply. He then swam around the boat, attempting to grab at the edge anywhere he could get a grip, as Sipi slashed at his hands and fingers. But Sipi stumbled on a net... my father got a good grip, heaved himself up, and pushed his weight down hard, nearly capsizing the boat. Sipi, already off balance, fell out into the water. He was a much weaker swimmer, and my father soon overpowered him with kicks and punches, and dragged him by the hair, almost drowning him. Finally my father managed to get aboard again and pulled Sipi out of the water to temporary safety.

He returned to the village, with Sipi captive. He showed all of the neighbors his wounds, and told the tale to everyone. It was decided Sipi should be killed. Then my father, my elder brother Damkats, my uncle Laat.el, and three other neighbor-men dug a deep trench and threw Sipi in, beating him with sticks to keep him in his place. After calling curses down on his name, the men buried Sipi alive and left him to suffocate.

Sipi's Family

Sipi was not the first man to fight my father, and he was not the last, but he was the most treacherous. I was very close friends with Sipi's children Ti'aw and Dini, especially with Ti'aw, who was closest in age to me. It was a tragedy to see my friends lose their father. I felt terrible sympathy for them as they witnessed his death. Sipi's execution upset me even more than knowing my father had been attacked. I was almost deaf and blind to the suffering my father went through during his difficult recovery from his wounds. I thought more, instead, about my own loss of my close companions. Though these events had a long-term effect on the later events of my life, I never found out what was the cause of the conflict that lead Sipi to try to kill my father.

Sipi's wife, children, and even his elderly mother were all driven out of town. They fled south—a dangerous direction to go. I heard later that all of their family but the two young boys were killed in a raid by a tribe of U.hulia people. The surviving brothers, however, lived to adulthood and eventually became very powerful men.

To give you perspective, you must understand that the execution of Sipi, though an important event for my family and village, was not a unique event. Death by homicide is common among the Wawli, either by murder, execution, blood feud, or warfare with neighboring tribes. The boldest men come to expect this as their fate. Many women die too, though they are rarely killed from within the clans of the Wawli themselves. It is a cultural taboo to intentionally kill any Wawli woman other than your wife.

Those men who aren't killed are often wounded. Those of us who occupy positions of power and wealth are more likely than others to kill or be killed, and it is a rare chieftain indeed who goes through life without at least one killing. Yet I did not kill a man until I was seventeen, and the time has not come to tell this tale.

I don't like the history of my people to be seen in only a violent context. I am an educated man. In my childhood I had a tutor, which is a very rare thing.

EDUCATION

When I was still nine years old, Olul, an educated outlaw, came to our village. He had been living as an outlaw for many years, since the time when he failed as a priest candidate and was sold into slavery to a traveling Twilak merchant. He murdered his ship's captain during his transport, and he and two other slaves escaped in a boat and steered back to the western shore of Wawliland. They separated and fled into the woods. Olul managed to stay alive by constantly moving about, finding refuge in various villages for brief periods, and sometimes wandering alone in the wilderness. He even spent some time among the Zatnimi, the mysterious wanderers of the woods, and learned to speak and interpret their secretive cant.

When he came to us, Olul asked my father for shelter, and my father agreed. Father insisted, however, that Olul earn his stay by teaching letters to me and my brothers. Little Anbi was somewhat interested in learning, but he was still too young, and he was easily distracted. He mostly liked listening to stories, whereas he typically ran off to play as soon as he saw Olul take out a brush, ink, and paper. Damkats, my elder, was very resistant to any kind of learning. He considered himself a man already possessed of courage, and this was the only value he thought necessary for success. Therefore, I was the best student in our family.

Besides learning the basics of reading and a little mathematics, I also learned a little bit about fighting. This was an alien concept to our villagers. No one had ever heard of studying or practicing for combat. It was always assumed that courage was an inborn trait and there were no learnable skills that could help a man in a fight. But Olul believed that fighting was a skill. He told me that I could improve the effect of my spear if I coordinated the movement of my whole body. He told me of the importance of speed, which no one had ever talked about before. He also told me I could improve my strength, just like any other skill, by practicing.

That summer, I cut more wood than any other boy in my village. Our village was full of expert woodcutters. Besides felling trees, we cut wood to the proper shape and size for the construction of roofs and other structures. The pieces were typically sold to farmers in the Hulan valley and city dwellers in Shamni. Wood work was our main trade besides brewing and hunting. We all knew that when one uses an axe, the axe does most of the work; one's body focuses on directing the energy to the axe head and aiming it at the point where it must strike. Olul told me that the same concept applied to fighting with a spear or knife. He made no mention of winning a fight through bravery, or of standing one's ground as though no weapon can hurt you. He emphasized motion. He told me it was possible to move defensively, and also to make false thrusts, to anticipate the movements of one's enemy so as to land a killing blow. He taught me that the constant application of effort to my work would build my strength, which proved to be true. We had always been told that the best workers were successful due to their strength. No one before Olul had ever said that they were strong because they worked.

Because I worked harder than necessary, because I cut more

wood than was needed, because I tried to learn fighting skills with Olul, and because I was studying to read and write, some village kids regarded me as weird, which is expressed as having '*clu*.' They often used a style of speech that, when speaking of people, is usually reserved for kings, gods, madmen, and the possessed. Since I was neither a king nor a god, this could only have negative implications, but I took it in good humor. Besides, I secretly nurtured the idea that having '*clu*' implied I was bound for great things.

I said to my father one day, "I know very little of the world beyond our village."

"Don't exaggerate," he said. "You've joined our hunting parties and traveled with us for trade."

"But beyond the festivals and ordinary expeditions…"

"What else?"

"Ik.hun of the wise words, son of Tanung, has often said that we should do labor outside the village."

"I know. Many sons of our village go out, but you won't. It's good to maintain ties with the farmers and fisher-folk. But right now, the only benefit we get is the exchange of wives. This is not an advantageous sort of marriage for someone like you."

"I can work hard."

"Sure. Work hard at home. And study. You can learn more of the world in your studies than any drudge learns from digging up yams."

For the first time that I remember I felt limited by what my father chose for me, but I couldn't rightly argue. Others went; I stayed. But my day would soon come.

A little over a year after his arrival, Olul moved on to seek refuge in another village, and I didn't see him for a long time after that.

When I turned eleven, my father got the idea to send me to the city of Shamni to further my education—to get a *real education*—as was sometimes done for the sons of wealthy village chieftains. Perhaps he had been planning this for a while.

I studied with the high priests there, even though I had no intention of becoming a priest myself. While I was in the city, I learned from several teachers, including the very influential high priest Mo'uh.

Mo'uh was a sort of idealist. He held a higher degree of prestige than any other person in the city, and thus the entire peninsula. Though he held no special title relative to the other high priests, who were officially acknowledged as peers with equally shared governmental authority, Mo'uh was still universally recognized as their moral superior. He could have exploited his position as the charismatic de-facto leader to establish himself as a new king of the land, but he stayed true to his ideal of a council of ruling priests with equal opportunity for any educated and qualified man to join the ranks of the elite.

Regarding priesthood itself, it has great potential rewards, but it's highly dangerous to apply for admission to the order. First, a candidate must have significant wealth, officially defined as enough to live continuously in the city for a minimum of three years without an income. If he can meet this basic requirement, then the candidate must pass a series of very difficult tests, and if he is selected and approved by the reigning priests, then his final test is a lottery. He must draw a single token from a leather sack. Half of the tokens are red, half are black. If he selects a black token, he's accepted into the priesthood. If he selects a red token, then he is rejected. All of his property is confiscated, he is outlawed, and he is sold into slavery to foreigners. Although slavery has not been legally permitted among the Wawli for hundreds of years, and it was rarely practiced before that, the priests willingly sell people abroad to foreigners who allow the practice.

Many people accuse the priests of corruption and dishonesty, but we all accept that the lottery is conducted fairly. The tokens are openly displayed to witnesses. The entire process is conducted openly, with the selection of the token being made by the candidate with his own hand.

Mo'uh's entry into the priesthood is legendary, and the story contributed greatly to his prestige. He came from a wealthy family and was the youngest of seven brothers. Each of his brothers before him, one at a time, applied for the priesthood and failed in the final lottery. Mo'uh's father then expended the last of his resources to give him an advanced education in the Twilak city of Lomaz beyond the Aldas Mountains, and when Mo'uh returned from his travels and completed his priest training, he came forward for his lottery and passed. Mo'uh gained tremendous personal wealth and power in the years that followed, but out of respect for the honor and tradition of the priests' laws, he never paid money to redeem his brothers from slavery. Thus a whole family was sacrificed for the success of just one man, and his rise to power is regarded as one of the most notable events of the seventy year period when the priest class ruled.

I spent two years studying with the priests, and they continued my education in reading and writing. I quickly perfected my basic grammar, and moved on to points of style. I learned a fair amount about versification. I also acquired some knowledge of music theory, and I was pleased to hear the harp and ensemble music for the first time in my life about four months after my arrival in the city. The blocks, timbrels, and buzz-flutes added an unexpected richness to the musical experience that was quite stimulating, and it was much more sophisticated than the harp-and-chant music I was previously accustomed to.

One of the greatest benefits of my education was that I was allowed to personally copy out the text of a book of wisdom. I made one copy for the priests, and I made one for my personal use. This book contained a lot of the religious history of our world, including the stories of Zodu and his creation of the world and life. It was good to see some of the stories I'd heard in childhood confirmed in a written text. The book also contained a collection of wise sayings including the quotations of Isay, the hero with four lives, and there were several articles on the proper composition of verse.

Yet I was taught a lot that had no value. This included a significant amount of agricultural training. Though this could be useful to a farmer, my village never farmed more than a few small plots of yams and vegetables to supplement what we could hunt or trade for. There were lessons in brewing, but my village had expert brewers who knew more on this topic than the priests, and I found that the priests were in error on many details in their lessons. Then there were deep discussions of the law, on the origin of human law, on the proper governance of the people, but it was all very abstract and incomprehensible.

Most strange was the priests' dedication to language analysis, and their newly devised theory that the instances of universals are corrupt. They claimed that beings which we consider divine, such as bear, are inferior to their immaterial and perfect original. They wanted us to use plural forms for words which traditionally could not be counted because they had *clu*. So "cloud" could become "clouds," "death," could become "deaths," and "devil" could become "devils." Can you imagine "darknesses," "airs," and "sceneries?"

It seemed the priests themselves had devised a new heresy and were prepared to make it law. The people, however, simply ignored the priests on this point. Most were even unaware of what the priests were teaching, and we students generally held to our old beliefs without regard for the teachings of our masters.

Then Mo'uh came to some of us students to explain that most of the people beyond our peninsula did not believe in *clu* at all.

"Lomaz is bigger than Shamni, and many people of other nations are wealthier and more educated than the Wawli people. They may respect our nation because of our history, our priests' advanced spiritualism and our intellectual advancement, but they find the backwardness of our *common* people quite risible. Only the enlightenment of our elite citizens can lead the people out of darkness. That's your task. To champion truth, we must eradicate ignorance."

I listened to what he said, and like my fellow students I kept silent in my contempt for his teachings. But when we were able to speak confidentially among ourselves, we all agreed that Mo'uh had betrayed his Wawli heritage in favor of foreign ways.

After my second year of study in Shamni, the priests did a

terrible thing. They hunted and killed three instances of bear, and displayed the bodies in the city center. They did this, they said, to prove the truth of their teaching. They proclaimed that the death of a bear was of no consequence to the immaterial ideal that a bear represented. The priests wanted the people to see that the flesh of a bear can decay and be consumed by flies and maggots, even like the flesh of men. This was too much of an affront to our faith, and we students who held to the old ways left the city in protest, to return to our people. This was the end of my formal education. It was also the beginning of a great deal of strife for all the Wawli people.

Scandal

I first went fighting when I was fourteen, after a scandal that affected all the villages of our land. Though we had formerly prospered, it was poverty that drove us to take what we needed from those we could take it from.

In the summer, the priests had summoned all seven of the mead bankers from across the peninsula to meet in Shamni. The bankers came expecting to be coerced into some kind of undesirable loan agreement, but instead, as soon as they arrived, three of them were condemned for bankruptcy and were burned to death within hours of their sentencing. The remaining four were ordered to cease lending at interest for the entire year. They were also ordered to sell a large amount of mead to the priests for silver, at a rate of nine jars for one silver, or nineteen jars for two. This was regarded as an unfair price, as the market was selling mead for an even price of one silver for seven jars, regardless of the amount exchanged.

Bankers were ordered and authorized to cash out all accounts and demand deposits by using silver at the new rate to compensate for any shortage in their mead stock. Meanwhile, the priests took control of the remaining stock in the bankrupted banks and used it to settle all accounts at a discount before dissolving them.

Despite these emergency measures, mead sticks from the

bankrupted banks were redeemed for only one-third of their guaranteed value, plus a token amount of foreign silver which our villagers had never regarded as real money. Those with mead at the four "solvent" banks were able to get about eight-tenths of the value of their mead sticks and guarantees. At the same time, all the debtors across the land rushed to repay their debts with unfairly appreciated silver, rather than the scarce mead which they owed.

A lot of suspicion fell on the priests. Stories circulated that the priests had redeemed all of their mead sticks at the insolvent banks in advance, at full value, before forcing bankruptcy. It was also generally known that the priests and their families were the largest debtors, as they were virtually the only merchants who did business with foreigners. Two ships had been captured by pirates that winter, and the investors were not expected to be able to repay their debts. It was also reported the priests had been collecting a "bank tax" for the last several years, which the bankers silently paid as they feared the potential consequences of talking openly about the tax or resisting it. This was blatantly unfair, as the villages already paid regular tribute three times a year. So we all concluded that we and the executed bankers were victims of the priests' corruption.

The star people who speak for Zodu say:
> "Drink mead and be happy
> The priests cheer the people
> The priest who despoils is a bad priest."

But our priests cheated us that year.

Many of the outlawed members of the banker's families, their agents, and associates were seen fleeing into U.hulia territory, bringing with them every bit of moveable property they could carry. I, myself, would never have trusted savages with my life or the security of my family.

My father lost much of his wealth in the bankruptcy. Our village brewers suffered even greater losses, and there was hunger among us.

Though our neighbors to the north, in the Hulan valley, had

grown plenty of produce and accumulated a lot of dried fish, they traded most of what they had to the city dwellers in Shamni, and even sold to foreigners, as they were better able to pay than we. With so much food flowing out of the valleys and the countryside, there was an increase in competition for the wild game we hunters depended on. Animals suddenly seemed scarcer than ever, and some clans experienced violent clashes initiated over hunting rights, though thankfully our village was spared the degradation of having to fight cousins over scraps of food. We were also fortunate that some of the farmers in the valley gave our village a little bit of untraded surplus as charity, because some of our men had worked as migrant laborers in the late summer. This increased the prestige of Ik.hun within our village, since it was his prescient advice which had yielded this result.

Li.nem

We travelled to our usual autumn festival in the trading village of Li.nem, but our village presented a pretty pathetic sight. We didn't even have a pig for the feast. Meat was our usual staple, but we had already traded away most of our meat for other necessities, except for the few scraps we had eaten for daily sustenance. We had some mead, but at the festival we consumed most of our winter supply in just one night, leaving us little to look forward to in the coming months. And, really, most of our "mead" was only yeasty dregs. My father, meanwhile, gave very poor gifts to the villagers, and everyone was very dissatisfied.

Dwaadwu

Several days after we returned from the festival, one night when many of our villagers sat outside their houses looking forlorn and showing deep despair, my father declared that the complaining had become too much. He ordered the women and girls to enter the houses and not to come out, and all the men who behaved like women were to do the same. Then he and the elders gathered to shake their bags and throw bones for luck.

They continued at this all night, some winning and some losing what little they had, while we younger men sat on the fringes watching, playing our own games, and sipping a blend of very weak mead and water with some wild berries and raw honey mixed in. Those who had no mead drank herbs and hot water, and some even boiled pinecones and slivers of green wood.

At the end of the night, the elders stated that the bones had fallen well. They put away their bags and sat to tell stories of our hero Isay, a great warrior king of a thousand years ago.

Just then, unexpectedly, Dwaadwu entered our village. Dwaadwu is the bear god, and he is every bear. He came among the men, and stood up on his hind legs like a man. He looked around at us all, then faced my father. He raised one paw, as if in salute, and dropped back to the ground on all fours. My father's face flushed red. We all watched as Dwaadwu walked fifteen paces backwards, with his head held low, before he turned and ran into the dark woods. No one had ever heard of a bear walking backwards before.

We waited for someone to speak, especially my father, but after a while he turned and went into our house. The other men remained mostly silent, whispering only a few words here and there as they too returned to their homes.

The next day my father declared that we would go on a raid in the South. This was the first time my village went into battle during my lifetime.

RAIDING IN THE SOUTH

All men of at least twelve years of age prepared themselves for the journey. First, we hunted for five days to collect meat for the departure feast, then we drew lots for the twenty percent who would stay behind to maintain the village and see to the safety of the women and children. Each head of household was also allowed to elect one family member to remain if they so desired, but in practice no one did this unless they had a seriously ill or disabled family member in need of care. One man who was automatically excluded was the eldest villager, Tanung, who was said to be 106 years old. No one could remember the last time he had drawn lots, but the other elders said that he had fought and killed bravely even in his late seventies. Now his mind was gone.

I was fortunate to be allowed to go on the raid, but surprisingly my older brother fell out in the lottery and had to stay. He gave me his knife as a side arm in case I might lose my spear in the fight.

There were about 240 of us. It took us nine days to cross down to the frontier lands and into U.hulia territory, until one late evening we came across a large village. The smoke of their fires was still a distinctly visible haze against the purple sky, so we proceeded cautiously even before coming close enough to smell the burning wood. We paused at a distance from the village, which was situated near a narrow but deep river, and we waited for full darkness to come. Then a party of scouts went forward to examine the situation.

The scouts soon returned and reported that the village looked rather poor, but there might have been several hundred men within shouting distance. My father decided that the main force of our men would bypass this village and proceed deeper into U.hulia territory. First, we would intimidate the villagers, and then a small group would hold them under siege for a few days so they couldn't interfere with our raiding plans.

To begin, our entire force of 240 men made loud noises, shouting, striking trees, blowing horns, and starting fires at various places in the woods, as we all ran in a wide circle around the outer fringe of the village. The enemy villagers didn't seem to respond at first. Then, some time later, we could see small groups of men running from house to house, gathering in groups, but seemingly uncertain of what action to take. They didn't mount any meaningful defense, except that the homes closest to the edge of the village were quickly abandoned, and the men rushed to lead their women and children towards somewhere in the center. But we kept running, circling, and threatening without an attack.

In the midst of the chaos we created, my father and his men took control of several abandoned fishing boats at the river's edge, and shuttled the warriors across—all but the sixteen of us who were selected to stay behind. Then it was left to us, who should have been terrified in that hostile place, to use fear to our advantage against men who outnumbered us fifteen to one.

It was relatively easy to keep the villagers contained at night. From their perspective it would have been too risky to venture out, not knowing what could happen if they abandoned the defense of their families. The fear and uncertainty of darkness were our allies. When the night dissolved into day, it was our turn to be afraid.

On the first day, we retreated to a greater distance and broke into groups of four to roam about, blowing horns at random intervals, shouting, sometimes gathering into a larger group to give the impression of an imminent attack, and so on. We didn't stay in one place for any time at all in case the villagers were provoked to rush at us. However, they did nothing for the entire day and simply held to their tight defense.

On the second night, after dark returned, we launched a quick attack on the abandoned buildings closest to the river, starting fires and fleeing quickly. About an hour later, we burned a few buildings on the opposite side of the village, and again retreated to the woods, all the time keeping up threatening sounds. We hoped that the villagers would be so occupied in rushing about, putting out fires, or reinforcing their defenses, that they would become exhausted and unable to launch out at us. If we tired them out enough, the next day might be safer for us. However, we too were very tired, and we had to work out a way to sleep in shifts. In a group of sixteen, that's not easy to do.

The second day delivered good luck our way. We reconfigured ourselves into three groups, and we had just split up when a small scouting party came out from the village. It was our fortune that they stumbled right into our midst. There were four of them together, and we spotted them quickly, though they were traveling carefully and quietly. My group of five was closest to them, and we hid and waited for them to pass. They were heading towards the river, where our other two parties had just gone to start their patrol, one group going upstream, the other going down. After the enemy scouts passed us by, we launched volley after volley of stones, throwing at their backs, at their heads and legs, and sending them running in a panic. They had no idea how many were attacking them, or where the attack was coming from. They rushed right into our companions who turned on them with spears.

Three of the enemy were soon driven into the river. The fourth bravely stood his ground, and though he was taken down quickly, he managed to wound one of our men with a vicious stab to the inside of the elbow. The others plunged their spears into him and he didn't last long. Meanwhile, those who had fled into the water were drowning, and our men stabbed at them and threw rocks any time they approached the shallows. We were afraid that their screams would attract a full battle-gang to assault our position, but it was only a few minutes before they were dead. It seems the villagers weren't well enough organized to quickly mobilize against us.

Those of us who had not killed a man with our spears were ordered to recover the bodies and decapitate them so we could throw the heads into the village center at nightfall. It was a good plan. Fortunately, there were several of us who knew how to swim (a skill that my father was certain to teach me after his fight with Sipi). After running a quick arc around the area to be sure an attack wasn't imminent, we swam out and dragged the bodies in, then took them into the deep regions of the woods. There, my brother's knife tasted blood, though not the blood of a living man.

That night, four hours after nightfall, I was one of the six men sent into the village. We stealthily made our way very close to the center, until we saw a large group of enemy gathered around a fire. As soon as we saw them, we screamed as loudly as we could to frighten them. They were startled, but very soon several of them rushed forward, and as they came we hurled the heads right at them. They fell back at the sight, and as they were occupied by what they saw, we disappeared into the dark. Half a minute later the whole village was howling as though mortally wounded.

We had no more trouble from anyone in that village.

A day and a half later, my father returned across the river. With him came the entire battle-gang, bearing with them a few of our men who had died. Our losses were happily limited to only five deaths.

MUHLOSANGKO

The villagers whom we had been keeping in restraint could have been easy prey for an all-out attack, yet father would not hear any discussion on the matter. Wibaw wasted no time and no words when he ordered us to withdraw immediately without further conflict.

As we made our weary way home, I learned from several of our warriors that they had successfully raided two wealthy villages and taken a lot of valuable goods: weapons, silver, furs, even spices and medicines. Some men had large skins of mead to carry in addition to their other gear. They all had a lot to tell us about the various battles and the difficulties they had faced and overcome.

Some of the men were pulling improvised sledges laden with heavy packages, and the bodies of our dead men were being born by two horses which had been captured from the enemy. This was the first time in my life I had seen horses, and the strange animals frightened me.

Yet, strangest of all, there was one tall captive man walking in the battle-gang's midst, with a section of rope in his mouth to stop his voice. His hands were bound behind him, he was shirtless though he wore luxurious and brightly colored pants, and he held a very erect and proud posture.

Only when we were a safe distance from U.hulia territory, after about three hours of walking, did my father approach the captive. He removed the rope from his mouth, and led him away to a private space behind some trees, with a small guard force, while the rest of us sat and rested. Very quickly, stories were circulated around our make-shift camp. The captive's name was Muhlosangko. He was a famous chief among his people. He spoke Wawli and, most shockingly, he had a Wawli woman for a wife! A banker's widow named Linay, who had migrated after the great banking scandal, had settled in Muhlosangko's village, and so they were married.

Half an hour after they had gone off into the woods, Wibaw and Muhlosangko returned. The enemy chief was given food to eat, though his legs were tightly bound while his hands were free. Then my father finally came and spoke to me directly for the first time since our separation at the riverside village. But his talk was all business.

"The enemy man is very strange," Wibaw said. "He told me some stories about their way of life, but I don't believe his words. Have you heard about his wife?"

"Yes, I think I have," I replied.

"She is one of our people. She came to me in person, when our fight was ended, and presented me with many gifts."

I simply listened. There was nothing for me to say.

"I will release him soon," Wibaw continued.

"That's good." I said. "But he seems dangerous."

"He is, but there's nothing to be done." After a pause, he added one more detail. "I saw their children. They don't look much different from the children of our village."

It was two days later, after much walking, that we released Muhlosangko in the middle of Wawli territory. If he were able to make his way back home, without getting killed along the way, then he would be allowed to live. So it had been agreed.

Then, a few days further on, with a successful venture behind us, we returned triumphant to our home village, and soon word spread to all the neighboring villages that my father was a great leader and a resourceful war-maker.

3.
An Intermission

By the time we had reached this point in Zhikbi's narrative, I had met with Randall nine times, and we were getting no closer to discussing the pertinent events of his life. In the evenings, whenever I was not occupied by other cases, I reviewed tapes and transcripts of our sessions and sought any connections which might exist between his tale and his experience—something to help me get a handle on my patient. No connections were immediately apparent. It didn't help that I knew only a few superficial details about his early life.

Here is what I gathered from his case history: Randall was born in Kansas City, Kansas, and remained there until the age of twelve. His family then moved to the neighboring suburb of Olathe. When he was growing up, "Randy"—as his family called him—was a mostly normal boy without any known traumatic experiences. He was one of the few black children in a mostly white middle-class suburban neighborhood. He may have experienced a degree of social isolation. By all reports, his family was loving and nurturing, and Randall was intellectually curious in his youth. He was also physically healthy, athletic, and somewhat taller and stronger than many of his classmates. He never ran into much trouble, and there's no evidence that he experienced any serious conflicts. Psychosis struck abruptly later in life.

The Glasper family unit was shattered when they received the news that Randall had been shot and arrested for an attempt to murder several police officers. His parents separated, and his other relatives disowned him. Randall's father remained his one devoted supporter, the only one interested in his ongoing treatment, the only one who was *on my side.*

These facts, and a glimpse of his fantasy life as revealed in his storytelling, were all I had to work with. Being a single man, I spent most of my private time reflecting on the cases that puzzled me most, and now it was Randall's case which dominated my attention. As I strove for understanding, nightmares started to trouble my sleep.

A Nightmare

Once, for instance, I dreamed of climbing across a dark and stagnant pool of water, hanging on to a tall plant with a flexible stem. It was something like bamboo. The plant arched far across the water. As I climbed further out, the plant dipped lower until I could just barely keep my back from touching the surface. In the murk below, I saw a giant black spider following behind me, waiting for me to fall. As I reached the other side of the pool, I grabbed a dangling vine to keep from falling, but the vine and the stem sagged under my weight, dipping me into the cold pool, and the spider, which was about fourteen inches wide, latched onto my back and bit me with a dull pain that felt like a human thumb pressed hard into my lower spine.

Investigations

It became necessary for me to launch into some private investigations. I contacted Randall's father, Nelson Glasper, and I also set up interviews with some of the police investigators involved in his criminal cases.

Nelson was enthusiastic about the possibility of finally communicating with his son through an interpreter, but he otherwise provided me with little useful information, and Randall stubbornly refused to speak with him by any means.

The police detectives frustrated my efforts by refusing to give me access to the evidence they had gathered. However, in my communications with the police, I made contact with Officer Evan Briar, who had experienced post-traumatic stress after shooting Randall. He was initially hesitant to talk to me, but, with some persistence, I got him to agree to come to my office. He then repeatedly postponed our meeting until I was nearly ready to give up.

Meanwhile I had some private meetings with Ned. Ned was quite willing, even eager, to discuss elements of the Wawli culture and language, but he knew little about Randall beyond his adventures as King Zhikbi. I was not at all sure he would be supportive of my efforts to cure his friend, as he had become so personally invested in Randall's delusion.

"I understand that you and Randall are very close friends," I said.

"Sure," he replied. "With all the time we've spent together, and all I've learned… he's fascinating. That's obvious."

"And you're the only one he can really connect with. Does he joke with you? Does he ask questions? Does he ever show any hint of understanding?"

"He understands plenty."

"For instance?"

"He understands principals. He understands honor. He understands human corruption, and greed, and kindness, and desire."

"What kind of desire might motivate Randall to kill?"

"What are you asking me?" Ned shifted about uncomfortably.

"Never mind," I said. "You can't get inside his head. But do you ever ask him about the fire?"

"No."

"Aren't you concerned about the possibility that your closest friend may be a mass murderer?"

"We don't talk about those things. If he wants to tell me, he'll tell me, but if I ask prying questions he just shuts down."

Ned, in his typically matter-of-fact way, was delivering answers which were sincere yet not deeply considered. He was not inclined to pry, and he was not comfortable with my attempts to pry. What was most puzzling about the relationship of Ned to Randall was not so much that Ned seemed to idolize Randall, but that he was genuinely disinterested in the drama surrounding his crimes.

Ned had been involved with Randall since early on in his

treatment, so I hoped that I could gather enough information to help me better understand the development of Randall's language, and perhaps settle a dark suspicion that was troubling me.

When Randall was first committed to a public hospital, it was noted that he spoke his own unique form of gibberish. The police possessed several notebooks in an alien-looking script, which they regarded as indecipherable. But no one could say for sure whether the sounds he produced were part of a fully developed language, and most of the doctors and nurses responsible for his care believed he produced only noises and grunts.

Then Ned Lincoln, a patient with bipolar affective disorder, was brought in. A manic impulse had inspired him to leap out of the moving car he was driving in midday downtown traffic. The uncontrolled car ran off the road and severely injured a cyclist and two pedestrians, while Ned himself suffered mainly from abrasions and bruising, with hairline fractures in his right shoulder and hip. This was his fourth hospitalization, and he was held for seven months of treatment and observation before his eventual release.

Ned was a highly accomplished linguistics researcher, with functional knowledge of several Indo-European languages—living and dead—plus Tamil and the related Kannada, Korean, Turkish, and Tsalagi (a.k.a. Cherokee). He was seen as a bit of an oddball in the linguistics community because his research was sporadic and unfocussed, and he often proposed and strongly defended radical ideas, only to drop them once they had reached a certain critical mass of acceptance among his colleagues. He described his specialty as "an analysis of the lexico-grammatical evolution of natural human languages, with emphasis on the function of language to meet communication challenges within a changing social environment." But Ned, the specialist in systemic functional grammar, whose main interest was the relationship between language and social environment, had accidentally met Randall in a mental hospital, and he discovered a complete "natural" human language that existed without any social environment whatsoever. At least that was his claim. He befriended Randall, he listened, noted, and learned, and they continued their friendship even after Ned's release from the hospital, through regular visits.

The doctors who first had scoffed at the idea of trying to speak to Randall in his own language finally came around to believing that Ned was their only chance to get through to him, but they had little chance to take advantage of this opportunity. When Randall was admitted into my program, Ned came along too, technically as a consultant and freelance translator—paid for his services.

My concern now was to determine whether Randall was the actual author of his own language, or if, on the other hand, Ned could have participated in its invention. To take the question further, I was not yet certain whether Ned could have been embellishing, or even fabricating elements of Zhikbi's tale as part of his process of "translation." If that turned out to be the case, then I and the psychiatric community would have been victims of a bizarre fraud. In any event, it felt time to apply a bit of scientific skepticism.

To reach an answer, I would need to learn a little more of Zhikbi's language, to test whether the recordings of his story matched the translations given. This, by itself, would not establish the truth, but it would be a step in the right direction.

"I've been trying to listen to Zhikbi's speech," I said. (Again he was Zhikbi, no longer Randall). "I was hoping to pick up a word or two of his language, but I've not been able to understand much of anything. Could you help me?"

Ned was instantly animated and charged with excitement. He plunged into some esoterica of the language. Several times I had to slow him down and ask for more general and easily comprehensible information. "Stop. Slower and more clearly, please." He responded well, but then he got carried away by his enthusiasm once more. Some of what he told me was quite interesting but difficult for me to follow. I took notes throughout our conversation.

I knew I wouldn't be able to learn a complete language through a short lecture, but in several meetings I gathered as much as I could of the grammar of Wawli, I learned the alphabet and associated phonemes, and I got a list of commonly used vocabulary words, broken down by parts of speech, copied from Ned's research notes. He cooperated as though he had nothing to hide, but I wasn't leaving such an important question to mere supposition. I had already had plenty of experience with people in other cases who were most effectively able to fool me because they had thoroughly fooled themselves.

In addition to learning more about Wawli, I gathered a few facts that I believed might be helpful in the progress of the case.

"Zhikbi won't speak to the man you call his father, because he's not his real father," Ned told me. "Zhikbi says he was assigned false parents upon his exile to our world. He denies all claims about his childhood and early life in America."

"But surely you could persuade him to at least meet with Nelson once and give him a chance."

"No. Zhikbi suspects that another child's life has been stolen, and that life is the basis of the false history you ascribe to him."

"Okay. But obviously *you* don't believe that."

"No, but what do you want me to do? Like I told you, if I pressure him, he shuts down. You can end the communication, or you can communicate whatever you have to say to him yourself. I'll facilitate."

But while Ned sometimes resisted helping me in this way, there were other times when he went out of his way to help. Once, for instance, he tried to warn me about his friend's emotional state:

"I don't want to make too much of a fuss out of it, but I think Zhikbi's sense of personal honor… Well, if you consider some of the stories of the hero Isay, and some of the events in his father Wibaw's life… I think Zhikbi could be potentially volatile and uniquely dangerous. Zhikbi is clever compared to others in his nation, but he's also more human and less exalted. He may even feel ashamed of his education and his wit."

"Yeah. Yeah…"

"In his own estimation, he has the sort of cleverness which is pragmatic but not... virile. In comparison to his heroes."

So piece by piece I was gathering information and impressions. And, with what I had learned from this conversation, I was then prepared to listen with fresh interest and attention to the further development of Zhikbi's story.

4.
Zhikbi's Tale: Troubles Arrive

A few years went by without major incident. Though there were rumors of some minor clashes between Wawli and U.hulia in the frontier villages, these conflicts did not involve me or my family. Ti'aw, son of Sipi, my childhood friend who was now seventeen years old, was gaining widespread fame as a powerful chieftain in one of the southern villages. The village was named Ti'awsuhn Shon in his honor. He was a successful raider, and he was good at defending his people from counter-attacks. His brother Dini was also regarded as a great man, but not quite the equal of Ti'aw.

A TIME OF CRISIS

Then a series of major events occurred one after another.

First, the high priests outraged our people by again killing bears. This time they killed six bears and had the bodies dragged through all the neighborhoods of Shamni. Word of this spread quickly to villages all across the land. Meanwhile, there was an increase in violence in the frontier territories. While the priests counseled patient forbearance, they requested a larger than normal tribute in order to deal with the conflict. Most Wawli found this disgraceful, especially the suggestion that we should wait and avoid any large scale confrontation with our enemies, whom we all felt had been occupying our land for far too long. It seemed, too, that the priests had no real plans to use this tribute money for anything practical for our defense.

The next major event struck my family especially hard. My mother was bitten by a snake while collecting water. Very quickly her leg turned swollen and black. She cried and shouted with pain over the next four days.

Her shouts at night were dreadful to listen to. It was especially unbearable to my little brother Anbi, who was not yet accustomed to confronting death. He and I lay quietly in our room, pretending to sleep, but I heard him sobbing under his covers. Though I felt awful contemplating the possible loss of my mother, and I wanted to cry because of her pain, I think the worst element for me was my feeling of guilt because no one, not even I, did or said anything to comfort my brother during this difficult time.

On the third night, I remember my father arguing loudly with my mother, and he shouted at her angrily to shut up and stop troubling the children. But this did not comfort us. It compounded our sense of guilt, and made us feel a sort of hatred for father. His words, which were well intended, seemed cruel, though he spoke this way only because he believed my mother would recover. He did not admit the possibility that she might die.

But finally the poison had done all the damage to her body that it could do, and she died. When I saw her for the last time, her dead body was contorted in a strange shape, looking puffy and discolored all over. It's hard to say which was more terrible, her death or the process of her dying.

And as most of the household was seized with grief, I finally slept, giving in to the exhaustion which I had carried for so many nights without relief.

In my sleep, I had a vivid dream. I saw a boat traveling on water. Surrounding the boat were four strange animals, dancing in a circle. One was a monkey, one was a horse with strange patterns on its hide, but the others were unfamiliar creatures, one with a long neck, and one like a fierce wild beast with a yellow beard and a black triangular nose.

When I awoke and told my family about my dream, they said it was a good sign. Our faith does not believe in an afterlife. When we die, it is our personal end. Yet our lives leave echoes that transmit effects across the future. The outcome of our lifetime actions is a sort of ripple of effects, and our children are the most visible extension of ourselves beyond ourselves. It was in this sense that my dream foretold bright events if we interpret the image as gods escorting my mother's echo through a safe passage into future times.

The same week that my mother died, another woman in a neighboring village was also bitten and died.

It was one of the principal responsibilities of the high priests to protect women from snakebite. No one had been bitten in over fifteen years, and no one who had been bitten had died at any time in living memory. Because of these events, many people said that the priest class was becoming too corrupt, and they would bring us all to ruin.

Then came the trouble with the tribute. The tribute collector came to our village two weeks ahead of schedule. Normally we would deliver our tribute at a gathering in Li.nem. Only if we were unable to attend the seasonal feast would a tribute collector be dispatched to our village. This time he came unexpected and unannounced.

He met with my father in front of our home and asked to be invited in for a drink. My father told him that it was impossible to meet inside, as there had recently been a death in the family. Instead, they met at my uncle Laat.el's house. I was not a witness to their conversation, but about half an hour after they began their meeting I heard a commotion.

I stepped out of our home, and looked across the village towards my uncle's home, where I saw Father and Uncle roughly escorting the tribute collector out. This was remarkable because, though my uncle was a big and powerful man, he was usually very patient and hospitable, even when dealing with troublesome characters. The tribute collector shouted something which I couldn't quite distinguish, but it sounded threatening. Then he walked away with slouched shoulders, looking dejected, and Wibaw and Laat-el went back in and shut the door.

An hour and a half later, I sat copying a poem from my book of wisdom and studying the style of the verse, when Father Wibaw, Uncle Laat.el, and Brother Damkats came in as a group. Laat.el was the first to speak.

"Zhikbi, we've made some big decisions, and your help is needed.

First, you'll want to know that your father and I have refused to pay tribute, on behalf of the whole village."

"Oh. Well, I'm sure you've made the right decision." This was all I could manage to say.

"The priests demand too much," my father said. "They want more tribute than ever before, they sent a collector early, they don't trust us, and they treat us like criminals."

"And they do nothing useful with the money" said Damkats. "Why do they demand so much, yet they keep telling us to wait and wait, and do nothing about the U.hulia."

"That's the main thing, Zhikbi," said Laat.el. "We have decided to attack the U.hulia ourselves, and support the border villages. It's much better than paying for a troop of guards and lazy priests who never leave the city."

"So, we're going to war again," said I.

"Not again, but for the first time. This is no little raid, this is much more serious. There will be great opportunities for honor and to increase our wealth."

"I see. But what is it that you especially need me for. I'm the youngest and weakest man here. I've never killed. I'll happily fight, but what else are you asking me for?"

"Ti'aw and Dini are becoming heroes in the south, but they resent your father, and all of us as his kin. We need to make peace. You know them best. You're also educated."

So it became obvious they needed me as a diplomat. Damkats and I were to travel with a small escort through the dark and dangerous wilderness, and walk into a potentially hostile village, to seek the help of men whose father had been killed by our family.

In fact, I told them it was a crazy idea, but if I were to do it, Damkats would be required to wait in a camp some distance from Ti'aw's village, and I would go in alone. Considering that Damkats himself had participated in Sipi's execution, I would only summon them if the brothers agreed to make peace. Then Damkats would be allowed to offer a truce as representative of our father. If we were not killed, then we would arrange a direct meeting and settlement between Ti'aw, Dini, Wibaw and Laat.el.

ZHIKBI THE PEACEMAKER

As on my first trip to the south, it took us just over a week to get down to the frontier area. Damkats and I were accompanied by six others: Wose, Gan.geun, Beunba, Kawlan, Lanna and Bikni, all of whom were to follow my directions and assist us in any way requested. Travel was somewhat slow paced, as we travelled cautiously in territory that remained largely unknown to us. Along the way, we debated my plan to enter the village alone, ahead of the others. Though I insisted on this, Damkats and the other men stuck stubbornly to one point: we didn't actually know where Ti'aw and Dini's village was. They said it would be foolish for me to walk unprotected into every village we encountered. I could possibly be killed even before we got to the right place, and our mission would fail. To prevent this, I should send scouts ahead to ensure we were where we should be. I argued against this for a long time, but ultimately came to the compromise that I would allow scouts to enter the first unknown village we came to, but only the first, and that once we gained our bearings I would be on my own.

Proceeding with this plan, when we came to a frontier village in approximately the right area, Beunba and Kawlan went in ahead of us. They returned shortly to report that this was Hongdaw. It was not Ti'aw and Dini's village, but the chief of Hongdaw wanted to meet me, and he would direct us to the right place.

Hebul, the chief, greeted and received us warmly. He gave me specific instructions on how to find Ti'awsuhn Shon.

"But you will not find Ti'aw or Dini there," he said. "There has been a raid, and the two brothers have fled in fear. They have abandoned their people."

"I don't believe it," I said. "They are known as great heroes. They would not run."

"I wouldn't believe it either, yet it is true. They were heroes once. Now they have forfeited their honor."

"How do you know there was a raid? Have you been there?"

"No, but there are some women here. They are refugees from the raid. They don't speak much. I've told you what I know."

I thanked the chief for his information. We made arrangements for Damkats and the other men to stay in Hongdaw for a couple of days and nights, while I went alone to explore further. Damkats was very annoyed with me, but he kept our agreement.

Before I could go, Chief Hebul gripped my forearm tightly and stared at me with a fanatical look in his eyes, quite unexpectedly.

"The world we occupy is more illusion than reality," he said, "but one misstep can cost you dearly. Your spirit seems strong for a young man. Don't lose your way."

He then released me.

I set out then for Ti'awsuhn Shon. I wasn't sure what to expect when I got there, and I didn't fully trust some refugee women whittling a birdsong. Nonetheless, I was cautious as I came to the fringe of the woods, where the trees thinned out to reveal a gradually sloping hill covered in sparse grass.

As I came out from among the trees, onto the field, I saw the ground had been beaten and churned as if by many hundreds of feet. There were signs that a few horses had passed as well. Clearly this was no ordinary raid which had occurred here. The village ahead, atop the plateau which was guarded by steep slopes on the east, west, and south sides, was utterly silent and still. A few broken fragments of wood and spear heads were littered about on the slope, and two dead men lay sprawled out, side by side.

I climbed the hill and made my way between the houses, into the heart of the village. Here I found more than sixty bodies, rude bloated corpses lying about the central clearing between the many homes that stood in a ring. The flesh of the bodies was putrefying, liquefying, melting into the sandy soil. Some of the corpses had the blackened flesh upon their faces run away, to reveal the broad white circles of their protruding eyes. In some cases, open spear and knife wounds were apparent, as the flesh had drawn away to reveal the skeleton below, or to vent the enlarged and overflowing inner organs. In other cases, there were no signs of the cause of the people's deaths, except for dark stains on their clothing and the surrounding earth. There was no shade in this clearing, and the sun beat down on them.

It seemed the entire village had been slaughtered, almost certainly by invading U.hulia fighters, and I didn't expect to find any survivors. However, as I made my way out to the western edge of the plateau, I was surprised to find a few teenage boys gathered there, digging graves. They told me they had escaped down the hill and run to the west as soon as the assault had begun, and now they had returned to see if any of their family members had survived. Sadly, the dead were in such a state that few of the boys were even able to recognize their parents or siblings. Nonetheless, they were digging graves for those they knew, and they were debating whether they should use a mass grave for the unknown ones.

I walked closer to the edge, and saw the great defensive advantage of the village's location. Not only were the sides of the plateau very difficult to approach, but the view from the top was clear for great distances all around. It should have been very easy to spot any approaching attackers. Yet the advantages of the terrain were not enough, as it seemed that an overwhelming number of men had come all at once. A lot of soil and clusters of stone had been torn away from the edges of the cliff faces, making it clear that attackers had scaled and attacked from all sides. The teenagers, and the few women refugees who had gone north, had to have been extraordinarily lucky to find an opening for their escape. That, or they had made their break very early, at the first sign of danger, perhaps without having the time to give warning to their neighbors. But the boys had nothing to say on this point, only that they had gotten away safely, which was clear enough in the circumstances.

Looking off to the west, I saw a nearby hilltop village, perched on a rise not quite as high as Ti'aw's Plateau. There was some rising dust and smoke there, and a few other signs of life, so I determined to go their next.

When I came to the western village, after determining that the inhabitants were Wawli people, I entered and approached the chief, Azpek, who met me willingly. He informed me that his village, Lishisuhn Imnu, had been spared in the recent invasion. He was hosting several more refugees who had escaped the slaughter. Some of the refugees reported that the invasion had been led by the famous U.hulia chief Muhlosangko, and their description of him agreed with my memory of the savage prisoner whom my father had ransomed.

"You've come the wrong way," said Azpek. "No one has passed through here. Rumor says that when Ti'aw and Dini fled, they ran for the safety of Isaysuhn Dozh."

Isaysuhn Dozh was a town of historical and cultural significance to the Wawli people. It was the only trading town in the southern frontier area. It had never been attacked or harassed, though it had little in the way of practical defenses. It was regarded as a sort of sanctuary, presumed to be protected by the spirit of Isay.

Azpek then asked me who I was, and where I was from. When I informed him I was Zhikbi, son of Wibaw, from Wibawdaw in the north, he was eager to determine the reason for my coming.

"Have you come to help us against the U.hulia?"

"No. On the contrary, I've come to kill Ti'aw and Dini."

"What? That can't be possible. What reason can you have to pursue a feud with the brothers now?"

I refused to answer.

"We need to fight to resist the U.hulia," the chief continued. "There's no time for personal feuds. Your father has already killed their father. It has brought the brothers shame that they have never taken vengeance. Now, how can you persecute them further, and why would you do so?"

"Don't question my reasons. I came to find out where they are. If you have no other information, then I can go."

I got up angrily, and turned to leave, then paused for one more comment.

"If anyone comes looking for me, don't tell them where I've gone. I will face my enemies alone, and want no interference."

"But please, don't be unreasonable!"

Ignoring him, I left at once. I marched back the way I came, but as soon as I was out of sight of any likely observer, I turned and ran north to rejoin Damkats and the men.

When I reached Hongdaw, I gave a quick report and very exact instructions that I wanted the men to follow.

"First, Lanna should run towards Wibawdaw as quickly as possible. If you reach a village and you're too exhausted to continue, send a relay of messengers ahead. Offer whatever is necessary to get the message through. If my suspicions are correct, there's going to be more than a frontier conflict. Tell Wibaw to gather as large a force as possible and proceed east to Shamni."

"Why?" Damkats asked.

I wasted a couple of minutes explaining. Then:

"Damkats, you need to take the others and go directly to Lish-isuhn Imnu, where I've just been. Stalk through the village angrily, mostly silent. When you meet with the chief, you should demand to know where I've gone."

"What's the chief's name?"

"I won't tell you. You haven't seen me. You've just barely managed to track me this far."

"What's the big mystery?"

"I won't tell you. You must remain mysterious, and give no explanation for your purpose for travelling. Then, stop and have some drinks with the chief and his villagers until you fall asleep. Fall asleep early. The next day, follow the chief's directions to find me."

"That's it?"

"Yes."

"Stupid!"

Damkats spat. Then he looked around. He saw me waiting for something. The other men were waiting too. He got up and left. Perhaps he was cooperating with my silent wish, as I really wanted to speak with the other men in his absence. Did he intuit this? But then, maybe he was just angry and offended.

"Now," I said, "Kawlan and Wose, you two are good drinkers. You stay awake longer than the rest of our people. If Damkats is only pretending to sleep, who cares? In a state of mock drunkenness, you can now reveal the 'secret' of our troubles to whomever is still awake. Ti'aw and Dini came north a month ago and captured our mother..."

"No, they didn't," Wose objected.

"Who cares!?... You should not use the word 'rape,' but it should be implied by the fact that my father killed her with poison shortly thereafter, to rid the family of shame. The villagers can conclude whatever they want from this."

They were horrified, but didn't dare respond. I also had no more to say. I stood up and set out at once in the direction of Isaysuhn Dozh.

SHISHNOMIDAW

A day and a half later along the way, I came to another small village which I had never heard of before. It lay in a low forested valley, with a thin stream passing through the center. I later learned that the locals called it Shishnomidaw (low country village). The village stood out quite visibly as I descended from the Western hills, as there was a blackened ring of burned trees surrounding it. Obviously the U.hulia had been there too.

Though I hesitated at first, I decided that I must explore this village before going further.

As I prowled around the edges of the village, I heard the sounds of voices speaking the strange U.hulia language, and the clatter of stone striking stone. I approached as cautiously as I could, dodging behind trees and the ruins of destroyed homes, until I discovered a group of three bowmen. One of them fired an arrow towards the window of a large stone building. He and his companions then stood awaiting some reaction. Several men, closer to the house, were throwing stones against the walls and the heavy wooden door.

Among the Wawli, archery was a rare practice. Most of our hunting was done with javelins and larger spears for thrusting. Military bows were almost always of foreign manufacture, and viewed with suspicion. The U.hulia, too, rarely used them, but here were three men, apparently well trained in archery, attacking a fortress.

Yet, "fortress" may not be the right word to describe it, as it was little more than a large single-family home, with a shallow trench dug in front of it. The trench had about seven dead U.hulia men in it, and there were four more corpses lying just outside of it. There were also some Wawli corpses in the vicinity. The stream passed very close to the rear of the house, where several other men had fallen.

"Try again!" cried a Wawli voice from within the stone house. Very briefly then, a man's face appeared at one of the unshuttered windows. An archer fired a shot, which was on target and passed directly into the house, but the man had already dodged to safety within. A shower of stones also beat against the face of the house, to no meaningful effect.

It was clear that a small number of Wawli men were still holding out against their attackers. The archers now seemed almost bored from a long day of taking shots, and they saved their arrows for only when a good shot seemed to present itself. They were in no rush.

I wished then that my brother and our men had accompanied me, but there was no hope that they would arrive until the next day or later. To wait so long was not an option, so I decided to hazard a chance.

I ran out from my hiding place and caught the archers from behind, completely by surprise. I thrust at the first man that I reached, striking him in the center of the back. Thus I made my first kill.

"Friends, come out now!" I shouted, as I turned against the second surprised archer. He tried to nock an arrow quickly to defend himself, but too late, as I caught him in the gut and the bow sprang out of his hand.

The third man had the time and the presence of mind to toss down his bow and grab a spear. Being busy with the man I had just put down, I wasn't able to respond quickly enough to get in the first thrust against my new attacker.

The Wawli concept of fighting tended to be very crude, and it seemed the same ideas dominated among the U.hulia. They fought against humans as they might fight against an animal when hunting. That is, they expected to take several thrusts to finally hit and kill the animal, but the hunter never had to worry much about the possibility that the animal would fight back. Consequently, all the attention was given to attacking, and none to defense, so that the first to strike in a battle between men was often victorious. Anyone who missed on the first thrust tended to continue the attack without dodging or evading or doing anything much to guard himself against a counterthrust.

Thanks to a very few lessons from my tutor Olul, I was a better defender than my opponent. I dodged, backpedaled, and after he had taken two more ineffectual stabs at me, I lunged at him in turn and struck him in the eye with my spear head.

It surprised me how easy it was to kill. In fact, I had often dreamed of fighting, and in my dreams people's bodies were almost impenetrable, as if a spear could only scratch the skin over the outside of the ribcage, without causing mortal injury. Though I had seen others kill men, in my own anxiety I imagined it would be nearly impossible, but in fact people yielded easily when the point struck home. They seemed like soft bags of blood.

A few moments before I blinded this man, there had been a loud bang, but I hadn't had time to process it. Now I turned and saw that the door to the stone house had been thrown down, forming a sort of bridge across the trench, and three armed-men had rushed out to the attack.

I also noticed a few fist-sized stones rolling around at my feet. Only then did it occur to me that the other U.hulia men, halfway between me and the house, had been throwing stones at me. It was my luck that they'd missed. Now the U.hulia turned to meet the three Wawli men as they emerged.

The archers were incapacitated and on their way to death, so I rushed to join the fight. To make the story brief, we easily defeated the remaining U.hulia men without any injury to ourselves.

TRUCE

When the battle was over, after we had looked about to be sure there were no other men to fight, the youngest of the Wawli men looked at me, smiling with relief.

"Thank you for helping us. Are you a man from this village?"

"No, I come from up north."

He was still smiling, but his expression seemed to betray a momentary doubt.

"Who are you, and why have you come?"

"Let's sit and rest, and I'll tell you my reason for coming."

I gestured towards the stone house, but the young one laughed.

"We'll gladly rest, but not there. I've had enough of that house."

We sat without ceremony on the dusty ground. The older man spoke.

"What a shame that one man could so easily give us relief, when none of the men of my village dared to return after the first assault. But it stands to your honor."

The silent one went to retrieve some pork and a pitcher of mead from their supplies. I then began the introductions. I addressed the eldest first.

"You must be the village chief."

"I am. My name is Ashan."

"And I am Zhikbi, a native of Wibawdaw in the north. I came to find Ti'aw and Dini, who are also natives of my village."

Their faces confirmed what I had suspected. These were they.

"Now that I've found you, let's discuss what we can do to help each other."

They were plainly amazed that I had intuited who they were. I told them briefly of my intention to make a truce with them on behalf of my father, but before discussing this further, we drank together peaceably and exchanged our stories.

I gave them some news from up north, and they told me about their recent trials and experiences.

"While residing in our village on the plateau," said Ti'aw, "we received an urgent message delivered in secret by a close confidante, whom we trusted implicitly. We were requested to come to Isaysuhn Dozh and to tell no one of our plans—neither where we were going nor the reason for our travels. The message detailed an assassination plot against Awngwu, the new chief there. We complied with the request, but when we arrived at the city, no one we spoke to could understand why we had come. The men we had been advised to contact were absent, and our confidante himself had conveniently disappeared. Suspecting a trick, we turned around to return home as quickly as possible."

Ashan continued the narrative based on his own experience. "Shishnomidaw came under attack by about ninety U.hulia warriors, coming from the west. My village was quickly captured, with most of my people fleeing into the woods to escape the conflict. The few brave men who stayed to defend the village were killed, with the exception of myself, my two sons, and three other fierce fighters. We went into the stone house and did our best simply to stay alive for a few hours, hoping to hold out as long as we could, and we sought to extract the greatest payment in blood that we could get in exchange for our lives. However, the large majority of the U.hulia fighters quickly left, and the fourteen who remained were content to keep their distance and engage in a contest of patience."

Ti'aw resumed his part of the story. "It was then that Dini and

I descended into the valley. On our approach, we crossed paths with a large group of U.hulia men, and we momentarily hid behind a dense cluster of trees to let them go by. Once we had evaded them, having seen the burnt trees and suspecting the village had come under attack, we ran to offer our assistance. Arriving in the midst of a struggle, we did our best to help break out those who were trapped within the stone house. Together, we fought well and killed many men, but in the clash, Ashan's supporters and sons were also killed.

"As the last three Wawli men standing, we saw we were failing in the fight, so we withdrew and barricaded ourselves in the fort once again, where we remained pinned and vulnerable to missile attack for most of a day."

Their story finished, it was then my turn to deliver tragic news. Ashan's elation at having come out of the battle alive was already subsiding. The great sorrow of having lost his sons and all the people of his village was fresh in his mind, and surely he must have felt shame too at the cowardice of his people. Yet Ti'aw and Dini had not yet heard the fate of their own village.

"Sad to tell," I said, "a much larger big-battle-gang came to your village on the plateau. The fact is you've lost everything. Very few of the women and young men escaped with their lives. Almost the entire village was caught within the enemy's grasp and cruelly slaughtered. Whatever wealth you once possessed has been plundered or destroyed."

Truthfully, they should have anticipated such news—the U.hulia had passed unrestrained through Tiaw's territory—but to hear it was still devastating. Now, crushed by the confirmation of their fears, the men became sullen and silent.

While they were oppressed by this great sorrow, I turned the topic to the advantages of making a truce with my father. His support, and that of the men of my village, were likely their only chance for revenge against the invaders.

"I've anticipated the difficulties you will face in making peace with our family, and I have contrived a way that we can restore both your honor and your wealth. I've already done what little I could to help restore your lives."

Dini broke his silence.

"It's true that you've done little to help us. You merely caught a few men by surprise who were, in practical terms, unarmed and unable to defend themselves."

I did not object, though it was obvious that my intervention had saved their lives. Only a moment before, Ashan had been praising me for this same action which Dini was belittling. However, neither my honor nor my pride was important in this case.

"Still, so long as we all agree not to tell the true story of today's events, you will have the full credit for rescuing the chief and killing all these men. The rumor is abroad that both of you fled from your village in fear for your lives, and abandoned everyone you knew, your women included, to be destroyed by the invaders."

I paused here for a moment, to measure the effect of my words. Then I continued.

"With your heroic action here, two men charging against fourteen, any rumors of cowardice will be silenced. If we include Ashan and his sons, we will say that the five of you defeated the fourteen U.hulia men, with Ashan's sons dying a heroic death in the defense. The other men of the village, we will suppose, had already died in the first assault."

As I spoke, I could see in their faces all the violence that my words were doing to their thoughts, as they learned first that their homes and their people had been annihilated, then that their honor had been hopelessly lost, only to learn in a few brief sentences that their honor would be restored and they would even be glorified as greater heroes if they only followed my plan. But Dini was not eager to show any appreciation.

"Again, you are not giving us any greater honor than what is due to us. We did charge, two against fourteen, and we did triumph in the end. Though your own assistance was close to trivial, we still thank you for it."

Despite the very somber mood, I was quite pleased to see a little smirk on Ti'aw's face, in reaction to his brother's answer. Ti'aw seemed well aware of how much I was really offering them. I continued.

"If you can first rally some men from these parts, especially from Isaysuhn Dozh, then unite forces with Wibaw, my father, and all the forces he can gather, we can eliminate every U.hulia man in our territory. And we can carry it further. If all goes well, we can take ten times as many men into the south as they brought north. We can push the whole nation of U.hulia out of our land, and the plunder will be infinite. Everything you've lost will be paid back with a bounty of wealth and near unlimited power."

"But..." Dini returned to silence, still resistant to any offer.

"We cannot accept anything," Ti'aw said. "Even our own lives are unacceptable to us, if we must purchase them with loss of honor. How could we make peace with your family? How could our people support us in such a case?"

"There is another rumor travelling with great speed across the land. This rumor will answer all your doubts. They say, and we will not deny it, that the two of you captured my mother in the north. What you did to her led my father to poison her to death. And the fact is undeniable that my mother is truly dead, and she died of poison."

"That... how can you even allow such a thing to be said? Yet you say it yourself."

"Rumors are rumors, but this one will benefit you. You see that there will be no loss of honor to make a settlement between equals, when neither party has had the advantage in our dispute."

"But you repay us with rumors for the actual death of our father," said Dini.

"Your honor and fortune rest with the people. Those things

114

will be restored to you. You will live to see great things. I cannot give back the life of your father. But you know the truth…"

I couldn't say more, but it was clear what I was hinting at.

Ti'aw had one more objection.

"I don't see how we can convince our people to accept a settlement. Even if we could make peace with you, we could never ask for it. To ask will lower us again."

"Don't bend a snake. The people will come to you and demand a truce. Don't ask for it. Resist it. But in the end, you will give in to their demands, and you will make peace with greater honor, as the people will know the sacrifice you make for their benefit. And the people will be sure to demand it, as they care most of all for what benefits them. Honor means less than life to most people. Our treaty will save their lives and extract a cruel payment from the U.hulia for all they've taken."

With this, no further words were needed to seal our pact. Our conference was concluded, and after a few more drinks we returned to the stone house to sleep for the night. Soon Damkats and my men would come, and we would go to raise a force in Isaysuhn Dozh.

5.
Second Intermission

Nelson Glasper: Randall's Father

Though Randall's father, Nelson, had visited our hospital numerous times, he was always so nervous and agitated as to be almost no real help in my investigation. He would hardly ever sit still for more than a minute or two before leaping out of his chair to pace, and he expressed a lot of his frustration by grasping at clumps of his hair and tugging on them violently. He frequently complained about the harassment he faced from people in his community, including racist epithets which he overheard when neighbors were careless in their gossip. He was known among his neighbors as "Mr. Spearchucker" ever since Randall's spear attack on the police station. While the black community avoided the use of this epithet, they were no more sparing in their judgment of the Glaspers. Meanwhile, Randall still refused to speak when Nelson was in the room with him, and he wouldn't listen to anything that Ned tried to say on Nelson's behalf. It was a cruel rejection considering how dedicated Nelson was, years after the rest of the family had drifted away.

"My life has been Hell since Randy's arrest," Nelson told me. "I've lost everything, and I'm still throwing the last scraps of my energy away, just trying to get through to him."

"I'm sorry. And how was your life before Randy's arrest?"

"It was hard then too."

But he wasn't forthcoming with the details.

It therefore surprised me when, after my fifteenth session with Randall, Nelson came to me with a new attitude. He was morose, he was weary, he was without much hope, but he was ready to be cooperative. He was resigned to sit down, to speak, and to listen, though he didn't seem to believe there was much that could be said. He simply saw me as his last chance to communicate with his son, even if the communication was one-directional and conducted entirely on Randall's terms.

"Tell me anything you can, Doctor. Tell me the good or the bad; just tell me something."

So I went ahead and told him a summarized version of Zhikbi's tale. He became excited almost at the start.

"That's me!" he proclaimed.

"What, you mean the whistle…?"

Nelson intoned a humming and whistling drone, just as Randall had described when talking about his infancy, carried in the arms of Wibaw.

"How could he even remember that?" Nelson said, with tears coming to his eyes. "I haven't done that since he was two or three years old."

"And… but he has no siblings?"

"No. He never had a brother, no sisters, even his cousins moved away when Randy was very young. So there were almost never any children in our house besides Randy."

"I didn't know he had cousins. They weren't mentioned in any of his case history documents."

"They're Lydell's kids."

"Lydell… Lydell your brother?" I flipped through some family history notes I had in the file on my lap.

"Yeah, but I don't even know them. Lydell's family moved away, what, twenty-four years ago? His wife divorced him."

"Why?"

Nelson was taken aback some.

"What, you've never heard of divorce? It's not uncommon."

"I hear about divorce all the time. But I haven't heard about it in your family, at the time of Randy's childhood. Was he close to his cousins and uncle? His aunt? What happened there?"

"Lydell was a gambler, that's all there is to it. Randy's cousins were girls, and he got along well with them, but that was long ago, and there's no way he could remember them now."

"You say Lydell was a gambler. Does that mean he overcame his problem?"

"I don't know, he stopped gambling for a few years, then went back to it… straightened out his life a few times, and fucked it up a few more times. I haven't seen him in years."

"He's disappeared?"

"Disappearing is a normal part of his life. I love him, but he's a bum. You can't rely on him for anything."

"You know," I said, "we've asked time and time again whether there was any history of mental illness in the family, and the answer has always been one-hundred-percent no."

"Oh. But Lydell never seemed to have any serious mental problems."

"Addiction that destroys a family, and causes a man to disappear for years at a time is pretty serious. It's the kind of factual information we need for a complete family history."

"All right, I get your point."

The first connection that we had found between Randall's delusions and a true experience from his childhood—the memory of the whistling lullaby—gave me a real thrill, and raised my hopes that there would soon be a major breakthrough in understanding his case. But as I proceeded to tell the story to Nelson, all hope for a meaningful interpretation vanished into a cloud of uncertainty and confusion. There was virtually nothing in Zhikbi's further story that meant anything to Nelson. The violence, the names, the conflicts, the places, none of it seemed sensible to him. It was compelling as a narrative, but it was otherwise entirely cryptic. True, Nelson told me that Randall had taken up beer brewing, then mead brewing in their home, but I had already been aware of this fact. It was in his file. Besides, he had only begun brewing after the start of his psychosis, probably as a development of his fantasy.

And then there was, perhaps, a false alarm. When I told about Zhikbi's dream of four animals dancing around a boat, Nelson leaped out of his chair.

"Fuck me, what is that!?" he shouted.

His right fist clutched his hair, and tugged hard. He stood there, deeply fascinated by some thought, then dropped just as suddenly back into his chair.

"No, no, no, I'm too old. I can't remember anything."

"What do you mean, are you sure? This seems to mean something."

"No, I don't know. But it's damned familiar. I just have to think about it. No, go on."

I still paused, but he had nothing more to say.

"Go on."

I continued the story, to the end of what I knew. Then it was over. And Nelson was flummoxed. He paced again, as he always had, and he raved about the absurdity of it all.

"It's ridiculous," he said, "I've told everyone, we had a decent house. There were no problems, no violence. My wife is as alive as ever. If anything, she was just driven away by the senselessness of Randy's behavior, and the shame his crime brought on us. Why talk about rape. He says I poisoned her?"

"Mr. Glasper, he didn't say anything of the sort. To him, you're not even his father. Wibaw is a delusion, there's no blame here, and even in his story the rape and the poisoning are fictions, fictions within a fiction. We can't dismiss them as meaningless, but don't interpret it as an attack on you or your wife."

"Yet he denies me as his father, how am I supposed to take that?"

He started walking out the door, with nothing more to say, but I called after him.

"You have to tell me about any connections you recognize," I shouted.

"I know," he replied distractedly. "The damned animals, circling the boat. What is that?"

He walked away.

THE JOE ALGER JAZZ DREAM

That night I had a dream.

Joe Alger, a black jazz player, perhaps a saxophone player, was standing in a jazz club; he had been invited to play one or two numbers with a local band. In the meantime he was in the audience area, amid the crowd that was forming in front of the stage. He seemed to be waiting for some signal. The club owner, standing elsewhere in the club, was preparing to listen to Joe's performance, whenever it was destined to occur.

However, no one told Joe it was his time to get on stage, and the band began playing without him. There were voices, but I wasn't always sure who was speaking, or who was responding. I had no 'self' in this dream. I observed events from various points of view as the dream unfolded.

A promoter explained to someone nearby, "Unfortunately, he's color blind, so he can't see the stage."

"If he was color blind, he could see. This man is blind," came the response from somewhere.

Joe was led through the crowd and up onto the stage, where he disappeared among the many performers. There seemed to be far too many musicians, and Joe was lost among them. Then the music came to a stumbling stop, and someone shouted.

"He's fallen into his own trap!"

There was a pause, and then the performers lifted Joe vertically out of a trap door in the middle of the stage. He seemed astounded by the experience, and very disoriented. Finally, after shaking out his legs and then crossing the stage from left to right, then right to left, and ultimately taking his place near center stage, he was ready to begin. Standing there with no instrument, he opened his mouth to sing. But I heard no voice, and no music. Then, after a few uncomfortable moments of silence, a faint and frightening whining sound came from his mouth, though he appeared to be singing energetically.

The club owner, wearing bright red-framed glasses, proclaimed, "Yes, man, he can play!"

The club owner's face became isolated from the rest of the scene, and black eyeglass frames shifted in from the left to replace his red frames. The dream ended.

When I awoke, my thoughts returned to Randall. I wondered whether Joe Alger represented an aged version of Randall, Nelson, or perhaps even Wibaw. But I couldn't resolve this question, and I had no more time to ponder. It was time to return to my meetings with Randall and continue listening to his tale.

6.
Zhikbi's Tale: On Our Way

A STRANGE ENCOUNTER

When my men arrived, though Damkats and the others had not had a chance to sleep, we could not waste any more time. We gathered our tiny force for the march. The U.hulia had left a couple of horses, saddled and with handling equipment. However, none of us were able to ride, so we loaded them up and used them as pack animals. I suggested that Damkats should try to get some rest by lying upon the back of one of the horses, but he refused even to get near them.

It was an odd affectation of the U.hulia to ride horses, which they probably inherited from their contact with the Twilak. For all we knew at the time, the south of the peninsula was not much different from our northern territory. With dense forests and narrow paths on rough terrain, horses should offer no real military advantage. There was no room for a massed charge. Furthermore, the sight range of a man on foot was the same as that for a rider. It's true that we may have neglected the value of horses for the delivery of messages, but, getting to the point, I had never met a single Wawli man who knew how to ride.

As we approached the outskirts of Isaysuhn Dozh, we noticed some smoke off in the woods, a short distance from our path. I sent Wose and Bikni to examine the situation, and they soon returned with their report.

"There is a single man with the look of a priest about him, sitting and weeping on the ground, just outside a woodcutter's hut with its door shut. The man is unarmed."

We went together in a group to see this priest. We caught him by surprise and quickly encircled him. As soon as the priest saw himself surrounded by armed men, he jumped up in horror and flung his arms wide, staggering about for a brief moment, then just as quickly he threw himself down again, prone on the ground, and cried out, "If you've come to kill me, kill me! I can't take any further persecution!"

I crouched down and lifted his head.

"Who are you, and why are you here weeping on the ground?"

"Why shouldn't I weep, when the sacred city of Isaysuhn Dozh has fallen to savages?"

We did our best to calm the priest and help him control his fear. We raised him to a sitting position. Then Dini took over the questioning.

"How did this happen? How did they conquer the city?"

"Do you mean you don't know? Where are you from?"

"We are survivors from Shishnomidaw. But now we'll ask the questions."

The priest looked around and spotted Chief Ashan amongst us.

"Ah, Ashan! I should have recognized you right away. They say you have an unmistakable noble aspect and a face like a stone idol of Zodu himself. And so you do. It's a wonder that at least you and these few men were spared. Well, if you haven't heard, the whole calamity started with those cowards, Ti'aw and Dini. They received some kind of warning that an attack was coming, and so they fled in the night, abandoning their people to die. If they had dared even to send out a message, perhaps the people of your village could have escaped or prepared themselves for a better defense. But there has been speculation that the once 'heroic' brothers are now in league with the enemy."

"Sit, relax, have some mead, and tell us more." Dini kept his emotions in check as he poured out some mead into a bowl for this slandering priest.

"Thank you so much, and if you could spare even a scrap of food of any kind… thank you… Do you see that cabin there?"

We looked at the unremarkable cabin, large enough for two or three interior rooms, which was backed up against a large natural stone outcropping. A few light wisps of smoke rose from a chimney at the back of the house. Nearby, we also saw the smoky embers in a stone fire-pit which the priest himself had likely kindled.

"My name is Dasik. Inside that house is a man, and that man is my brother. Emot. I've been coming here for seven years to help him in any way I could. I've brought him money, clothes, food, tools, anything I could think of that he might want. He's spurned me every time and left my gifts strewn around the ground until they were taken by thieves or eaten or destroyed by animals. He doesn't speak to me. The people of Isaysuhn Dozh know him as 'The Mad Woodsman.' They say he speaks only in a mysterious language of his own which none can interpret, not even the Zatnimi. He is most certainly mad, and his madness is mainly my fault. But now that I'm in my most extreme hour of need, I've come to beg a little help from him. It's no use. He won't even offer me the skins of his yams to boil for a broth. He's barred the door to me when I have no place left to turn."

"We could force the door and bring him out," Damkats offered. "We'll find out if he really doesn't understand our language."

"No, don't disturb him. He can't help the way he is, and I'm sure he has his right to refuse me, though I wish I could persuade him to forgive me."

I spoke up at this point and asked, "What does he have to forgive you for?"

Dasik's Tale

When we were children, my brother Emot was a very sensitive boy. Too sensitive, I thought, and I'm ashamed to admit I was very cruel to him. I didn't know better, being so young and hot-headed.

Emot loved animals, and he was easily upset when he saw an animal hurt.

"How could you be so cowardly?" I asked him. "We're a race of warriors and hunters, but you cry when you see a bird with a broken wing."

I made a point to hurt animals when I could, just to shame

124

my brother further, and maybe toughen him up. Sometimes he fought me when he couldn't bear my teasing, but I was bigger and stronger than he, and I beat him easily.

When Emot foolishly adopted a squirrel that he had found picking through scraps behind our house, I took the first opportunity to kill it, and I left the skin of the squirrel in the house, under his bedclothes for him to find.

I was trouble all around in those days, and wicked ideas always filled my head. But I never meant any serious harm. My father often beat me as punishment for the big and little things I did to bring trouble to our home. My brother was sometimes beaten as well, but not as often and not so seriously. The whole family knew he was too soft for a really serious beating.

The chief of our village was himself a strange character, and he had a pet monkey that he had bought from traders who had travelled to distant lands. Everyone was a little afraid of that monkey, whom they called *Shrunken Grandfather*. Emot spent a lot of time playing with girls, and he especially liked the chief's youngest daughter. One day I was simply fed up with my brother, and I told him I was going to kill the chief's monkey, and I was half serious too.

Even though he wasn't sure I would have the courage to go through with my plan, Emot begged me not to hurt the monkey, for the sake of my own safety and out of concern for the poor beast. I warned him that I would do it unless he followed my commands slavishly and did everything I told him. I abused this power by making him steal mead from our neighbor for me to drink. I told him to spit into our father's food bowl. Father caught him doing this, and gave him the first serious thrashing of his life, but Emot never told that it was my instruction that made him do it. I continued my threats, and manipulated my brother into stealing a chicken. When I'd wrung the chicken's neck, I ordered him to clean it, and then I made him eat some of the intestines raw, ostensibly to teach him to be less squeamish, but I honestly recognize now that I got a thrill from pushing him and seeing how far he would go.

Then I decided I would kill the monkey anyway. It was more trouble than you'd imagine, and before I set out to do it, I got outrageously drunk off of stolen mead, to build up my courage. I planned my attack for a time when the chief and his family were out of their house, when *Shrunken Grandfather* was out in the yard behind the house, restrained by a long cord tied to a post.

While the monkey was scampering around the garden, I walked up to the post, took up the cord, and started to reel him in. As soon as he saw he was being pulled, *Shrunken Grandfather* ran and circled wildly, raising more noise than I'd counted on, but I was drunk and determined. When I had the monkey close, all the tugging and jumping were making me crazy and inspired a sudden fear in me, and just then it leapt at me, biting and scratching. I got my left hand around its neck and one shoulder, and pressed the monkey to ground. While fumbling around in an attempt to un-hook the hatchet I had tethered to my belt, I heard the shouting of my brother nearby, who was running at me and demanding I stop. Before he could get close enough to stop me, I chopped off a large chunk of the monkey's tail, then released it. *Shrunken Grandfather* screamed and ran, and Emot tackled me. I threw him off of me and stood over him as he cowered.

"I'm not going to kill it, you idiot. But what do you think of this?"

I tossed the two-hand-span-length section of tail in Emot's face and laughed.

That's when I heard more shouting, and men approaching rapidly. I then realized what a suicidally foolish game I'd been playing. I ran off in an instant, and before I knew it, they had my brother.

I told myself that Emot's punishment would be far less serious than what I would have faced if I had been caught, so it was best to stay quiet and let him take the blame. He was a child of nine, whereas I, at the age of twelve, could be maimed, mutilated, banished, or killed. The villagers generally were less sympathetic to me as well, as I had a reputation for trouble and I had made several enemies. Emot, apparently, had too much pride to give me the blame I deserved, and his character was stronger than I'd imagined, though it did him no good. He refused to say that he'd cut the monkey's tail off, but he also refused to give any explanation or defense against the accusation.

Emot was stripped the next day and beaten publicly with sticks, then tied and left in front of the chief's house for four hours, for public shaming. He was insulted and humiliated by all. As for myself, though the whole spectacle horrified me, and I couldn't bring myself to speak any libel against him, I slapped his face to cover my own guilt. But the worst for him was when he was confronted by the chief's daughter, his playmate.

"You sicken me!" she declared. "You're an animal. I'll love a no-tailed monkey before I care for a no-dick coward."

Public shaming by a female is, of course, the most vulgar and dishonorable, but yet I told myself that he would someday forget a few hours of punishment, and I'd be very grateful and kind to him after that day for saving me.

Sadly, as soon as he was freed, he fled the village forever, and it seems his broken pride never recovered. I bore the burden of guilt for many years.

I tell you this, but you must also know that I absolutely reformed my life. I've lived with honor, discipline, and absolute devotion to decency and kindness since the day I escaped my punishment and recognized the extent of my crime. I wanted to learn the strength of kindness that my brother had shown, rather than the strength of cruelty which I had tried to teach him.

In order to regain some measure of family honor, to compensate for the shame that my brother brought to the house (and my father always believed that Emot was to blame, since I never openly confessed), my father struggled to the utmost to raise and save money to buy me an education and a priest's candidacy. He succeeded in raising the money, and I succeeded in becoming a priest through diligence, zeal, and ultimately through good fortune. I held the position of temple visionary and associate minister at Nu'a Temple.

In the years that passed, I never forgot my brother or my debt to him, but when I searched I could learn nothing about where he had gone, until one day I heard the story of a strange man living in the woods outside Isaysuhn Dozh. They said he cut wood far from the city and dragged it into town on a sledge, to sell for firewood to the lame and elderly for a pittance, though woodcutters who inhabited the city were able to supply the same service with less effort at an already low cost. He gathered and sold enormous quantities of roots and herbs which others considered quite scarce, and he accepted any trivial price from medicine men, though he could have easily demanded much more if he had any sense. He ate no meat, but only vegetables which he raised in his own tiny woodland plot, and odd fruits and fungi. Finally, they said he spoke no human tongue, but had a natural affinity for wild fowl, varmints, and even foxes. These last details made me think of my brother, the lover of animals.

Convinced I would find him, I came south to search the woods for Emot's forest retreat. After several fruitless attempts, I finally stumbled upon the mad woodsman as he was foraging for herbs, not far from where we now stand. As soon as I saw his face, I was sure he was my brother, though he had changed quite dramatically, having become much rougher, nearly wild as a Zatnimi, and he showed no recognition on seeing me.

"Emot," I asked him, "don't you remember me? I'm your own brother, come to find you after so many years."

But he behaved as though I were a transparent being, neither seeing me nor hearing me, but carrying on his business at an unhurried pace. I tried desperately to attract his attention, and even shoved him, but he picked himself up and didn't react. I followed him as he finished his work and slowly made his way back to his home, where he entered and silently barred the door.

I observed him a few more times after that, and I followed him once as he went on his rounds selling wood in the city. I could say for certain that he was my brother when I witnessed his interactions with others. Though he doesn't speak with them, he communicates through gestures and other signs, while sometimes babbling to himself in his own alien tongue. He's friendly enough, in his way. It is only I that he completely spurns, and thus he demonstrates that he recognizes me, as he treats me differently from any other person.

On returning to my home, I demanded that my superiors in Shamni transfer me to a post in Isaysuhn Dozh, so I could be close to my brother and attempt to help him. I was refused, at first, but eventually I was able to get an assignment merely as a deacon to the priest of the Shrine of Memory. This represented a major demotion in terms of prestige and authority, but I was thankful nonetheless.

Through the years, I have tried to devise many ways that I could assist my brother, but have never succeeded. When I found that the food I brought him was left to rot, and the tools were scattered in the woods, I devised another plan. I contacted some of his customers and offered to supply them with money to buy his wood; they should just offer him three times the usual price, and I would pay them even more as a reward. Emot was astonished when he was presented with what seemed extravagant sums for a few pieces of wood. He stopped doing business with these customers at *any* price when he suspected their motives.

I've continued to try to court his favor, even just to get him to acknowledge my presence, and I've pursued every route I could imagine to enter his heart, until, just two days ago, all my plans went to ruin when Isaysuhn Dozh fell to U.hulia invaders.

We had already received word that a fight in the villages was getting underway, when a small group of travelers came running to Isay's Shrine crying out that a large group of enemy men was approaching and would arrive imminently. Panic spread, and several prominent citizens, including myself, went to Chief Awngwu to recommend immediate surrender. If we could avoid the profaning of our shrines and relics, and prevent the slaughter of the mostly unarmed populace, we would do best to submit to a temporary occupation.

A small deputation was quickly assembled. I was not among the selected. They marched out to meet the enemy on the road, to surrender arms and invite them in without resistance. Three hours later, the U.hulia entered the city, leading our peace ambassadors now in chains with their ears cropped and faces branded.

But the enemy did not stop. The majority simply passed through our town, only pausing to gather supplies for their continued march. They left about thirty or forty fighters to seize Awngwu in his estate and gather up the surrendered arms of our populace. No one dared oppose them, but as evidence of the extreme irrationality of the masses, the townsmen turned against *us*, those of us who had advised upon the surrender. We were called traitors. I witnessed the cruel killing of one of our priests by a mob armed only with gardening and digging tools, and then I fled into the woods, hoping at least to find shelter with my own brother, begging that even without forgiveness for my adolescent taunts, he would be moved to the least degree of mercy just to spare my life. Yet he remains indifferent even now.

The Priest's End

The priest was startled by the splintering of wood when, at the end of his story, my brother Damkats suddenly smashed down the door of the woodsman's hut.

"Lying priest!" Damkats shouted when he reemerged within half a minute. "What lies are you telling us, and to what purpose?"

Amazed, we went in turns to enter the house and discovered there was nobody there. There was no sign that anyone had been there in a long time, and even the ashes in the fireplace were cold, which made us wonder where the bit of smoke had come from that we had seen earlier. But there was no smoke now, and perhaps it had been an illusion.

"Everything I told you was true," Dasik protested. But Damkats simply kicked him in the gut, and he tumbled down onto the ground.

"Sleep!" Damkats commanded.

Night was already falling. We all looked about us, and wondered. Unable to make any sense of any of it, we muttered a bit to each other, then made camp and prepared to sleep.

As I was starting to doze off, I heard a whisper.

"Are you really who I think you are?"

The priest had dragged himself to within a few inches of Ti'aw's face, and was staring down at him in the semi-darkness, as Ti'aw silently stared back.

"Yes, I think you are" Dasik whispered, and nodded his head.

"Sleep!" my brother commanded once again. And, with a start, the priest threw himself down and shut his eyes.

A few hours passed, and then Bikni awakened us. His voice was ragged, he was breathing heavily, and blood stained his legs and feet.

"I've killed the sneaky devil," he declared. "Though it was my responsibility to watch the camp, I decided that when all was quiet I would pretend to sleep, and see what would happen next. As I suspected, the priest too was only pretending. After rolling about for a while, to see whether he would awaken anyone, he became bold, got up to his feet, and sneaked out of the camp. I gave him a three minute lead, then I rose too and followed him into the woods. It wasn't long until he started running noisily, and he ran directly down the path, back towards Isaysuhn Dozh. 'What could he be planning?' I wondered. But soon we came within close range of the city, and I couldn't afford to wonder any longer. It's sure that he would have gone and told someone about us. I quickened my pace, and though he heard me at the last moment before I caught him, it was too late for him to escape. I cut him down."

Just as Bikni finished his tale of the death of the mysterious priest, I noticed a horrifying sight. *On top* of the house, illumined by the faint light of a waning moon, a man was sitting up and smiling. Looking closer I saw that, despite his smile, there was also a copious flow of tears from his eyes, down both cheeks. The man then made a sudden movement and leapt down from the roof in one bound.

"Hello, friends," he began. "I've made some soup, and though it's gotten cold, if you bring a ladder, you can have some."

A Battle in Brief: Isaysuhn Dozh

Through a combination of wit and bravado we then liberated the city of Isaysuhn Dozh from the occupiers.

After that, Damkats, Beunba, and I departed for Shamni, where we expected a full-fledged war was about to be fought. Ti'aw, Dini, Chief Ashan, Gan.geun, and Wose stayed behind to muster a fighting force from the surviving citizens of the city. Kawlan had died, and Bikni had received a wound in his side and a broken foot, so I dismissed him.

During battle, Damkats had striven to make himself the hero of the day, but in his eagerness to win glory, he had fallen twice and had proven largely ineffectual.

7.
Third Intermission

OFFICER EVAN BRIAR

Minutes after I had concluded a session with Randall, I sat at my desk, and my mind was in a whirl contemplating events that Randall had related. I was not prepared to see anyone, and I wondered whom I was now confronted with as a strange man came into my office with a large cardboard box under his arm.

"The receptionist told me you were expecting me—Evan Briar. You insisted yesterday on the phone that I come."

Oh, the cop!

"Yes, of course, thanks." I raised my hand to my forehead and shielded my eyes for a moment, then resumed a calm and friendly demeanor. "Please have a seat."

Evan sat and placed his box on my desk. He was dressed in ordinary civilian clothes, semi-casual, though his shirt looked dressy.

"I just saw him—Randall—in the hallway," Evan said with some excitement. "He seemed all right. It was strange seeing him, though. Does he talk about me?"

"Ummm, I'm sorry Mr. Briar, I'm not sure that Randall even knows who you are, but I wouldn't be able to tell you about the details of our conversation in any case. We enjoy the legal confidentiality of the doctor–patient relationship."

"And yet you expect the police to assist you."

"Exactly. I don't often get much cooperation, but I remain hopeful," I said with a laugh. "Now, if you've spoken with your colleagues, you know that there have been a few instances when one of my patients, after successful treatment and release, has voluntarily confessed to a crime in open court."

"Yet they were still declared not guilty despite their confessions."

"I'm not trying to start an argument with you. You've had a difficult recovery from the stress of your involvement in this case.

If your interest is in the truth, then helping me can bring out the truth and bring closure." I paused. "What's in the box?"

"Well, you're in luck today," Evan declared. He opened the box to reveal a pile of photocopied documents, and an album of photographic prints. There were also several magazines of all sorts, from nature, to fashion, to science, to hunting, to news, to softcore pornography. "You can't retain any of these materials, and you can't read them without my being present. If you have any questions, you can ask me."

"But… is this evidence from his case?" I asked.

"None of it is original material, but I've been doing my own investigation. I got copies of some things, I got a few photo files of his home…" Evan paged through the photo album. "…Then I got a list of some of the books and magazines he had, and I've purchased issues of the ones I could find. It hasn't helped much, but maybe it can help you."

"Oh, my God!" I declared. I had just come across photocopies of Randall's own writings, from a notebook written in his Wawli script.

"What? Does this mean something to you?" Evan asked. "Can you read this?"

"No, I can't. But maybe I can figure out a little bit of it. Have you shown this to Ned Lincoln yet?"

"Who?"

"Never mind. Listen, we're going to have to look at this together for a while after we talk today. Do you have time? As much time as you have, I'll need it."

"Sure, sure. You know, no one in our investigation has been able to make any sense of this at all. The only thing I've seen is that some groups of symbols repeat, but seriously we're at a loss."

"Maybe it means nothing, but hasn't some F.B.I. language expert or cryptographer gotten involved?"

"No," said Evan, with a simple shrug.

I understood. Who has the resources to study scribbles in a notebook by a psychotic?

A Few Investigation Details

I asked Officer Briar, "Is Randall still being investigated for the gentlemen's club fire?"

"There's been no active investigation in the last couple of years. The newspapers have it right. The two principal suspects can't be charged, for lack of evidence. Investigations still technically center on Carla Black and Grace, but there's no actual progress, and Randall was never designated as a viable suspect for investigation after the first few months of looking over the evidence. But I know he did it."

"Hmmm."

"That's mainly why I'm talking to you. There's no case to compromise. Anyway, look at this."

Evan showed me a close-up picture of a mostly burnt wooden sculpture.

"When they were investigating the ruins of the warehouse space behind River Dancers, they found the remains of this tiny wooden carving, in the shape of a crocodile. Only the head and one hind leg were distinctly visible, and a photograph was taken before any attempt to move it. Unfortunately, the figure broke when it was removed from the site, and somehow the head was lost before entering the evidence locker, but we still have the photograph."

"I see."

"There were also, strangely, the bodies of several dead bees in a small heap. Anyway, no one knew what to think of it exactly. One profiler on the case suggested that the crocodile could be some kind of 'calling card' left by the criminal, which kind of gave us a laugh. Then, after Mr. Glasper's attack, when we examined his house all kinds of pictures were taken. It's only by dumb luck that one evening, while organizing some of our photo files, an intern came across this picture."

Evan showed me one of the pictures from Randall's room, which included some small pieces of wood carved with animal figures. No close-up pictures were taken, for some reason, and the figures were not identical to the burnt crocodile, but it was conceivable that they were sculpted by the same person.

"The intern happened to be the same guy who filed and noted the River Dancers evidence," Evan explained, "and he figured there was a strong resemblance between the carvings. That's about it, really. Once he brought it to the attention of the crime scene investigators, and they looked at the crocodile photo, they pulled out Glasper's stick carvings again, compared, and said 'That's the guy.' A lot of investigators had rejected the profiler's idea about a calling card, some said it seemed ritualistic, and a psychology expert argued that the leaving of the sculpture and the bees was consistent with a psychotic criminal. The detectives took it all very seriously, they did their job, but no one could turn up any other evidence."

"Nothing physical?"

"Nothing physical, no motives. We can't even talk to the guy. So there's no progress."

"Were you the one who leaked the story about Randall being a suspect?"

"No way. I don't want anything to compromise our chances of solving this. We don't know how the story got out."

"And what have you personally done? Why are you convinced Randall is guilty?"

"I know you probably think I'm obsessed because I'm the guy who shot him. But you don't know. The brutality of it, the sheer irrationality of going from chatting with the guys in the office to life and death struggle in an instant… nobody talks about how ridiculous it is, how it makes you sweat so damned hard. You want to laugh when you think of this… there was no sense in any of it."

Evan was really possessed for a moment, but he calmed himself and proceeded. "But that's got nothing to do with it. Most of the guys agree that Randall Glasper burned the club. His carving was found at the scene, and the crime seems fundamentally irrational, once the two other suspects are eliminated. Only, the profiler proved to be a real pain, since she claimed, based on no real evidence, that the criminal was probably a white man pursuing a revenge motive, and that this was likely his first fire. I think the profiler's a quack. Real profilers aren't so broad and general, or so insistent on one interpretation until there's more of an accumulation of evidence. People accord too much credence to so called experts sometimes."

"Yeah, I'm sure you're right about that. Now, are you sure that nothing else turned up to connect Randall to the crime?"

"Nothing in the official investigation, but the only thing I found on my own was this model."

Evan pulled out one of the pornographic magazines, and opened to a page near the back. It was the image of one nude woman massaging another with oil.

"The brunette is Sandra Kenley. She was close friends with one of the victims, and she was interviewed as part of the investigation. There's not much in that, though. People all through the sex industry have common connections, there are friendships and enmities, and she didn't have anything at all useful to say. Glasper didn't know her personally, he'd only seen her in a porno mag. So really it's nothing at all, but it's the closest I've come to a connection between the suspect and a person affected by the crime."

"To tell the truth," I said, "I was surprised to hear that you found anything pornographic in Randall's room."

"The laundry room, actually."

"Ah. Well, it's probably a good thing, in some sense, that he has a kind of human sexuality. Up until now I've seen no sign that he has sexual desires of any kind, so I've tended to think he would not commit a crime related to sex or jealousy. If he has no connection to the victims, well, however irrational you think a psychotic may be, I wouldn't be so convinced of his involvement."

"I don't know why he did it, and I can't prove he did it, but he did it," Evan countered. Then he stood, for no obvious reason. "What else can we talk about?"

"I'm not sure, but I'll definitely need your involvement, going forward" I told him. "Now, though, I'd like to give some detailed attention to Randall's notebooks."

Evan stayed with me for another two and a half hours, as I examined the Wawli writings, thumbed through some reports, and I asked a variety of questions about every other aspect of the case. The investigation of the notebooks was thrilling, and it answered many of my doubts. I couldn't read much at all, except phonetically, but finding one simple sentence which I was able to interpret, based on Ned's teachings and notes, revealed that Wawli really was the language of Zhikbi, and Zhikbi alone. The sentence "*Geginwe solimshas,*" meaning "It's getting darker" demonstrated a fully developed grammar that was entirely consistent with what I had learned. It indicated comparison, the marking of the subject, the use of the general change verb for "becoming/getting," and it properly conjugated the verb for agreement based on the subject-noun class. It was also demonstrably written before Randall had met Ned, as the notebook had been taken into police evidence before their meeting. I had been listening carefully recently and reviewing the tapes, so I had already convinced myself that Randall really was saying some of the things that Ned translated, and his grammar was in line with what I understood of the language. Now, with this early writing sample, I could say for sure that Zhikbi's tale was really all Randall, that the culture all existed in his mind, and that Ned was being faithful in his interpretation. To top it all off, by examining several fragments in various sections of the book, I concluded that this was, in part, the "book of wisdom" which Randall claimed he had hand-copied from a text in Shamni during his early education period.

I thanked Officer Briar profusely, and I explained as well as I could the import of my discovery. Against my expectations, he allowed me to retain a copy of the complete notebook on the condition that only Ned and I should look at it, we would not let any additional copies or translations go out of our possession, and I would give him a report on its contents. I warned him that I was limited in what I could tell him if it was too damaging to Randall. He disagreed, arguing that the information I received from the notebook did not come from treatment. He was willing to leave the book with me anyway, in the hope I would eventually discover something meaningful and tell him about it. That was the end of our meeting.

8.
Zhikbi's Tale: War in Shamni

When we arrived in Shamni, the city was in chaos. Many homes, buildings, and ships in the harbor were burning. Many more were in ruins. Shouts could be heard echoing from groups of men engaged in invisible clashes amid the tangled alleys of the priests' district. A frightening din was also heard among clusters of trees, and the city itself emitted a confusing and persistent buzz. Meanwhile, there were mobs of men scattered here and there, mostly idle. The groups ranged in size from nine or ten men in a pack, to several hundred standing in ranks. Yet none seemed certain of what they should be doing. We made our way from group to group, asking questions and exchanging news, hoping to find some men of our village along the way.

Most of the men had travelled from outside the city to oppose the invaders. There was no central authority, and there was little communication or cooperation between the men of different villages.

Several men, especially in the larger groups, had minor wounds and injuries. They were the survivors of battles who were preparing to reengage the enemy. Those who had been more severely wounded or killed had been removed to other parts of the city, and some had been carried into the countryside to return to their homes.

The first major news we gathered was that Mo'uh, the high priest, had been killed. The first assault, which took the city largely by surprise, overwhelmed him and his household. A few other wealthy and powerful priests had also been killed in the first day, along with their supporters. Any local men who had attempted to organize and resist were entirely wiped out.

After the initial carnage, the priests reacted mainly by gathering defensive forces, issuing orders that no one venture any aggressive action. They insisted that the townsmen abandon even the defense of their own homes to mount a "common defense" which mainly benefitted the wealthy priests themselves. People had reacted in varying ways.

One man whom I stopped to question had seen some of the early action right after the enemy arrived.

"There was a local man named Gweudam who was famed for his courage and good sense. He was a cousin to the chief of my village, so when I and eight of my people came to Shamni and met Gweudam, we joined him. He was defending the property of High Priest Zhomhet. But Gweudam resented Zhomhet's selfishness. When we repelled an U.hulia assault, we pursued those we had put to flight. We went far in the pursuit, but we soon were caught in an ambush, and few of us escaped alive. I am the only one of my village among the survivors, and I have since joined this band from my wife's family's village. I have been told that while Gweudam was leading us astray, another surprise attack came, and Zhomhet and his family were killed along with the few guards who stood loyally by them."

We continued on, asking questions to those we met, until a more detailed picture of the situation emerged.

The remaining high priests were now mostly shut away within their estates, or gathered within temples, defended by the remaining loyalists, hired men, and those neighboring villagers who had first arrived to help. Few of them could be tempted to risk any avoidable conflict. Stories of cowardice, and defenders who broke and ran at the first sign of trouble were now spreading.

Muhlosangko, the hero of the U.hulia, was reported to have killed many men with his own hands, both on the first day and in several following clashes. The men he commanded were regarded as a devastating, irresistible force, even after five days of fighting in virtually all quarters of the city. Everyone who had opposed Muhlosangko was defeated. This included my father and the men of Wibawdaw.

One man told me, "Wibaw disregarded the well-known example of Gweudam's slaughter. He led his men, plus allies from Womsho and other groups, to break away from Hinen Temple and directly confront Muhlosangko. This was day three of the fight. The Wawli outnumbered the main force of the U.hulia two to one, but the U.hulia fought in a strictly disciplined and coldblooded style that none of us have ever encountered before. They put the Wawli to rout, killing and injuring a great many. But the U.hulia did not follow through. Instead, they broke away and moved rapidly to another region of the city."

"Do you know where the survivors of my village went?"
"No."

Another man whom I encountered shared some of his reflections on the tactics the U.hulia had been using:

"They're not just tough, they're clever. They're not swayed by failure or success, and they resist being drawn into any unknown danger. They give us no time to rally a defensive force or set a trap. They hit and run, and keep their necks out of the noose."

The enemy were said to be uncanny in their instinct, or else remarkably lucky in their encounters. Time and time again, they managed to isolate small groups that were beyond the reach of support and annihilated them. The various roving mobs throughout the city were easy prey for U.hulia attacks. Yet, when small advance groups were deliberately organized and set out to lure U.hulia forces into dangerous areas, the enemy consistently avoided the bait.

Against all expectation, the U.hulia seemed not to fight for personal gain, nor personal glory. They were determined only to fight. They didn't loot. They didn't surrender to superior numbers. They were intent only on destroying property and killing men, especially the killing of priests. By all signs, though their numbers were rather small compared to the city that surrounded them, they had no apparent intention of leaving off the attack until they were all killed… or, if by some chance they could never be defeated, they might go on rampaging forever… mad dogs, yet disciplined beyond all degree.

The men who had travelled from far outside the city were preoccupied by another kind of rumor. They were half-fascinated and half-outraged by stories of the incredible treasure stores, on ships and in the priests' warehouses, consisting of vast quantities of mead, dried fish, cut wood, spears, homespun cloth, all forms of crafts and the product of thousands of men's labor, all assembled for foreign export, exchanged for foreign silver. Some men wondered aloud whether all of the fires around the city were caused by the U.hulia, or if perhaps there was a wider-spread rebellion.

So much for rumors.

REUNION

We found the men of our village as darkness was falling. The first whom we met was Ik.hun, who was well known for his directness and precision in speaking. He was never known to speak a false word, and his opinions were never overstated nor understated. He confirmed the stories of their battle and their defeat.

"Welcome, we're surprised by your arrival."

"Thank you, we've been searching for you, and only luck brought us to you so soon. Do you know where my father is?"

"I'll take you to him. You'll notice that the mood is generally grim, and morale is low. We've suffered a serious defeat, and lost several men. Many believe we face an impossible challenge, but your father is holding out hope. Here you are."

Ik.hun gestured towards a circle of men who were in a meeting, my father among them.

"Your brother was among the injured," said Ik.hun. "You'll want to ask your father about that."

We entered the circle and interrupted their meeting, though the men were in a deep discussion. My father, who had an intense and determined look upon his face, looked up and greeted us with surprise and some warmth in his words, though his face didn't animate or match his tone.

"Here, at last, a good sign! My sons have returned."

Damkats embraced him first.

"We've returned with good news to report. Your faith in Zhikbi was justified. As for myself... I'll vindicate myself in the coming fight."

I also embraced my father, but I was preoccupied.

"What happened to Anbi?" I asked.

"You've heard already," he noted with surprise. "He was wounded when the enemy routed us, but don't worry too much. He's one of the lucky ones. Many others were killed, but Anbi will recover well. We've sent him with some companions to return to our village and relax in safety and comfort. Several of us others, I'm afraid, should never expect to return alive and intact."

His words were designed to assure me of Anbi's wellbeing, and I rested my worries. (But several weeks after this, I finally heard the truth. Anbi's back and leg had been broken in a stampede of men who trampled him while fleeing Muhlosangko's assault. Several of the men who stumbled were killed, and their corpses were literally heaped upon him. Anbi would live, but he wouldn't live well.)

Meanwhile, my uncle Laat.el drew Wibaw, my brother, and me aside for a private conference. My father made sure to thank me for the quickly relayed message which I had sent via Lanna, warning of the impending attack.

"We mobilized immediately. It's true we were unable to prevent the initial attack, and we arrived only after many people and priests had been killed. But our efforts have prevented the overthrow of the city, and we've done damage to the shrinking numbers of enemy men. Despite the brutal cost of Wawli lives, I believe the endless skirmishes and battles must be close to exhausting the U.hulia."

"What about the report that Ti'aw and Dini's village was destroyed," Laat.el asked. "Were the brothers killed as well?"

"On the contrary," I said, "Ti'aw and Dini are alive and well. They are coming with a large force to support us, fresh from a heroic victory in Isaysuhn Dozh."

"This is amazing," my father replied. But he was not quick to say more on the subject.

"I've avoided spreading the news. I'm afraid everyone might simply stand still and wait for the heroes to arrive. We have large numbers of supporters on the way, but our men must be ready to act at any time. I leave it to you to decide what to do with this information, when and how it will be used."

Now I finally saw a smile on my father's face, for the first time since our arrival. I could think of three possible interpretations for that smile, but its true meaning eluded me. Still, it seemed a good moment for a smile.

We then returned to the circle of men and they concluded their discussion. My father persuaded them that we could prevail by pursuing a simple, crude plan.

"I have communicated with the chiefs of seven villages. We have all agreed to full mutual support. Force of numbers will be decisive. Each chief will lead his own men to stay active and mobile throughout the day. We will patrol the streets methodically. Units will be ordered to engage the enemy on sight, without hesitation and regardless of circumstance, and you must raise a cry so nearby units will be able to respond, each raising a cry in turn, bringing a cascade of men until our entire force shall be concentrated on the point of conflict. If we encounter the main force of U.hulia men, or if they are attracted to the fight, then the war will be speedily concluded. Otherwise, in the worst case, there will be a lot of noise and little action."

With the discussion concluded, men prepared to sleep. Night had fallen, and the sky seemed like an inferno. Clouds shifted quickly over the city, blown by stiff winds and mingled with smoke, ash, and burning embers, as they reflected a pulsing glow of brown and orange.

As I stared at the sky, one of my old companions told me of the changes he'd seen. "The city and neighboring woods were frightfully dark in the first nights of the conflict, black as though the air were a thick rich soil, and the nights were moonless. The enemy camped in silence and darkness, with no fires, making it impossible to trace them. Now there is always light, and the burning city continues to draw men out of the woods and down from the eastern mountains.

But no fights occur at night unless they've begun in twilight. The U.hulia win those fights."

When everyone was finally settled down, I looked around and was unable to find my father. I suspected he had gone out to do his own nighttime scouting.

On Patrol

The next day, we went out patrolling as planned. Our men were divided into five groups. Wibaw and Laat.el each led a unit, and my brother Damkats was also given a command. Hang and Watez, two elders selected for their prestige within the community, were assigned their own groups, and I was placed in Hang's group. Beunba and Ik.hun of the Wise Words were also under Hang, along with about sixty-five other fighters. As we went, Ik.hun did his best to advise me, whereas he said very little to Commander Hang, who was too proud to seek his counsel. The five groups were ordered to move within reasonable distance of one another so we could respond quickly to any encounters.

We established rendezvous destinations for meetings every few hours, so that our groups would not be separated too much. We could not signal one another before meeting with the enemy. Our planned rendezvous were sometimes delayed, as none of us really knew the city, so it was easy to stray a bit out of the intended path. For this reason we had runners backtrack occasionally and try to locate any groups which had fallen behind in the overall progress. We did not send runners forward into unexplored territory.

We did not experience anything noteworthy for the first few hours, though we did hear some troubling noises in regions too remote to safely approach. These noises were vague in terms of distance and direction. As many houses had been torched, and many locals were shouting to one another or loudly mourning the deaths of family members, we did not go chasing every sound which reached our ears. We listened for our established call of "*Uswewe tizdalo*," ("Fox in the bag!") but we would have responded to anything that sounded like a loud outcry from a group of our men.

As we walked, some men chewed on bits of dried squid. For some it was salt-fish. They had brought scraps of food from the camp, which had come our way via barrels unloaded from one of the intact cargo ships remaining in the harbor. Our men had little time to attend to necessities, so they nibbled on whatever they could get, in whatever time was available.

When the suspense of patrolling in unknown territory started to lose its edge, I then unexpectedly heard the tromping sound of galloping horses' hooves rapidly approaching. I almost shouted out our signal phrase, but Ik.hun stopped me.

"No, don't. Wait. It's probably not an attack."

Still uncomfortable with any hesitation, I called out to our commander for guidance.

"Hang!"

Hang looked about a little uncertainly, and a few men near him approached and mumbled some words, then he stepped back a bit and directed his attention towards the approaching horses.

"Stand at the ready, and withdraw to the side of the road!" he called. We all obeyed.

In a moment, three riderless horses came running out from an alleyway and circled in confusion upon seeing so many men. Beunba and I exchanged bewildered glances, but the rest of the men soon ran out and stabbed the horses with their spears, as though the killing of stray horses were a matter of routine in the city.

The horses screamed as they died.

We continued on our way, though two men were left behind, one to guard the horses' bodies, and the other to run back to camp and find someone who could help butcher and transport the meat in exchange for a share. As we walked on, Ik.hun offered some explanation.

"No one has seen any riders since the second day. The strays run about confusing everyone and adding to the noise."

"But it's too strange to imagine the U.hulia would bring all their horses so far, only to abandon them."

"They must have been useful in the first surprise attacks. But then it is said, the day after Mo'uh was killed, some city men decided to follow the horses' tracks in the evening, expecting to locate the U.hulia camp. The tracks, instead, led them to a field where several horses wandered freely, and no enemies could be found. They scattered the remaining horses, then returned along the way they came, where they fell into an ambush and were slaughtered."

After a successful rally of all the units from our village, we split up into groups again and continued our patrol. It was about half an hour later when we fell into trouble.

As our group came through yet another narrow alley, and we were about to emerge onto a broad square, a large stone came down and struck one of our men dead. Then more large stones came down, and we saw six U.hulia on the flat roofs of the houses beside us. For a moment the majority of our group backed up a few meters out of the range where boulders could be cast, while the head of our group moved forwards. The forward group was partially separated from those of us in the middle and rear. Then a small cluster of U.hulia rushed into the alley against those who had been isolated at the head. We raised the alarm. Several of us pushed forwards to try to rejoin Hang and the lead warriors, while the stone throwers kept the majority back. Several of our men scrambled up to climb on the low roofs, while those of us who had advanced from the middle were not effective in helping our leaders, as the narrow alley limited our motions.

There were a few more people injured on both sides, plus one more of our men was killed. At that time, somewhere well ahead of us, we heard a loud shout of alarm from another of the groups, but we were too occupied to respond.

Then we heard several more enemy warriors rushing in, this time from behind us. Though there were nearly seventy of us, and we fought as well as we could, we were pinned and struggling ineffectually. Most of the men in the middle could do nothing more than try to boost their friends onto the roofs. Fortunately the stone throwing was brought to a stop and a few of the enemies were driven off their rooftop perches, but they put up a brave fight with their spears.

At the head of the group, Hang called for us to move forward, just as the men at the back were starting to get cut down. Hang himself was able to spear an enemy in the chest, but he was killed in turn by two men who speared him multiple times in the legs, then stomped on him and stabbed his face and chest. As our group recoiled once again, we finally mustered the force for a massive push forwards, and drove all of the enemy out into the square where we could engage them more freely. A few of the enemy who were too slow to move were wrestled down and killed with short daggers, though this also delayed the progress of about half of our force who remained clogged in the mouth of the alley.

Our men on the rooftops prevailed, killing most of the men they encountered, though two of the enemy got safely into the square to rejoin their companions. And now we were set to finally triumph, as Laat.el and his group of seventy came thundering into the square to assist us. Together we destroyed our remaining foes.

Finally, the last of our men extracted themselves from the alley, and those who had attacked us in the rear fled back the way they came. As I soon learned, that group was caught and killed by Watez. But more noise of battle continued ahead of us. Somewhere.

While Watez arrived on our heels, a group from another allied village soon arrived. At the same time, Laat.el's men went forwards, out of the square, towards where the noise seemed loudest. Checking first to see that our square was no longer under assault, Watez set off behind Laat.el, while we survivors of the alley fight gathered together and prepared to follow them, leaving the corpses where they lay. Altogether ten of our men had died, and many more were injured, against the nineteen U.hulia whom we had killed.

Just before we could set off, from somewhere deeper within the city, two bloody Wawli men with great wounds upon their bodies emerged shouting "*Liton nakopzlikol pwim! Awsokwe solibishas!* We have lost! Disaster has come!"

Ik.hun questioned them, and they explained that they were perhaps the last survivors of a battle against a large force who had attacked Damkats and his unit. We set off at a run towards the place that they indicated, and we were followed by the allied villagers.

As we ran, I felt exceedingly hot, even beyond what I would expect after a fight. I was also feeling very disoriented. Touching my face, I found that I was thickly coated with blood, and I also found my hair was sticky and saturated. A spear point had slashed my scalp without my even knowing it, except by some dim awareness I could hardly remember. My arms too were very achy, probably due to great exertion during the fight. Yet I had been almost entirely unaware of my own physical self, only noticing the press of men around me and the passage of what seemed like hours, though perhaps it was much shorter than that. And now here I was, running off to find if my brother was dead.

Six to eight minutes of running brought us past a few scattered bodies in the alleys, until we came out into a large clear space where bodies were heaped all around. There were many unfamiliar Wawli men standing here who had arrived a few minutes too late to take part in the battle. Many more of their companions had already departed, looking for the enemy. And here, Damkats had died among sixty-five of our men. It truly was a disaster for our village, the second disaster of the week, as I had been told. And there were very few dead U.hulia.

But then the battle was upon us once more.

From the West came Muhlosangko with a force of hundreds who had somehow bypassed or scattered the groups that had just set off to meet them. Those of us who had come for a fight got caught by the forceful and immediate shock of their attack. Hardly knowing what was happening, I managed to get my spear stuck deep into a charging U.hulia man's abdomen, down near the top of his hip, then something blunt hit me near the outer corner of my eye socket and knocked me to my knees. My spear was wrenched from my hands, and quite to my surprise, when I recovered enough to look up, I saw the man with my spear in his gut still running along with companions, until he stumbled about 80 meters away, and he was set upon by several Wawli.

Shortly after that, another of the passing U.hulia warriors lunged out of the mob in my direction, and stabbed at me with his spear, which I aimed to block with my left hand, being otherwise unprotected. The spear point passed straight through my palm and out the back of my hand, driving back on me hard, and cutting my cheek and shoulder. The next thing I knew, he was yanking back on the spear, dragging me with it over the backs of a couple of fallen bodies. Then a few more of my companions ran forward all around me and struck him down, and the spear point came dislodged from my mangled hand.

Wawli men were still tumbling down on all sides, but the U.hulia hadn't come to stay. Rather, they kept on trotting, running off to some unknown quarter of the city. Soon the square was mostly empty again, except for the dead, the dying, and the few of us who were less critically wounded. Many of the survivors on our side had scattered in the face of the onslaught, and now they came trickling back from the side roads and alleys, some even emerging from houses in which they had barricaded themselves for shelter.

Ik.hun had received a wound which punctured his lung, so he was out of the fight from that time forward, though against all odds he ultimately survived this wound. Beunba, meanwhile, was one of the very few who were still standing, uninjured and holding his ground. I don't know why this made me as happy as it did. Of my travelling companions, he was the one I liked least, and I had hardly had any conversation with him. But at least there was one man I knew well who hadn't tasted personal defeat.

It was about ten or twelve minutes later when my father came jogging into the square, followed by his demoralized companions. In his train came Laat.el and Watez with their men, and several of the men of other villages. All of them had been caught up in a minor skirmish of no consequence. They then found themselves running in contrary directions until Wibaw had finally commanded the attention of the majority and brought the units together into a single force. They were too late, unfortunately, to catch Muhlosangko.

The first thing my father did, after surveying the scene of our massacre, was to call for Hang. When he was informed that Hang had died, father then looked around until his eyes found mine. I must have been hard to recognize in that moment. But, giving no special attention to my injuries, Wibaw marched right up to me and declared:

"You should have held them longer."

He turned away from me again, to look about among the bodies of the dead. He rolled over a body here and a body there, until someone called his attention to the place where Damkats had fallen. Wibaw walked over, lifted up the heavy corpse, and flung it over his shoulder. Then he marched off to the south, saying no more. In our own time, the rest of us followed him, bringing with us the wounded men who were unable to bear themselves. Thus we returned to camp to eat our horsemeat.

The Great Battle

That night I got less sleep than usual. My hand felt as though it were being crushed between two massive stones which were slowly grinding together. I felt sure the wound would be permanently maiming and might even turn out to be fatal. However, though the bones internal to my hand must have been fractured and partially dislocated, nothing was crushed beyond the body's ability to heal. I had my hand tightly bound with a long strip of absorbent cloth, though treatment may have been superfluous. Beyond the first hour, there was little bleeding and no other significant discharge, and the wound seemed to close itself up very tightly as though the muscles were gripped in a cramp. My fingers were curled down in a rigid clump, constricted around the wad of cloth which had been forced between fingers and palm during the application of the bandage. Though the pain kept me awake for much of the night, I eventually lapsed into a couple of hours of sleep, and in the morning I awoke with significantly less pain. My hand felt then more like a block of wood than a hand.

The events of the new dawning day were like a falling stone. There was a lot of noise and movement in the camp, and I began to vaguely remember some of the conversations which had occurred around me during the night. As I tried to focus my thoughts, however, I drifted off to sleep once more, in disregard of the bustling activity that surrounded me.

Uncle Laat.el woke me abruptly.

"Grab a spear in your good hand, and move."

I was soon up and running at my uncle's side, with all of our men massed together. We were running towards the sound of a battle, which sounded like the fiercest clash I had heard yet. Meanwhile, I had left my shoes behind in the camp, having moved out too hastily to put them on. My uncle was raving.

"I can't believe he left me behind. The pig goes off to die, and he leaves the hardest task to me."

I didn't see my father anywhere, and presumed he must be "the pig." I asked Laat.el what was happening, and he told me succinctly:

"*Gamsesno la.wawzh*. He took twelve men with him, and I wasn't one of them."

The phrase "*Gamsesno la.wawzh*," meaning *obligatory sacrifice*, explained everything.

In the previous night's conversation, there had been a lot of talk of taking two days' rest without a fight, to recover our strength and to express our grief for those we had lost. My father went into a rage at this suggestion. He told the men that there would be no rest during daylight hours, no one was even to bury their dead, and if there were any more grumbling he would personally find Muhlosangko and lead him back to the camp to slaughter us in our sleep. He then went off on his own.

Most of the men were quick to excuse him, while not taking his threats very seriously. They said he was entitled to his anger after the death of Damkats, that most of the men felt the desire for revenge as he did, but that he was still bound to compromise. Some of the more shameless men in the camp, however, dared to suggest we give up the fight altogether and return to our village. We had already sacrificed enough for the weak city people, they said.

And now we were rushing into a fight that was almost sure to kill us all. None of us could refuse to follow the village chief after he had taken the suicidal plunge. Least of all could I, his only surviving and able bodied son… able at least in three of my limbs. As I kicked up the dust of the road with my bare feet, dashing forward, I felt and saw the men around me adjusting their pace, allowing me to pass and gain the lead. Watez and other elders, and the men who accompanied them, also stepped aside for me. My uncle too, in the end, let me take the lead before him, and placed himself a half pace behind me on the left, as I rushed into what felt like the first true battle of my life, the one that counted most, the one I expected to be my last. Then we were in it.

We passed through a narrow street darkened with the stains of blood, dead bodies tossed aside with heaps of debris, pressed into the corners and the doorframes, critically wounded men writhing, hobbling, and staring wide-eyed at our charge. Then we suddenly merged into a roiling mob of men, both our allies and our enemies, who were crowded together in a chaotic mass in the nearly impassable street. There was no order to the battle, suggesting that the rigid discipline of the U.hulia had finally been shattered, and isolated groups were fending for themselves. While some of the warriors on the fringes were trying to push themselves into the midst of the conflict, others were struggling to extract themselves. The momentum of our charge carried us on and through. Those we couldn't push forward were pushed aside.

We emerged into a very broad square, which was packed with more men than seemed reasonable or even possible. The scale of the fight was becoming apparent, as we saw fighting in all directions, down every alley and every street, with shouts and the sounds of colliding forces audible behind every building. Yet quite close by there seemed to be a more urgent commotion, as a circular motion of men seemed focused on one point of the battle.

There was no opportunity to give immediate attention to this neighboring conflict, as our group was soon caught up in a fight of our own. Several U.hulia men crossed our path, and we fought. They turned to block us, showing great courage and self-discipline. Though their lack of mobility made them easy targets, they didn't fear death and gave no ground for as long as they could stand and resist us. My one-handed spear thrust was sufficient to wound one of them, and I was able to stay clear of his counter-attack, as his aim was precise but his thrust was too short. Because he was sharply stung by the wound I had given to his belly, the other Wawli men around us were quick to finish him. His companions were soon falling at his side.

Then there was a thrill of energy which suddenly passed through my body… I could hardly account for its source. It was my own mind stumbling over an electrifying *fact*. The name "Muhlosangko" entered my thoughts, or, as it sounds in the animal-like jumble of noises that constitutes the U.hulia language, "Mlosanko". Perhaps someone had really spoken his name somewhere beside me. My eye caught the sight of something that I could hardly be aware of seeing. I still cannot summon up a clear picture of what I saw, but I am aware only of the startling *fact* of it, that a low and rising spear thrust had caught the enemy hero under the chin, and in an instant he was transformed from an infinitely menacing presence, to a crumbled and pathetic dying thing. And the man holding the spear shaft was my father!

Somehow Muhlosangko had been isolated from his supporters in the melee, and a scattering of men all around made it impossible for his supporters to come to his defense. I was remarkably close to the midst of it all, and I felt that I must reach out and do something, but I was frozen and inactive… and all for the best, as I might have been killed had I taken a single step. I saw one Wawli man spear another Wawli man in an accidental and instinctive motion to prevent *anyone* from interfering. No one knew who was who in that moment. The sense of awe gripped every one of us in the vicinity. I felt it.

My father's spear had passed up through the flesh under Muhlosangko's jaw, through tongue and soft tissue, but had not broken through the palette into the brain. Muhlosangko writhed as Wibaw pushed his fallen body for several meters across the dusty ground, striving to press the spear point deeper for the kill. Then Wibaw withdrew the spear, and Muhlosangko still had the energy to turn himself over, gripping at his throat to retain any portion of his life's blood that he could hold back. My father struck two jabs with the spear into the back of his neck, and one more through the center of his back into his heart, stamping Muhlosangko underfoot and ensuring his death.

We were in motion again. Our men grabbed Wibaw and pulled him away, before the enemy could fall on him in a mass. He was the hero of the day, the victory was ours, and we wouldn't allow the advantage to be snatched back from us. Yet the battle raged on in all directions. Only little by little did people get the news that Muhlosangko had been killed. His body was swallowed up under the swirling storm of deadly strife. But, though our battle had been won, my father had come with the intention to die, and he would not withdraw. Thus we fought on, though for us the fight had become more of a pushing match than a true war. The walls of men around us were dense, while the enemy were becoming scarce.

"Ti'aw and Dini have arrived" Laat.el told me. Where had my uncle come from, and where had he been? "Ti'aw and Dini, with their hundreds of supporters." There was nothing left for us few individuals to do, as the vast numbers of our allies crushed the few remaining enemy whose ranks had been broken into fragments. But Ti'aw and Dini were too late for the real glory. The death of Muhlosangko was universally accepted as the event which turned the war in our favor.

9.
Fourth Intermission: The Pivotal Question

The Gentlemen's Club Fire

Before my next session with Randall, I felt it was necessary for me to review the details relating to the Gentlemen's Club Fire, bringing together my file of newspaper clippings, my personal notes, and the reports included with the papers Evan Briar had given me. This is the summary of the event, and the investigation which followed:

No one has ever been charged for the highly publicized arson attack which killed seventeen people. All of the dead were trapped in a loft space upstairs from a newly opened Crossroads-district strip-club called "River Dancers," famous for their all-nude shows. The public reporting on the case focused on two suspects, both women, but evidence was lacking and arrests had not been made. Both women seemed strong possible candidates for having started the fire. One suspect, known by the pseudonym "Grace," was a prostitute who worked in the upstairs private club that functioned as an illegally operated brothel. It was not visibly connected to the strip club on the ground floor but it was managed by the same owners and it employed some of the same security staff. The other suspect, Carla Black, was the jealous wife of a man who may have frequented the strip club.

"Grace" had a proven history of arson, and she is currently serving a prison-term on an unrelated murder charge for having killed her husband in Oklahoma seven years before the club fire. (Her conviction for that crime came only recently.) News reports proclaimed that she had a clear motive for burning the club, as she had complained several times—both to friends and the police—that she had been raped by one of the club regulars, yet the club manager did nothing to protect her, and he continued to admit the assailant to the club. The accused rapist was not among the victims of the fire, however, and appears not to have been present that night. No witnesses were able to say where Grace was at the time of the fire, and she offered no alibi. There were no reports of threats made prior to the event.

Meanwhile, the "jealous wife," Carla Black, had come to River Dancers several times and created a disturbance, looking for her husband and shouting that she would kill him, once proclaiming, "You'll all die for this," before she was bounced from the club. It is unclear whether her husband had ever actually attended either the strip club or the brothel, and it's believed she was unaware of the existence of the separate club in the loft above, as she had never appeared there nor threatened any of the patrons. She had a history of violent conflict with women she suspected of sleeping with her husband, though no one could say whether there were any grounds for her suspicions.

While the public was fixated on the two female suspects, and they each had several additional circumstantial connections to the crime, the police had never taken Carla Black very seriously as a suspect after their initial interview with her, and they were unable to get beyond motive in their investigation of Grace or produce concrete physical evidence. The police then turned to Randall, and his name was leaked as a suspect, though most details were not disclosed to the public. When the police felt there was nowhere else to go with Randall, they turned back to Grace for further investigation, and then they stalled out completely. The last word from the news media had Randall as the likely killer, while a spokesman for the district attorney's office denied he was being considered.

The fire was started within a locked warehouse space behind the club. No one knew what method the killer used to access the warehouse, or whether it may have been unlocked before he or she arrived. An accelerant was used to burn a pile of books and papers gathered together and heaped in a pile under a stairway that accessed the loft. The only method of exit from the loft, other than the burning stairway, was a manually operated freight elevator. However, after several patrons and security staff escaped, they abandoned the elevator on the ground floor, stranding everyone else upstairs without a way out.

Some of the survivors ran down through the fire and were badly burned, until a section of the stairs collapsed and two men fell through and died. Strangely enough, six of the casualties upstairs were men in wheelchairs. Among the people with disabilities in Kansas City, River Dancers was known as the club with the best accessibility, and the upstairs brothel had a reputation for catering to disabled men. The terrible denouement was that, with their one point of access cut off, they were trapped without hope of rescue. Other victims of the fire included prostitutes and customers. One customer who died was a Missouri state assemblyman.

The downstairs club was destroyed, but all of the patrons successfully evacuated in the early stages of the fire.

After reviewing the facts, and considering the horrible fate of the victims, I felt I had to once again confront Randall directly, and force him to give an answer regarding his guilt or innocence in this crime. I met Randall and Ned the following afternoon, and before they could go anywhere in the further development of Zhikbi's story, I told Randall what I knew about the physical evidence linking him to the crime scene.

RANDALL'S CONFESSION

"It seems like damning evidence to me," I said. "Regardless of everything else, this one point seems to prove your involvement. I think the police officer was right in accusing you."

I thought Randall would dodge the question again, but instead he came right out and surprised me, saying (through Ned), "You're right, I did it. I killed them all."

I wasn't sure I could even believe him now. But yet... I did believe him. I do believe him.

"But... why?" I asked.

"I saw the heart of a bear within. The bear called out to me. I did the honorable thing."

This just floored me. I don't know why I expected a rational answer from a psychotic. I wanted something sensible to *click* here. I'd had a lot of patients before who were quite disturbed, but this man had done more harm than I was used to confronting. After so much time spent trying to understand and relate to him, I was troubled by where my sympathy had lain.

There was no more conversation between us for a while after this. Randall would say no more about the fire, about his childhood, about his family history, his dreams, his desires, about anything else I wanted to discuss, whereas I had run out of patience for his distracting story that seemed to lead nowhere. We were in a standoff for two weeks. A little more than that.

Then, when I found myself at the height of frustration, and I was having more difficulty sleeping than ever, Ned came to me and said "Zhikbi would like to tell you more of his story." I could resist no longer. We resumed our meetings and the tale continued.

10.
Zhikbi's Tale: Fallout

When the war in Shamni was all over, Wibaw was held in high esteem. The fact that he had gone to face sure death—yet survived—made his accomplishment near legendary. Yet there was truly little for us to celebrate. The U.hulia had brought around 1,200 to 1,400 men to the city, all of whom had died in the conflict. The very few who had not died in battle had killed themselves to avoid surrender. On our side, throughout the many days of fighting they had killed over 4,500 of our fighters, while leaving thousands wounded. An unknown number of women, children, and weaklings had died in their homes in all quarters of the city, and vast amounts of wealth and property had been destroyed.

The surviving priests were afraid, and with good reason. Much of the public sentiment was against them, and they were especially hated by many of the village chiefs and warriors who had come and sacrificed so much. We had seen how cowardly our nation's leaders were, and how rich.

Still, several of the city-dwellers supported the priests. They feared that the country-men and the poorer classes of city-men might overturn the structure of authority. They insisted that the produce of the northern farmers and the system of trade that the priests had established must be preserved and protected. They reminded the people, in speeches throughout the city squares and in the camps, that the priests maintained peace with Twilak slavers and other foreign forces.

One remarkable memory for me is seeing a beautiful young woman screaming passionate injunctions against rebellion.

"The priests are the spiritual center of faith for men of many races," she shouted. "They are our guarantee of safety. The priests must rule with free access to their ranks available to all men. They are not merely your representatives, they are literally the best of *you*. Why disturb that state which is *neither loud nor quiet*? Would you rather run from extreme to extreme in the *uncentered whorl*? Do you think your protection lies with kings? Would you find *warmth in the hands that are bathed in your own life's blood*? In the age of kings there was no need to buy wood for a funeral pyre; they stacked the corpses one upon another and the flames never expired. Ground burial, when it was preferred, was no problem; the grave pits were never covered. You could be securely buried eighty men deep, down where your most disgraced ancestors still lie in carrion bogs. Do you think the kings would bring you warmth today? Maybe they will… Warmth in excess!!! When Zodu's starvation was fierce enough that he ate his own hands, *the blood that poured out from the wounds became fire and molten steel.* Can you endure the scalding of your flesh? Your misplaced ambitions have called down the vengeance we see today. To further defy the priests would bring unparalleled supernatural destruction of which this is only the mildest hint. *You've had the broth, will you try the meat!?*"

Speeches such as this seemed highly influential in their effect on the citizens of Shamni. As for those of us who had staked everything in order to preserve them from their enemies, they all thanked us with their mouths, but they kept fear in their stomachs. With that devil Muhlosangko no longer menacing them, we, their saviors, were quickly seen as the greatest threat to their comfort.

We country warriors scoffed. We knew at what cost the comforts of the city had been bought. We saw that war had come despite the priests' claims to be protectors of the people. We knew the full history of their corruption, their abuses, and their violation of our traditions.

It was manifest that the priests could not maintain their hold on power without at least giving superficial acknowledgement of the debt they owed to our fighting men. They called upon my father, the hero, to meet with them, and they presented him with rewards and honors for his bravery and leadership.

Tipsnu, the most respected of the surviving high priests, said to my father, "We have heard that you planned a union of forces to invade the U.hulia lands. We know that the men of Isaysuhn Dozh have called upon Ti'aw and Dini to end their feud with you and join your cause. We encourage the proposed peace. We will reward the two heroes of the south for what they've done, and we will place them under your command, along with all the forces, weapons, and supplies you need to drive the U.hulia out, or neutralize their threat. You are the supreme hero of the people, and we, the voice of the people and the echo of Zodu's voice, praise you and authorize you to act under our guidance."

They then conducted a private conference of some length, with all the involved parties, and the truce was resolved. But this was not the end of it. The priests insisted on one dishonorable condition, which again defied the tradition of the people. They demanded that Wibaw make a public pledge of future conduct, to ensure his loyalty, and surprisingly he accepted their terms.

Wibaw's Pledge

Wibaw met with the High Priests in a public assembly at Hinen temple. They questioned him, and demanded that he make a series of pledges to ensure that he would not seize power or oppose the priests.

"What pledge can you offer to demonstrate that the fighting forces under your command will be used only to defend our nation, and uphold our authority? How can we be sure that you will not seek to become king?"

"I would rather be a beggar than a king."

"Tell us again what you pledge."

"I will beg a single coin from a man much poorer than myself before I seek the throne."

"Whom will you defend and support."

"I will defend and support the Wawli people, and I will defend and support you, the high priests."

"Tell us again what you pledge."

Wibaw gestured out the north window, towards the high peaked Etol Mountain which sheltered Hinen temple from the sea.

"I will protect you from your enemies for as long as Etol Mountain stands to the North of this temple."

"You will not seek to rule this land?"

"May I be cast down by the people if I seek more than your grace would grant."

"Tell us again what you pledge."

"If I ever violate my oath to you, either in word or in spirit, the people should cast me down on the same day I take the throne."

This last pledge satisfied the priests, and they assigned military command authority to my father, though they issued a final warning that every man must be held to the same pledge, and that Wibaw was not to violate his promise in any way. Then Wibaw was officially made the leader of the people's fighting force, the first great-battle-gang assembled in our country in more centuries than we could remember.

Several months were given to training, planning, and equipping, and many resources were expended. Wibaw had been highly impressed by the courage and discipline of the U.hulia force which we had faced, so we learned to imitate their character and tactics. Wibaw also counseled with me privately.

"I've been very pleasantly surprised by your skill in fighting and leadership, including everything I've heard about your performance while we were apart. I'd say the lessons you've learned from your tutor, Olul, prepared you well. So I will assign you to the training of troops. I will also order that word be sent throughout the land that Olul should come out of hiding and join us. His safety and freedom will be guaranteed."

Yet Olul never came.

Wibaw, my father, did express misgivings on one point however.

"I heard a terrible rumor about your mother," he said. "It caused me great embarrassment in my negotiations with Ti'aw and Dini, though they were consequently willing to forget our feud. Nothing was spoken openly in the conference, but there were insinuations. Do you know anything about this?"

"As you know, the people of the south are gossips," I said. "Their words never come to anything."

From that point forward, we focused on our new mission. When we were ready, the people marched behind us. My third trip to the south would prove a decisive moment for two races of men.

War of Nations: Campaigning

Wibaw's doom was our doom. We were honor-bound to follow. Many people said the priests were sending us off to die. My father was not yet through with *gamsesno la.wawzh*.

Because we had been so impressed by the fighting spirit, courage, and cold ruthlessness of Muhlosangko's men, and we would soon be fighting the U.hulia in their own territory, we anticipated meeting a very difficult, perhaps even hopeless challenge. However, it was not long before we discovered the true nature of our enemy. They were, to a very large extent, weak, passive, indecisive, and undisciplined.

Muhlosangko had to have been brilliant beyond compare as a commander and teacher. He had rallied the very best of his nation, men of superior character in every way, while those who had stayed behind completely lacked the fighting spirit. With the main strength of their force already defeated, they could hardly resist us. They should have anticipated that breaking the peace in Isaysuhn Dozh and the attack on our great city of Shamni would provoke a strong reaction, but when we fell upon them in reprisal they seemed to have no idea we were coming. This made the attack on Shamni all the more mysterious. What had they been after? They had, in effect, committed national suicide.

I have speculated, but can never confirm, that the more powerful leaders in the deep south of their land must have been deluded, even superstitious in their belief that the Wawli people would submit to terror, that we would not organize or fight back, that our society would be shattered at one blow. Then, I have also considered the possibility that some kind of internal pressure, conflict, or crisis had made them desperate. It is regrettable that reliable historical records do not exist. The U.hulia were almost entirely illiterate, and in our campaigns we so thoroughly wiped away any vestige of their culture that the truth may never be recovered.

This does not mean that the war we waged was without adventures and great risks for our fighters. Rather, we had more adventures than I can reasonably relate. Though they were disorganized, their numbers were far greater, and their weapons were stronger. We faced horse fighters in relatively large and flat clearings—in contradiction to our assumptions regarding the southern terrain—when they attempted to intercept us and slow down our progress. Their use of military bows by trained archers also caused us a great deal of trouble, while we could never turn such weapons against them due to our lack of training and experience. Our limited use of small-game bows for hunting at very close range, of course, counted for next to nothing. But through it all, we prevailed.

The overall progress of the war came about through two swift movements, starting with a deep penetration of the south, accomplished in a couple of weeks along the eastern extreme of the territory. We then swept west out from the rough foothills of the Aldas mountain range, and pressed the U.hulia hard towards the western limits of the peninsula. Success came about as a consequence of three principle factors.

First, we remained cohesive. The necessity of holding together to ensure our survival prevented any power struggles from arising which might divide our efforts. Ti'aw and Dini showed incredible maturity and self-restraint in their cooperation with Wibaw's plans, without introducing any new, dangerous rivalry. I had been quite impressed by the way the two brothers always shared in one another's glory without any overt competition. But I was always anxious that a rift would occur between them and our family, and if our truce ended, our entire campaign would be defeated. Somehow, such a rift never occurred.

Second, we were relentless and energetic in our constant driving of the enemy before us. I don't boast much of my own accomplishments, and I know I have never been much of a hero on my own. I've never displayed the kind of fierceness or courage that I've seen displayed by our very best warriors. But I will credit myself with this element of our success. I absolutely insisted on constant motion. Even when my own father, Wibaw, our most determined and impassioned leader, three weeks into the fighting once suggested we give our men a few days of rest and relief from their struggles, to regroup, to re-plan, and to reconsider our options, I wouldn't hear a word of it. "We must double our effort!" I demanded on the spot, astonishing everyone by my stubborn determination. Wibaw quickly agreed, in contradiction of his own hastily spoken words of a moment before. We would only enjoy as much food and sleep as was necessary to stay alive, and no more! No comfort. Move, move, move. I had learned about the power of a force in motion from my studies with Olul, and Muhlosangko had shown us how much could be accomplished by keeping the enemy in a state of confusion and uncertainty. I had more faith in these lessons than in any idea of the power of simple courage. "Courage dies a fool's death," I told my father, "unless it is focused by a plan. And the plan arises from fundamental laws…" As I found myself lecturing, I saw he looked upon me with pride. I had forgotten my humility, at least for a moment.

The third element of our success was the morale benefit of our early victories. As stories of our campaigns were reported back to the north, many groups of men, without any central authority or planning, started flowing down to join the fight. The increasing pressure they placed on the already harried U.hulia ultimately broke the enemy's will. We knew that something had snapped when we found ourselves marching against no resistance, through many abandoned villages and trading towns, meeting only with fleeing refugees who had moved too slowly to avoid our path, and sometimes stumbling across the unexpected presence of friendly Wawli encampments.

We wanted to avoid all delay, but each time we came upon a group of our allies, they called out to us to pause, rest, help one another with food and supplies, and exchange valuable information. In order to ensure our forward progress, our force continued on its way, while we left only a handful of men to communicate with the chief or chiefs, try to persuade them to join us as reinforcement troops, and then the liaison group would race to catch up with us and deliver messages. Some of the groups we met had fought brief but successful battles against the enemy, while others had been swept aside by the movement of unexpectedly large forces. But they all reported a general withdrawal of U.hulia towards the western shore.

Hebul of Hongdaw

We were passing through just such an encampment on a rapid march, and we were approaching the shore where we expected to fight a climactic battle, when I was told by one of our liaisons that Hebul, the chief of Hongdaw was nearby, and he was dying. He remembered me from when I'd travelled through his village, and he requested to see me.

I sympathized, but I thought it ridiculous that I would be requested to stay behind now, just at such a critical time when my help could be most useful. Reports from forward observers told us that the enemy was near, in a state of extreme panic and confusion, and it was essential that our force proceed without hesitation. My father, however, insisted that I honor the dying chief's request.

"You can easily catch up and join us after a few hours' delay. Perhaps you will learn something important here. You're the clever one, and I've been told that Hebul has no sons. He may pass his learning on to you before he goes."

Old time ignorance, I thought. *A man has a lifetime in which to teach, if he has anything to teach at all. Why should he wait for his dying day? If he leaves an echo in this world, he'll do it when he's vital, not through a few parting words at the end.*

Still, I stayed behind and met with Hebul.

Amazing to see, the dying chief was lying on a blanket, barely clothed, insect bitten and raw-skinned, with profound wounds on his face, arms, and torso, in a small clearing in a wood beside a narrow creek. He was among several other critically wounded men who all had been left out to die.

"Hebul, what is happening here?" I cried out. "Your people are dining nearby. They are sheltered, they are well dressed. I even heard singing in your camp as I passed through. How can you, their chief, be reduced to such a condition?"

"Don't pretend you can see my suffering, because you cannot. What you see is nothing next to the pain."

I was silent, but inwardly I condemned him for wallowing.

"Zhikbi. Do you remember what I told you about the cost?"

"I only remember you warned me to be careful, and make no mistakes. I've seen a lot of danger, but so far I've come out of it."

"I'm talking about the cost. Our desire to triumph is a plague in itself. We ignore the true values. I led my people here to share in the reward of a Wawli triumph, and we've been shamefully defeated."

"And these men are the cost?"

"No. Don't forget what you witness today, but you won't see the true cost of our pride here among our men. Look instead to the enemy."

"Why are you lying out exposed to the sun, with your wounds untreated?"

"You could hide me away, take me inside, clothe me and feed me and sing me a sleeping song, but you can't hide me from death. You can't create an illusion strong enough to blind me to what's coming."

"And these other wounded men? Where are your medicine men? Where is the help that could save their lives?"

"We follow the ways of the ancestors of our village, those who came from the deep lands. When the chief sees his end is near, there will be no help for other sufferers."

"So you would counsel me and teach me true value, yet you choose to condemn your own men to a needless death."

"Your cleverness has already blinded you. Your sophistication…"—he said this word like a curse—"has destroyed your understanding. Of the strengths of man, strength of body is the least, strength of mind is of little consequence, and they are both dwarfed by strength of spirit. That is what your father has, while all you have is cleverness. Spirit is what our people as a whole once had, and our lost strength of spirit is the cost we have paid to enter this new chaotic age, when men grasp for glory with both fists, while it trickles away between their fingers."

"Tell your men to get help for their wounds, before it is too late for them."

"I've made no choice here. The elders themselves, and my accursed rival, my mother's son who will succeed me, they have invoked the law of our ancestors. I have carried three men across that stream today, and soon I will carry a fourth. Since ancient times, no chief but Chief Senay ever saved another while he himself was wounded. Senay saved his infant son by crossing the stream, and he died from the effort. But I have now rescued three vigorous warriors who will carry on my faith when I am gone. I have no son, but today, *that one*, he will be my son."

Hebul indicated a pale giant of a man, lying unconscious and nearly bled to death, with a wound upon his neck.

Hebul struggled to rise for one last great effort. I tried to prop him up, but he refused me. Then, blood flowing fresh from his own wounds, the chief lifted up the man he had selected, and heaved him up upon his back. I stared in disbelief as he forced his frail and damaged body to bear the great weight of the dying hero, whose eyes cracked open just a little, but who showed no other sign of life as his limp body dangled and waved like a hunk of deer meat in the jaws of a wolf. The other injured men looked on in envy.

The chief took one step into the stream, and his foot sank

down between two stones. Then there was a "tasak!" as his leg sheared and broke. As Hebul fell, he flung the man from his back and propelled him forward onto the dry bank on the other side, just a meter away from where he stumbled.

I rushed forward, as did several other men who I didn't know were hiding in the wood nearby. We pulled the chief, groaning and gasping, out of the water, while others came out to rescue the man he had thrown across the stream. The medicine men were now allowed to attend to him, according to this strange tribal custom that none of us Upland Wawli were familiar with.

I stayed with Hebul for several hours more, watching him slowly die. He didn't say much after this, except to remind me not to believe too strongly in the superficial, to keep my eyes open to the essential. There were several long stretches of time when he sank into a kind of stupor, but when I became impatient to go, he struggled to revive himself and fixed me with a stare that said, "Not yet."

Finally, when he knew he could keep me no longer, when it was apparent that his death agony would last longer than either my sympathy or interest, he grasped me one last time.

"Do you know why your father let you stay behind to watch me die? It's because he didn't want you to see *him* die. He's sparing you that."

I knew that he was speaking the truth, that I had ignored the essential all along! I ran out of there as fast as I could. I chased after the men I really cared for, my own people.

On the Beach

But there was nothing to fear on that day. By the time I reached the coast, our men had already won the fight. My father won the fight, perhaps exceeding his own expectations.

I came to the beach. Here, on the sand, some U.hulia men were still busy dying, falling under the spears of our friends, while all around in the expanse of water, as far out as I could see, there were thousands of bodies, some moving of their own will, many moved only by the tossing and churning of the sea, and no one could know how many more had already been swallowed by the waves. I knew then that we had accomplished something quite remarkable.

Return to Shamni

On his return to Shamni, at the head of the big-battle-gang, Wibaw planned his assault on the High Priests and their defenders. First, however, he assembled the men to perform a ritual and offer a pledge in support of his insurgency.

As part of an arranged spectacle, I stood at the end of a tremendously long line of men.

A soldier at my side turned to me and said "Will you spare one coin for a man in need?"

I gave this man a silver coin, saying "I will, and may it relieve you of your need."

Then another man asked the one who had received the coin "Will you spare one coin for a man in need?"

"I will, and may it relieve you of your need."

The soldier passed along the coin I had given him, and added one of his own, so now two coins passed down the line. Following this pattern, each man among us added one coin to the rapidly amassing fortune. Eventually, porters were needed to carry the gift in large jars, and then a cart was employed to transport it from man to man, until it reached a poor man dressed in tatters, standing beside my father. He was not a soldier, but a lifelong beggar named Bayshen. He had been especially selected for his extreme poverty. He possessed only one coin, which he had borrowed at interest, though it represented more than all the yams he could beg in four months. It was the first coin he had ever held in his life. My father asked him "Will you spare one coin for a man in need?" The poor man looked sick, seeing all the silver on the cart before him, but after a moment's hesitation he added his coin, saying, "May it relieve you of your need," and presented countless thousands to my father.

Wibaw received the treasure in humility. Then he called for his own possessions to be brought forward. He added enough silver to quadruple the amount that he had received. He added, besides, all of the mead sticks he had collected, and heaped up in a mass all of the furs, and weapons, and jewelry, and every thing of value he had seized from the U.hulia. He added golden ingots, and precious foreign medicines. Speaking to the crowd, he declared "All of this shall be divided among the men on the day I am made king." No man had ever seen such a treasure assembled in one place. As a final gesture, Wibaw gave Bayshen, the desperate beggar, twenty silver coins from his own pocket and declared "Never beg again, and I will give you the rich home of the first priest whom we capture." This, at last, brought a smile to the poor man's face.

Regime Change

At the conclusion of this spectacle, the morale of our men was very high, support for my father was tremendous, and we all felt that we were on the verge of a new age of prosperity. Thus, no one openly voiced an objection when Wibaw appointed large bodies of warriors to simultaneously descend upon the homes of the priests, taking as many into custody as possible and seizing their estates and property. Only the priests themselves were entirely surprised by this, as they counted too much on the support of the public, their own interpretation of Wibaw's pledge, and the degree to which he was bound to it. In fact, virtually no violence was necessary in the capture of the priests, as the townsmen and estate guards were unwilling to throw their lives away for a hopeless resistance. In several cases, it was the estate guards themselves who restrained those priests who attempted to flee or hide themselves.

Wibaw then ordered an accounting and inventory of all confiscated properties, after giving the estate of High Priest Winshaw to the custody of beggar Bayshen.

When my father saw the decrepit state to which the mansion of Mo'uh had been reduced, he was outraged. None of the furniture remained, and the precious treasures which had undoubtedly adorned the halls a few months before had all vanished. It was a testament to the greed of the priests that, after the great battle, they would strip the home of their most respected peer upon his death, when even the U.hulia men who had killed him had not dared to loot his home.

My father called upon his troops to gather furnishings from the homes of the neighboring priests and do their best to restore the mansion to a livable state, as he planned to make it his own residence. Then, unexpectedly, while Wibaw was having his possessions brought into the mansion, the famous beggar Bayshen arrived with a gift.

"Sir, I humbly thank you for lifting me out of poverty, and providing for my future with such generosity. I hope it will please you to receive this robe which is rightfully your own. I believe it is the robe of Mo'uh, a treasure looted from this very mansion, which was found among the property of Winshaw, whose house I now occupy."

Wibaw, Ti'aw, Laat.el and I were all gathered together, and we came closer to examine the robe.

"It truly is a treasure," said Laat.el.

"Most certainly made in foreign lands, and the jewels which adorn it must be worth a fortune," said Ti'aw.

"I will accept this," said Wibaw. "But I will not wear it until the day when I am proclaimed king."

Bayshen seemed disappointed, certainly more so than one would have expected.

"But sir," he said, "surely no one would deny that you are already our king."

"I'm no more than a war chief. It is not yet time to claim such a title as king. Now, as you say, you have returned property which is rightfully mine. You have already received your reward, as you know."

"Of course, I could never ask for more than I have received."

"Then I free you to go."

And so Bayshen was dismissed. I felt he had shown true loyalty and a simplicity of mind in his desire to see my father made king.

"He's not alone, Wibaw," said Ti'aw, "in expecting you to become our king. Why stand on ceremony?"

"First we must bring justice to our captive priests," said my father.

Then Laat.el spoke, still intently eyeing the precious robe.

"But it is not an honor for a great man to receive a gift from a lesser man. Rather, the junior should receive his honor through gifts from his master."

"And so I give this to you," said Wibaw, handing the treasure to Uncle Laat.el, "in recognition of your accomplishments in war. You are guaranteed a secure position as my deputy, my brother and my most trusted friend."

They embraced. If Laat.el felt slighted by the implication that he was junior to his younger brother, his face did not betray his emotion. He seemed fully content.

I departed, to go and have a look around the city, which was still largely in ruins. As I left, I heard the men talking of going to the bath, but I wasn't accustomed to such city luxuries, which I had never enjoyed even when I'd studied there in my adolescence.

I wandered here and there, among the unrestored remains of buildings, weaving my way between heaps of rubbish and fallen roof timbers, and along the way I saw some idlers peeking out from windows or standing in doorways. I saw one boy of nine looking out from his home, and he had a broad smile on his face. At least here there was a family who was thankful to see the rule of the priests overthrown.

I took it as a good sign, and imagined that there must be many people who would support my father's claim to kingship, if he were really to go so far as to claim it. Wibaw had an enviable position now, and my family was about to become not only prominent, but epochal. With that in mind, I turned my thoughts to wondering about my own role in the family and our future.

By chance, as I wandered, I crossed a square and then saw Bayshen once again, in the shadows of an adjoining alley. There I found him talking to Ti'aw's brother Dini. Before I could interrupt them, I saw Dini strike Bayshen in the face. Now I was angry. I was about to come to Bayshen's defense, when I heard him speak.

"He wouldn't wear it, but it can't be long before he puts it on."

All of a sudden I realized their treachery. Dini grabbed Bayshen by the collar and roughly shook him. Then they noticed me and looked frightened, knowing they had been caught.

I turned and ran in the direction of the mansion, to give warning. The two I left behind were slow to act, and unable to detain me. I arrived before the mansion and almost entered, momentarily confused about which way to turn, when I heard horrifying screams from within the neighboring bath house. I stopped, wheeled around, and ran into the bath, afraid I might be too late.

As I entered the bathhouse, I found Ti'aw lying on the floor, with his right forearm lying several yards away, the lifeless hand still gripping a spear shaft. My enraged father stood before him with the wood axe he had grabbed for an impromptu defense. A small party of soldiers who had responded stood about doing nothing.

In the waters of the bath, my uncle Laat.el stood wearing the poisoned robe which clung to his body like a second skin. Howling in agony and splashing about, he struggled to peel the robe from his flesh, but it gripped him too tightly to be removed. The water around him, and the blood which flowed from his flesh, were boiling with the heat that he radiated in his death-throes. Twice he slipped down into the water, then raised himself up again to continue his hopeless struggle. I rushed into the bath to rescue him, but he pushed me away for my own sake, then he turned away and covered his face with his hands to restrain any further screams or cries. He struggled no more, and submitted to his death, suffering now in complete silence as he went. It was a few minutes more before death took him.

In the aftermath of this assassination gone wrong, the guard successfully tracked down and captured Dini and Bayshen. Ti'aw only barely managed to stay alive through the night following the loss of his arm. The next day, my father commanded me to execute my childhood friends. As I prepared to kill them, Wibaw stood to curse them.

"Your envy drove you to treason, and so you have chosen to follow your father. By my command you too shall die. You were raised to greater heights than he; your heroism was all the greater, so your villainy is the greater shame. Let you leave no echo in our world, and no offspring to commit any further crime."

I then raised the wood axe which my father had used in his defense, and I struck each of the brothers on the crown of his head, destroying the top of his skull and the brain within.

Bayshen, who observed this, expected to die a similar death. But instead, my father said to him:

"I return you to your poverty, and I will help bring your suffering to its natural conclusion. You will be chained to a tree, in a quiet shaded spot and given two cups of water a day, but no food will be given to you. You are condemned to die of starvation, in whatever time it takes."

11.
Final Intermission

The Most Dangerous Sport

As Zhikbi's tale heaped violent act upon violent act, approaching what seemed like a possible final climax, I couldn't help thinking that Randall was likely guilty of even more crimes. Meanwhile, I discovered something quite remarkable in Randall's connection to the Gentleman's Club Fire.

I had felt that I should give more attention to the question of who had been killed or injured in the fire. Officer Briar's one tenuous connection, the pornographic model that Randall could have seen in a magazine, led nowhere. It had turned out that the magazine in the laundry room was Nelson's, and Randall had most likely never seen it. But after poring through the list of victims again, I had picked up another lead and followed it.

One victim's name, Noah Lippenschott, reminded me of the name of High Priest Mo'uh, so I researched what I could find related to him. I discovered that he had been featured in an article titled "The Most Dangerous Sport," in *Outdoor Adventure* magazine. Randall was an *Outdoor Adventure* subscriber, and it seemed plausible that he had read the interview. I therefore placed an order for a copy of this issue.

Now, as I was absent-mindedly sorting through my mail while daydreaming about the murder of childhood friends, I froze when I came across the *Outdoor Adventure* back-issue, with Noah Lippenschott on the front cover, legless, in a wheelchair, holding a hunting rifle.

"The Most Dangerous Sport," it turns out, is bear hunting from a wheelchair. Noah was the captain of a club for paraplegics, amputees, and otherwise disabled hunters, many of whom had been mutilated by bears but were unwilling to give up hunting. Noah himself had had his legs torn off, with the bones irreparably splintered and crushed, when a bear dragged his body through a narrow cleft between two rocks. The bear dropped him and fled when it got spooked by the sound of gunfire from other hunters, and Noah was rescued. A year and a half after this incident, Noah founded his club, the Arctophonus Fraternal Order, which employed fully-able assistants to push, pull, and sometimes carry the hunters and set them up in ambush positions.

On the night of the Gentleman's Club fire, Noah entertained five club members who had joined him to celebrate his recent kill of a bear in the Missouri Ozarks, not far from the city of Rolla. All but one of these men died together in the fire.

I interviewed surviving club member Geoffrey Lessing, who had attended the dinner but had not joined the others at the brothel. He had gone directly home to his family. I learned from our conversation that the men had feasted on bear meat. They had concluded their celebration by eating the heart.

Pondering all this, I proceeded to my next meeting with Randall, and one can imagine how distressing it was to listen to the continuation of his story while the fate of his victims was running through my mind. On top of it all, I was hopelessly puzzled by the question ,"How did he know?" I still have to wonder to this day: How did Randall know what was in the stomachs of his victims on the night when he killed them?

12.
Zhikbi's Tale: Consolidation of Power

The priests were bound and shackled and held prisoner in a dark enclosure on the ground floor of a small house, with all windows covered. Despite their protests, they were held captive for four days without food or drink. Then, on the fifth day, they were fed on a few scraps and given goat's blood to drink, and they were led out into the bright light, squinting.

The priests demanded protection, as the people all around shouted for them to be killed on the spot. They expected to die at any moment, but their legs were unchained and they were driven forward with whips, to limp along a road to the northwest, until they came to a small neighboring town. There, Wibaw came out and chastised his soldiers.

"Don't beat these men, and don't kill them. Give them peace and rest, and feed them well. I've pledged them my protection."

He walked away, and the priests called out to him, declaring that this was not enough, they should be free, they should rule and he should give up his military command. But he pretended not to hear, and disappeared among the other men assembled in the square. Meanwhile, the priests were led into a better furnished room on the ground floor of a rich home, where they were fed good food and given mead... but not given their freedom.

On the fifth day following, they were suddenly and unexpectedly deprived of food again and starved for the remainder of the week. Then they were stripped of their clothes, beaten with whips, and driven out of town. Finally they came to another town. When they arrived near the town center, Wibaw appeared once more and told his men "I gave you orders to treat these men well. Bathe them, give them medicine for their wounds, give them rich clothes to wear, and prepare a great feast for them. I've pledged to protect them from their enemies, and you are clearly these men's enemies."

The priests cried out "This is not enough! It is obvious these men follow you. Tell them to set us free!" But again Wibaw ignored them, and walked off.

The priests were led into a very rich home, where they were treated with all the luxury and care which Wibaw had ordered, and they were given a magnificent feast, but again they were not allowed to leave.

Not unexpectedly, on the fifth day they were stripped of everything again, starved, and driven on, now weeping in despair as they trudged for many miles due north, towards the sea. The whips beat them mercilessly, and several came close to dying on the road, but whenever one would fall he was propped up and supported to keep him marching with the group. Filthy, bloody, sweaty, bitten by insects and burned by the sun, they came to a large clearing in the woods. There were no buildings there, no shelters, and Wibaw stood there alone to greet them, along with the guard that drove them.

At this point the priests gave in completely.

"Let us go," they asked. "We don't want anything more. Just let us live, we grant you the kingdom. As to the letter of your pledge, that you would not seek more than our grace would grant, we will grant you everything you ask, all the wealth and possessions, the rule of this land, if only you graciously allow us to walk away with what little skin we have left."

But Wibaw said, "I don't want to hear you speak," and to the guard, "Drive them on."

Now the priests felt they were absolutely without hope, as they were forced on further and further, until the road rose up a hill, and then at last they broke out of the woods into the open, at the crest of a rocky cliff by the sea, and there they discovered... Hinen Temple! All around the temple, hundreds of witnesses were gathered, including all of the village chiefs. The priests were forced to climb the steps and enter the shrine, where they looked and confirmed that Etol Mountain was no longer visible out the north-facing window. It was now in the east. Wibaw had cheated them, not by moving the mountain, but by moving the temple.

Wibaw and a small guard of men walked up and entered the temple behind the priests, and the temple was set alight. The flames raced like shadows. Inside, with the walls burning around him, Wibaw walked down an aisle between the priests who had been shackled into two rows of chairs, the seats affixed to the floor. He proceeded to a small balcony, set just outside the north window of the shrine, where he mounted a specially prepared throne that faced in towards the assembled prisoners.

"I hereby take the throne, and with it I claim rule over all the land of the Wawli people. The authority of the High Priests is abolished."

Deaf to the protests and pleas of his victims, Wibaw was then pushed with poles over the edge of the balcony, throne and all, and he descended on prepared ropes down to the deck of a ship moored below the temple at the base of the cliff face. Thus Wibaw was "cast down" on the same day he took the throne. His guard descended behind him, and all ropes were pulled away, so the priests were left to burn.

After twenty minutes in the blaze, one of the priests managed to drag himself to the window and fling himself down into the sea, where he drowned. It is said he looked like a black and red skeleton, with hardly any flesh, and that one of his legs still had a hunk of wood shackled to it, while the other leg had no foot at all. All the rest were reduced to ashes.

Finally, the treasure which Wibaw had promised them was distributed to all of the men, and Wibaw had additional gifts of great value given to the chiefs of the villages, as they all proclaimed him rightful ruler and king of the land.

I heard about these things from my father and the men who witnessed them. The details of the priests' final days and final minutes were retold a thousand times, and the story spread to all the communities of the Wawli people. They could only call it justice.

13.
Mysteries and Developments

A Moment to Ponder

Randall fell silent. A minute or two later, he communicated through Ned that he was tired and ready to return to his room. This ended our session earlier and much more abruptly than usual. As Randall showed himself unwilling to answer any of my questions, and I felt I had enough to think about as it was, I let both men go and sat quietly alone in my office for the next twenty minutes or so.

Deeper Language Mysteries

My colleagues and I had lately done some laboratory work with Randall to clear up some questions I had about Randall's language ability. Our tests had shown that Randall was not merely refusing to acknowledge his native English language; his brain wasn't processing it. In an Evoked Potential experiment, we monitored his brain activity as he listened to some specially prepared recordings. The recordings alternated between provocative spoken statements in English, more prosaic English fragments from a series of lectures on the process of manufacturing furniture, disordered and meaningless statements based on the English lexicon with no syntax rules, equivalent phrases spoken in Portuguese and Arabic, as well as Wawli translations of the same, and finally a randomized collection of vocal sounds. All samples were spoken with minimal inflection, nearly monotone, so that vocal tone and pitch would not reveal meaning. Randall's brain reacted differently to the random, non-linguistic voice-sounds than it did to the samples of actual human language, and he could perceive a difference when we switched from one language to another. However, he could not differentiate between the types of spoken English samples any more than he could distinguish within the set of Portuguese or Arabic samples, and there was no evidence that he was processing any information while listening to these. This was clearly contrasted to the Wawli samples, which produced significant reactions indicative of his understanding, showing clear distinctions between provocative statements, prosaic statements, and jumbled syntax.

Medical examinations, including CT scans and MRI, were never able to find evidence of brain tumors or other physiological damage that could account for language impairment, so though we knew he couldn't understand English, we didn't know why. But lingering doubts remained in my mind regarding how he used and processed language.

While sitting in my office, now I stumbled upon a question: had Randall actually read the text of the *Outdoor Adventure* magazine, or had he only observed the pictures? Both possibilities presented additional challenging questions, and I knew I could not go further in this line of inquiry unless I conducted another test. Then I came up with a little experiment—a shot in the dark for which I had high hopes and low expectations.

THE EXPERIMENT

I prepared my experiment thus: I had a sign printed in large black text on a white panel, and hung it over the desk in my office. The sign read, "I'M ON TO YOU."

When Randall and Ned visited my office on the following afternoon, they both caught sight of the sign. Ned appeared annoyed, but Randall looked me in the eyes with a mysterious look, challenging but also inquisitive.

I said to Ned, "Randall has obviously noticed my sign. What does he think of it?"

Acting through Ned as interpreter, Randall said, "You say you know my secret. But I don't have any secrets."

This was incredible. In planning my experiment, inspired mainly by intuition, I hadn't actually prepared myself for the possibility that Randall could read English.

"Did he actually use the word 'secret'?"

"Yes, 'twoeshgal' means 'secret.'"

This immediately changed the direction of my investigation, and the next week and a half was dominated by further tests and consultations with a variety of experts. (However, I did meet once with Nelson Glasper, when he delivered a child's mobile to me. This mobile, and its significance, will be considered in its proper context.)

It was soon demonstrated that Randall could read the meaning of English texts without comprehending the phonetics of the alphabet. He was not a good reader, having an ability comparable to a third-grade elementary student's, though in his school days his reading and writing had been judged exceptional. But Randall now unconsciously translated what he read as though it were written in his own Wawli script, and he understood several idioms without stumbling over literal word-for-word translations; his versions were all expressed in Wawli syntax. When he was confronted by fragments of words, or individual letters, he became confused and could say nothing. When he was asked to copy one letter of a word at a time, by sight, he copied a few very slowly, as though roughly drawing an unfamiliar figure, but two or three letters into a word, when the letters should come together to indicate the sounds of a common English word, he would stop. On two occasions, when we were able to get him to copy out an entire English word, and then we asked him to read it, he couldn't do it. It became a cipher to him despite the fact that he had previously been able to read the same word in the context of a complete sentence.

Though there had been precedents of patients with partially lost language ability, including those who could read but not comprehend speech, and some who lost the use of one spoken language and not another, such impairments were always associated with traumatic brain damage, and none had been accompanied by the development of a completely synthetic language.

Nonetheless, renewed medical testing on Randall did not uncover any evidence of stroke or other brain trauma.

After a while, he became annoyed and uncooperative amidst

the new routine of testing and interrogation, and Ned informed me that Randall was becoming more withdrawn in their private conversations. He was showing signs of depression. Now that I knew he could read, I attempted to communicate with Randall through written letters, but he rejected this approach and discarded the letters without reading them.

Then I started to miss our old storytelling sessions. My curiosity regarding the continuation of Zhikbi's tale became greater and more pressing than my expiring interest in Randall's English reading ability. The new direction of our research seemed merely distracting. I reflected that months or years might not be enough to resolve the questions related to Randall's language processing, but the story he chose to tell could reveal much more within a few hours if I could only find the right way to interpret it.

I suspended research, and scheduled a day of rest and recreation without tests or questions. On the day that followed, a Thursday, we had another story telling session, which turned out to be our last.

14.
Zhikbi's Reign

A Footnote to His Own Tale

Though I'd hoped that Randall would take up the continuation of his tale with the same enthusiasm he had shown in previous sessions, I was disappointed. It turned out that Randall considered his tale, as he had already told it, complete. He was only minimally interested in talking about what followed Wibaw's rise to power, even though this included his father's tragic end, his own kingship, and his transportation from Wawliland to the United States of America, the very details I was most interested in learning. I pressed him, and I was thankful when he continued, laconically, as follows:

The First Disaster

Wibaw died soon after his rise. His life was bound up in violence and his end was inevitable. Though a lesser man, if he had achieved all my father had achieved, would have been content to live comfortably and securely with the blessing and support of his people, Wibaw was determined to pursue a more heroic self-destruction.

He assembled a force of U.hulia men from the few adult survivors, and placed them under Wawli officers. He also ordered that all of our countrymen who had taken U.hulia women as captives make a choice: they must marry the women and abandon their first wives, or else they must release the captive women and stay faithful to their families; slavery would remain an outlawed practice. A surprising number of men chose to marry their captives and abandon their Wawli families. These men were then pressed into service in the newly formed U.hulia Relocation Force, to serve as foot soldiers with our former enemy who were now their peers.

Wibaw led his big-battle-gang to cross the Aldas Mountains into the southern frontier region of Twilak territory. His declared intention was to relocate all U.hulia survivors here, outside the limits of our peninsula, and establish it as their homeland. It was said this was a return to where they had migrated from in the days of our weakness, after the passing of Isay. The newfound country, if successfully established, would become a tributary power under the rule of the Wawli.

Two weeks into his campaign, Wibaw was killed, along with the majority of the men fighting at his side. Reports tell that on the fateful day, enemy men came down from the hills like a storm of hail, the shafts of their arrows and spears brought the darkness of night at midday, and their spearheads sparkled like stars. When the killing ended, true night had arrived, and two moons appeared, one in the sky, and one reflected in the lake of blood where our fallen men were submerged.

Our invasion had been anticipated. Wibaw's preparations had not been very secretive, and the enemy received advance information. It's the only way to explain this disaster.

The specifics relating to Wibaw's death are unclear. All witnesses have said that he died heroically, with courage, fighting to the end, but exactly how he met that end has been told in as many different ways as there have been men to tell the tale.

ELEVATION

Upon my father's death, it fell to me to take the throne and title of king. I did so proudly, though I knew I would soon be a target. Intrigue surrounded me from the start, and my first fear was that the survivors of the priest class would betray me. Meanwhile, Ik.hun, with whom I would have liked to consult, had disappeared just when I most needed his advice.

Two days of asking questions led me to an honest man, Panna, Ik.hun's drinking partner and confidante, who was able to explain his absence.

"Ik.hun's honored father, Tanung, died this week. They say the old man drowned on dry land! It's a sign of our world's disorder."

"Why should the world be disordered?"

"It's not my thinking, but some say... well, now that Wibaw has died, some speak against him."

"And what do they say?"

"The crime of his usurpation of power—again, these are not my ideas—it's being revenged by supernatural events. Anyone could be the next victim, even our most honored and revered, even the most innocent. Ik.hun wanted to speak with you, but he was turned away from your home by a man with a message signed by yourself, saying Ik.hun's family was cursed and you would no longer associate with him. He was a liability to your rule."

Who was this mysterious bearer of forged messages? Obviously some plot was underway. Before anyone took the opportunity to attack me, I made the quick decision to visit the priest Somgay at his estate. I would stay with him as his guest.

Somgay was rich and quite influential among the surviving priests, a class which I could not entirely eliminate, as the priests had so far been the only ones to effect peace with our foreign neighbors. Somgay had openly called for a reconciliation between my father and the priests, and I believed he had contacts among a secret order who had gone into hiding. Rumors said that this secret order was attracting new recruits to the priesthood and had plans to stage a return to power, but as of yet nothing could be discovered with certainty regarding this conspiracy.

It was a radical step for me to go out from my manor and stay in the house of a priest, but I believed Somgay would not allow me to be killed while I was his guest. He was a weak sort of man who might even wish me dead, but who would not compromise his own safety and public reputation—would he stain his own hands or risk a confrontation with my guard? As a pretext for my visit, I told him I needed advice for the planning of purification rituals at several reconstructed temples. It was not the best excuse, but it was good enough to begin with, and by chance, on the third day of my stay, I found a new pretext.

The priest had a young and attractive daughter, named Nelati, whom I met with in the garden that afternoon... and then she fled. But that was not the first time she brought comfort to my world-weary eyes. In her, I recognized that same fiery-spirited woman whom I had seen preaching in the streets of Shamni about the horrors that would befall us if a king came to rule. And here I was, king. She seemed gentle and mild in the moment before her eyes met mine, untouched by any care. Then I frightened her.

Once I'd seen her, I'd found my pretext, and I let it be known to her father, first by hints, then by more direct speech, that I was seeking a wife. The one I chose to marry would be my companion, my partner, and the mother of future kings. She would help me build my dynasty.

The effect of my proposal was remarkable. Somgay entertained me more lavishly than ever, and he spent as much time as possible by my side, to promote his daughter as the perfect match. He invited many guests each night, so they could witness any possible development and testify if I made a choice.

One evening, when I tired of being the center of attention, and I withdrew to eat in a side-room, my meal was interrupted by an unknown messenger who approached me and whispered:

"An old friend is looking for you. He waits for you now in the garden."

Did I hear correctly? Would I be allowed to taste the fruit before the purchase?

"Did you say 'he,' or 'she'?"

"He, sir. He awaits."

It wasn't Nelati. What was this?

"Leave now, and don't trouble me," I said. "Your life will be at risk if I see your face again."

A few guests turned their frowning faces on him and he left, only to return the next night.

He approached. "Your old friend is Olul," he whispered.

What? Not what I was expecting. Olul, my tutor from childhood!? But what a ridiculous claim. This time I shouted loudly, "Leave me alone!".

My outburst caught Somgay's attention; he peeked into the room and asked, "Who is this?"

"I have no idea," I replied. "He seems to be some kind of storyteller. I thought he was a friend of yours."

"He's no friend of mine," Somgay countered.

He had the messenger taken out by two armed men, who I am told gave him a severe beating. I'll admit that some questions troubled me that night, but overall it seemed most probable that the messenger was part of a plot to assassinate me.

I continued my vacillating courtship of Nelati for as long as I could, expressing guarded interest, then expressing uncertainty, inflating hope and then deflating it, until one night at a dinner where the guests included several priests, wealthy merchants, and farmers, I declared finally that I would marry the girl.

"I mean to have Nelati for my wife."

There was no other way to further protract my courtship or my stay, and… I wanted her. Not only did I engage to be married, but I also made promises to appoint some priests as ambassadors to foreign states, I told them I would establish a new center for religious learning, and I hinted at many possibilities for roles for an elite class of priests, not as they were in the high-priest days, I would forbid the selling of slaves, the killing of supernatural creatures, interference in banking, but there would be room for some compromises. And Nelati was given three days to prepare for the wedding. I was on my way to forging alliances that would maintain me as king and secure my life. With an exchange of gifts and promises, I then felt for the first time that I could safely return to my own manor house.

Yet, as soon as I arrived home, I was confronted by an oddly dressed man. Ik.hun was there, presenting himself in disguise.

"Why didn't you respond when Olul approached you?" he asked.

"What? Is he really alive? I was cautious because I feared a trap."

"You may be wiser than I to a degree, but your wisdom did you no good in this case."

He went on to tell me how his own life had been saved by

a messenger from Olul just a day before his intended arrival in Wibawdaw.

"The messenger intercepted me in the woods. 'Are you really such a fool?' he asked me. 'The very minute your king needs you most, you go running off to get yourself killed?' With a sudden awakening, I was like the man who 'found his drunken face at the bottom of the cup.' I realized my father was surely not a victim of supernatural vengeance. Far more likely, some priests' assassins had drowned him in a barrel to draw me out, and here I was about to run upon their spears. I was outraged, but my anger could not supersede my responsibility, so I foreswore my vengeance and quickly returned to you."

"I've engaged myself to Somgay's daughter. We marry in three days."

"You've made a great mistake!" he said, "But it is a mistake *they* will have to pay for."

"I didn't see any other way to ensure my survival."

"There probably was none, but it was a mistake nonetheless. Now there's no backing out, and there's no trusting any of them in a compromise arrangement. I'd heard rumors you were seeking a wife. Mmmm.... And Olul and I have discussed what to do. So here it is, if you have any faith in my best advice: You will go ahead with your marriage, but you will not have sex with your wife."

"Why not?"

"First, you don't dare get her pregnant. If she has a son, he will be a threat to your authority; any child may be so, even before it is born. Second, Nelati already has a lover. Your best hope is that she will attempt to meet with him, and you will be able to kill her with honor. The final consideration is that you may soon have to murder her father. You cannot allow your resolve to be weakened by any sympathy she will stir in you."

I swallowed painfully as he continued to plot:

"After the marriage, when a suitable amount of time has passed, we can discover who are the greatest threats to your rule. You will then appoint a special deputation to visit Lomaz. All of your enemies will be placed aboard a ship. It will be arranged for them to depart almost immediately so that they will not have any pretext to refuse, and there will be no opportunity for escape. They will bring gifts gathered from the richest class of city dwellers as offerings to the Twilak, including a valuable gift from yourself. This will give them the false security to believe in their safe delivery. Of course, we will remove all these valuables from the ship during the night, along with all trade goods. Olul will then secretly board the ship, and he will kill them all at sea."

The plot was so well conceived, I couldn't object to any part of it, and I discovered that my own talent for plotting was no match for what Ik.hun and Olul contrived in consultation.

"This plot is in no way safe for you personally," Ik.hun continued, "but it is the best way to prevent a return to the rule of the priestly class, and the best chance to establish your dynasty. If, some day, you must resort to a mass killing, your future will depend on the public's reaction, your military ability, and your effectiveness in suppressing enemies. In the worst case, you may have to go into exile until you can return honorably and with support. Your brother Anbi, then, will rule in the interim."

"He is sensitive, innocent of the ways of war, and physically broken. If it comes to that, you will have to guide his every step. Meantime, keep him safe."

I met with Olul only once in person. We had remarkably little to say after so many years, so many events, and so much to look forward to. We enjoyed some good mead together, and then he went.

Unraveling

Our plot yielded mixed results. Nelati was frustratingly faithful after marriage, and she always kept servants and acquaintances nearby, so we could not slander her. I'm not sure whether she ever understood the reasons for my coldness towards her, but she accepted it. At times I thought she was grateful for it, and I was jealous. Soon, we hardly saw each other, and we never spoke. But I sent her gifts from time to time—jewels, toys, trinkets and gems—in the hopes of making her happy in some small way.

We identified the greater number of my enemies, lured them aboard the ship as planned, and Olul drowned them all by means of a trap he had rigged in the hull of the boat, but for reasons unknown, he was unable to escape to a nearby boat held by his accomplices. Thus he died among his victims.

There were many public expressions of outrage regarding the sunken ship and the "lost" property, but to maintain power, I leaned on the support of veterans who felt national pride and the romanticists who still believed the spirit of Isay would bless a new age of kings. Yet two tragic events soon occurred which would undermine me.

First, there was an outbreak of a disease among the wild game in the woods, particularly deer, many of which came wandering into villages on wobbly legs and collapsed upon the ground with open sores visible upon their flesh—flesh which no one dared to eat. This reignited fears of supernatural punishments.

But the greater shock came when I was publicly rebuked by the wife I had failed to love. She brought an outrage upon her own flesh to condemn me. While she and I were in Isaysuhn Dozh to visit a shrine to Isay, Nelati staggered us all by stripping off her clothes, throwing herself naked upon the consecrated floor, and cutting her own throat with a dagger, calling down curses upon me and my family! I tried to restrain her, to grab the knife and take it away, but men all around pulled me back, more concerned for my safety than for hers.

"*Blind, cold, and alone!*" she cried out as I was forced out the door. "*Blind, cold, and alone!*".

A fright caught me then, and I couldn't stop shaking. My thoughts dragged their hooks through my mind all night, but there was no way for me to undo what had been done. I could hardly speak, and no one had answers to console me.

Even Ik.hun was without advice.

After I fell asleep, I soon awoke in the locked cabin of a sailing ship, rocking on the sea. My exile had begun without warning.

Again I slept, and again I awoke in unfamiliar surroundings. My skin had been tattooed black, from the tips of my toes to the top of my head—perhaps it was intended as a disguise—and I felt that I had aged many years in a short time. I then found myself in a house, awakened by strangers who took me for their son—a lie expressed in gestures and through actions, as we had no common language to speak. And now you know the story of how I arrived in your land.

15.
Provocation

And thus Zhikbi's tale reached its conclusion. Then Randall lapsed into silence. I asked several unanswered questions, then I decided to give up for the evening.

When I stood and suggested Randall go back to his room, he had Ned ask me about a box I had sitting on my desk.

"What do you have there?" he asked.

I had intended to show him the contents of the box earlier, but now I felt it would be better to let it go for another day. We had already talked enough. Yet Randall insisted. Now I started to feel I should not open the box. Again he asked me to show it to him.

"This is something your father, Nelson, searched for and found among some old items from your childhood, which he's kept in a storage locker. It relates to a dream you told me that you had after the death of your mother in Wawliland. You probably should have no conscious recollection of having seen this item in your infancy, so maybe it will mean nothing to you."

I lifted an infant's mobile out of the box. It was an arrangement of tiny plush animals on strings, suspended from a tented roof, circling around a boat in the style of Noah's ark. There was a lion, a giraffe, a monkey, and a zebra.

As soon as he set eyes on the mobile, Randall flung himself with all the strength of his arms and torso, straight out of the wheelchair in a desperate lunge at me. He couldn't reach me in one go, but he grappled with the edge of my heavy desk, which he pulled down with a loud crash. I leapt up and recoiled, and Randall, in a murderous rage, scrambled across the carpet, dragging himself over obstacles. I had to flee my office for safety, as he glowered and grunted like a beast.

Nurses returned Randall to his room, sedated him, and monitored him closely for two days. I, meanwhile, fell into a sort of depression, and blamed myself continuously. Very often in my prior cases, when I would speak with psychotic patients and listen to them attentively, non-critically, appearing to be credulous, as I gained their trust, sometimes cracks would open in their delusion, and they would become semi-lucid, move on to discussing elements of their life and cooperating somewhat in their therapy. There were transitions, there were changes; there were inconsistencies as well in the things they said; and when the patients became aware of their own confusion, they would start to trust me as a sort of guide to help them out of their confusion. But none of this ever happened with Randall. And now this.

Though I had other cases to work on, many appointments and issues to occupy my mind, I was suddenly deeply frustrated by the fact that I had spent so much time learning about Randall on his own terms, I had learned everything I could hope to learn from him through direct conversation, I knew everything that could reasonably be known about the crime investigations, yet I was no closer to really understanding, and I had no plan of action for moving towards a cure. I hadn't gained the trust I'd hoped to gain, in fact I had squandered the little trust he gave me through a couple of ill-conceived stunts. Randall, after confiding so much in me, now viewed me as an enemy.

It was with these thoughts in mind that I fell asleep late one night in my office, and had the following dream:

THE "TRAPPED MAN" DREAM

In my dream I was at home alone, unable to sleep, though I was quite tired. My eyes hurt because I was unable to close them. I decided to go to the kitchen to look for a beer to wash my eyes with. When I opened the refrigerator, I found it was empty, except for some ham and some crackers on the second shelf. The air from the refrigerator blew on me coolly, and I was able to blink. I next went to open the door of a secret pantry, which I had never seen in my kitchen before. I entered it, and I descended to my "beer cellar." The beer cellar turned out to be an empty bar with a stage, with wooden floors painted black, and the whole bar echoed with the noise of my clomping feet. I smelled old cigarettes. I soon realized I was in the jazz club where Joe Alger had done his show. I saw there was no one in the club anywhere, no one behind the bar, but I felt someone might come in and find me at any time. In a state of curiosity, I climbed up on the stage to investigate. I found the closed trap door near the center of the stage, which had no apparent handles or hinges. I heard crying, and I knew somehow that Joe Alger was trapped under the stage, forgotten. Just then I was startled by the loud voice of the club manager, who came out from a doorway behind the bar—a doorway which I hadn't seen before.

"This club is about to move underground. You'd better go before it's too late!" he called out to me in a loud, but confident voice, betraying no sense of urgency regarding his own safety. In fact, I didn't think he cared much, one way or another, whether I stayed or went.

But I hurried off the stage and back up the narrow flight of stairs towards my apartment, where I emerged into another hallway. My head itched.

I proceeded into the bathroom, planning to take a shower, and as I entered, I saw an open bottle of beer sitting in the basin of the sink. The bottle was unstable in its placement, and I made a grab for it just as it was falling back and starting to spill. In my haste I caused the bottle to strike the side of the basin and the glass smashed in my hand. The beer was cold, and some of the bits of the bottle still adhered together, connected to the partially crumbled and wet paper label. The label showed the brand name: "Very Lucky Seven."

TRAGEDY

I was abruptly awakened. Officer Evan Briar was standing in my office, looking scared. My secretary had failed to intercept him.

"I killed Randall. He's dead. I'm sorry Doctor." He blurted this all out as I was trying to shake off the dream I had been awoken from.

"What?" I wasn't sure where I was, and stumbled a bit as I rose from my chair. "What? What are you talking about?"

Evan Briar was really there, standing in front of me and trembling.

"I killed Randall. I came home, and he was there waiting for me. I shot him." Evan fell to the floor, weeping.

It took me quite a while to sort out the details and find out what had really happened. Between what Evan told me that night, and what I discovered from discussions with nursing staff and police staff in the following week, I learned that Randall had escaped from our hospital without his wheelchair; he dragged himself across the city with just his arm strength, until he found his way to Evan's house. Several pedestrians had witnessed him, but only one had bothered to call the police, and he had only done so a day after the incident. Other witnesses who could be found, including regular customers at stores and bars along his path, reported that they thought Randall was a homeless man, or they otherwise felt it best to mind their own business.

When Evan arrived home from work, at 2:30 in the morning, he found Randall sitting in the dark in his living room, with his hand resting on a side table, clutching something that Evan believed to be a knife. As he told me confidentially, he was so frightened to meet Randall in this uncanny context that he didn't pause long enough to sort out fantasy from reality; from the perspective of his fear, it didn't matter what sort of weapon Randall may have held. He fired five rounds into Randall's face and chest, killing him on the spot. Before this moment came, he almost believed that Randall was indestructible, that he could not be killed, and so it went against his emotional expectations when Randall died from *only* five bullet-wounds.

He recalled after the shooting that Randall seemed to have been chanting something, and Evan had a strangely vivid memory of hearing a phrase starting with *"kaskekol..."* perhaps followed by *"...swelli..."* or something with a similar sound or rhyme. He had no way of understanding the meaning of what he heard, but the *sound* of it stuck in his mind and left him with an unsettled, unresolved feeling. He was sure he had heard something quite close to that, but he couldn't recall any other detail.

It also turned out, when the scene of the shooting was analyzed, that Randall had not been holding a knife, that his hand was empty, and perhaps his hand hadn't even been resting on the side table as Evan had supposed.

Randall had broken into Evan's house by smashing out a wooden panel at the bottom of the back door, using a claw-hammer he had found in a toolshed out back. No one had reported the noise disturbance. Evan lived alone, without pets, and did not have an alarm system.

I participated in Randall's autopsy, and though large amounts of his brain matter were destroyed or damaged by gunfire, the matter which remained intact showed no irregularities which could account for his mental illness.

Following the autopsy, I communicated openly with the police about Randall's confession and the details of my investigation which linked him to the Gentlemen's Club Fire, and I expressed my firm belief that Randall was the perpetrator of the crime though I couldn't assign anything resembling a rational motive to his actions. I also reaffirmed my conviction that Randall was severely psychotic and mentally incompetent to be culpable for his crimes.

A MEANINGFUL CONNECTION

But the investigation had not entirely come to an end. There remained at least one more detail to be discovered. In reviewing my notes and my memories of all that had come to pass, I realized that, through my dreams, my subconscious was hinting at something. I had to puzzle it out.

I gave some deep thought to this, until it finally occurred to me that the "lucky" gambler ("Very Lucky" as the trapped-man dream would have it), the man symbolized by the jazz player under the stage who remained lost and forgotten... he might have been a stand-in for Randall's gambling-addicted uncle, Lydell Glasper, whom I and the police investigators had so far neglected. Lydell had not been seen by his family in half a decade, but no one had ever filed a report on his disappearance. It was simply assumed that he'd gone off on his own rambling way.

When I asked Evan Briar to look further into Lydell's disappearance, it led to a remarkable revelation almost at once. Most of the family's more recent photographs did not include Lydell, but he appeared in the background of one picture taken at a family picnic. When Evan examined this picture closely, he recognized Lydell, and it was again a very uncanny experience for him. *This* was the same anonymous man he had seen dead in the police morgue just a few weeks before Randall's attack! Evan was really shaken by this unexpected connection between himself and Randall's family. He had always firmly believed that Randall's attack was random and unmotivated, but this latest discovery demonstrated some kind of connection. A sensible one? I can't say that it is.

One day, an unidentified and unidentifiable elderly black man, apparently quite poor, dropped dead of a heart attack while playing a hand of $30/$60 limit Texas Hold'em poker in a riverboat casino. He died right after winning an unusually large pot against several opponents. On the table he had about $5000 in chips in addition to the $900 or so in the pot, and there was $14,000 in cash in his pocket, but his shoes were worn out, he was unwashed, he had no credit cards, no car, no house keys, no hotel registration, and the identification he had used to enter the casino (required by local law to limit the amount of money a gambler may risk in one visit) turned out to be a fake driver's license with a false name. The man could not be matched to any missing-person reports, and there were no other records to help the police identify him or locate his family. This mystery dead man showed up in the morgue, and one of the investigators called Evan in to take a look at him.

"Meet Evan Briar," the detective said, and he laughed.

"What do you mean?" asked Evan.

"He's got your name. Well, probably not really. But look at the coat he was wearing when he came in."

The coat which the detective held up was Evan's coat, labeled with his name. Evan hadn't even known it was missing from his closet, and yet now it belonged to a dead stranger lying in the morgue.

When he had a chance to reconstruct events, Evan discovered that his wife (he was still married in those days) had taken some of his old clothes and donated them to the Salvation Army, a charity to assist the poor. Among the clothes she had donated on his behalf was this old coat that had his name sewn into the inner lining on a cloth label. This poor washed-up gambler then wound up with Evan's coat and nothing else to trace him by, but it was a dead trail; the man was buried anonymously.

The incident was probably worth a laugh, and not much more. For a few days, Evan joked with his friends about the oddity of the event, and the uncomfortable feeling that he had barely escaped his own death, that the coat would have killed him first if his wife hadn't gotten rid of it.

This little incident was easily forgotten when, a few weeks later, Evan was confronted by the madness of a half-naked Randall thrusting a primitive spear into his side, the chaos of bullets, and all that followed upon it; and now, such a long time later, these events had culminated in Randall's death in Evan's living room chair.

Nothing we know can explain how Randall learned about Lydell's death, or the coat, or Evan Briar. Had he overheard some gossip somewhere? Had he known enough English to even understand anything he heard? Had he seen a written account somewhere that he was able to read? Had he known more about his uncle's life and whereabouts than any other family member knew? These questions will not be answered.

16.
The Echo of a Lost Culture

As for Ned Lincoln, after some time spent in grief over the loss of his friend, he came to see me.

"Now I'm the only one," he said.

Yes, it was clear that Ned was the sole heir to the worthless treasure of Wawli language and culture. The little I had learned of the language myself was not sufficient for conversation. My knowledge of Zhikbi's tale was in fact just a summary, and there were many incidents, anecdotes, and elements of Wawli lore that had been passed on to Ned, which I would never have time to learn. I was not about to make Zhikbi's fictional past the subject of my life's study, and neither would anyone else. For Ned, Randall's death had taken a close companion; it had also taken the fullness of his fantasy and turned it into an emptiness.

Ned helped me, however, in pursuing one final thread of my investigation into Randall's life and death. Together he and I attempted to uncover the meaning of Randall's last words. Yet there was no clear and conclusive way to interpret them, and the tantalizing results of our investigation remain an open mystery.

The "kaskekol" that Officer Briar had recalled was unambiguous: it meant "vision," as an object. But "swelli" has no known meaning, and the officer did not have a distinct and certain memory of this part of the phrase. Ned and I discussed this in the context of what Randall, or Zhikbi, might have wanted to communicate. Evan had reported that Zhikbi's words sounded like a chant, so we had to consider poetry and songs as potential sources. But had he said "Swelli"? "Zwali"? "Swani?" What sounds followed?

Ned soon recalled a passage from one of Randall's notebooks, which included verses from the famous writings of the mythical hero Isay. There was a poem titled "Ge'ene'ast," which used the phrase "kaskekol zwe'ilishas," meaning "frustrating-" or "confounding the vision." The poem relates to fearlessly confronting death, so this seemed like a perfect fit for what Randall would likely say before dying.

This "perfect fit," did not turn out to be the *only possible* fit, however. A couple of days after presenting this poem to me, Ned came back to tell me of a fragment, not quite in verse but a kind of "prose poem," which he recalled Randall had recited. It used the phrase "kaskekol swalim," meaning "to give sight."

In the meantime, I had been so inspired by reading "Ge'ene'ast" that I struggled to learn more of the language, and I read through several pages of the notebooks, until I came across *another* verse containing a phrase starting with *kaskekol*: "kaskekol shani…," which means "to regain one's vision." But, more precisely, it was "shani*gu*," if you include the verb ending. How much could I presume Officer Briar was mistaken in his hearing or memory of this short phrase?

Ned's fragment had no apparent bearing on death, nor on Randall's specific circumstances, while the verse I had stumbled upon (which Ned assisted me in translating) seemed very relevant, but also contrary to the tone of the first poem.

I repeatedly interviewed Evan Briar in an attempt to determine which of these poems he thought sounded most like what he had heard, but he was unable to recall or to distinguish among them. Even when we attempted to use hypnosis, the results were entirely ambiguous. Evan was inclined to take any suggestion we gave him, and said, "Yes, that is certainly what I heard," until we suggested another of the verses, and then he was just as certain that *that* was the one. I had to give up trying.

Evan, after this last meeting with me, went against my advice and made the regrettable decision not to pursue any PTSD treatment or therapy. As far as I know, he is getting no psychological treatment anywhere. He has retired from his police duties.

I must now conclude my account with the three translated verses and fragments, though I cannot help the reader choose which among them is a fair representation of his intended final message. I even freely acknowledge that none of them may be quite what he intended. This record, therefore, will merely preserve a few last elements of his lost culture which I am able to share with the public.

GE'ENE'AST

> *Hawswe e.mawsuhn hil.suhn ohawkuht*
> > *Huzaaz hwizhlo azdim*
> *Igemno gwamno li ge'ene'ast*
> > *Gomgelno sung.lest gwoezh.i*
> *Gozlayno gewe su.kobon neu.les*
> > *Kaskekol zwe'ilishas*
> *Gimkatsa longwe lokno zi'aalkol*
> > *Lison masdolo deukesh*

INTO THE VOID (GE'ENE'AST TRANSLATION)

> *Few see the image of life's glow*
> > *within death.*
> *I turn the sharpest gaze*
> > *into the void with abundant hope.*
> *Purple darkness, with all its mystery,*
> > *confounds my vision.*
> *And yet, the blackbird will find*
> > *no tears in my eyes.*

Untitled Fragment, "Prose Poem"

Kwilsuhn ezolwe
  Izhdukol swalishas
Emawno maswe
  Kaskekol swalim
Manno galswe
  Azlimkat ibulkat
Koldawsuhn inbakol
  Gosako swalishas
Luzoluno i'ay'u
  Tipemno kigaw
Awnuwe kido
  Hwizhlo kulimishas
Zhlaysuhn adem
  Hagalba dagalba
Nedamshi uhklo

Untitled Fragment, "Prose Poem" (Translation)

The closeness of a woman
  Gives pleasure
The living eye
  Gives sight.
A drink of mead
  Tumbles and whirls
Gives us the dance
  Of intoxication
Echoing sadness
  Mad dreams
Despair
  Reel among the stars
A pig's feast
  An orgy of the living and the dead
On a heap of dung

Untitled Verse

Gosaksis lumgan nazkwino tiwe
  Wekluno ma.zwemto ne.
Emaw.we kigawto ne'ishasul
  Gawsisis zhidarimshas—Zhamha!
Hwoesh.woesis go'ano onuhluwe
  Lokishasu nomishas.
Baltseklo taasno bingwawsis mintgan
  Palawe palak.ishas—Wadis!
Pulayshal lano tazido kate
  Pilikwe awna'ishas.
Implusuhn saylsis eudiwe dison
  Kaskekol shanigu pwim—dayltgan.

Untitled Verse (Translation)

The things we pursue
  Are a dissipating mist.
Some wonder whether
  Life is a dream—Deceit!
Hunger tells me
  There is no awakening.
For a warrior, courage often comes
  From stubborn blindness—A cut!
Only the sting
  And the bloody fingers are true.
The terror of dying helps one
  To regain one's vision—too late.

207

Seth Rookard

1.
Seth and Kira

Seth Meets Kira

The birds seem annoyed with me. They keep giving me dirty looks. They drop seeds from their mouths, as if disgusted, and scratch the ground, wishing I was a worm so they could eat me. They leap up and fly with a loud, threatening flutter of their wings. I live in a city. I'm supposed to be safe from this kind of assault.

The wind blows bits of ash and gum wrappers at me. I have to guard my eyes from a piece of dust, or it might get in. Then I might not be able to get it out for days.

But the people ignore me. I'm safely anonymous. I could probably grab one and kill it, and the others would continue to walk by in blithe indifference, their heads slightly bowed. I almost tried it once, but that was when my mind wasn't as clear as it is now.

I spend about an hour hanging around in Cancer Survivors Park, but it finally becomes unbearable, so I hike over to the Neptune statue on Wornall and just sit myself down on the edge of the fountain. People don't *just sit* in Kansas City, but hell, that's what makes me different.

Now, I know you're not going to believe me when I tell you how beautiful this woman is, but goddamn, if the earth were to just split open right now, and you found yourself plummeting through space, with not even enough time to scream before you fell, you could not be as surprised as I was by her. Her looks could kill a man, and I was sure she would destroy me, but knowing that to be true, what point would there be in resisting.

She was simply engaged in an everyday act; she was buying a newspaper from a corner vending machine. Before I knew it, I was already making a fool of myself. I shouted "Hey, Hello!"

She looked at me in confusion, struggling to determine who I was. By then I was up and walking in her direction. She noticed my bandage, and that may have frightened her, but she acted as though she were concerned.

"Oh, hey, are you all right?" I think she was trying to cover for the fact that she didn't recognize me.

"Yeah, look, I don't know you, but I figured I'd say hello and then think of what to say next."

"Oh." She looked away, then back again. "Well, that makes some kind of sense, but…" She glanced at the folded paper in her hand.

"Hey, I'm not from a church or anything, it's just I noticed you're very beautiful and I wanted to tell you that."

Though she responded with a little laugh, and "Thank you," she also started walking rather briskly, and I walked alongside her. She laughed again. "It's nice of you."

"Well, I'm sincere. I don't normally talk to people, in fact, I'm very reserved. But I thought you might have some time…" I trailed off, looking for a reaction, and then I was a little unsettled when she smiled at me, very naturally and confidently, though she kept up the pace of her walking.

I saw that she was walking away from the more populated area, and we turned onto a narrower more secluded roadway. It was as though she actually wanted to encourage me to speak confidentially. This was quite upsetting to me, naturally, but I kept my cool.

I wondered whether her beauty might be a disguise. Might she even be a man?! Had she been sent to distract me? I had been thinking very deeply a few minutes before, but now I had forgotten the whole thread of my thoughts. I'm pretty sure I had stumbled onto a very important idea, something I should act on right away… but now that idea was gone.

I didn't want to let dark suspicions set me on the wrong path though, so I decided to play a little trick on myself. I would imagine that our conversation had happened long ago, and my only task was to remember what we had said and repeat it.

So I asked her if I could take her out some time, just to talk and get to know her, and I told her she seemed smart, like someone

I could have a meaningful conversation with. Then I admitted that I didn't really know what she was like, but I wanted to find out, and I apologized for speaking so directly, but the circumstances demanded that I be direct, or else I'd let an opportunity slip by.

She stopped walking and gave me a sympathetic look. "You seem very nice, and you're a great talker. I'm really quite amazed by your approach, actually. But I'm living with a man, and I have someplace I have to go, so I'm sorry that I can't date you."

"Well, yeah. Hmm… that's too bad for me, but I hope you have good things happening for you, and that people treat you like you deserve to be treated. Be happy if you can."

"I am happy. You've cheered me up. I was just thinking there are no real gentlemen. But I have to go."

"Sure. Hey, it's a small town. If you see me, you can shout 'Hello' at me like I did to you. My name is Seth."

"I don't think I *will* shout when I see you, and if I don't, I think you'll understand. I just might though. My name's Kira."

And that was the end of the conversation.

I found I was very angry at her after this. She was quite stupid to allow me to talk to her at all. If she allowed me to talk to her like that, she had probably allowed other strange men to talk to her too. That's dangerous. What if she were my girlfriend, living with me, and some other "gentleman" decided to talk her up?

Despite my anger, I spent all of my free time for the next two days, including my break time from work, and in the evenings too, walking around The Plaza area, hoping to bump into her again. I didn't.

It was a couple of weeks later that I heard her call out, "Hello, Seth!" I was in the bookstore, shelving some books, and she was standing so close. Looking at her was like an embrace. I felt her trembling with me. The intensity of that moment was such a thrill, I've never felt such exhilaration. She seemed vulnerable, as shown by her expectant face, yet she was also innocently unaware of how she completely dominated the situation, how I was ready to become her slave if she would even allow the thought to cross her mind. But I was also enraged on her behalf. How could she be so foolish as to approach me?

I turned away and said nothing.

2.
Seth and Women

Seth Rookard, a twenty-three year old white patient from Nashville Tennessee, told me the above story during one of our interviews, as I was treating him on an outpatient basis. He had recently migrated to Kansas City to pursue treatment in my program. He was now telling me that he loved a woman he had recently met, and this was the first time I had heard him use the word "love" without prompting. When I had previously asked him to discuss love, he generally used the word "love" only in such phrases as "I don't love…" and "I've never been loved."

After a long pause in Seth's monologue, I asked about the conclusion of his encounter with Kira in the bookstore. "How did she react?"

"I assume she was mortified. Other customers had noticed her loud greeting and my refusal to respond. She hurriedly tossed a book on the floor and left.

"As soon as she was out the door, I rushed to grab the book, to be that close to an object that had touched her hand. It was Cyrano! My beloved Cyrano, the play that I've read with such devotion."

Seth had the incessant habit of talking about Cyrano de Bergerac. It came up far too often for this coincidence to be plausible. "I'm sorry," I said, "It's hard to believe that she was reading Cyrano."

"It was Cyrano! And perhaps because of me, she won't read the play now. I've cheated her of so much already."

"But why were you so angry as to refuse to answer her greeting?"

"Can't you see? She has to learn how foolish it is to trust a man like me. Other men, if she allows herself to be so open, could exploit her. They could rape her. They will."

"It sounds to me like you were overreacting out of guilt regarding your own sexual feelings towards her. You said she is beautiful. Describe her in more detail. What about her body? Is it slim? Voluptuous?"

"I refuse to talk about her in that way. But if I tell you she is a goddess, do you imagine her figure to be anything less than perfect?"

"Is there such a thing as a perfect figure?"

"I didn't use to believe in such a thing until I met Kira, but now I know the ancients were right: There is such a thing as a perfect form. But, despite your suspicions, I tell you once again that I have no sexual impulses whatsoever."

"I can never accept that based on the things you have told me. You should try to come to terms with your true feelings."

Denial of Sexual Impulses

"I have no sexual impulses. I told you, I've only had sex with nine different women, and every time I was so disgusted by the experience… several times I failed to perform adequately, and the other times I just forced myself to go through the physical act, while I closed my eyes and pretended it wasn't happening. It was like sticking my dick in the knothole of an oak barrel, you know what I'm saying?"

"But actually, nine different sexual partners is quite a lot for someone your age, especially when you claim to have no interest in sex."

"And by that you mean, how could this guy, who is so messed up, so socially awkward, such a filthy pariah, have managed to bed so many women? Because a normal guy can do that, but not I!"

"I wouldn't say that, but you know you've spent most of your life afraid to approach people or even go out of your home. You were practically a hermit for several years."

"But those women I was with were just garbage, you know? It was just like picking up a piece of garbage, a rotten burrito, a tin can, an egg sandwich, and doing something filthy with it in my pants. I hate them."

"The women you were with are people. Some of them may have gone on to fall in love with someone, or perhaps they will someday, regardless of your contempt for them. There's no cause for you to show such disrespect in your attitude towards them."

"I know that, and that's why I hate myself too."

"How do you meet the women you have sex with? They're not prostitutes, are they?"

"No. I'd never have sex with a prostitute."

"Why not?"

"It's too cruel, and besides, what's the point?"

"Well, a lot of men go to prostitutes."

"Have you?"

"I'm not talking about myself, but the point is that men go to relieve sexual feelings, or for a thrill, or as a compulsion, or to fulfill a fantasy. There are reasons why men do it, so why don't you?"

"I don't have a sex drive, like I said. But let me tell you a story."

ATLANTIC CITY EXPERIENCE

"I met this woman, and oh my god, her ass was so nice and perfect. I couldn't take my eyes off it. I met her in Atlantic City, when I was walking along the boardwalk, on the day before the Bolden versus Chatman fight. She was showering off the sand from her body, while wearing a very revealing swimsuit, just near the fringe of the boardwalk, and she was accompanied by two others, a young woman and some guy.

"I go insane when I see swimsuits. It reminds me of when I was in junior high school, and when we did swimming for gym, or I went to a public pool, I really liked looking at girls, and I fantasized that I could follow them secretly into the girls' dressing room and watch them shower naked. But then, I was always afraid at the swimming pool that I might get sexually excited and embarrass myself, so I had to pretend like everyone else that there was nothing to be excited about. I generally hated swimming because I felt some shame about my body. But I always had a secret pleasure after swimming in thinking about what I would have done or could have done with those girls.

"So, getting back to this girl on the beach, well I'm really scared of girls, but I walked right off the boardwalk and said to her in front of her friends 'Hey, don't be a typical boring girl. Come and have an adventure with me.' She laughed, of course, and so did her female friend, but the guy who was there was probably trying to play up to the other girl, so I saw I had a chance.

"So, she says to me 'What kind of adventure?' I just put it straight and say 'a sexual adventure. Come on, I'll make it good for you.' She turns bright red, holds one hand up over her face, which was smiling in a shocked, almost frightening way, while she reaches out her other hand to me, almost like she can't believe she's doing it.

"Her girlfriend screams, and I lead her away. 'Oh my God, Melissa!' her friend calls out, and that's the only way I know this girl's name. Before I can drag her away, she grabs a bag off the sand, and quickly pulls on some gym shorts and a big oversized shirt, and then she says 'Take me gambling first.' 'No,' I say, 'let's go to my hotel.'

"Actually, I didn't have a room yet, but I took her to the nearest hotel's check-in desk. The only thing Melissa could think to say was 'You're crazy,' and I said back 'No, it's not like that,' but meanwhile I was thinking 'You don't know the half of it.'"

"Do you think you charmed her?"

"No. Don't you see, she would've gone with anyone that day. There's a lot of women like that, they're just waiting for someone audacious enough, someone who isn't a part of their social circle, as that could produce embarrassment, but an interesting stranger who makes them think they're daring, someone to give them a thrill. She would have fucked a dog that day if it came up to her, so I know this isn't an accomplishment.

"Anyway, we got to the room, and I pulled off my pants, and she went to work on me with her mouth. At first I just thought about sand, and the rainy weather we had been having just a week before, and then I tried to think about oranges because I like the smell of orange skins, and that sometimes gets me excited, but I couldn't look down, and she got me off physically in a short time.

"Then I tried to give her a little pleasure with my fingers, but it was kind of awkward. After a few minutes, she went 'Oh,' like she just remembered something. Not like an orgasm. But I knew it was my signal to stop.

"She said she wanted to take a bath and asked me to get some drinks. I got her some whisky from the shop in the lobby. I drank a bit, though I never drink, and we watched T.V. We didn't talk much. She was kind of boring."

"But you didn't get any sexual satisfaction from the experience?"

"No. She was just the right type, you know, really dark hair, a beautiful ass, breasts that were shaped just right, and shook just right. But it was all for nothing."

"Did you ever think that you might have other sexual interests, besides women?"

"What, you mean gay? No. Don't get me wrong, I like vagina too, I was just talking about those other body parts to be polite."

History

Seth's psychopathology is complex, and at the time narrated above, Seth suffered principally from a compulsion to cut and otherwise injure his hands and arms, especially his left arm, which he typically kept wrapped in bandages. He had been hospitalized on several occasions due to severe injuries and related infections. He had twice crushed his fingers by slamming them in the space between a door and its jamb on the hinge side. This was in addition to blunt injuries from punching or otherwise striking hard surfaces. I regarded the condition as life threatening.

He also exhibited a form of obdurate paranoia, he experienced frequent anxiety which was only partially managed through drug therapy, and he tended to pick up new interests which developed into temporary acute obsessions. These obsessions sometimes threw his already unstable life into a greater state of chaos.

He did not, however, display any mood disorder, he did not engage in abnormally frequent suicidal ideation, his intellect was intact, and he did not tend toward psychosis, though there was a family history of psychosis.

Yet, despite his persistent and difficult to treat psychological maladies, Seth was already regarded as one of my successful cases. When I first met him, he was a severe agoraphobe who had lived alone from the age of seventeen to twenty, during which period he only left his home between ten and fifteen times a year, mainly to visit a library where he felt moderately safe. He had only one notable break in his routine, when he attempted a trip out of Tennessee for five days, which he had to abort due to anxiety.

I cured Seth of his agoraphobia, in addition to an array of other exotic phobias which had plagued him from an early age, by using my *shadow-into-shadow* technique. The theory is complex, but in basic terms it involves the creation of subconscious psychic *guardian entities* which suppress the fear causing agents within the patient's mind. It is effective in the treatment of specific phobias, while generalized anxiety is managed through more conventional drug-based therapies. The treatment method is described in detail in my book *Freed from the Fetters of Fear*. Two months in my program was enough to help him overcome a truly crippling mental condition. His world has been expanded, and he's discovered new possibilities. He was able to find employment upon moving to Kansas City, and he improved his ability to relate to others. Thanks to my program, he was also able to endure a four-month jail term without any undue trauma.

UPBRINGING

Seth was raised by his mother, Avery Rookard, a paranoid psychotic who has gone largely untreated though she did undergo two brief hospitalizations in psychiatric wards. He never met his father, but Avery claimed that Seth's father "had no name," and he was "kidnapped by Mexicans and executed for selling bad drugs."

Avery married once when Seth was seven years old. The marriage ended within two years, and though the step-father, Jack Kolakowski, was generous, kind, and sympathetic, Seth never heard from him again. In fact, though Seth didn't know it at the time, Jack attempted to contact him and to communicate through letters, but Avery turned him away and destroyed all his correspondence before Seth could learn of it.

Seth's mother had a constant fear of coded messages which might be written about her and her family, or messages that could be used to tempt Seth into some kind of criminal conspiracy. When Seth developed an obsessive interest in crossword puzzles at the age of nine, Avery forbade him to "participate in any wordplay or word game of any sort," and she once pulled him out of school for three weeks because she heard that he had told a riddle. She did not permit newspapers or computers in the house, but Seth was allowed to watch television and listen to the radio, as long as he avoided "anything with numbers" such as financial reporting.

Though Seth never said so explicitly, his mother was most likely very promiscuous. Whenever Seth talked about Avery's "boyfriend," or "someone she was dating," or "a man who visited the house," the man had a different name—I counted fourteen different names—or Seth mentioned no name at all, so there is no means of accounting for the total.

Avery was always looking for a cultured, rich, well-educated husband, and though sometimes, by some means, she managed to get hold of significant sums of money, she always spent her money frivolously. She never worked a regular job, but on two occasions she started her own private business which failed: she once opened a costume jewelry shop, and once a vending machine company. In each case, her business partner was a boyfriend who financed the business.

The partner in the jewelry shop was named Peter. Seth believed that he may have been a married man, and the business relationship was an attempt to hide their adulterous affair. However this may have been, Peter was also interested in turning a profit, and Avery had to convince him she had a sound business plan before he put up any money.

The vending machine company partner was a man named Winston, who was also quite serious about his business venture.

Avery bilked each of the men, mismanaged the companies, bankrupted the businesses, and blamed her partners for the business failures. She also sued Peter shortly after the liquidation of the jewelry shop, claiming sexual harassment. Seth believes the man paid her a small sum as a settlement.

Seth was quite different from his mother when it came to money. He was very frugal. At times when his mother schemed a way to get some money, from a man or some other source, if she was feeling generous Avery bought Seth gifts, which he invariably sold. He sold his bicycle. He sold a video game console. He sold his new shoes and bought old ones from a thrift store. Avery was outraged every time he did this, and she wouldn't speak to him for days after, but Seth kept his money closely guarded. Because Avery was impractical and irresponsible, Seth extorted an allowance out of her to use on groceries and household expenses, but he always skimmed off ten percent to add to his personal stash. He also stole some of her jewelry and sold it.

In hard times, when Avery was broke, she demanded money back from Seth and searched the house from top to bottom. She had his school locker opened six or seven times in order to search for hidden cash. But he never gave her anything, and she never discovered the many hundred-dollar bills that he stuffed into the hollow space of a disused (but not broken) fishing rod he kept in an old chest of tools and toys.

One day he came up with an ingenious lie. "I'm a gambling addict," he told her. "I can't help it, I've been trying to get a bit of luck, but I can't catch a break." He said he was always losing money on sports bets. This she could easily understand, believe, and forgive, so she stopped searching for cash. She continued to give him gifts and grocery money when she could, and he managed to survive the lean and lonely months when she was absent or neglectful.

The one obsession that Seth has had for most of his life is professional boxing. Seth can't explain why. He's never been very physical, he doesn't like other sports, and none of his family has ever shown an interest in boxing. Seth was able to watch some matches on TV, but he was only able to find out the results of most matches by reading the papers in his school library. He memorized a lot of historical information and statistics that he gathered from books and magazines, since he didn't keep notes, clippings, or photocopies, assuming his mother would discard them.

Seth's grandfather and grandmother were sympathetic towards Seth, and they knew that their daughter Avery was troubled, but they weren't very practical or sensible, and they said there was little they could do to help him. They assisted financially a few times by making payments against Avery's mortgage when she was unable to do so herself. However, they had very little money of their own, so there was a limit to their ability to assist.

They invited Seth to stay with them for a few days at a time when Avery disappeared or "went on vacation." Seth sometimes accepted his grandparents' invitation, but it never worked out and he couldn't stay for long.

Seth's uncle William, Avery's oldest brother, was a little person, and Seth was terrified of him. His grandparents thought it was very cruel to scream and make a scene whenever he met his uncle, and they repeatedly attempted to reconcile Seth to William, but it was hopeless.

Seth also disliked sixteen of his seventeen cousins. The one exception was his cousin Anna, William's daughter, whom Seth really enjoyed talking to and spending time with. She was very intelligent and imaginative, and they had deep and interesting conversations on many subjects. Anna had a darker complexion than his other relatives, and most significantly, she did not closely resemble the rest of the family. (Seth never clearly explained what constituted a family resemblance, or how Anna differed beyond skin tone).

In contrast to Anna, some of his other cousins teased Seth quite a lot, and sometimes they tormented him with his fears. They couldn't understand how someone could function with a "fear of broken things." Sometimes they accused him of faking his phobias, and other times they claimed they were trying to help him solve his problems by confronting his fears, "like they often do on talk shows." However they justified it, they routinely confronted him with bits of broken glass, a dead bird, a doll without hands, to see his reaction. He was always thrown into an extreme panic, sometimes passing out after a bout of hyperventilation or uncontrollable screaming fits. Flexor spasms sometimes rendered it difficult for him to use his hands or feet for several minutes after a panic attack.

Because of these confrontations with family members, because his grandparents were already overburdened financially, and because their house always contained several broken things which they neglected to get rid of, Seth always wound up back in his house alone again. He discontinued all visits to his extended family after the age of eleven.

Eleven years old was also the time when Seth's mother finally admitted to him that she had received and destroyed letters addressed to him from Jack Kolakowski. She justified herself by saying, "They were written in a secret cipher and could have had a corrupting influence." Seth hadn't forgotten his step-father Jack, and from this incident he lost what little remained of his trust for his mother.

There seems to have been a violent conflict of some sort between Seth and his mother at this time, but I've been unable to determine any of the details. Seth always refused to discuss it when I approached the subject; then he transitioned to other topics.

For the next couple of years, whenever Seth's mother was home, she alternated between grand promises of a better life and despondent tales of how she had been cheated or betrayed by those she depended on. Seth reports that she developed the habit of speaking to herself a lot, or speaking to people she imagined were present, and she often complained of the cold—even in hot weather. She also continued with her periodic unexplained absences. She avoided communication with the rest of her family, except to sometimes beg some more money to keep up with her mortgage.

Seth's grandfather then became sick with an illness whose nature was never openly discussed, and he was forced to retire from his job as a loader and driver for an automotive glass company. The family came under further financial stress, until finally the grandparents filed a lawsuit against Avery to get ownership of her house. They claimed that all of the mortgage payments they had made on her behalf were loans, that she was incapable of avoiding future foreclosure without their assistance, and that she had borrowed large amounts of money for other purposes over the years without repayment.

When they produced loan agreement documents that Avery had signed, she at first insisted the signatures were forged. Then she said she had signed them only because she had been hypnotized. She said that while she was in a trance, her family also sold her as a prostitute. Then she claimed that she was entirely unable to read because they had burned her retinas with an ultra-violet ray. She had not received any money, and she had signed the papers only because her parents had asked her to, without her knowing the contents of the documents. "Only people who understand secret codes can know the true meaning of written words," she declared.

Avery instructed Seth to destroy any letters that came to the house from law firms or the courts, without opening them, and he did as he was told for several years thereafter.

When he turned sixteen, Seth dropped out of high school. Though he didn't finish his schooling, and he had always had serious difficulties in his social and academic life, Seth was very intelligent and well informed due to the enormous amount of reading he did privately. He had done well on standardized tests while nearly failing most courses due to frequently missed classes and incomplete assignments. School counseling services had not made an adequate intervention in Seth's life to help him escape the troubles of his home life and integrate him into academic society.

Emancipation, Agoraphobia, Jail

That same year, Seth's mother disappeared for good. Seth was left alone for several months until his grandparents came and announced that they had won their suit, and they were taking possession of the house. They allowed Seth to stay until his seventeenth birthday, and then they sold the house and arranged to relocate him to an apartment in the basement of a private home in East Nashville.

They helped him become a legally emancipated minor, paid his rent in full for one year, and gave him fifteen percent of the price they got on his mother's house "to help him on his way."

Though they were legally appointed as his guardians, he never lived with his grandparents, and they left him to otherwise fend for himself.

After moving, Seth attempted to live a somewhat active life, and to maintain a civil relationship with the two women who lived in the house above him, a middle-aged lesbian couple who were outgoing and friendly to all the neighbors. However, they made him very uncomfortable in a variety of ways.

"I think they almost never had sex," he said, "but they always joked about it. They always told me they thought I was living a single man's fantasy by living in a house with lesbians, but they generally creeped me out with all their talk. I never knew a straight couple who spoke so vulgarly. Later I concluded that they were only compensating for the perception that the neighbors were too conservative and judgmental—that they merely tolerated a gay couple in the neighborhood but didn't really welcome them.

"Then one day I figured out that one of my housemates, Sandra, was nagging, controlling, and sometimes violently abusive of Christie. She once threw hot coffee on her at about nine at night. I only knew about it because they took their fight out into the yard, where Christie threw a screaming fit and Sandra punched her around, calling her a 'frigid, recalcitrant bitch' whom she was going to 'thaw out even if it takes three pots of coffee to do so.' When a neighbor shouted from halfway down the block 'I'm gonna call the police if you don't shut up!' they took it back inside, but the screaming continued for another hour or so.

"After that, they tended to look at me with a little bit of hate in their eyes, as if they thought I was to blame, just for knowing their secret, though in fact the whole neighborhood had to be aware of what was going on."

This alienation from his housemates wasn't necessarily profoundly affecting in itself, but it did begin his trend towards isolating himself again, and this time his isolation developed, within about six to eight months, into a serious case of agoraphobia. The terror which used to grip him when a moth was killed, or an egg was broken, now rose up every time he considered venturing out among people, especially into unfamiliar circumstances. By the end of his first year in the basement, he was unable to go out of the house at all, except, as mentioned, on a rare excursion to the local library.

Neighbors, who at first must not have given much attention to Seth's seclusion, eventually noticed that he had standing orders for a pizza to be delivered to his backdoor entrance five times a week. He sometimes overheard laughter and comments from neighbors, some of whom may have deliberately spoken loudly for his benefit.

"This isn't paranoia." Seth explained to me. "It's natural they would notice after a while that I didn't come out, but it bugged me that they were paying attention to that fact. I didn't see why it was any of their business. All I was doing was eating pizza, plus I had regular deliveries of other groceries and essentials, so there's nothing to be ashamed of. But one time I shouted at the walls 'Mind your own damned business what I eat! You all eat your own shit!' It was just about the only time I raised my voice while living in that place.

"Mostly, I enjoyed my life there, except for the self-consciousness of knowing how the neighbors viewed me, that they considered me an odd hermit. I watched a lot of TV, including boxing matches that I got on cable, and I could special-order some fights on a pay-per-view basis. I read a lot too, and I pretty regularly read Cyrano De Bergerac. Sometimes this also made me a little self-conscious; I think I was guilty of fantasizing that I was a kind of Cyrano—except I couldn't find myself a handsome double. I didn't outwardly exhibit much panache, either, as there was no one for me to exhibit it to."

When I told Seth that, as a young man, he actually was quite handsome, he laughed pleasantly.

"Well, I guess I could have been my own double, then."

But, to continue, Seth locked himself away, and by virtue of his isolation he attracted the unwanted attention of strangers. On two occasions, he was paid an unexpected visit by a neighbor.

The first visit was from a housewife and mother of two from up the street, a woman named Gloria, who was a regular church-goer. Seth invited her in for a brief chat—partly to reassure her that he was quite normal and nothing to worry about—but he mainly wanted to get her inside and away from the door because he had an anxious suspicion that a friend of Gloria's was waiting somewhere, lurking nearby, and this frightened Seth.

Gloria told Seth that she had heard a lot of gossip and rumors about him.

"Some people at the church and I thought you might need some kind of help," she said.

"No, I'm fine."

"I'm sure, but you're very young, and it's obvious you don't go out, you don't socialize… and where's your family?"

"Uhh… really, I'm just a bit shy."

"Well, I wouldn't say that. You seem pretty self-assured now that I've met you."

"You know, I read a lot. I'm sometimes nervous out of doors, or I just don't prefer it. But my Transcendental Meditation helps me a lot."

Seth had suddenly stumbled upon this lie, which he thought might defer any religious questions, and Gloria seemed to take it as a sign that Seth was eccentric but non-threatening.

"You keep your house real nice," she said. She had an expression of relief, suggesting that she had expected him to live in squalor. "So… anyway, I'm sure you're doing just fine. My friends will be relieved to know that, and I'm sorry to have worried you. But if you ever feel the need to come out and meet some good and helpful people, you could visit me at my home or come to our church some time."

"Of course," Seth said, "I'll probably come see you someday just to say hello and see how you're doing."

He never went to see her.

About two years later, Seth received a second visit, from a somewhat angrier mom, Bessy Moreland, who lived just one house away.

"I hear you've been looking at my kids."

"What? What are you talking about?"

"Look, I don't know you, but you're making people uncomfortable, and I don't know why you're looking at my kids."

"I'm not looking at anybody. You know, I don't even go out much to talk to people."

"That's the thing. You don't talk, but you watch. The kids say they see you peeking out the space between the curtains."

"Hey, look, I don't bother anyone. But sometimes people come around; they look *into* my window at *me*. Once or twice I've looked out my window to see what's going on; I hear people talking about me like I'm some kind of unnatural wonder or something, when I'm just reading a book or something, and I hear 'He's in there, what's he doing?' Why does anyone even care?"

"People care because we're human beings, you know. You should be happy if people care enough to want to help you, but it's not normal being locked up all the time. If you wanna be locked up, you should be in one of those places where the locks are on the outside of the doors, you know?"

The conversation ended pretty badly, but there was no more trouble for a while.

Along the way, Seth had occasional brief exchanges with his housemates, particularly if he bumped into one of them going in or out while he was en route to or from the library, or on one of his rare visits to the bank branch where he made cash withdrawals. He recalled having a long chat one afternoon with Christie. She was a reader too, so they discussed books, but years later he couldn't remember any details of what they said. He came away with the impression that she was boring and conventional beyond her relationship with Sandra.

Then, one day, Seth hatched a plan to go on an adventure. He was going to leave his basement for five days straight and take a trip to Las Vegas. Somehow he convinced himself that he could ignore his fear and bully his way into riding a bus for nearly two days each way to attend a heavyweight boxing match, the Ray Coaster versus Shiloh Gillins fight at Mandalay Bay, a game in which he expected Gillins to pull off a major upset victory.

Seth made his plans carefully. He knew that he would need to make two transfers: one at St. Louis, and one at Denver. But he was frightened about taking the first steps. He expected great difficulty in getting to the Nashville bus terminal, buying his ticket, and sitting in an unfamiliar public area while awaiting his departure. He did his best to imagine each of these steps in detail before setting out, but he found it all impossible to visualize. Nonetheless, he somehow motivated himself to go, and he controlled his anxiety well enough to get himself onto the bus. He got along through the first seven-hour stretch, plus he made the St. Louis transfer, and he still held it together for another seven sleepless hours on the road. But, in the full light of day, he could not face the open plains of Kansas.

"I thought I would be all right, far from the city and far from people, in a mostly calm and peaceful scene, but it was horrible. From all across the fields, as vast as the wide world, I imagined a plague of insects like a boundless ocean rising up with me at its center. It just tore me to pieces."

He couldn't remember all the details of his consequent fit, but he certainly screamed and cried a lot, creating a bit of a hysterical reaction among his fellow passengers. They found him with a lot of blood smeared on his face and shirt and more blood running out between the fingers of his left hand. Passengers cried out "He's cut off his dick!" "His ear!" "He's ripped out his tongue!" but these were all absurd conjectures. In the months prior, he had started cutting himself in his basement, and amidst his panic on the bus he had bitten the unhealed wounds and scabs on the flesh of his hand and arm, causing copious blood to flow. That was all.

After a long and terrible delay, pulled over on the side of the road, Seth was escorted off the bus by a police officer, who cuffed his wrists and used a *lateral vascular neck restraint*—or *chokehold*—to control him and prevent self-injury and threat to others—though at this point Seth was no longer resisting. The police officer delivered Seth to a hospital, where the doctors responded to a renewed anxiety attack by tranquilizing him and sending him to a psychiatric ward. He was confined for four days, then released.

While he was in the hospital, Seth learned from another patient that his prediction had been correct: Gillins won the fight. But he'd missed his chance to see it.

Doctors noted profound bruising on both of Seth's hands, with pus emitted from several cuts on his left arm, which also exhibited cellulitis. He received proper care for his infections. His psychiatric doctor at this time, Dr. Sung Pil Kwon, happened to be an old friend of mine from medical school, and you will soon see why this is relevant.

This visit to the hospital was Seth's first experience of psychotropic medication. He was initially sedated with Midazolam, then treated with Clonazepam over the subsequent days of his hospitalization. The drugs enabled him to travel back home by bus on his own. "But," as he said, "the real reason I was able to avoid a breakdown was because the fear of another encounter with a police officer was more frightening than anything else I could imagine."

Once he returned to his basement, he went off the drugs, sought no further psychiatric assistance, and avoided even visiting the library for the next several months. He resumed cutting himself.

In the next year he delivered himself to the hospital emergency room twice due to self-inflicted injuries. He was treated for a sprained wrist, two broken fingers, and he received antibiotic treatment for apparent staphylococcal infection. Beyond this, his life returned to its earlier routine. He did not refill prescriptions or make any follow-up visits to his doctors.

Then came the real crisis.

Food Crisis

It had become Seth's practice to place money in his mailbox for the pizza deliveryman, and not to come out to collect the food until a few minutes after the deliveryman left. Thus he was able to avoid even the minimal social contact required to exchange money for food through a half-opened door. The kids in the neighborhood became aware of this practice, and soon they started stealing his money out of the mailbox. At first the theft was periodic and rare, but then it became increasingly common as the kids were emboldened. Even when they suspected Seth was watching, if they could guess the right approximate time to come by the house in the evening, they would run up to the box, make a grab for the money, and run. If they came up empty handed, they'd just try again the next day. Seth's shouting did not deter them, and he was afraid to take any more assertive steps, knowing that the parents in the neighborhood were not sympathetic and the police would regard the "prank" as too trivial to pursue.

Soon the pizza restaurant refused delivery, and Seth started to starve, until he arranged to make a large advance payment for two full weeks of delivery. That went off fine, until the kids started stealing the pizza, and sometimes destroying it. When they followed up by intercepting his Wednesday morning delivery from the grocery store—one child was brazen enough to cut school for this very purpose—the situation became critical.

Seth reacted inappropriately.

"Very early one morning, when I felt confident enough that no one was waiting outside my door, I ran an electrical wire out the window and connected it to the metal mailbox that was mounted just up the steps and to the right of the basement entrance. I cut a wire off a lamp and stripped the end of it, and I placed the exposed end of the wire in the box so that anyone who might grope around blindly might brush or grab it.

"Later that afternoon, when many kids were out playing after school, and I figured the neighbor kids may be watching for another chance to steal from me, I went out and conspicuously placed a thick envelope inside the mailbox. Then I went in, plugged in the wire, and waited.

"It's just my luck that the sickest kid in town was the one who tried to steal that night."

There was a loud shout, a stumble, and a crash against Seth's door, when fourteen-year-old Philip Redding was seized with a heart attack. The boy, who had a congenital heart defect, had an implanted defibrillator. It appears that, perhaps because he was quite short for his age, he had been leaning with his left hand on the metal banister beside the steps, while he stretched his right hand out to reach the mailbox. When he touched the wire, the shock—rather than traveling harmlessly across his hand—traveled through his chest and produced ventricular fibrillation. Fortunately, his defibrillator was able to revive him within a minute, but it is uncertain whether a healthy child would have experienced a heart attack at all, or whether the defibrillator itself contributed to the emergency by conducting the initial shock across the heart muscles. A device malfunction may have been the true cause of his medical crisis.

Seth shouted out for help, then called the police, and some neighbors came to rescue the fallen boy, all before anyone could put together exactly what had happened. Philip was transported safely to the hospital and recovered.

As Seth explained, "There was good reason for me to fear a lynching when the neighbors reconvened behind my house and started kicking my door, as some of the men called out that they would tie me up and drag me around town behind a truck."

The police broke up this conflict and threw one of the mob into jail for the night, a man who had a history of assault arrests. However, Seth was not spared. The police dragged him off to jail too.

Six hours after his admission to the Davidson County jail, Seth was transferred to the Middle Tennessee Mental Health Institute. The corrections officers at the jail had determined it was "inadvisable to hold him in the detention facility, as his extreme panic and unrestrained behavior make him a danger to himself, corrections officers, and other inmates of the facility."

REFERRAL, TREATMENT, PRISON

After several days of isolation and heavy sedation, Seth was able to subdue his anxiety and began to ponder the strangeness of his circumstances. He laughed when he was informed that the guards in jail had regarded *him* as dangerous.

"It seemed remarkable that a person who's deemed unsafe for jail would be sent to a *hospital*, as if the nurses are better equipped to handle dangerous people than the jail guards. But then I realized the potency of the tool which hospitals wield: the drugs.

"Then, the hospital did not seem like a much safer environment than the jail, at least when I thought about it. A lot of crazy stuff was going on in there. I tried to stay as calm as possible and let the medication help me burn through the days."

Seth's sense of danger was heightened because he was surrounded by a constant rotation of emergency admissions, mostly involuntary commissions, many of whom were violent, psychotic, some of whom were criminal. Even in isolation, there was rarely more than a few minutes of undisturbed quiet.

Seth did not yet realize that he was caught up in a sort of feud between politicians, the department of corrections, and the psychiatric facilities. Historically, in most cases like his, the system preferred psychiatric treatment and probation to jail time. It was regarded as both cruel and dangerous to imprison the mentally ill on the basis of minor crimes, especially those people who were young, had no criminal history, and had not previously been given treatment and a chance to reform. However, recent events were causing changes to the way such cases were handled.

In a highly publicized incident in Tennessee, a mentally ill prison inmate named Leo Alexander committed a horrific crime which strongly swayed public opinion. Alexander was serving a fifteen-year term for rape and aggravated battery after he attacked a neighbor, Janice Callaway, whom he had stalked and obsessed over. Though he had been judged competent to stand trial, and the jury had convicted him despite a defense based on insanity, four years into his prison term, Mr. Alexander's lawyers and his prison psychiatrist successfully got him a temporary transfer into a psychiatric hospital. He escaped from the hospital shortly thereafter, attacked Ms. Callaway in her home once again, and killed her.

Amid the public outcry over this incident, Tennessee Governor Oscar Coronado declared that he would not "allow people to take advantage of their psychiatric conditions to avoid jail time." He issued a mandate to the prisons that they should not transfer anyone convicted of a violent crime out to a facility that is less secure than the prison in which they were incarcerated. That, of course, meant no transfers at all. The police started arresting more psych cases, but the county jails—which held non-convicted criminal suspects—were not constrained by the new regulations, so they were shuttling most of the less violent cases back out to the hospitals. The hospitals, which were facing greater overcrowding issues, were responding by holding people for shorter duration and then turning them out onto the street again.

As for those who were ultimately convicted, though, the situation was much grimmer. Thus, as soon as Seth was released from the hospital, his lawyer strongly urged him to take the first deal he could get. He was offered a one year prison term for a guilty plea to the charges of *reckless endangerment with a deadly weapon* and *assault*. If he would not plead, the prosecution intended to charge him with the same crimes plus *aggravated assault, attempted voluntary manslaughter,* and *mailbox tampering.*

Seth consulted a second lawyer, and this lawyer also advised him to make a plea deal, though he kept open the possibility that Seth's mental condition could still be a factor in his defense. He dug into Seth's short psychiatric history, and contacted Dr. Sung Pil Kwon in Kansas for some details to assist him. Dr. Sung took an immediate interest in the case when he recognized what was at stake, and because he knew of my recent success in the treatment of phobias, he referred Seth to me and my program.

I was not able to prevent Seth's criminal conviction, nor could I permanently defer his incarceration, but after I testified in a court hearing and spoke in consultation with the prosecutors and judge, it was determined that Seth would accept a one-year term and that he would be permitted a temporary transfer into my program for treatment, until such a time as he was deemed fit to survive in a prison environment.

As has been previously described, Seth responded to treatment very quickly, and I was able to declare him fit within two months, at which time he was returned to the Tennessee Department of Corrections to serve his sentence. On my advice, he was kept in segregation for protective purposes. He was not treated with psychiatric medication during his incarceration. Unfortunately, he did witness one violent assault, but he was not directly affected, and he had access to the prison psychiatrist for counseling. After four months and three days in the prison, he was released.

4.
Romance vs. Therapy

It was half a year after his release from prison when I next saw Seth. He came to visit me in the center and told me that he had just moved into town so that he could receive further treatment. He had already gotten himself a job at a bookstore and set himself up in a tiny apartment. Again, he was in a basement. He began studying for his General Education Development test to receive a Certificate of High School Equivalency.

At first I was reluctant to accept him as a patient, but I saw that his problems were still quite severe.

"I've been trying to live a stable and productive life, you know. But I don't know when some whim is just going to take over… I just really need help to keep straight and avoid trouble." His personality kept producing difficulties in his relationships. He was still hurting himself, and some elements of his fantasy life were quite troubling.

"Now, I don't want to complain too much," he said. "You've done a lot for me. Thanks to you, I was able to get over my fear of Uncle William. He's the one who helped me the most after prison. I lived with him for a while, and he mostly let me come and go as it suited me. I found I had a lot of freedom. I also had my first romantic kiss. It was with my cousin Anna. But don't worry, it wasn't anything incestuous because we didn't have any other, you know, sexual contact. And Uncle William never found out."

Released from the terrors that had constrained him, Seth took several road trips, and finally lived out his fantasy of watching real boxing matches in the arenas of Atlantic City and Las Vegas. He did not fly, as he was still too anxious to travel by plane, but busses and trains were sufficient. He had his various adventures along the way. In addition to what I've already related, he also told me about his first sexual encounter, with a woman he called a "retarded girl." I objected to his use of that term.

"She was kind of repulsive in her appearance, and very out of shape," he continued. "She sat next to me on a bench in a public park, and after a quiet minute she said to me 'Do you want to have sex with me?' She spoke in that retarded voice they have…"

"Seth, you know that's not appropriate language."

"Oh, hell. Half your friends are retarded, so you always fuckin' stick up for them!" Seth stormed out of my office.

I omitted to ask about the continuation of this story the next time I met him.

However it is that he made use of his newfound freedom, Seth soon used up the greater part of his money; he admitted he had held on to a few "crumbs."

After he reestablished contact with me and I accepted him as a patient, I put him in touch with one of the benefactors of our program, who began assisting him in his preparations for university. Seth was given an education stipend, a recommendation to the University of Missouri, and the promise of a scholarship if he were to be accepted into their literary studies program. Seth declared it his goal to go on to the Masters in Library Science and Information Technology program, and ultimately to seek employment at the Linda Hall Library of Science, Engineering, and Technology.

All in all, things were looking pretty bright for him, when compared to the conditions he could have found himself in. Though, he did continue to slash his fingertips occasionally with an X-acto knife.

Now let me bring us back to where we started:

Hard to Get

When Seth snubbed Kira in the bookstore, this was only the beginning of things. Nine days later, Seth was in my office, looking as though he'd been touched by God.

"I was visited by her scent! Oh, glorious transports. Mere inches, perhaps millimeters had separated us. I heard a rush, and turned. I was on the street, I couldn't find her. But a hint of perfume lingered in the air, she had been so close. Poets call their beauties 'moon,' but Kira is a radiance that surpasses all heavenly objects.

Beauty stands abashed, admitting Kira to be her mistress. None can compare! One need not see her to know the perfection of her face and form, the glory of her soul, but just to stand and feel the vibration of her aura would make a slave of any man."

We made no progress in Seth's therapy that day.

Whether or not Seth had scented Kira's perfume in the spring air, she did reappear in his life shortly thereafter. One day at work, Seth was walking across the store when he made unexpected eye contact with her. He had just emerged from the stacks when there she was, sitting about fifteen yards away, with three of her friends, in the bookstore's cafe. Seth froze, then retreated between the shelves, but in that instant she called out:

"Seth! Get over here!"

He felt frightened, but not being able to think of a good escape, he overcame his hesitation and came out into view once more. He walked over to the table.

Kira's friends were mute, their conversation abruptly interrupted, and they simply looked uncomfortable. But Kira was smiling with a hint of mischief.

"Hi, Kira."

"Hi. Are you finished ignoring me?"

"Yeah. Sorry."

"Good."

Kira looked with impatient hostility at her friends.

"Oh, grow up, y'all. Go back to your conversation."

Kira got up from the table, came very close to Seth, and started to lead him by the elbow—the right elbow.

"Hey!" one of the girls cried out. (Seth has described this woman as *a social misfit with an aggressive urge to entertain*). "Why do you always try to hide your men from us?"

Kira took Seth further away, amid the bookstacks, but there was no truly private space to be found, and Seth felt very uncomfortable about flirting in his workplace. He was also a touch disoriented.

"Do you have a lot of men to hide?" he asked.

"It's a joke, Seth."

"Not a very funny one."

Kira was leaning into Seth, with her head down. He was numb, still, and euphoric. She looked up and kissed him. Then stopped. He had given himself entirely to that momentary contact. As he says, "The whole passage from first touch, to kiss, to gentle glances, was an eternal moment of intimacy. And I didn't care what it meant."

The sensation of shame only came a few moments—or an eternity—after. It was a mild shame that told him that it was she, not he, who had been truly bold—and that she was the one in control. (But he was wrong).

Kira turned away again, with a playful giggle and hands to her face.

"I'm sorry for what I was thinking… I don't know…" She turned and led him by the hand a little further away, across the shop.

"Why are you pursuing me?" Seth asked. "This is incredible. I was so stupid."

"Honestly, I came here to ridicule you because I was so angry at the way you treated me. But I also got an odd kind of thrill when I met you. I don't know about you."

Seth couldn't respond.

"I brought my friends for sport. I thought I would see you. But actually, it was they who suggested I should try to tease you a bit."

"Ummm, wait."

"But I really just wanted to see you, and I shouldn't have brought them at all. How…" she leaned in close again, almost whispering. "How can you be such a mystery to me?"

"You have me confused with someone…some other kind of person. I'm not so deep or fascinating as all that."

Seth, seeing that he was being clumsy, picked up some courage and determined to turn the situation around. He had fantasized about her, but she had never been the one to take the lead. In a way, it was almost emasculating.

"If you see me as passionate," he dared to say, "if you can see the burning inside me, it's only the passion you've inspired in me. Just being close to you…" He didn't complete the thought, but wrapped his arm around her waist for a bold and firm embrace…but she resisted kissing him and it became a fumbled gesture. Then: "I'll take the lead now," he continued. "Tell me when I can see you again."

She withdrew from his embrace, and seemed a little shaken as though she had not expected him to respond so aggressively to her flirtation. But when he was disarmed, she leaned in close once more.

She whispered now with lips just a breath away from his ear "You can see me any time. You just have to find me first!" Then she broke away and ran to rejoin her friends.

Seth, coming out of his reverie, saw his supervisor, Janice, looking at him from the other end of the aisle. Then she looked away in disapproval. He wanted to murder her.

"Work just pisses over everything," Seth told me.

THE CHASE

That month turned into a strange game of hide-and-seek. Seth realized he knew nothing about Kira, and it seemed that if she didn't come to him on her own, if she didn't somehow let herself be found, he'd never be able to find her. Nonetheless, when she failed to make another appearance, Seth began a desperate search. He decided to go out on a Friday night, when many young men and women go to bars and restaurants, and he would drop in on all of the popular spots to see if he might cross paths with her.

At the first bar that Seth visited, he felt very out of his element. When a waitress asked him if he wanted a table, he said he would sit at the bar. Once there, he felt compelled to buy a drink, as a sort of cover. But the bar was rather small—crowded—and though it was dimly lit and the walls were darkly colored, he had felt that Kira wasn't there from the moment he entered. He hadn't spotted her in his first glance, and he didn't believe she would allow herself to be lost within this dull and ugly crowd.

He had no real experience of drinking alcohol. True he'd sipped a bit of whisky with that girl in Atlantic City, but he had since sworn it off. Now he sat with a pint of tap beer on the bar before him, sneaking an occasional peek out of the corner of his eyes, but trying to be as unobtrusive as possible.

In an attempt to blend, he took a few sips from his beer, but didn't swallow them. Rather, he held the beer in his mouth, and the next time he lifted his glass he spat the beer back out while attempting to appear as though he were drinking it. Several minutes later, he realized that he'd taken enough sips that the glass should be empty, but it was as full as ever, and he felt too embarrassed to leave the bar without finishing his drink. By now he was sure that Kira wasn't there. He asked the bartender for a glass of water, and drank down about a third of the water very quickly, thirstily. Then he went back to the routine of sneaking sips of beer into and out of his mouth, only, for variation, he started spitting the beer into the water glass. He realized he'd made a mistake. He should have drunk more water first. Now, if he wanted to drink a little water to make room for more beer, he would have to swallow the mixed-in beer too. Well, to hell with it, he went ahead and drank the mildly tainted water, figuring it was better to do so early, rather than late. Then he continued transferring beer from beer glass to water glass. No! The water was turning yellowish, and he'd only reduced the amount of beer in the other glass by a small amount. It was useless.

Seth noticed then that several people sitting at the bar were watching him. The bartender was very intentionally *not* watching him. He'd created a mini-sensation. In haste, Seth put six dollars on the bar, placing the money into a damp spot where a bit of water had splashed, and he walked briskly out the door.

One would think that Seth would have the sense never to repeat such a performance, but he repeated it twice that same night in other bars. In the third bar, he'd opted for the less conspicuous choice of sitting at a table a bit out of the way near a wall close to the bathroom. Now, no one took notice of his strange sipping-and-spitting routine except for the waitress, who came around after a while and gave him a funny look.

"Will some friends be joining you?" she asked.

The table was big enough for four, but Seth was alone in a crowded bar.

"Um, no. They won't," he said.

But as he left, he silently shouted *brilliant!* in his thoughts. Now he had a new plan. He visited several more bars that night, announcing as soon as he entered each place—if confronted by any wait staff or hostess—"I'm joining some friends." He walked from table to table, group to group, getting a quick look at everyone before exiting with the remark—if the hostess cared to hear it—"Sorry, they're not here."

Finally, after walking through a particular bar for the second time that night, Seth announced to the disconcertingly familiar hostess, "They're not here."

"Isn't she?" the hostess asked.

"They, I said! They!"

The hostess had seen through his tricks, and identified him as a desperate man in search of a woman. How? Was this common? Did every bar have occasional visits from such men as him?

Seth went home and crushed the second joint of his left ring finger with a nut cracker. There was no bone damage, but serious bruising, a gash on the inside of the joint, and crushed cartilage required splinting for about a week.

That didn't stop his search, but he made a point to avoid returning to bars and restaurants he had already visited. Although it disturbed him to think that Kira might be sitting in one of the places that he'd already crossed off his mental list, he recognized that, mathematically, it didn't matter. Since he didn't know which kind of place she was likely to frequent, and he was unable to visit all of the bars and restaurants in one night, then there'd be no point in backtracking. One bar was as good as another for his purposes.

But then, that wasn't right either. She'd be more likely to be in a big bar than a small bar, and he could see a greater number of people in such places in a shorter amount of time. And popular places, especially those which were popular with a young crowd, could provide him with special opportunities: if he were able to stay in such a place for several hours, then almost everyone who was out that night would be likely to flow through, even if they soon moved on to other places, so he could save himself the trip of going here there and everywhere. Thus he changed his tactics. He gained the confidence to walk into and through most places without talking to anyone, unless spoken to first. It had been his fool impulse to announce "I'm looking for someone" that had drawn unwanted attention. In most places no one cared if a person sometimes walked through and cased the joint, except when he acted like "a character." He also decided to sit down comfortably, order a meal, and buy a few colas in a popular bar so that he could reasonably stay long enough to observe those who came and went.

Surprisingly, he discovered, in one or two places, some lone individual would sometimes sit and read in a bar. He had never considered doing that, but once he'd become aware of the practice, he started bringing a copy of Cyrano with him, and it made him much more comfortable.

Once, Seth saw a loner with a book who was obviously sneaking peeks at every beautiful woman who crossed by his table, and he ogled the legs of some women standing near the bar with their backs to him. This made Seth less comfortable. Now he imagined that carrying a book could get him labeled some kind of pervert. Or it might be interpreted as flirtation. Someone, someday, might come and ask him, "What are you reading?" and he wouldn't like that. He wasn't interested in meeting anyone but Kira.

Despite all his efforts, Seth never found her in any bar or restaurant. He spent money—on food and unfinished drinks—that he could hardly afford to spend. And eventually his nightly wandering saw him walking outdoors more and more and sitting indoors less and less. His evening walks—and sometimes afternoon walks—and sometimes morning walks—became less focused and purposeful too. He'd lost any hope or expectation that he would meet Kira unless she decided to find him, or perhaps they would meet just by some ridiculous chance, maybe years in the future. But he couldn't sit still at home, so walking about and peeking into dark corners, loitering near newspaper vendors and watching the people passing by was the only remedy for the misery he felt when he was alone.

It was while he was out on one of these walks that he heard a voice shout out behind him, but it wasn't Kira. It was one of her friends.

"Hey, dummy!"

"What?" He turned and recognized her. "Oh, hi!"

This was "the aggressive entertainer" whom Seth had seen at the bookstore cafe. She was a notably unattractive girl with big feet and sharp eyes. She also seemed dangerously intelligent at first, though Seth later concluded that her intellect was dull. It was her self-confidence and sure opinion of herself that gave a false impression of intelligence.

As Seth described this woman and related their conversation, she reminded me distinctly of a former patient of mine of the same approximate age. She also had the same first name. If she was the person I believed her to be, she was a psychopathic personality case. Her successful treatment is detailed (under a pseudonym) in my book *Treating the Untreatable: Seven Breakthrough Cases*. However, due to my extreme fidelity to the rules of patient confidentiality, I was not able to warn Seth about her condition.

"You must be Seth," said the woman.

She gave him a manly handshake. *Am I in a farce?* Seth thought.

"Yes, I'm Seth. Who are you?"

"My name is Estelle. And don't go drooling when you look at me. I'm a virgin beauty, the object of many men's desires, but I don't go for guys like you. Heeheeeheeeheehee." Her laugh was hideous. "What's with the arm?"

"Oh, this? Well, it's injured."

"Clearly. Skiing accident? Skateboard?"

"No. Look, where's your friend Kira?"

"Ha! Are you looking for her?"

"Well, no… but… Could you give her my number?"

"I could, but if she wanted to see you she'd have gone back to that bookstore you work at."

"Maybe she has. I don't work there. I kind of quit."

Estelle gave Seth a penetrating look, then asked a strange question.

"Do you like books?"

"Of course."

"So, I guess you're a rich guy who just works in a bookstore for the love of literature, then. Minimum wage job with a million-dollar bank account? Or working your way through college?"

"Neither. I'm broke. No college."

"Oh Christ."

She walked away. Seth wasn't sure if it would be a crime for him to follow. Kira had invited him to stalk her, Estelle had not. Besides, he wasn't sure he could handle her. But Estelle turned back after several paces.

"Aren't you coming!?"

Seth sprinted to catch up with her. As soon as he did, she resumed the conversation.

"As a matter of fact, Kira's disappeared. None of us have seen her in weeks. I assumed at first that you were responsible, but I'm guessing now that you're not. Right?"

Seth stopped in his tracks while his heart raced. Then he realized he should answer. "Right!"

"Yeah, I figured. The fact is, she's disappeared before anyway. She's really crazy. No one can figure her out."

"Is she really crazy?"

"Oh, yeah. A lunatic. I guess that's what inspired your pursuit. Hehehehehhheeehehe."

"Listen, how are you and she even friends, I mean…"

Estelle put on an offended look at first, but it was greatly exaggerated, and she dropped it in a second.

"Yeah, you're not the first to ask. They say we're nothing alike. But I'm not that bad, once you get to know me. Besides, why wouldn't I be her friend? She's hot! Hehehehehhheheeeheee."

Estelle noticed that Seth didn't even make a polite effort to laugh along with her jokes.

"You're a boring guy Seth. And there's nothing I can do to help you. Unless you want to help me with my virginity problem."

Seth looked down in embarrassment.

"True love!" she cried, "It's true love, I swear to God! That's the only way you'd turn down my offer. Hehehheeehehe. Goodbye, Seth."

"I think you're the lunatic."

"Oh, I am. That's the one thing Kira and I have 100% in common. It's the foundation of our friendship."

This time she walked away for real.

Starting Again

The next day, as Seth was out wandering and searching again, Kira *found him.*

"There you are," she said in a soft voice as she appeared just beside him and slipped her hand into his. It nearly startled Seth out of his skin.

"Were you looking for me!?" he asked.

"Just recently. Estelle told me you were wandering the streets with a crazed look about you. I felt guilty, so I came out wandering myself."

"But Estelle said you had disappeared."

"She lied. She does that. She's..."

"She's what?"

"A theater major."

"Ah!"

That explained everything.

But nothing mattered anymore. Seth was ecstatic.

"Kira. I've died a thousand deaths, now give me hope! Do you have an infinity of men, crawling and creeping in corners, searching for a glimpse of you? Or am I a special case? Is there any sincerity in the tenderness I see in your eyes now? Or do you live to slay men with your charms, laughing in scorn behind those lovely features?"

She looked disconcerted, and even humble, as if she hadn't known the potency of her beauty and grace.

"I've treated you terribly, I guess. But I couldn't imagine I'd make such an impression on you. I thought I'd come see you again, after letting you suffer for a while, and maybe we'd go out once or twice. But I hesitated. Then I had personal matters to attend to, and then… I thought you must have forgotten me by then. At the same time, I've had a thrill, imagining you out there pursuing me, wondering what would happen if one day you found me, but I haven't believed in the impulse, I haven't trusted the attraction. I've punished you for my doubts."

"You have."

"But honestly, you've been chasing a fantasy."

"False. I only care for the real you. Let me know you, and you'll see."

"What are you imagining?"

"Do you think I'm a fantasist? I'm a cynic, I come from a low station in life, and I don't live on dreams. But you've awakened something in me."

"How low is your station?"

"Low enough."

"You're also a little scary, to tell the truth. But take me out on a date. If money's a problem, I'll pay, but you'd better listen and find out who I really am. Men lose their minds sometimes."

"Money is sometimes a problem, but I won't let you pay. And as for losing my mind, well… I guess you'd better find out some things about me too."

The Date Gone to the Dogs

Seth met Kira at a restaurant that he picked based on customer reviews, never having eaten in such a place himself. He was twenty minutes late. She was twenty-two minutes late.

"Hi, so sorry I'm late!" she said, as she came in the door. When she saw he was standing and didn't have a table, she asked, "Were you planning on leaving without calling me first?"

"No, certainly not! I'm glad you came. I was late myself."

"Oh." She was annoyed with him for being late.

They got through the business of requesting a new table (their reservation had been cancelled), getting seated, ordering a meal, and engaging in casual chit-chat.

Then Kira asked, "What's your excuse?"

"For what?"

"For being late. I mean, you acted like this was some life-changing event, I'm an angel on high to you, and you stare at me like a starving man looks at a morsel of food. So how could you be late?"

"Well… it's not easy to talk about."

"Yeah, okay."

"Seriously."

"Look, I'm not really interested in excuses anyway. I've heard them all."

"Really? All of them?"

"All of the typical ones. An atypical excuse is liable to be lie."

"Well I'll tell you an excuse you never heard before."

"An *honest* one?"

"Yeah. You see… I don't want to go through the whole routine of trying to convince you of my sincerity… but before I came here I had a kind of vision."

"Oh, God."

"No. It's not that I hallucinate, but sometimes my anxieties are so intense, I get wrapped up in a daydream of sorts that has all the convincing elements of reality."

"So what happened in this vision?"

"I came to meet you. I saw it in my mind's eye…"

"You imagined it… and got nervous."

"Don't trivialize. Call it what you like, but it had more significance than that. I saw myself approaching the restaurant. I entered. It didn't look quite like this…" He looked around to compare his vision to the reality. "I saw you sitting at a table in a dark corner…

not even a corner, sort of a nook, with three walls and just a single table-for-two in it with all the dinnerware set out. There were no other patrons in the restaurant, not even wait-staff… you were smiling. But, as I approached, you and the table and everything were lifted into the air. The three surrounding walls raised suddenly and unexpectedly to reveal a pack of hungry, ravening dogs, which howled and gnashed their teeth as they leapt forward to eat me."

"And… you thought this could really happen?"

"It was more real to me than this table that I'm resting my hand on right now. It was as real as your face that I'm staring at. And I'm coming to realize that everything is a mask of sorts. The interior, or the hidden, is full of such potent horror… that is the stuff… the essence of everything."

"So… basically you think I want to murder you? With dogs."

"It's not beyond the realm of possibility."

"Well, I'll grant that's an original excuse."

They muddled through a few more minutes of eating and managed to talk about other things.

Then Seth asked, "What's your excuse?"

Kira looked at him with a teasing glance.

"I don't need an excuse."

Love Blossoms

Seth didn't tell anything more about what happened that night, but somehow, despite the awkwardness of his manner and the strangeness of their interaction, something must have gone very right. From that time he regarded himself and Kira as a couple. Love had brought them together, nothing could divide them, and he believed theirs was the most romantic of relationships.

Meanwhile Seth was unemployed. He had no income, and he had no routine to ground him and occupy his time. He couldn't have had much money left, though from time to time he had unearthed another sockful of cash from somewhere. That, I was sure, could not last forever.

Seth was almost unreasonably honest with Kira, and though

he believed she was equally honest with him, he wouldn't share any details with me. I mostly got his side of conversations and his impressions—impressions which showed that he could be very gullible.

He told Kira all about his lack of prospects. He told her he had been to jail. He was surprised that this upset her; she had already told him she had spoken to many convicts, so he thought she would be more open-minded. He told her about his phobias too, his family, his lack of education. And he admitted that he wasn't keeping up with his studies, so his chances for university were threatening to slip away.

They had their disputes, and there were times when Kira distanced herself from him for a few days, or a week at a time. Then there were times when she drew him close again. In the time in between, Seth had a habit of falling apart.

When I considered Seth's difficulties and how his condition was deteriorating, I wondered whether he should be admitted to my center as a resident patient on a short voluntary commitment, but initially I felt it would not benefit him. I felt the clinical environment would be a step backwards for him, and I was also concerned that exposure to the more troubled patients would be a bad influence if he began to identify with them. I was not sure whether I would continue to feel that way in the case that Seth became homeless. Would Kira support him financially and make him a dependent? She had family and well-adjusted friends. They were relatively affluent. How much would her social environment tolerate a mentally ill live-in boyfriend (if she took him in), and when would the strain lead her to abandon him?

Certainly I've had numbers of patients whose lives have taken a very bad direction, who have lived on the streets or even in worse situations. But it's a tough call to decide whether a patient is likely to benefit from commitment—whether their life conditions are deteriorating due to mental illness or are merely the result of miserable circumstances and bad decisions.

On the positive side, from the time he started dating Kira, Seth stopped injuring himself.

A Short Separation

Kira had a two-week break from work, and she went on vacation with her family. There was no room for Seth on this trip for somewhat obvious reasons (she had not yet introduced him to any member of her family). Kira also told him that she would need to do some thinking about their relationship while she was away.

"*Thinking*. What a damned curse word," he said. He was deeply distressed during her absence, and he struggled hard to resist cutting himself.

One phobia I was unable to cure Seth of was his fear of erotic imagery. Thus he made no use of pornography to distract himself. He remained chaste and faithful while Kira was away, even in his deepest thoughts. He also refrained from masturbation because, as he said, "I don't believe in it," and because he feared that he could break his penis. As a matter of fact, I've only heard of two cases of men who broke their penises from excessive masturbation, and that takes a lot. I didn't mention these cases to him as it does no good to let such a patient know that this horror is actually possible.

While he was waiting, his inevitable bankruptcy came very abruptly. Seth was completely tapped out on funds. He hadn't been able to get a regular job of any sort, partly because he was speaking and behaving more eccentrically, and largely because of his lack of previous employment and education.

"I tried to make some money," he told me, "but I couldn't even get regular day-labor work because my bandage makes me look physically incapable of handling the work—though I did get two days of work collecting and sorting advertising flyers from the street to resell to the advertisers. That job paid one dollar for every fifty flyers or seventy-five business cards collected and sorted in good condition (no water damage, no tears, and no footprints). But I got muscled out by one of the regular bums who does the job, after the guy got released from three weeks in the county jail.

"I soon realized that I wasn't cut out to compete in that job anyway when I discovered that the regulars routinely steal entire stacks of the flyers from supermarkets, building lobbies, apartment mailboxes, and some of them make deals with the flyer distributers who prefer to unload their flyers on the collectors in bulk, rather than make the effort to distribute them properly. That approach requires a bit of finesse because you have to mess the fliers up just enough to give the impression that you collected them off the street, but not so much that they become worthless. They say it's a good idea to mix in some really trashed ones, so the buyer can deny about five percent of your pay, but you still turn good money. But I just wasn't made to be a hustler."

He fell behind on paying his rent, and he ate up the various canned foods and snacks that remained in his kitchen—canned peaches, tomato sauce, ramen noodles, and a bag of potatoes that he boiled. I then arranged to allow him to eat in our institute's cafeteria once a day.

Kira returned, and they got together a couple of times, but she now seemed noncommittal and said she was "confused" about their relationship.

Seth begged some money off of his uncle William, who generously assisted him. Then, shortly after he got the money, Seth got robbed by a kid with a knife while he was crossing a pedestrian bridge over Brush Creek. The robber was inept, and Seth was able to grab him and toss him over the rail of the bridge, where he fell on the edge of the footpath below and bounced into the water. But half of Seth's money was in the robber's pocket (the rest of the money, Seth had already paid to his landlord). Seth considered going down to drag the kid out of the river to get his money back, but then he got frightened and ran.

I decided to accept Seth into our hospital on a voluntary two-week commitment when he told me he truly believed that Kira had been hiding *in the water* of Brush Creek at the time of the attempted robbery. He said she was orchestrating all the problems in his life.

Commitment

It appeared to me that Seth was rapidly undergoing some kind of psychic transformation at this time, but in uncontrolled and unpredictable ways. His anxiety was taking new forms. He was making a good effort to resist his self-harm compulsion, but it was hard to claim that he was making overall progress in light of his recent erratic behavior and fanaticism.

Seth agreed to try more intensive treatment because he felt that he was at risk of losing Kira, at the same time that he feared she would do him some terrible harm. He told her about his plans to be committed, and she supported his decision. But she did not promise to wait for him. She said she loved him and she wanted him to do what was best for him.

"I told her that I would get better for her," Seth said. "But she didn't want that responsibility. She said I should get better for myself, regardless of our future together. *Regardless*. It's really a hurtful thing to say, honestly. But I'm still resolved to get better *for her*."

The Hard Work Begins

Those who are familiar with some of my work with personality cases from reading books such as *Treating the Untreatable* might guess that I saw this transformative stage as an opportunity to apply some of my more radical techniques. However, it should be remembered that those techniques which have been demonstrated effective in the treatment of other personality disorders have so far been ineffective in the treatment of patients who tend towards paranoid personality. This is because the jarring nature of my treatments—which have been repeatedly referred to as unorthodox in a pejorative sense by critics of my program—has the undesirable effect of confirming some patients' belief in their own persecution.

That is so, and there is also the danger that a patient will get a heightened sense of his or her importance. Patients of this sort experience an effect nearly opposite that which is intended. Rather than being thrust into a condition that makes them vulnerable to an applied effort towards personality transformation, the patients become radically aware that something is demanded of them as an individual. The ego is ossified, the patient's suffering attains a new poignancy, and his or her personality becomes even less tractable.

Another deterrent to my use of radical therapies at this time was that our center was being audited by the Missouri Department of Health on the basis of some complaints by families of patients who had voluntarily transferred to our center from a state hospital after receiving an order of commitment.

The therapy for personality cases that I found most effective at this time was the-striking-with-a-bamboo-rod. I adapted this practice from a book I read about Zen, though I've never had any other association with Zen. I was able, in many cases, to identify the precise moments when a sudden and unexpected strike, usually on the back or shoulders, would have the correct startling effect on a personality patient. This would often produce an immediate positive effect, while in some cases it needed to be followed up quickly with a several-hour speech-and-babble session, physical disorientation therapy, or radical sleep adjustment. I continued this therapy approach in our center even during the audit, though I did not employ it with Seth.

The more radical therapies that I put on hold included the "toilet startle," in which I gathered a large number of nurses, both male and female, to rush into the bathroom, turn out the lights, and laugh and scream hysterically while the target patient was in the middle of using the toilet. This was sometimes followed up by light caressing of an ambiguously sexual nature, then physical disorientation therapy and sleep adjustment.

In one case, a vigorous and prolonged beating-with-iron-rods was very effective in the treatment of a borderline personality case, but I discontinued this therapy entirely due to threats and pressure from outside agencies. I was regrettably unable to continue research into this treatment principally because of the risk that the center's funding could be cut off and law agencies could interfere with the other operations of the hospital. Sadly, prejudice and closed-mind-edness once again stood in the way of scientific progress.

But none of the above therapies would have been suitable for Seth. I instead subjected him to a more experimental and newly developed therapy, the "citrus startle."

In this therapy, I had Seth placed in a dimly lit room, seated in a chair, facing a window out into a sort of airshaft. In the airshaft, there was a large mirror, which was angled in such a way that, in coordination with other mirrors on the roof of the center, it could shine the light of the sun directly into his eyes. The mirrors were pivoted by computer-controlled motors on a timer, and the whole system had the effect of his staring into the sun while simultaneously feeling isolated from nature and the outside world. The light was, of course, very intense, and we placed the glass of a car windshield about seven inches from the patient's face. This had psychological value because it gave the patient a sense of safety from the risk of blindness, as the windshield glass would prevent the passage of ultra-violet rays that could damage the retina—but in fact we doctors knew that this was unnecessary beyond its psychological impact. The ultra-violet rays were not significantly reflected in the rear-surfaced mirrors, and thus the windshield was superfluous.

While the patient (Seth) stared at the sun for several hours, he was instructed to self-apply saline eye-drops to his eyes once every forty seconds. Sometimes, at unpredictable intervals, a technical assistant would squeeze a lemon close to the patient's face at exactly the moment when he was applying the eye drops. Though the lemon juice would hardly ever strike the patient in the eye, the perception and anticipation that it *could*, coupled by the strong citrus smell, had a striking effect upon the mind. This effect was more like an "aha" moment than an experience of threat or perceived danger, and it was calculated to render the paranoid-personality-patient less self-aware and more "out-of-self aware." The hypothesis was that the patient would then become semi-pliable and have more effective follow-up talk-therapy sessions.

Fragments from a Therapy Session

"Communication with the eyes... you can't warn me of danger... if you tell me I'm about to back my way out the window, you've doomed me... I'll take the fatal last step face-first... It's nothing to do with my past... There are cowards... Most people... I won't allow myself to live a long life only to regret the opportunities that I've allowed to slip by... Do you understand, it's better to blame the universe than to blame myself?... It's nothing to do with my past... There's Kira, a miracle... Why play games?... I know, I know... She's as deeply involved as I am, we each pursue our own reckless course... the other is the fatal object... You can see it in her face, there's no doubt... She's just getting spun around a bit by some trivia... There are external pressures and circumstances... Weakness stands in the way... It just means I need to be more assertive... Who cares about money and jobs?... I have the will to turn the world upside down... You don't frighten me with your chamber of horrors... There's a connection between us now that can't be broken... And if I'm wrong, so what?... We all die... But to not have played the game, that's the coward's way... She's not a child... She knows better... This is the way she hooks me... Nothing satisfies me like knowing that she is satisfied... If she wants to swat at me, knock me about a bit, why not?... I'll grovel if I have to... She can pull my eyes out, I'll lovingly give them to her... It's not masochistic... Masochism is undergoing your useless therapy... She doesn't wish me harm, but my passion takes strange forms when I give credence to my imagination... There's no fear there... But there is horror... This is pointless, why explain?... I'll master her, I'll master you, I'll master fear... There's nothing to doubt... I don't want her to fall and get hurt, of course... I don't want her to fall and not get hurt, or get hurt without falling... To be unconventional is to be a realist... All you suckers who are limited... That's the end of all... Such fear and cowardice among you... We all die someday, you know... Broken in a thousand pieces... Your program... It only exists to divide me from Kira... You fooled me into committing myself… A doctor can never bear for his patients to be cured… But I'll defy you… I'll defy you… You won't make an emotional cripple of me… I visualize her face, and my strength returns a thousand-fold… The first night… Together… After… I had more energy… We went out again… I said, 'I love you very much, and I plan to keep you.' She doesn't want to be kept? Fine… She'll have to go then… She doesn't want to go…Is it so easy for me? she asks… 'What easy? I do the most difficult things with suddenness and conviction.' … She's persuaded of my sincerity… She'll love me forever… But no, maybe not… Things change day to day… We've made a *physical* pledge… She'll break it whenever she wants… If she wants luxury, give me time, I'll get her that… But respectability?… Fuck that… She's not a child and her parents don't matter… I'm not without my strength… I could tell her one day to spit in their faces… do you think she'd refuse?"

Seth had a lot more to say than this, but it was never more coherent. Still, these fragments paint a picture of what was going on in his mind. He was stubborn and resistant. There was little hope of changing him while he was so obsessed with Kira. He knew I had nothing to gain personally from treating him; my livelihood didn't depend on it. But he increasingly saw me as an enemy. Therapy was stalemated, and it wasn't my purpose to break his will.

One could argue different.

But I wasn't able to elicit the kind of cooperation I was aiming for. I carried on, day by day, and I thought perhaps, in his volatile condition, a new change would occur, and a new opportunity would arise. I'd seen more stubborn cases than his that took a spontaneous turn for the better. But I was frustrated, I must admit.

LOVE TRIUMPHS

One day, when Seth and I were about two hours into a planned four-hour session, we took a break and I decided to walk outside for a moment to relax. Seth was permitted to stand up for a while and blink his eyes in the dark.

While I was outside under the breezeway that runs to the parking lot, I saw, across a street and further across an open meadow on our campus, at a distance of about 150 yards, a woman. Even at that distance, I could instantly recognize that she was beautiful. I was convinced that this was Kira. Seth hadn't lied about her. She was standing still, just looking in the direction of our hospital and apparently waiting for who-knows-what. There was no good cause for her being there, just looking. I was tempted to run out to her, but before the impulse could pass from brain to muscle, she was suddenly running, and then she was gone.

When I returned inside, I felt a slight tremor in my legs. I felt cheated by not having had even the chance to take one step in her direction before she fled. I told Seth that we would cut the citrus treatment short and proceed immediately to a brief talk session.

Once we'd entered my office and taken our seats, Seth said, "You saw her, didn't you?"

I felt pale and nearly transparent. I couldn't deny it. "How did you know?"

"I knew it! You're rattled hard. Where was she?"

"I think she's... well... She was just... watching."

Seth leapt from his chair.

"You've got to release me."

"I've got you committed for one week more."

"It's voluntary."

"Not any more. You checked yourself in, and I'm not checking you out until I see progress."

"Bullshit! Check me out now. If you don't, you'll get no more cooperation from me. You'll be responsible for the failure of my treatment if you coerce me into staying."

"You can't come up with a threat that would rival half of what I've heard from other patients. And you're not ready."

"Release me."

I pondered for a moment. I wavered.

"Tomorrow," I pronounced, surprising myself.

The next day, he was very agitated. He got his little bundle together, and I gave him the papers for his release, and when he had been wheeled to the exit by a nurse—with me following along beside him—Seth got up and looked across that field. And she was there again, waiting. He ran to her.

"What the hell?" I thought.

I saw him draw close to her. They seemed to exchange a few words. Then they jogged off together, and I expected I would never see either of them again.

5.
The Next Phase

MY OWN ANXIETY

One day I was out of the office, riding a bus across town, when I found myself standing beside an Asian high-school kid who was wearing a drab grey Catholic-school uniform. He was listening to music through headphones connected to his phone, and he was looking with absorption at something on the phone's screen. I was lost in my own thoughts, and I hardly gave him any attention until my eyes were drawn to his high-top sneakers, which were covered entirely in a shiny gold metallic foil. Then, for reasons I can't understand, I looked up at his mild face, and I burst out screaming "Gold-Shoes!" as though it were the most vulgar insult. The kid was astonished, and so were the other passengers. The bus came to a stop a few seconds later; as soon as the door opened I made a quick exit.

Some kind of stress—perhaps relating to my patients—was getting to me and prompting a collapse of sorts. But why was I especially stressed at that time, and why did the stress affect me in that particular way? Thinking about it, I realized that I had hardly slept in the past week. I thus made the decision to take a four-day break from work at the center, and go on a trip to clear my mind. I flew down to Saint John, in the Virgin Islands, and my four-day trip turned into seven days. But when I returned, I was more exhausted than I had been when I left. The sea and sand had done nothing to clear my mind. The natural "beauty" was too garish. The sun was too bright. The women on the beaches made me ashamed of my desires, my age, and my solitude. The couples were too desperate in their happiness, and the palm trees were disturbingly phallic.

In other times and other circumstances, I had often had vivid and memorable dreams while working on my most troublesome cases. While working with Seth I had not had *any* memorable dreams at all. Reflecting back, I could recall several long stretches when I got by on minimal sleep, but I could also recall several periods in which I was able to sleep "well," and apparently "restfully." Still, something was troubling both my waking and sleeping hours without giving me any hints as to why.

There was one thing, however, that I was able to work out intellectually; it pained me to be honest with myself about it. Whatever there was in Seth's case that had upset my emotional balance, the effect of it had tripled once I'd seen Kira with my own eyes. It also troubled me to think that—even though it was so obviously irrational the way Seth swung from loving Kira, to fearing her, to throwing himself at her with no care for consequence—though this was so, on an emotional level it *made sense* to me. It shouldn't have made sense. I, myself, had never been love-mad.

SICK

Anyway, Seth was not gone for long. I was alerted when he turned up in the emergency room of Truman Medical Center, with vomiting and a high fever, muscle aches, shortness of breath, and cellulitis on the forearm. He had several untreated puncture wounds, which he confessed he had inflicted on himself with a sharp two-pronged barbecue fork.

I met with him at Truman after his third day of intravenous anti-biotic treatment, and he was recovering reasonably well from what was diagnosed as systemic infection. Shock had been averted. But, as the hospital's medical staff had told him and I reiterated, he had come very close to a life-critical situation. He should be very thankful to be able to walk away with his body intact.

Seth was more concerned with getting released early so he could keep his job. One of Kira's friends had helped Seth get employment as a movie-theater projectionist in a sixteen-screen multiplex. He told me that his job required him to thread and start the projectors an average of forty times per shift, to write between sixty and eighty "scratch reports," to correct any framing or sound errors, and to run from place to place constantly to keep on top of his responsibilities—all for one dollar above minimum wage. He loved it.

Lying in his hospital bed, Seth challenged me for not having helped him enough.

"And why couldn't you or your friends have hooked me up with a job like this?" he asked me. "You managed to pull plenty of favors for me before, but no one could help me in finding even a subsistence level job?"

"You know," I explained, "the world has its ugly side. Even wealthy philanthropists start to shy away when the recipient of their aid is hitting bottom. Certain... cases..."

"You mean *people*..."

"Certain cases take all the people around them to their limits. And everyone has limits. You're lucky I was able to convince your benefactors not to stop supporting your educational goals... *if* you get yourself on your feet and show a basic commitment to helping yourself."

"You're starting to sound like a social worker."

"Hey, better than a prison warden! Now... what happened?"

A shadow crossed Seth's face; then his calm and unaffected demeanor abandoned him.

"She's playing games with me! I'm just... one of the men... who..." He whispered the rest, "...that's it. I'm only *one* of her men."

Then he laughed, painfully, as an attempt to be cavalier about his own misery.

I was rather upset to hear this. Until now it seemed that Kira was... more sensible than that. But I didn't know her.

"Well, you don't have to let that happen. You don't need her. Come, check yourself into my program, we'll resume our therapy and we'll help you work out the serious issues that trouble you. Besides, this affair of yours could literally kill you."

"No. I can't commit myself. I have a job."

"You'll get a job again."

"I don't count on that. And I've got it together now."

I had to push a point with him, and get him to speak directly, literally.

"What is the nature of your relationship, anyway? You talk so passionately about her, but you never come right out and talk about the sex."

"Don't ask about that! It's… not appropriate."

"After all you've told me before…"

"I won't talk about her that way! She's a lady."

"Not if what you said is true, about other men…"

"Fuck you! Don't talk about her that way, you…" He was seething. "I don't know why you think you can know anything about this… She's so much beyond you, beyond me…"

"She's a human, and you say she's cheating on you."

"It's probably my fault! It's not her doing, she can't be blamed. And I'm… you know, pretty messed up. It's weird that she even considered dating me, but she gave me a chance. Why should someone… so faultless… be constrained by normal ethics?"

"Before you'd met her, I'd never heard you acknowledge another person as even being worthy of you. At first I thought it might be a good thing, finally, with this woman… you saw something of value out there in the world, even if your response was a bit exaggerated… something that didn't exist just for you, just as you wanted it to be, but… now you're debasing yourself."

"But you don't know… the euphoria… the transcendent bliss."

"You mean sex? You've finally had a good sexual experience? That's good, but you can have that in a relationship that gives you more."

"No, you filthy head-shrinker, don't sully it. Get out!"

Knowing that it would be wrong to push further at this time, I suggested we end the conversation and meet again when he had calmed down. But he changed tack.

"No, wait. You don't get off that easily. Let me tell you that I've discovered the potency of a love supreme, something of the quality that only our most sublime poets have ever glimpsed. If you see me humiliate myself before this miraculous phenomenon, it's only because it's right to be humble in the presence of the divine. And men like you… the lowly… you tear apart everything beautiful because it's denied you! You mock a man who's fallen, one whose life swings from bliss to beautiful torment, moment to moment, while burning in the flame of all-consuming love…"

"Maudlin!"

I reached for my bamboo stick to strike him, but then noticed that I didn't have it with me.

"…But you can't 'cure' this. Nonetheless, you can help me. You *must*. You must help me master myself and make the sacrifices that must be made… make them willingly."

"No."

"You have to. It's your job. I can straighten out my life and convince Kira to be faithful, and then I'll be happy."

"It's not my job to secure your happiness. I don't care about your happiness. I care about your mental health."

We made an appointment for our next meeting the following week, at my office. I resolved to maintain my professionalism from that point forward.

More Revealed, and More Doubts Raised

Seth finally started to tell me more about the real Kira without hiding so much behind abstraction and romantic fantasy. He and she were currently living together in her apartment. He had moved in after negotiating an early release from his own rental agreement, which his landlord was willing to agree to since the alternative would probably have been eviction. "You can't get blood from a turnip," said Seth.

Kira McFee was a professional court reporter in the Kansas City Municipal Court. She had briefly studied History at University of Missouri, Kansas City, but in reaction to the continual pressure from her family to prepare for law school and to follow in the footsteps of her father—who had been a lawyer for twenty-seven years—Kira dropped out of university after only two years of study. She thought that studying law sounded "unappealing." At the same time, she had befriended several "artsy" students on her campus who attempted to influence her towards some kind of performing arts career, or perhaps modeling, to cash in on her exceptional good looks. Kira, however, did not believe she had any genuine talent for any kind of performance, and she feared the rivalry, struggle, hard-driven competition, and interpersonal conflict she imagined a modeling career would entail.

After a three-month temporary job in a customer service call center for a bank, which left her feeling like a shell-shocked veteran, she resolved absolutely to avoid any career that would require frequent contact with the general public. She also hoped to keep interaction with other employees to a minimum, to avoid office politics and hopefully to avoid sexual harassment. When she heard about the possibility of working as a court reporter, from a cousin who worked in a court in Louisiana, Kira decided this sounded like a dream career. She pursued and acquired her certification, and her father helped her with a recommendation, though he did not let up on the pressure to "get over this slumming phase and grow up to be a professional." Anyway, she got the job.

The job was not quite a dream job, but it wasn't very disappointing either, and people mostly let her be. She listened a lot, spoke little, and got through the day while earning fair pay. She felt pride in her exceptional skill at this mostly mechanical job, and she believed she was developing a special, deeper understanding of language and its varieties while transcribing the rhetoric of lawyers and the idiom of the criminal class. She was also developing an interest in learning about communicating with the deaf and hearing impaired, which would be a career asset if she wanted to move into Communication-Access Real Time translation services.

Seth was worried that Kira was being exposed to disturbing

images and corrupting influences during the criminal cases and depositions of sexual predators, perverts, and other varieties of rapists. This made him terribly anxious, but he was in no position to try to influence her career choice. She was the breadwinner. He was the breadloser.

Before living with Seth, Kira had had a few different roommates. One of them had been male. Kira said that her relationship with this roommate, whom she wouldn't name, was strictly "just friends." Seth was very jealous. "He did like to talk about sex, though," she told him. "It was funny and provocative in a 'silly' way, but nothing serious."

"Oh my God!" Seth ranted during counseling, "When I hear something like that, I want to cry, then vomit, then vomit tears and weep vomit. Is there a single woman on this planet with an ounce of sense? She was practically molested on a daily basis by this sicko who thought it might turn her on for him to talk about blowjobs or something... and what about when she was dressing in the apartment... or showering? What did he see of *her body?* While she trusted him so much... holy Christ."

Seth was euphoric one day and despairing the next. He was convinced that she now cheated on him routinely, and he even portrayed her as hypersexual. He accused her of manually stimulating herself in court. He said that she had sexual relations with judges, lawyers, witnesses, court clerks and security staff, that she exposed herself on video during taped depositions, and that she sometimes attempted to have herself sneaked into the prisoner holding cells in back of the courtrooms. When Seth and Kira went out in public, if she wanted to go to the bathroom he would often follow just to be sure that she didn't go into the men's room. He believed that she had an obsessive fantasy about being gang-raped and humiliated in a public toilet, and several times he got her to admit to this fantasy.

Seth also mentioned that he feared that Kira was planning to acquire and distribute nude photos of him.

Yet, when I asked for details about his own physical relations with her, he said that it was something he dared not talk about out of respect for her. He then sang her praises as a living embodiment of perfection, pure sensual pleasure, absolute beauty, a marvel to see, a paragon of ethical purity, faithfulness, sincerity—love incarnate, yet too noble and sacred to be sullied by "mere carnality."

At one point I began to wonder whether, perhaps, their relationship could be entirely platonic—whether, in fact, Kira was engaged in sexual activity outside their relationship, while Seth meekly sat on the sidelines and only *talked* love. Was he avoiding a direct discussion of the subject because he was bluffing me? Yet there was that "sensuality" that he let slip in his speech, from time to time. Then I thought my hypothesis was ridiculous. Surely there was sex between them.

I had to resolve this, so I finally approached the topic in reverse, asking in effect whether he was *not* having sex with her. I thought this challenge to his virility would force a confession.

"Has your lack of a sex drive been an impediment to your relationship?" I asked.

He didn't give any verbal response to my question at all, yet he radiated a sort of calm pride and contentedness. It was visibly apparent that he was still enjoying the sensation of her body. It was then that *I* was unaccountably inflamed with jealousy, and I felt ashamed.

When, on a later occasion, he told me that he sometimes felt a physical *hum of satisfaction* with no interruption for a day or longer after "being with her," I had my answer, and I felt a new unease. It was then he dared to tell me that, sometimes, his hands and fingers could not be stopped from stroking and caressing every bit of her skin just to arouse her to a trembling, as though his body were not his own to control, and his mind was a willing but passive recipient of the thrill that it gave him.

He said all that, but he acted as though I were insulting her to use the word "sex," or to ask even about their "love life." He was infinitely protective of her honor, but he alone retained the right to challenge that honor as an expression of his helplessness and the anxiety that could not be restrained.

He refused to entertain any discussion of a connection between sexual anxiety and compulsive self-injury.

He talked often of his suspicions and suffering, he sometimes spoke about his bliss and boundless happiness, but he revealed very little about their real emotional exchanges, their everyday conversations and activities, or even the thoughts or opinions which they had exchanged. He thought nothing of the future, and quickly retreated from any discussion of his past. Kira, in the abstract, was the only thing he cared to talk about.

When he was exhausted or frustrated by my questions, he broke off abruptly, and sometimes he skipped a session. Once, he disappeared from treatment for a stretch of several weeks. I finally resolved to turn him away from therapy upon his return, and I suggested we discontinue entirely.

Freeze Out

"Seth," I told him, "I'm sorry to say you've become an obstacle to your own recovery. You're uncooperative in the extreme, you refuse to talk about topics that are an important part of your treatment, and I feel that your new therapy routine is becoming another a phase of your sickness."

"I... I'm sorry. I just need your help, but... you've done a lot for me, I'm just not quite logical sometimes. And your curiosity seems just a bit... well, I'm not sure why you want to talk about some things."

"So this means you don't really trust me, which means this just can't work. But you can't use my program as a kind of service to patch you up from time to time so you can go out and self-destruct repeatedly. Are you cutting yourself?"

"Sometimes."

"Often, I think, and you no longer talk about your past, your feelings, the reasons why..."

"I have something else on my mind!"

"Well, anyway, since you're not willing to check yourself in for a long period, and outpatient treatment is failing you..."

"I know, I know... it's me... it's my fault."

"I'm not blaming you or talking about fault. I'm talking about a new approach. We have to be pragmatic. I think it's time for you to try going your own way. Not for a few weeks. For a long time. Or forever. Come back only when you're ready to confront the hard facts."

"Is this normal? To turn away a patient in need?"

"I have my program. Normal has nothing to do with it."

After I sent Seth away, he had a few minor crises that prompted him to call me. When I had time for a brief telephone conversation, I listened to what he said. But our communication was kept to a minimum. Nothing really changed for a while, as far as I could guess. Anyway, he was still with that woman. I thought about him a lot in the quiet times. And I kept thinking soon he would ask to be committed again, and we could start again in earnest.

He had yet another crisis, a bigger one that was hard for me to ignore, but I stayed uninvolved. A police officer called my office to say that Seth had been brought in on a new assault charge. The department wanted to know whether he was currently in treatment. I reported that he was not.

BLIND LOVE

I received something strange in the mail one day. In an envelope I found an advertising business card of the sort which is sometimes thrown on the ground in alleys for lonely men to pick up. It was a sexually suggestive personals advertisement.

"For your hands only: I want to love you with your eyes closed. My face is too beautiful for you to behold, but my body is yours to be held. Send msg to Kra@blind-sightful.info, with 'nosee' in sub line. If U say teh right thing, U get #".

Frankly, I often get strange messages, texts, voice recordings, and all kinds of handwritten scrawls from patients; from former patients; from friends, family, and associates of patients; and from public cranks. But it would have been hard not to think that this message had something to do with Kira. Did it? "Kra." And Seth had always said she was hypersexual. Well, he didn't say it in such words. But what could this be?

After pondering a while, I responded. I sent a message titled "nosee." The body of the message was "teh right thing." I used one of several email accounts that I maintain for anonymous correspondence.

Thirty-five minutes after I sent my message, I got the response: *"Name yourself now. No funny business. The first letter is 'P.' Lie, and you don't get to touch me. Tell the truth and you don't get to see me... but you get more. I'll protect your secret if you protect mine. Don't disappoint."*

I told myself, out loud, "This is only to benefit Seth. I won't cross any lines." I was feeling a bit jittery while I thought about my next step. A bit too jittery.

I sent the message: *"...ercy."*

The next message I got gave a phone number. I called it. The phone picked up before I could hear it ring.

"I knew you'd call," came the whispered voice at the other end.

"Um." I hesitated. "You know me, or you've heard of me. I'm calling out of sincere... It's strange to call you."

"Tell me what you want." The whispered, breathy voice was ambiguously feminine. A little too ambiguously.

"Seth!?"

The phone call ended. I didn't try to call again.

RETURN TO THERAPY

The next day, Seth came into my office and I agreed to meet with him if he would talk seriously about committing himself for a longer hospitalization period. He said he was willing to consider it.

Before allowing him to talk about Kira, I insisted that he talk about some of the other elements of his life. He said he still had his projectionist job, and he was working steadily. He had gotten his shifts covered by other employees on the days when he was forced to miss work due to illness. And there was his arrest. He was now saving money—even though his wages were quite paltry—by continuing the miserly habits he had acquired in childhood.

"Kira and I had an argument," he said, "when she discovered I've been saving some of the money she gives me to do the shopping..."

"All right, stop now. If you're going to talk about Kira, let's talk about that strange phone call we had."

"Yeah. Okay."

"Why did you send me that message, and why..."

"You have to know what Kira's really like."

"But that wasn't Kira's business card. You created that whole situation."

"But that's the kind of thing she does to meet men."

"How do you know? I have my doubts, Seth. A stunt like that isn't going to convince me of anything. Now, I want to hear about other things in your life. You're not going to live a healthy life until there's *more* to your life than this one obsession."

"I'm being cruelly mocked and ridiculed behind my back by coworkers. They pretend to be friendly, but they secretly despise me."

"Why do you think so?"

"I overheard them laughing," Seth explained, "two projectionists plus the asshole concessions manager Todd, from downstairs. He was getting projection training from our boss Charlie. And so I stayed behind the platter tree of projector fourteen, in a darkened corner of the first projection booth, and listened to see what they were laughing about."

"What did they say?"

"Charlie said 'We don't really like him,' and after they laughed some more, the others replied in unison 'We're fooling him into liking us. Ha hahaha.' Then Cruz said 'Now we're laughing at him because we think he's stupid.' Finally, after another burst of laughter, Todd said 'He's Seth.'"

"But that's a completely implausible dialogue!"

"It's a fact. Why would I make it up?"

"Maybe you got some of the facts wrong, or you may have forgotten the exact manner of their speech."

"They said my *name*. I couldn't have gotten confused, and this leaves no room for misunderstanding. They were laughing at *me*."

"Well... tell me about the arrest. That's the biggest thing. Why did the police call me?"

"Oh, it's nothing. They wanted to charge me with assault, I guess, but now they've dropped it... though I might have to go to court in a few months."

"But why? What did you do?"

"I got in a fight. But it's not my fault, and the guy I fought with is bigger and stronger than me, and I was injured."

"How?"

"I got my hand broken."

"Let me guess. The left hand?"

"Yeah. And I sprained my knee."

"But how did it happen?"

"I punched him, and that broke my hand, and I fell down when I tried to kick him in the head but he dodged and pushed me off balance. That's how my knee got hurt."

"Explain. What were you doing fighting with this guy?"

"Well it was raining. Kind of raining, slightly... well, no, it was just raining. And this guy was walking along, and he was carrying an umbrella, but his umbrella was not open."

"And?"

"And he was obviously mocking me! You see, I had an umbrella too, and it was open. But then I see this big guy with his folded umbrella, and it's like he's rubbing it in my face that I'm some kind of coward for using an umbrella, when he doesn't think it's raining so hard."

"And then... and then you hit him? No words, you just attacked him for not opening his umbrella."

"He was making fun of me!"

"How?"

"With his actions and his attitude."

 Pause.

"Seth, you came here because you know that you're dangerously close to seeing everything come apart. You're out of control in your behavior. You need to commit yourself for a month."

"I know what you really want."

"What's that?"

"You want to end my love for Kira."

"I don't know. If you want to get better, you have to face the facts that there may be some big changes in your personality and in many aspects of your current life. You may or may not end up leaving Kira. It might prove necessary."

"But you won't do it. You won't split us up."

"Will you commit yourself?"

"Yes. But you won't do it. I'll hold out against you. I need to fix my life, and overcome a few hurdles. But I won't give her up."

"Maybe in a month…"

"…She won't give me up either! I know that for a fact. In some ways I don't trust her, but she won't give me up."

"We'll see."

6.
In For a Month

The First Few Days

Seth checked in, and we spent the first few days getting him acclimated and dealing with impulse control. He was significantly more agitated than in his previous commitments—at first—but he soon became more cooperative and pliable.

A Woman's Greatest Desire

Throughout the month of Seth's commitment, I applied a variety of therapeutic techniques, including those mentioned previously, with longer periods of isolation and sleep adjustment, but our discussions and talk-therapy sessions offered the greatest opportunity for understanding Seth's thought processes and gauging his emotional and psychological progress.

Seth was more lucid after readjusting to our routine, and we soon began to discuss some matters in more depth. Our first serious discussion dealt with his jealousy.

"What does it mean to you to contemplate Kira cheating?"

"It's… it's enough to make me want to end everything."

"What do you mean *everything*? Would it end your relationship?"

"I mean everything. The world. I just want to see it all come to an end."

"Tell me explicitly what you're talking about."

"I haven't thought about that. No, I'm not talking about… self-harm. It's just cataclysmic, something out of my hands. I can't contemplate it really."

"Please. Don't tell me you can't contemplate it. You contemplate her infidelity all the time. You tell me she's been cheating on you from the beginning, but the scenarios you describe are… at the very least exaggerated."

"But I can't contemplate the real consequences of it, I mean if I were really to confront the meaning of it."

"What consequences? I can't fill in the blanks here. You have to be the one to do it."

"Stop pushing me, goddamnit."

"But you're jealous. Frequently."

"Constantly."

"And you believe that you have a reason to be jealous. It's not just some... hunch or anxiety?"

"Don't talk to me about hunches. Listen. She's cheated on me. I don't have to guess. She told me so."

"Why? Why would she do that?" I heard a strong note of anger in my own voice when I asked this, and I hadn't known I was feeling it. My voice was almost a thing that was bigger than myself.

In a few moments, Seth surprised me by weeping for the first time that I had seen (other than the tears produced by staring at the sun). It was quite unexpected.

"Oh God! You can't know the degree of my hopelessness... it's all... it's all too bad to be false."

As he cried, I wondered, *What Kind of woman is Kira, really? What if she is truly unfaithful? What if he has actually fallen into the hands of a woman who... despite knowing his vulnerability...*

"Thank God she's not here," he said between sobs.

"So... you're glad to be away from her at last?"

"No! I'm just glad she isn't here right now. You know, women have this fantasy. It goes beyond the desire for sex or money. It's the desire to see a man cry."

"You've never cried in front of her, even in an argument?"

"No. How could I? Some men, the cruder ones, desire most of all to give a woman an earth-shattering orgasm, one that will represent an absolute conquest and total dominance in the relationship. But for women, a man's tears are sweeter than orgasm. They mean that she has won!"

"You claim to love her. Why do you portray love as a contest with only one winner?"

Actually, this notion was not novel to me. Many male patients had told me something to the effect that women love a man's tears most of all. Perhaps it's a common paranoid fantasy.

But Seth didn't answer my question. He continued to weep for a time, then dried his tears, and his face took on a countenance of rage. His eyes made rapid darting movements, as he was undoubtedly starting to visualize Kira having sex with other men. Minutes more passed, until he shook himself out of the day-nightmare he had indulged in. Then he turned his glance to mine, a hard look still dominant in his eyes. And for a moment, I think I really did see a fraction of his pain.

No Visitors

The terms of Seth's commitment were rather severe, and one restriction was that Seth was not to receive visits or communication from any unapproved parties. Kira, of course, was not approved.

Seth asked me on the ninth day of his commitment whether she had tried to contact him. She had not, and I told him so. He seemed disappointed, and slightly skeptical.

Right after this session, as I was passing through the secured doors of the ward and returning to the central lobby, I had a very strange, giddy and electric sensation that I can't quite describe. The receptionists were—almost inaudibly—discussing an unusual *happening*. Something out of the ordinary.

When I asked one of the nurses standing beside the desk, she told me that they had just turned away a guest who was seeking to visit Seth. It was Kira McFee.

I embarrassed myself somewhat by immediately running out after her. I passed through the front doors, out and along the pathway that leads towards the public street. I saw, on the left, a car pulling out of the small front visitor's lot. I also saw, pulling around from the other side, on the right, an SUV coming from the long road that leads to the larger lot in the back by the meadow where I had previously encountered her. Was one of these her car? There was no reason to think so, and I couldn't think where else to turn my eyes. Where the Hell was she?

I walked with purpose back inside to the reception desk, and I explained unnecessarily to the chief reception nurse that Kira should not be allowed to enter the hospital again.

"I think that she and Seth Rookard have somehow established communication, and I will order him into isolation for the rest of his commitment period."

But there was no need for me to report my further plans, so I returned to my office feeling rather foolish for having squandered my words. *Let the receptionists think what they want.*

Isolation

We kept Seth in isolation for the remainder of the month. I did not tell him that Kira had tried to visit. Soon his personality started to unravel. After a few days, he said he felt as though he had been in the hospital for years, or even centuries.

"I have to admit," he said, "in life, generally… I'm simply miserable most of the time. Not profoundly, just pathetically. Hurting myself doesn't even help much anymore. There's no kick. I feel like I'm playacting; my heart's not in it."

This was a hoped for but unexpected development. We had been working a lot on the causes of his self-injury compulsion, but for all his facile attempts to appease me by talking about his relationship with his mother, etcetera, I didn't think he was close to making any real behavioral change. Now it seemed his energy level was declining and he was becoming less engaged—troubling developments if they had occurred in the ordinary course of his life but unsurprising in his current environment—and at the same time he was losing his destructive urges.

I contrived, shortly thereafter, to leave a large retractable box-cutter in his room before having him locked in for the night.

I calculated that there was no way to disguise my intention. Still, intent wasn't the point. He would be alone with temptation with nothing to distract him.

If he was going to survive in the world outside the hospital, with ready access to sharp implements whenever he wanted them, then he'd have to survive this too. I had a rotation of nurses watching him through a concealed light-amplifying security camera so they could intercede in case he cut himself. But, though he didn't sleep much that night, he didn't harm himself. He merely scratched the wall with the blade.

When I visited him in the early morning, when his room was unlocked, I found that he had cut the words "Fuck this hospital" into the wall. He handed me the closed knife.

"I see you're making progress," I told him.

Strangely enough, I perceived that he was a little *disappointed* in himself that he had not slashed his flesh. There was no pride in his recovery, but he was recovering, and he had some of his fight back too.

To test his mood, I engaged him in a conversation on the topic of love right after he had undergone disorientation therapy. During the conversation, I made an off-hand comment about the "emotion of love." He responded with vehemence and strongly objected to this term.

"Love is not an emotion. How can a so-called scientist—a psychiatrist, of all people—be so sloppy in his use of language? But it's no surprise. The elemental... that which is most critical to our understanding of human beings and their nature... that atom which virtually defines us, completely eludes the understanding of the scientifically minded. You imagine you can test it, define it, probe it, or reduce it to a mere chemical reaction within the brain, a hormone rush... or you use fanciful terms like 'libido'... But you can't resolve such a simple question as 'What is love?'"

"You call that a simple question? It's been a challenge to every class and profession of man since the dawn of civilization."

"Well, I can certainly tell you what it's not," Seth insisted. "It's not an emotion. And you can't test it or measure it, but it's an absolutely real phenomenon. Tell me this: what is a lie detector?"

"Um… ok. I'm not sure why you ask, but a lie detector is a device that measures physiological reactions to determine whether a test subject is lying, or if they show signs that they are likely to be lying."

"Is it a *liar* detector?"

"What?"

"Is it a *liar* detector? No, don't answer; I'll answer. It is *not* a liar detector. You may be able to detect a lie, but you can't detect a liar."

"I frankly don't see your point."

"No, of course you don't."

"Being obscure doesn't prove higher intelligence. Explain yourself, and maybe I'll learn."

"You certainly have a lot to learn, because I don't think you know the first thing about love. Look, if you've got a suspected criminal strapped with a polygraph, maybe—maybe!—you can say 'He's lying now… and now he's telling the truth,' but you can't say 'This guy is a chronic liar. It's his nature to lie, it's his character.'"

"Hell, if I could make a machine to detect personality or psychopathology, it would save me a lot of trouble in diagnostics."

"Right. But you can't. Now, when some pseudo-scientist sits down and measures dopamine, or vasopressin, or breathing rates…"

"Hey, you didn't tell me you had studied up on the topic. But I should tell you right now, I've never subscribed to any chemical explanation of love."

"Well then you should be careful in what you unconsciously assume."

"Hah! The patient is becoming the therapist."

"Did Freud teach you to mock your patients during a therapy session too?"

"I'm not a Freudian."

"That's what all psychiatrists and psychotherapists say."

"I didn't think you had spoken to all psychiatrists and psychotherapists."

"You're argumentative! Listen, you can say Bill is happy right now, you can say he's sad right now, or even that he's aroused. You might even find a way to electronically 'detect' these things. But love is like a faith, a belief, a fear of spiders, a psychological inclination or tendency, a persistent state, but not an emotion."

"Okay, love is different from happiness." I made a note of this.

"Also, love does not have to be an absolute, any more than a belief in aliens. In some cases, people have a total certainty, in others their 'belief' expresses only a tentative compromise between conflicting arguments. Some can never be converted. Others may change their belief over time, or in different circumstances. But it doesn't switch on and off like the sensation of pleasure or pain, or the ephemeral condition of happiness."

"And how about your love for Kira? Is it tentative?"

"It is absolute."

"There are never any doubts?"

"There are *always* doubts. But the faith is always greater than the doubts."

I turned the conversation on this point, hoping to expose some of his doubts and find if his "love" was vulnerable to persuasion.

"Now," I said, "I've always seen you as a kind of skeptic, so answer me this: what did you feel when you first met Kira? When you first saw her?"

"Love."

"Arousal, which you interpreted as love. You're not going to tell me that it's coincidence that your love found a remarkably beautiful woman as its object? Especially as your love was confirmed before any chance for conversation, any chance to really know her mind?"

"Call it what you will. If it was arousal at first, it developed into love, and that progress shows that the first faith—that was born in an instant—was well founded."

"So you're saying that, *retroactively*, it was love at first sight. Because you *claim* you love her now."

"Yes exactly! You think you're arguing with me, but you're just proving my point. And what's with this 'claim'? You think that an undemonstrable 'claim' is somehow contrary to 'faith'? The faith was there. It is there. It persists."

"And what is that faith founded on? When have you progressed past the tits-and-ass phase of your 'faith'?"

"Faith need not be founded at all. But I will tell you exactly what it is founded on tomorrow, and I won't be baited by your crude reduction of love to just a physical act."

Well, the next day he did not take up exactly where we left off, but he did set out to explain why he loved Kira. He also strayed more into poetic and metaphorical expressions such as he was accustomed to use before his hospitalization.

"When you last released me from the hospital, I realized how wrong it was for me to run from Kira. She had terrified me, but the terror was an ecstasy—something a brave soul could never turn away from. I found courage in my desire to embrace that terror and ecstasy. And when, as I exited the hospital and rushed to return to her embrace, I approached her, I saw her gripped by a passion to surpass my own! True, its physical manifestation was subtle, a quiver of the lip, a shift of the eyes, a discomfort and hesitation detectable in the tension of her voice as she began to speak the words 'I don't care if you're dangerous.'

"'You're speaking my heart and mind,' I told her. I wanted to go on, and tell her that I'd go through anything, face any challenge, just to possess her. But she didn't require any declarations. It was the unspoken understanding that passed between us in an instant that confirmed our love. She knew me. I knew her.

"Our passion that night was physical and intense, but I've sworn to speak no more explicitly about that. And that too was merely an expression of a far deeper spiritual passion that was infinite in its desire to hold, and infinite in its generous desire to please, even if it meant sacrifice, even if it meant death.

"We spoke inspired words of sincere love, and we spoke in a sacred language I can't share with you.

"Starting again, we talked of everything trivial too, as we did in the early days, our little hobbies and interests. And in the way she *saw* me, in the way she tensed, and relaxed, and laughed, and shrugged, we knew and understood each other even more, by knowing that the superficialities were of no consequence.

"I've made many confessions to her, and she's made her confessions to me. I told her of my old life, hiding nothing that was shameful... though I didn't dwell on women... I couldn't talk about that other than to say that there *had been* women... and to speak the truth, which was that they never touched my heart even for an instant.

"She could not believe it was so, and she accused me of exaggerating my love for her, denying my love for others. At the same time, she had to confess that she *had* been touched... she had loved. But everything she thought had been wrong and deficient in her 'cruder, more childish affairs,' she swore that I surpassed all her other loves, that I could not know the true extent of how much she loved me and how she now abandoned herself entirely to me.

"I wanted to know why. Why would she do that for someone like me? She couldn't explain with logic. But she could persuade. I know now, as I knew then, that it was true. We had reached a higher love.

"That was not enough for me though. The wound in my heart is incurable, knowing that she actually *loved* before she met me. It hurt more, even, than her subsequent infidelities of a purely physical nature. It hurt more than the knowledge of her secret whoring.

"Her parents hate me. We've never met, but they hate me. Kira's too honest when she speaks to her family. I can't blame them for wanting her to have something more than what I can offer—superficially!—but that ineffable passion, that intense certainty that she and I *must* be together... that she and I, by being together, redeem everything that was wrong... fix everything that was broken in our lives before we met... Her parents are fools not to know how much this joy means to her and me. We swore an oath—unspoken, but still spoken in other words and other languages—that we would not be separated for the world, though we suffer for it… we will not be driven apart.

"The truth is that Kira's friends have all given her up for lost. We socialized together at times. They let me into their circle, and I tolerated their little jokes. I tried to be 'fun,' and 'normal.' We went to movies, we sat in pubs, they drank and smoked, I nibbled snacks and tried my best to be patient. But at times it was just intolerable. I only wanted to be with Kira, and I couldn't get over the feeling that the others were… going to ruin things somehow. She didn't say and do what so many other women might have done. She didn't insist that I try harder, that I relax, that I "blend." She socialized with her friends less and less, she spent her time with me more and more. We were in our world. Estelle joked about Kira's eccentricity, and made a brutal comment about how she was 'mad for man-flesh.'

"The only thing Kira didn't compromise on was her responsibility to her job. The job kept her away a lot. It made sense, obviously, neither of us can survive without some kind of income… and she says she's good at what she does. That's when I came upon the idea that she could be cheating."

"You *came upon* the idea?" I asked. "You know that you have a lot of 'ideas.' Why did you trust this one?"

"She confessed. I asked her, and she confessed. Not to everything, but to many things. She told me that she cheats."

"Then…" I hesitated, wondering.

"Don't bother to tell me. You know what I told you from the start. Nothing will separate us."

FURTHER DEVELOPMENTS

Now that Seth was showing more of his old spirit, I repeated the experiment with the box-cutter. Again, he spent the night safely without giving in to the temptation to cut himself. There was no guarantee he would continue this way after a release, but this was still encouraging. From this point forward, he had an option each night. He could sleep with the box-cutter, but he'd have to be locked in for the safety of other patients and staff; or he could sleep with his door unlocked but with no sharp implements. Most nights he preferred to be locked in with his knife.

Kira attempted to visit again, and she was again turned away. This time she left a handwritten message for me.

The message read: "You need to let me talk to Seth, or talk to you. You surely have misunderstood him, and you can't really understand me. He has no one else to advocate for him here. Meet with me and you'll see that I'm good for him. I can help him."

As I'd expected, there was no useful information in this message, and it was not something I could respond to, so I filed it away. I did not tell Seth about this visit either.

Seth's mood was changeable, and at times he became despairing. I think he was also processing a lot, and starting to draw some sensible conclusions.

One day he took up the topic of the time he spent in prison.

"Prison was worse than this. But at least then I had something to look forward to. Freedom seemed to have a lot of potential. But it was a horrific place. I don't care if you think segregation is safer than living in the general prison population, I'm sure it is, but they can never keep you completely safe. One guy got his lower lip cut off—I mean, completely. And the scream he made... you can't imagine it, and the effect it has on us. Our cages stank with the horrible musk of fear for at least a week after that. There was already a fear, we all knew that something like that and worse was likely to happen to us... it could happen at any moment. And trapped in our cells with that... You can't trust the guards either, obviously. Some of them were sadists of the worst kind. They have less respect for us than for animals. Not all of them, but... they're a part of the prison culture too, and us guys in segregation are part of the lowest caste. If the guards didn't have their own fear of consequences for going too far, they'd probably massacre us all in a day.

"But I knew my term was not going to be very, very long, and there was a whole world of experience on the outside that I hadn't had yet. Maybe not *everything* was possible, but *some things* were possible. I still hadn't had any experience with women, so I didn't have any stories to tell. And stories are pretty important inside. Some of the stories I heard… inspired me.

"But now I've had my taste of 'free' life. I realize there's nothing in it. Nothing but Kira. If she were not waiting for me when I got out, there'd really be no point in it.

"The real trouble, I think, is that I'm starting to realize I'm no good for her. I'm taking away her potential. How dare I expect her to make sacrifices or limit herself? For what?

"This is a very serious dilemma for me. Something I've got to work out."

Shifting Perspectives/End of the Month

A lot can happen in a month, we spoke about more than I can relate here, and he responded in a variety of ways to therapy. He alternated between reasserting his pledges to spend his life with Kira and reflections on his own inability to provide a happy and secure life for her. He would not *blame* her for having affairs, in the sense of holding her morally responsible, but he couldn't really come to terms with this behavior and its implications for their relationship. At times he spoke of *disappearing*.

As time passed, it was clear that not all of these issues would be resolved, but Seth had his compulsion under control and he was capable of rational discourse. He did pull one disturbing stunt when he used his box-cutter to cut his own hair. I thought that this testing-of-limits was a dangerous game to play. But he was overall cooperative and showed a desire for self-improvement. In the final judgment, it appeared safe for him to give the outside world another go. If only he would stay away from Kira!

Seth's mind was occupied by his expectation of imminent release, and two days before the end of his commitment term, he said, "I'll be out soon. Then I'll be back with her."

"How are you?" I asked him.

"Unbroken."

"Does that mean that you're *still* committed to Kira as the most important thing in your life? You know, *you* are the most important thing in your life. Your first step out the door doesn't have to be a permanent life-defining decision. Most people, in their relationships, just try things out to see how they feel. They leave the big decisions for later."

"I already know how it feels."

"I'm not just talking about the good things, you have to consider the pain and chaos that constantly threaten to turn your life upside down."

"When has my life been right-side-up?"

"That's the way people speak when they've gone beyond their emotional pain-threshold. But you have known some good times, some stable times... But think again. Really think..."

"I'm thinking."

"About her. Whether her life needs to be turned upside down too."

"Yeah..."

And then his final day arrived, and I had him brought into my office again.

"Seth, you should go away for a while. See what your life is like away from Kira and away from me. Do you think you can afford a trip?" (I knew he had gotten a little money from his Uncle, and he'd put some other money aside as well).

"Maybe. If I travel cheap. But it's kind of... wasteful to do so."

"Just plan carefully, and I'll do my best to get you a referral for a job of some sort when you return. You could see your uncle, or go see a boxing match. Something you enjoy for yourself."

He didn't respond, but he seemed to be considering it. And I wondered if he would really discover the strength to make the big sacrifice, to ultimately let Kira go, for her sake if not for his own.

It was only a few hours and a few formalities later when he was released, though I didn't see him go, as I was attending to another patient.

7.
The Final Reversal, Plus One

KIRA SPEAKS

The very next day I was sitting idly in my office at the other end of the center when Kira McFee walked in on me, and the reader can imagine how shaken I was by her unheralded materialization.

Immediately, as she walked in, my phone rang, and as I fumbled with the receiver I was told by reception "Kira McFee would like to speak to you. She's waiting in the lobby."

"No, she isn't. She just walked in."

"Oh! Sorry Dr. Shieling," said the receptionist, "I..."

I hung up, and I half-rose from my seat, embarrassed.

"What did you do to Seth?" Kira demanded at once.

"I... I didn't do anything. I treated him."

Her beauty was terrifying when she stood so close. No, Seth hadn't exaggerated at all. I sat back down in my seat, and she remained standing.

"Listen, you have to bring him back. I'm desperate."

"I don't really understand. What are you desperate about? I released him yesterday."

She looked around the office, confused.

"There's a chair right in front of you."

"Oh."

She sat. Her thoughts were wandering. I glanced, without intent, at her body.

Kira's fingers touched the dark wood surface of my desk. Was she really hypersexual? Her fingers of her left hand unconsciously moved to her own right forearm, and she caressed her skin while her mind was... elsewhere. It was somehow the most unanticipated and spontaneous erotic moment. She was with him in her mind, panting slightly, and pink in the face and neck. Her eyes pinched closed and a tear fell. I've witnessed every kind of behavior when alone with patients, or even in group settings, but I was unprepared for this.

"Christ! Christ, don't let me lose this. I can't."

Her eyes opened, and she looked into me with a burning intensity.

"You can't let me lose him, Percy. You don't know... he has transformed my life. The sadness that filled me... the emptiness... has been filled with such a passion. This world is very petty, very small, and hurtful, if you want to know the truth of it. But it sparkles in Seth's presence, he brings me such hope and such happiness, like something I never thought possible. I'm sure he's told you everything about me and him, and I don't care. No one should dare to take this away from us. It's like... to murder a child."

"I... I would never have expected to hear anything like this. I wanted Seth to find something like the happiness you speak of, but be honest. Hasn't it all been miserable? Don't you see how hurt he is, and how helpless? He's not capable of the kind of human connection you're after..."

"Don't tell me what he's capable of."

"...and your infidelity will drive him to his death. If not that, he'll do something reckless and be imprisoned."

"I won't let him go, not for my life, and not for his!"

I leapt up. I couldn't stand it.

"Why are you here? Are you telling me he's gone? If so, thank God. You're more fanatical than he."

She laughed a bit at the absurdity of my statement, and wiped away a few tears.

"You've only learned about me from what he's told you. You've only learned about *him* the same way. But he doesn't know himself at all. He's fragile, he's self-pitying when he should be proud, but when he's proud, when he thinks that he is a great man, he doesn't love himself as much as I love him. And when he praises me... it's absurd... I feel high and giddy, but I can never live up to his image of me."

"No one but you would say that." Could she see herself? Did she know how the world looked at Seth, and how they'd compare the two?

"You're just like all men. You're superficial. You imagine that I am something wonderful. I'm not. But when I'm with him... I almost rise to the level of his dreams."

"But then you turn to other men for your fulfillment."

"Do you believe that? What have you learned about Seth in the month you had him here?"

"Not as much as I'd thought." I paused. Had Seth completely imagined her infidelity? "Enlighten me."

"Of course Seth believes I cheat. It's what he expects. He's a jealous man, that's all there is to it. And once, just once, in the midst of his badgering and accusations, I said 'You're right. I've cheated on you, and I'm gonna do it again!' But... that was just vicious words spoken in anger. Can he never forgive this normal human impulse to lash out... just once? When I think of it, it tears me to pieces, I feel so degraded. But never in my life will I have even an unfaithful thought. My devotion is unshakable."

"Those are strong claims. But why do you force the issue? Aren't you able to see... he's not cut out for such a turbulent affair. Let him be wrong about you, or let him know the truth, but let him go."

"There's something about this guy, you don't see it, but I see it. He's not just a human wreck. He's exquisitely beautiful, a whole soul, under the pain he's something... I won't lose that."

"If he left the hospital and didn't go straight back to you, perhaps you've already lost it."

She threw herself down in a heap. It was like seeing someone throw a precious vase upon a marble floor, and I gasped. Then she lifted herself up slightly and glanced at me through her tears, in a nearly manic state.

"Listen," I said. I tried to keep my composure. "Human relations... love relations, have such intensity and such turbulent passions involved that no one on the outside can fully fathom them.

But you and he are a danger to yourselves and each other. And *he's* my patient. It's his interests I have to look out for. You may want the best, but if the only way to keep him from ruin is to see the two of you separated... you are the one who can more easily rise, get yourself together, and start again.... The best he can hope for is some degree of normalcy. If he can get that without you, you have to let him go."

She rose. How tall was she? Had she grown larger?

"I told you I wouldn't. And you must know where he went. You're the lowest bastard if you won't tell me."

"I thought he was going to run to you. If he hasn't... I have three ideas of where he may be," I said. "But I can't tell you any of them. You have to leave now."

She took her seat again. She muttered to me, she pleaded, and she told me of all the sweet things he had said and done for her, the beauty of his soul, the honor of his character, all repeated, all again, with more details piled on, she demanded and cajoled, but after all that she left...when *she* had decided that going was right, when she had finally concluded that my stubbornness had put me beneath her contempt.

When she rose from her seat, I did not hold out my hand to help her, not because I was not a gentleman, but because I didn't dare to make even the most casual physical contact. I didn't even dare to touch the door as she passed through. Though I had been stern, I was nonetheless awed by her, and I ached with an unspoken desire... and—I'll admit it—envy for what Seth had had.

SETH'S DECISION

Seth was gone and life went on. New troubles with other patients dominated my attention, while I had not heard from him—or from Kira—for some time.

When, one evening, my mind was on other little things, as I was walking in the neighborhood near the hospital just daydreaming about the ingredients of a meal I was going to cook for myself, someone suddenly stomped the heel of his foot into the back of my knee, and I tumbled face-first onto the pavement. There was no time to wonder what was happening. Next I felt a fist pounding me, then I was forcefully rolled over. Seth was standing there, over me.

"She walked in," he said, "in the dead of night, thinking I was gone. How ashamed I was of my momentary lapse. How could I explain to her why I didn't run to her at the first opportunity?" He was short of breath. "But I will never hurt her that way again," he continued. "I'll abandon myself before I abandon her. She's suffered a lot for me. Why should I turn away now? You've failed, doctor, and righteousness has won. Some might call my life choices regrettable, but I say that every act is regrettable… only if we choose to regret."

I was very shaken, as you'd expect, but when he'd gone and I'd recovered my wits, I felt sorry for Seth.

I never heard from him again after this—not directly. But I did get an update on his medical history, not long ago. After another infection brought on by self-injury, his arm was amputated above the elbow to save him from the rapid spread of gangrene. He suffers a profound suffering. He's made his choice.

The Wisdom of Tameka Williams

1.
An Unknown Patient

A Brief Sketch of Tameka

There is not much I can say about Tameka Williams. She was not my patient, and I only met her once. Her doctor was one of the fellows at my hospital, the talented Dr. Miguel Moncayo. He made his best effort for her, but three years of therapy produced no results.

Tameka never spoke about herself, her problems, or her life. She instead made only philosophical pronouncements—or *pseudo-philosophical*, abstract pronouncements. Moncayo noted that she seemed to rely on a repertoire of self-composed aphorisms. But every day the phrasing and sequence of these aphorisms changed. She spoke to anyone she could grab by the sleeve, and she cornered me this way a few times. Sometimes she was observed mumbling to herself, to an invisible audience, or to the walls. Dr. Moncayo suspected there was a deep and complex pattern within the sequence of her pronouncements, but I could detect nothing of the sort.

Dr. Moncayo, after consulting with me a few times, requested I meet with Tameka personally. Which I did. Once.

I asked Tameka, "Teach me." She spoke as if she were pronouncing a *received wisdom*, and the following is what she said:

2.
What She Said

A pocketful of coins is one thing, but a pocketful of people is another. Watch me turn, see me bend, observe the grace with which I spring. No applause is sufficient reward for my performance. As a girl, I collected dolls. Now artists, poets, and the greatest intellects have become my playthings. I would strip you of your skin to wear it as a coat. I would strip you of your thoughts and string them like beads upon a necklace, to wear as an adornment.

Pride reclines on a comfortable couch in a house with no mirrors.

Philosophers strive to discover the truth, but the powerful merely define it. The deep-rooted, strong-limbed tree is not troubled by a little wind. Power and prestige stand most firmly on a foundation of experience.

Place your knowledge on one pan, and a loaf of bread on the other pan. Which way does the scale tip? When they are exchanged, who profits? One must be aware of one's culture, learn it, profit from it; but don't be defined by it.

Any conclusion can be supported with reason.

On the other hand, the stars were not placed in the sky merely to teach us when to plant.

The crocodile king swallows chickens whole. Some would teach the world one value above all: accumulate. When ambition is not guided by a great intellect, it is wisest to subdue the passions. Disaster may be averted by opening just one eye.

The stone idol is noble without passion. Unmoved by cries of joy or sorrow, it is adored. An enlightened leader is gracious, bounteous in season, but never lavish, while remaining deaf to praise or criticism. In short, he is a fruit tree. If we pluck cherries from the cherry tree, it might rain.

Deep within the mind-well, the explorer gets lost in infinite ramifications.

There once was a man who had ice-water for blood. He was dirt poor, but his heart was clean. Desire nothing, and you'll get it. I trample upon my own passions. I scorn even scornfulness. The way opens up before me.

The "old hat" is immune to injury. People are eager to go nowhere when he serves as their guide. There are even those who forget to feel. They omit themselves from their own ideals. Crystal castles keep out anything that could move them. The ones whose faith is cold enough to freeze, they choose choicelessly to follow fate. In their eyes, fortune is seen over every horizon. Some poor souls, tossed hither and thither, rising then falling, resign themselves to the tempest. "Surely something good must come of this," they half-believe.

When the weather gets cold, draw close to the fire. Let others gather wood.

What must it be like to look down the world's longest nose?

Knowledge is a personal journey, it cannot be shared. Ignorance is the first step on the road to knowledge. Apprehension is preceded by misapprehension. The hermit equates physical distance with spiritual distance—what a mistake! Wisdom is an ecstasy that can lift one out of the world. The master shows the way by walking straight through mountains and rivers. The human psyche can be seen clearly within the shape of a stone carved by the river's flow.

Has the sun ever eaten corn?

It is greater to nurture the spirit before the body. Trust in nature's provision. Those around you will stand amazed. The eagle's beak is blunted, its talons broken. A winged rabbit flies: pure awareness.

What can we say of the Idealist who embraces neither wealth nor comfort, who is neither leader nor follower? This one remains unshaken as cities crumble. The earth opens beneath his feet. When you scorn the gold with all its weight, it is easier to take flight. This is certain.

The moth seeks the flame. Can we deny our sympathy for this creature's naïve and impotent sacrifice?

Look into the distance; who is that who now leads the charge, and why are we not following in the restless surge? He is a naked man with a sunburned back. He has discarded his wisest reservations, along with his clothing. Millions raise their eyes and sigh to see the spirit's rise toward heaven. The celestial pathways are not to be trodden by mortal foot, nor can the mind of man comprehend their windings.

Look at the prodigal king. He leads by his ruinous generosity. He tips his coffers out and scatters his substance. He will burn brightly and quickly before turning to ash. "Tear down the palace walls!" cried the prince of poverty. "Let us all be equal in our misery." The crowd lifted him on their shoulders. He was wearing a tin crown.

What's that throbbing sound? What's that din? My God! He's arrived! The ecstasy will consume you if he catches you with his glance. Value? What is value? Try to teach it to the romantic youth. Whatever you hold dear, he accounts as nothing. For one thrill, the stirring of his heart, he'd trade his very life. Passion intoxicates. Its victim is torn to shreds by violent spinning.

The aesthete strives to make the mind an analogue of the universe; will this analogue include an analogue of the mind itself?

Some appreciate society as theater. To them, message is nothing, import: everything. Others find their pleasure—and advantage!—in social engagement. Some are whipped into a frenzy by their own passion for experience. They spend their nights in brothels and die on the wheel of St. Catherine.

The heart, in fact, flows only with blood.

Experience is not always the best teacher. To feel much and understand little is the mark of the false sage. A general stood on the frontier. He received the order from his president: "Push the border as far as it will go." He did so, but he pushed it in the wrong direction! The winner of a horse race is skillful in wielding the whip. A rich man with no ideals can surely afford to rent them. Even without knowledge, one can possess the fruits of knowledge. Great power can be found within the pages of a bankbook.

In a dirt field, one clod of earth got kicked around more than any other. Was he, thus, the king of clods?

Select, then, to believe only that which suits you best. To break the rules is easy, once you've learned the rules of rules.

A merchant is an expert at reckoning value. The brightest gem is darkest in its heart. Sometimes real gold can be found in a fake goldmine.

If the energy of sexual climax were a substance, how well could one sleep upon a bed of that substance?

The most accomplished plunderer sometimes loses a prize, and the prize he does get loses its relish. One who never sleeps never dreams. When knowledge is complete, ideals are forgotten.

Thoughts turn in upon themselves—a psychic maelstrom.

There are those who are deaf to everything but echoes, which they believe can tell a truer story. Do you possess life, or does it possess you? Is your life merely an island in the vast ocean of death?

The boys like to play wizard. Watch them wave their magic wands; conquered ladies are their pride and pleasure. Seduction is akin to enslavement. Snake-charmers eat little children.

In every society, opinion comes from one or two. Consensus is a form of tyranny.

I sit where I am. I remain content. "Pssst." There's a whisper. "Look behind this door. What lingers in the shadows here?" Now, how can I resist?

There is a thrill to be found in leading a mob of angry men. Sensitivity threatens the intellect. Then the fruit of knowledge goes overripe. Is the very substance of the soul sordid, or is there something transcendent within? The most crippling affliction is to feel the suffering of others as well as one's own.

On the night before my death by hanging, I had a brilliant insight. I suddenly saw the beauty of a world without gravity.

What a piteous plight to be invested in human affairs. In such a state, foresight is no better than hindsight. Does the mind delight in discovering the final element of a mystery? The mind's work is accomplished through focus, fortitude, and isolation from distracting elements. Privateers leave humanity behind when they set out from port. Turn the earth inside out, or bury oneself alive—what's the difference? Every treasure offers three thrills: the anticipation, the discovery, and the possession.

Some engage in private enthusiasms, which can be all-consuming. There are those who would read messages even in the shape of the ocean's waves. This becomes their private poetry. Some are led by their dreams to roam in the wilderness, till every wood and every field swarms with lonely wanderers. You can meet idealists anywhere, at any time. I once met one outside the supermarket at 9:39 on a Thursday night. He said, "I don't give a damn what you think of me, lady." "Really?" I asked, "What do you care about?" "Got a cigarette?"

In the earth's deep recesses, the hot-blooded serpents lie. With a thousand claws they swim in liquid gold. The very rocks around them burn with hatred.

The universe delights in its own self-possession. What need is there for more than one mind?

There was a miserable wretch who was generous within his means. One lucky day he got a taste of comfort, and it cured him of his charitable thoughts.

There are those who fling themselves into the waves upon a boat without a tiller. They trust the tide to lead them to salvation. Without a battering-ram, one method for breaching a wall still presents itself: dash your brains against it. I will not call this a wrongheaded approach. It is suitable for mules. If you glance upon a cipher dressed in rags, contempt closes your eyes. Yet he too has lofty ideals and a raging pulse. Sink low, but look high. From the bottom of the well you will see the sky. Cast all the world away—or be cast out!

A corpse may be animated, without a will. It goes where it is accustomed. Puppets too can enjoy the dance upon strings. But what of the man who stares eternally into the eternal light? There is no self there. Upon his vanishing, will you mourn? If so, for whom? The universe in all its apparent complexity can surely be understood by a determined, inquisitive mind. To discover truth, one must seek without desire.

For some, belief in their own superiority is a faith bordering on certainty.

When peace comes, the once-thundering heart falls silent. At the end of the race, the winner doesn't mind a few blisters. To believe that a chicken in every pot will end man's hunger is to forget the stomach's tendency to expand. Even the ignorant know their own desires.

The mountains, the oceans, the fields and streams, the cities and their occupants, are only drops of a precious liquor which the lord sips from—from time to time—according to his pleasure.

One cold winter night, I entered a bar where I was a stranger and ordered a drink. When I finished, I stood up to leave. As I reached the door, a man sitting at the bar called out, "Where are you going? It's cold out." Was he flirting? I was annoyed by his question. "Anywhere...," I said, "Everywhere!" But the man at the bar was no longer interested. He had just been served another glass, and his face was suffused with contentment. Then: "Where *am* I going?" I wondered aloud.

I once asked a fool what he thought. He's still answering. I should have asked him what he knows. Stupidity walks on two legs. A mind plagued by misapprehension is a comic tragedy. In obscurity, the one-man crusade pursues its own ideal. By dumb luck, the ignorant can stumble into an earthly paradise. Grasping what can only be felt with thick fingers, they declare, "Society be damned!"

Architects of Utopia see their creation by closing their eyes. Holding out their hands, they touch a whisper.

If you trust neither heart nor mind, black acid will drop into your eyes. Visions of goals will be erased, and frustration will be forgotten.

The man whose head is aglow with faith and passion proves thoughtless. He aims at lofty goals, yet leads the way into a blind alley. An Idealist—living passion—leaps into the inferno. He comes tumbling from the tower's peak. No thought stands between him and the decision to shatter his frame and discard his very flesh.

The brightness of my lover's face turned all the world to shadows.

Some people's charm is all context. With the right ambiance, they appear divine.

Burn the books, and bury the scholars. I am the beginning of history. And what of the man who dares compare me with Emperor Qin Shi Huang? Burn him too.

Look at the ruler who plays the clown and makes a sorry spectacle. His example is a warning. "Do not go where I lead." In battle he runs to the head of the crowd through the blackest night and falls into a chasm. A golden crown must be fitted carefully to the wearer, or there is a risk that it may slip down over the eyes.

When the social machine produces well, the lords can be seen to smile. They never ask "How?" They only ask, "How much?"

Bernard Williams

1.
Crisis of Faith

All of my colleagues would laugh to scorn the idea of an *intellectual madness*. But Bernard Williams, a former skeptic and former Catholic monk, was the only patient I've had who came close to convincing me he could be cured by reasoning alone.

Bernard's story, simply told, is that he was convinced of the existence of God because he had seen a ghost, he devoted himself entirely to the Catholic faith, he became a monk, and then he experienced a psychic shock that shattered his faith when he witnessed the face of God. In that moment, Bernard became extremely and permanently dizzy.

While I have encountered some cases of chronic dizziness from psychological causes, it is relatively rare, usually intermittent, and tends to occur only under stress. Significantly more common are the cases of temporary vertigo brought on in the wake of a major trauma, or as part of an attack of anxiety. But Bernard's dizziness was without respite, and was severe enough to be crippling. He was unable to walk unassisted, and he tended to roll his head and contort his neck, shoulders, and arms unless he was allowed to sit or lie prone and grip the edges of a bed or other furniture. His eyes darted about rapidly, and he often complained that his dizziness produced odd illusions. He reported seeing distant objects passing in front of closer objects, and sometimes he saw the reverse side of an object such as the back page of a newspaper lying front-page-up, or the back of my chair while I was facing him directly.

There was no point in trying to correct his perception by, for instance, turning over the newspaper on the desk to show him a headline he couldn't predict. He knew he was seeing an illusion, but he couldn't prevent it.

During our conversations, Bernard routinely closed his eyes

for a few minutes at a time whenever he wanted to concentrate, but this never lessened his physical sense of vertigo. It merely cut out some of the distracting and unreliable visual information that he experienced with open eyes. He was no more able to walk blindfolded than with unobstructed vision.

It should be unnecessary for me to point out that several doctors had run many tests to rule out any likely physiological causes for Bernard's dizziness. We did not neglect to consider stroke, inner-ear trauma, neurological disorders, epilepsy, drug abuse, reactions to medical treatment, environmental factors, and so on. It *should* be unnecessary, but I have learned that it is sometimes necessary to state the obvious or else be accused of negligence, incompetence, or quackery. I will not permit the less generous readers to thus accuse me, while I expect the more generous readers will forgive this *unnecessary* tangential disclaimer.

One would imagine that many months of extreme vertigo would make a person incapable of structured rational thought, and the horrifying prospect of a lifetime feeling the world spin, as though one were tumbling down a mountain in a barrel, would lead to a kind of ego annihilation. But Bernard liked to talk, and as a conversationalist he seemed like a mostly normal, though highly intellectual, perhaps overly meditative man. His speech was occasionally interrupted by a gasp, but he otherwise communicated well.

The Nature of Ghosts

Until he was twenty-six year old, Bernard was an atheist—a second generation atheist whose parents had never exposed him to the inside of a church, though his maternal grandparents were Catholic and his father's family identified themselves as Christians of no particular denomination. Bernard was a skeptic who rejected all magical thinking and belief in supernatural phenomena. Then he saw a ghost, or so he says. In fact, he says he was bitten by one.

"A ghost is not what you would imagine a ghost to be," he told me. "No. Rather, a ghost is a kind of animal. It's a living, breathing

thing—solid. There's nothing ethereal about it, but it has all the terror you associate with ghosts. It is a human spirit, to be sure, but when it manifests in our world, it is a thing with muscle, sinew, and bone."

I think it best now to let Bernard's own voice report the major events of his life before hospitalization.

2.
Bernard Tells How His Life Was Transformed

Ghost Sighting

A ghost, or at least the ghost I saw, is a kind of hair-covered thing, with odd white and black—or very dark brown—patterns. It's kind of like what horse fanciers call a *tovero* horse, in terms of coloration pattern, though of course a ghost is not horse-shaped. You have to imagine this creature with dark spotting, stark whiteness and a dark, not quite symmetrical "medicine hat" over the top of the head and ears… but also a bit more stripe-like than a tovero horse displays, sort of an echoed medicine hat… the analogy is not perfect.

The limbs of the ghost that I saw were sort of indistinct, solid to be sure, but due to the unfamiliar hair patterns, the unexpectedly large number of joints which are quite different from those found in a human or horse limb, and their rapid movement, it was hard for me to perceive their precise shape or even their number.

The face was only vaguely humanoid in shape, and only vaguely equine, while momentarily appearing as something closer to a hyena or badger. The genitals were large and stark in their black coloration against the otherwise paper-white surface of the lower torso and groin. They flapped about in a flaccid and vulgar way. I wouldn't say that they exactly resembled a male member. They were something fleshy or rubbery with an unusual shape in the region where one would normally expect the genitals to reside.

Oh, of course I should probably mention the circumstances of my encounter, and how I concluded that what I was seeing was in fact a ghost. Well, I was in New York City, walking briskly up Broadway at about four in the morning, passing through the mid-twenties… I mean crossing the streets around twenty-fifth street. I didn't take note of exactly the street number. It was a cold autumn night, I had just been drinking and smoking in a dive bar on east fourteenth, and I was walking up towards Penn Station to wait for the morning trains to start running. I felt uncomfortable being alone at this time of night, in this commercial area, when there was virtually no one out except the homeless and a wandering maniac or two.

I walked past one side street, where I considered turning west and cutting across to Seventh Avenue, but I saw a tall dark-skinned man walking along the sidewalk practicing martial arts moves, kicking his leg high, and shouting "Hah motherfucker," at no one in particular. I'm not going to say he was black. I don't know. Maybe he was Latino.

Anyway, I avoided him and kept on my way up Broadway, when two blocks further up I saw some thuggish-looking kids with sticks, poking at a dead body in the middle of the street. Where they got sticks that looked like tree branches, in this part of New York City, I have no idea, nor do I have any idea why the guy was dead. He was a bloody mess though, with his abdomen open and his intestines slightly uncoiled. His face was pretty much gone.

I shouted "Hey" at the guys who were poking the corpse. It was kind of an instinct. I wanted to walk away, but I shouted at them against my own better judgment. Strangely, the guys—who I think were maybe in their late teens, or maybe just a few years younger than myself—well, they talked to each other in a mumble and retreated with no particular haste. Then one said to me, so I could just barely hear him, "Do you know this guy?" meaning the corpse. Well, I said, "That's irrelevant."

Then the kids, whose faces I hadn't seen so distinctly because of the distance and the bad lighting, well they just turned and walked away. I stood still and watched them go to the end of the block and round the corner, and though I wanted to flee and leave this scene behind me, I found I couldn't. I walked cautiously towards the dead man. There were taxis passing up Broadway behind me, but none were driving along this street. I saw a man and a woman over on the next avenue turn towards me, then pause—perhaps they could see something strange was going on—and they turned back.

So, I was alone with the dead man, but as I approached, the dead man rolled himself over and crawled, dragging his guts and broken legs, very rapidly into the space under a parked car. The car was too low to the ground for a normal person to crawl under, and certainly no one could get under it so quickly, even if his head was tiny or pressed nearly flat and his body was unnaturally thin… and this guy had looked pretty big and bony.

I now knew that I was witnessing something supernatural, and I froze. There was then a loud and grotesque farting sound under the car. I know it sounds both silly and absurd, but I'm just reporting the facts. And then the ghost came out from under the car. I realized that this ghost was not the man I had seen, but he had been eating the man, or a part of him. The ghost's body was intact, and he had a piece of intestine in his mouth, which he swallowed up. While the ghost and I were looking each other over, I saw the hand and arm of the dead man reach out from under the car and flail about in an effort to grasp the ghost's foot. The dead man's voice, sounding like his throat was full of viscous liquid, gurgled "Give it back!" But then the ghost turned and shat on the man's hand, and when the shit hit the man's hand he cried out 'Oh my God, I'm dead!' and he vanished completely.

My eyes suddenly flowed with tears, and I was free to turn and run, but the ghost ran me down easily, knocked me to the ground, and bit the flesh of my back. I thought he'd kill me, but he just stamped a bit upon my head and body, then ran on to somewhere in the east.

I crawled quickly to get out of the street and, again by a sort of instinct, I tried to crawl under a parked car near the curb, but I couldn't fit under it. Then I realized that I was still alive, and I laughed at the confusion that had made me identify with the dead man for a moment. I picked myself up and ran out of there.

On Broadway, I flagged down a cab. The cabbie stopped, but he wouldn't let me get in the taxi. He drove across to the other side of the avenue to keep some distance from me, then got out of his cab and called over to me.

"I'll get you an ambulance, but I'm not taking any bloody guys in my cab. I'm sorry." Then he called an ambulance on his cell phone. I felt rather helpless and stupid. Then he called across to me again, "What happened to you, did someone stab you or something?"

"I was bitten by a monster!"

"A monster?! Oh, fuck!"

He was panicked. I had expected that he wouldn't take me seriously, or that he'd think I was a nut, but he just took it for a fact that there are monsters in the world. I was tempted to call him a credulous fool on that account, but then I realized with suddenness that I was no longer in a position to challenge someone else's beliefs. It had been my own stubborn *incredulity* which left me unprepared for the event that befell me.

The cabbie then crossed to my side of the street.

"Let me see that."

He approached and looked over the wound on my back.

"Oh, man! You've got some kind of ghost saliva mixed into your blood!"

"What? What are you talking about?" I tried to look over my shoulder, but couldn't see my wound or bloodied clothes. "What do you see? Are you some kind of psychic or something? How do you know what ghost saliva looks like?"

"I don't know nothing, man, but this ghost saliva is showing me pictures or something. There's this dead guy, he was a lawyer, but he also did strange sexual things… he stole a lot of money, and the day he died he was unrepentant. That's just what the pictures are telling me…"

"You sound like a lunatic," I told him. "Get away from me!"

"I'm going man, I can't look at this anymore. But the ghost told me through the pictures in his saliva that I should warn you of the necessity of finding God. He said you were lucky to still have your soul in your body. Hell has almost claimed you. Oh, fuck!"

And then he ran to his cab and drove away.

The ambulance then arrived. While the paramedics were helping me get into the ambulance, and as they applied first aid to my wound, I noticed that I was having difficulty hearing them, though my hearing had been clear a minute before. When I told them this, one paramedic looked in my ears.

He pulled something out of each ear canal and said "What the Hell is this, some kind of voodoo? You've got a dead man's fingernails in your ears." He showed them to me, and sure enough he had two whole fingernails in his palm.

"How do you know they're from a dead man?" I asked him.

"There's signs of decomposition and mold upon them," he declared. "But we also found a dead guy two years back with fingernails in his ears, and they weren't his either. The police matched them to DNA from the severed fingers of a lawyer they had shot to death while he was trying to escape from a courthouse jail—a crooked lawyer they had up on some kind of fraud charges. His left-hand fingers were blasted off in the shooting, but four fingernails were mysteriously missing. The fingernails we'd found were two of them. Now I'm guessing the ones in your ears are the other two."

"Do you see any ghost saliva on my back?" I asked him.

"What the fuck is ghost saliva?" he said.

PHILOSOPHICAL CRISIS

Before that day, and for several years after, I never saw anything otherworldly. In my younger days, you could not have convinced me to regard ghosts and goblins as anything but the products of stupid superstition, and religion appeared to me as a form of mass-insanity where people allowed their lives to be guided by fairytales and wishful thinking. Once I had seen definite proof of life after death, though, it forced a total rethinking of everything I had believed before.

The first challenge for me was to determine whether I actually had seen such proof. Was it possible that I had been mistaken? But what I had seen could not have been brought to accord with any "natural" explanation. Even allowing for the possibility that fear or shock caused me to slightly misperceive or misremember some details—though I'm convinced that my perception and memory were quite reliable—still, allowing for the possibility of some slight distortion of the facts, there was no circumstance or series of events which could naturally occur that would even vaguely approximate what I had seen, heard, and felt. Either something supernatural had occurred, or the entire episode would have to be regarded as a false experience or false memory. If it had not really happened, then I'd be forced to regard myself as insane, and that would be the end of any reasonable contemplation.

But I actually *was* wounded, and the wounds upon my back were mysterious to the doctors. They told me that the injury to my flesh *almost* corresponded to human bite marks, from teeth that resembled human teeth rather than any other animal's, but the jaws were spaced in a way that is entirely unnatural to a human jaw. They wouldn't credit my report about the creature that had bitten me, yet they had to admit that the wound was completely out of the ordinary, beyond their experience, and it produced great curiosity among doctors.

I must also assert here that, though I was a sinner, though I smoked, drank, and occasionally fornicated (very occasionally), I did not use drugs, and I wasn't very drunk that night. I sipped my beer slowly, as was my habit. More importantly, as I need not truly persuade anyone, but I must only come to terms with myself: *I know what I saw.*

The police interviewed me because of the strange fingernail evidence. It was confirmed: a dead lawyer who had been shot to death had lost his fingernails, and two of them were found in my ears. No one could explain it. Though no one believed a word of my story (and neither would I have, if only…), the available facts and physical evidence were enough of a mystery to baffle investigators.

My experience has become just another weird and laughable spook story for the officers to tell their families and friends, or else they've written me off as a madman. But I've had to wonder from time to time: what will happen if the police stumble onto another dead body somewhere or some mutilation cases involving bites or missing fingernails? When it's time to look up some of the psycho-suspects, will they include me in the list? Am I the first on that list?

If it had not been I—if I had not personally experienced this—then I would probably assume that there was some fiction in it; someone was lying somewhere. But having experienced it myself, having the testimony of my own senses, I was incapable of walking away from the questions that arose. The absence of any natural explanation left only a supernatural explanation, something to account for what I saw with my own eyes, heard with my own ears, and felt as it pierced my skin, tore through muscle, scraped the surface of bone. I had encountered a dead spirit, reincarnated in the flesh, a supernatural entity—*proof* that the soul lives on.

Once I understood this, it was clear that I was facing the biggest crisis of my life. I could not become a wishy-washy wonderer. I could not become one of those millions of people who claim to believe in paranormal phenomena, yet who continue to live their lives in daily concern over trivia. If the soul persisted, and had an existence beyond the bounds of our daily search to satisfy our mortal bodies, then it was vital that I devote myself to understanding that persistent soul. But my experience had cancelled the "if" out of that statement. The soul *did* and *does* persist. It *did* and *does* have an existence beyond the bounds of the physical. Thus the urgent need to understand the soul is undeniable. Trying to satisfy the desires of the body has been revealed, at the same time, to be a fool's distraction to be avoided at all cost!

Who has devoted millennia to understanding the soul? Who gives priority to the soul over the desires of the flesh? Among others, there is the Church. Among others, there is the Christian tradition which dates back to the Apostles and which is founded upon the older faith of the ancients, which has been transmitted by learned men and women, through centuries that have witnessed the rise and fall, not only of individuals, but of the frail and ephemeral kingdoms of man and his perishable cultures and races.

A learning has been passed down that exceeds the narrow limits that humanity has imposed upon its own knowledge in our modern "enlightened" age. Our rediscovery of science, as practiced by our ancestors, but which has been expanded to become a sort of lord over our minds, has allowed us to make great discoveries regarding this fleeting life—at the expense of closing off our investigation into the grander and more permanent spirit of man! In fact, we've begun a process of dismantling, forgetting, and blotting out the knowledge of the soul which we once acquired, because it does not submit itself to the new Lord Science.

I have always admired science, I have learned extensively about physics, at least to the level of a good university-level dilettante, though I can't pretend to understand the higher-level theories and the mathematics which support them. But since awakening to the truth of the soul, I have been distressed to see how our knowledge of the physical (which is nevertheless always incomplete and insufficient) has come to displace our knowledge of—and even interest in—the spirit.

While there have always been God-fearing science theorists and researchers, the masses have been converted to atheism, and worse: a-spiritualism. By what evil influence has this new "light" been construed to blind us to spiritual values? How has the conjuring of sticks into snakes and silicon into cell-phones convinced the mass of humanity that *it doesn't matter what will happen after you die?* And, when the greater values are considered, how have we convinced ourselves that trinkets and toys are worth the sacrifice of the eternal soul?

No sound-minded skeptic can look at the world in which our bodies reside, and claim to see happiness, joy, satisfaction… a material heaven on earth? We see a temporal and mostly miserable existence with a few minor distractions and cold comforts, ending in tragedy billions of times over. But when we consider that death is not in fact the "end…" Well, our material obsession is incapable of bringing lasting joy to body or soul. It's sheer emptiness, the definition of illusion… what a poor deluded species is man, and more today than perhaps ever since the day we were born unto this earth.

I'm racing ahead, because what has become clear to me through years of thought, reflection, debate, consideration, seems so intuitive and obvious, but anyone who does the work to consider what is *essential* will reach similar conclusions, though I've omitted to exhibit many of the necessary steps.

I am not a St. Augustine, and though the spirit is willing, both the flesh and the *mind* are weak.

This last fact is at least partially explained when we realize that our latest conception of the mind is forced by definition to conform to the tasks of performing science. That is, our materialism has despiritualized the mind and denied it any non-material function. And madmen today even propose to *map the mind* in material, chemical, electronic terms! They are defining spirit out of the equation. No wonder scientists proclaim themselves the winners of a debate in which they have defined the terms, the field of battle, and outlawed the intellectual tools of the opposition.

But once again, I am getting ahead of my story.

Considering Religion

While I lay in the hospital, I spent a lot of time in contemplation without reaching any satisfactory answers. I thought about many of the things I had been told in the past but had rejected out of hand because they conflicted with my atheistic faith.

I asked myself whether Buddhism might hold the answers. I had studied Buddhism as an elective academic subject in university, strictly out of curiosity. But it had seemed so wrong to me. Its claims that fatalism and the recognition of cause and effect necessarily lead to the proof of reincarnation and a cycle seemed... they seemed ill founded and unproven. The emphasis on mysticism, the way in which the Buddhists appeared to run away from reason when reason confronted their faith with difficult questions... well, this all seemed disingenuous. Meanwhile, if all is illusion, then that undermines our understanding of even the basic terms "all" and "is". Buddhism's world of illusions doesn't account for either natural laws, or supernatural occurrences. And I could make no sense out of the idea of consciously striving for non-striving, unconsciousness, the effort to achieve what already is, the active strife in a fatalistic universe where there can be no "active." I couldn't see it as more than an intriguing abstraction or game when I studied in university, I couldn't see how any person could embrace it as a faith, and now... now it was still of no use to me.

Could some kind of polytheism explain it all? Were Thor and Loki, Apollo and Athena, Vishnu and Hanuman running about, pursuing their own vain pleasures, and were we humans in constant danger of the consequences of their arbitrary wills? But there was no way for me to square this anarchic view of the universe with the mostly rational workings of the everyday world, as I had perceived it every day of my life.

I could find no answers, largely because until this point in my life I hadn't been willing to ask or even consider the right questions.

For some reason, while I was in the hospital, I avoided even considering Christianity, as though it were necessary for me to exhaust every other possibility before turning to this last resort. One of the men who shared a room with me during my recovery was an active Christian, and when his wife visited she asked me casually about my faith. I simply smiled and shrugged the question off as I always had when confronting *people of her type*.

My mother visited me in the hospital on the day after I was admitted. I was embarrassed to try to explain to her what had happened, but I couldn't entirely avoid discussing it. I told her that I had seen something strange, something mysterious and unexplainable, that I had been attacked by something... unnatural. She looked deeply concerned, as though she couldn't decide if I was lying to cover up a shameful secret, or else I may be suffering some kind of strange breakdown. But she was *not* concerned about the possibility that I had actually had a paranormal experience.

Clearly that was out of the question. She had never heard me speak about such things, and frankly she didn't want to. So she kept the conversation on the topic of my health and recovery, the pain medications, and the expected time of my release.

My father didn't come, and I don't blame him.

Every night that I was in the hospital, I had the same dream. I was a child again, lying in the dark in my old bedroom, lying on my side in the dark room, lying with my forehead and nose close to the cold surface of the wall, running my hand over the surface of the textured and cold wallpaper, imagining the red sports cars and skiers that decorated the wall, sometimes touching my face to the wall, and then feeling the bed rising and falling as though I had just come from a rollercoaster and my body was still experiencing vertigo as an aftereffect, and I wanted to vomit.

This dream vertigo was nothing like the extreme vertigo which I'm experiencing now, it was more like the vertigo of doubt, but perhaps it was a sort of precursor of my current illness.

Anyway, when I'd recovered I was released from the hospital, and I walked out on my own. The sun was bright but the air was cold. I wandered, still feeling a grave sense of doubt about pretty much everything. I walked along the sidewalk, uptown, mingling among the pedestrians.

As I walked, I saw a young woman with a sort of heavy-metal look, with black hair, black eyeliner, and she was wearing a vulgar rock 'n' roll t-shirt. It read "Boiled Cock at St. Vitus," and its logo was an upside down rooster plunged into a kind of cross-section view of an iron cauldron bubbling with oil, over a wood fire.

It meant nothing to me except that I felt a kind of sorrow and pity for this young woman (not much younger than myself, though), and the mention of the name of a saint forced me to ask myself, "Why aren't you considering the Christians? What is it about your own heritage that's making you ignore the Catholics?"

Well, I resolved to go directly to the library and read something, anything, about this Saint Vitus. It was a name I had heard before, but I was otherwise entirely ignorant.

Well, when I read the story of St. Vitus it forced me to confront some new, very uncomfortable questions, but it also pushed me towards some answers. A twelve year old boy withstood torture at his father's hands to maintain his faith. He later cured the pagan emperor's son of demon possession, but yet he was condemned for sorcery because he would not give thanks to pagan gods for this miracle, rather than praise his own Christian god. As punishment, he was thrown to the lions to eat, but he tamed the wild animals (which is why he is now called upon for protection from animal attack). After this, he was boiled in a cauldron of oil. Different versions of the story give variable continuations, either he died in the cauldron, or he survived and was transported away while a thunderstorm rocked the city and then he later died from the torture he had endured. The uncertainty of the conclusion does not take away from the central fact that he was martyred for his faith.

Of course I'd heard of martyrs before, but now I suddenly asked myself the question I'd been avoiding. Why? Why did a pre-adolescent boy willingly die for his faith, and in such a miserable fashion? Was he delusional? Maybe he was, but then where did the delusion come from? The church? This church was founded by apostles who also willingly died as martyrs. So again we face the question, why? Had they lied about the miracle of Jesus from the start? Would *they* too have been willing to suffer and die for the sake of what they *knew* to be a lie, because they were the ones who had created the lie? Did they pursue their own violent deaths for no purpose, with nothing to gain personally, and without even fearing that their lie would soon be contradicted and their false faith rejected? Which, in the end, is more plausible? That the apostles had truly witnessed a miracle with Jesus, and thus could not deny the truth of Jesus' teaching, or rather that they had conspired against themselves to get themselves killed for no reason at all, just to maintain an absurdly fabricated lie?

When you seriously consider what it takes for a man to willingly die, and consider that the first martyrs were the very founders of the faith who all agreed in their accounts of the miracles of Jesus, so that they could not be said to have been deluded or misguided by someone else's teaching, then it's no longer so easy to dismiss the central tenets of Christianity.

Upon reaching this conclusion, I decided it was time to open my mind and my heart, and to finally listen with suspended judgment to what the Catholics had to say. I would go uptown to hear a sermon at the Cathedral of St. John the Divine.

First Service

I could not bring myself to return to my parents' home on Long Island, where I had been living for the past two years, until I gave some time to trying to answer some spiritual questions. Thus I stayed in a hotel in Manhattan. On the morning following my release from the hospital, I left my hotel and made my way to the subway station, to go uptown and attend a church service. It was a Tuesday morning, around 7:45.

As I was passing through the subway station, along the platform, I saw a homeless man sprawled out, asleep or unconscious, with his legs blocking half of the space necessary for passing. Passengers were awkwardly maneuvering to get around him without stepping on or kicking him, and without colliding with one another. Next to the man's head, there was a filthy baseball cap lying open like a bowl, with just a couple of coins in it.

On impulse, I reached into my pocket and discovered around thirty-five dollars in cash. I hastily deposited the cash in the man's hat, and moved along. In passing, I saw that the man's right shoe had a big rip and the sole was separated from the top, hanging like a flap. His left shoe, while in slightly better condition, was also rather tattered. When I'd found myself a place to stand and wait, about twenty yards on, I turned back and saw the homeless man move his hand towards his hat, grab the cash, and pocket it, without otherwise moving or betraying that he was conscious. I suppressed a little laugh.

I was still thinking about the man and his shoes. Feeling a sudden desire to help him further, I walked back to him, removed my shoes, and placed them near him, while attempting not to disturb his feigned sleep. He surprised me by shouting.

"What are you doing!?" he thundered.

"I saw the condition of your shoes, and wanted to help."

"I don't need no damn shoes! Get those things out of here."

I backed away a bit.

"I just saw your need," I explained. "Look, I just gave you about thirty-five dollars…"

"I don't have any thirty-five dollars! Shut up. Get your shoes outta here."

I walked away, but he called me back.

"I said I don't need no damn shoes. I'm with the police academy. We arrestin' people and shit. Now hustle!"

I went back, grabbed my shoes, and threw them on the subway tracks, just as a train was pulling in.

"I don't need them either," I explained. Then I boarded the subway.

Uptown, I arrived at 110th street and started hiking. I felt strange walking around in my socks and dirtying them, so I removed them, tossed them in a trash can, and continued barefoot on my way. I noticed several people gave me strange looks.

So, New Yorkers aren't as blind to one another as I'd always thought, I reflected.

I came to the church and entered a surprisingly crowded nave, which I had not expected to see at a Tuesday service. I found my way to a pew, and settled down, uncomfortably. I felt the same kind of alienation I had always felt in churches: the sense that this is all for someone else, and if people could see into me, they'd know that I don't belong here. I was pleased when the sermon began because it took me out of myself and my own personal discomfort. The attention was focused on the preacher.

The preacher told us about our endless search. "You're looking for a job that pays. You're looking for a lover who makes you feel fulfilled, complete," he told us. "These are common things that we all seem to desire, yet they never fulfill us. Our natural spiritual desire to come to God—God who is our true aim—is neglected as we direct our search to the things of this life, the things which we naïvely believe to be the source of our future satisfaction.

"If you have searched, and searched in vain, or searched and found what you thought you wanted, only to be dissatisfied, the reason is simple. You have neglected God's command to *stay awake*, just as Peter, John, and James neglected Jesus. In your weariness, you have lost sight of what you seek, and in the illusion of your dreams you have substituted false values for the one true value of God."

He went on this way at length. I wasn't particularly moved, but I attributed this to the unfamiliarity of the circumstances. Looking around at the faces of the congregants, I saw several attentive listeners. I had to admit, though, that I felt I was being patronized.

I sat through the entire service, but didn't participate in the sacraments. When the service was over, I made my way to the front, and attempted to speak to the priest. I wasn't sure if that was allowed, but I had to try.

As I approached, I saw one of the parishioners speaking to the priest. "Thank you for the sermon, Father, it really touched me today."

"Thank you as always, Mrs. Benson," the priest replied.

"Father," I blurted out. "I'm sorry, I've never been to a Catholic sermon, and I don't know what to say…"

A few people near me had gasped, giggled, or grumbled at my outburst, though I didn't know why. I thought I saw a few looking down at my feet.

"I need guidance, or something for my spiritual troubles," I continued. "Can you speak with me?"

"Of course," the priest replied. "Call me and make an appointment. There's a leaflet in the atrium, and my name is Father George Eckenrode." As he walked away, he paused and turned back. "By the way, we're not Catholic here."

"What?" I was stunned. He looked Catholic to me.

"We're Episcopalian."

"Really? What's the difference?"

"That's something else we can talk about."

He chuckled slightly, perhaps anticipating the difficulty of explaining such subtleties to me, but I felt a little put off by the reaction. As he left, an old woman nudged me.

"You'll probably want St. Patrick's, downtown," she confided.

The whole thing had been my mistake, but I felt swindled. It was almost scalding for me to realize that I was in a protestant church which I had imagined was Catholic, and I hastened to leave. I waited until that following Sunday before attending my first genuine Catholic service at St. Patrick's.

THE WORD OF GOD

At St. Patrick's, I had a new feeling. Although I was still quite conscious of my inexperience, and I felt "outside the flock," so to speak, I was beginning to feel positive about the church experience, as though I were starting to recognize that this strange house was my home. I avoided touching the holy water near the entrance, still not knowing or understanding any of the rules. I participated in all of the group rituals, including making the sign of the cross, up to and including the prayers of intercession, but I avoided the Eucharist. I was fully attentive to the readings and the homily. My initial stance was, as usual, one of skepticism, yet as the mass proceeded, I felt I was being converted, and I felt this was a good thing.

I cannot remember every word of the service, but I can reconstruct a large part of it, because it moved me profoundly, and because I have since spent years studying the Bible and returning to some of the passages that we heard that day.

The first reading was from Wisdom 17, through the first four verses of Wisdom 18. To tell the truth, I hadn't even known there was such a book in the Bible as the Wisdom of Solomon, but I soon came to deeply appreciate it. The reading addressed the great terror that comes to the ignorant and wicked who do not possess the wisdom that comes from God. This reading touched me very closely. It told us that, like the Egyptians under the plague of darkness, we can be frightened unto death by our own imaginings when we reach the limits of our understanding and perceive the potency of the supernatural. I felt a glow of shame as I heard the verse *"And no power of fire could give them light, neither could the bright flames of the stars enlighten that horrible night."* I felt that I was in the midst of just such a night.

We then sang Psalm 34. This addresses the trials of a righteous man surrounded by troubles, who is persecuted by the wicked, but he has the comfort of knowing that God is there to defend him and overthrow his enemies. He need not fear, as he trusts unto the justice that God will render. While singing along with the congregation, I almost laughed when we came to the line *"they gnashed upon me with their teeth."* It was a giddy sort of laughter that I had to suppress, full of more terror than cheer, but there was an inkling of hope in it, as I felt for the first time that this was a special service just for me.

The second reading was from the beginning of the Epistle of James, a passage that dealt with the patience taught by our trials, and the final reading was from the Gospel of John in which God's Word is identified with Christ and the Holy Spirit. After this, the priest's homily brought the elements together, and the theme became apparent: Wisdom is the path out of fear into the secure knowledge of God's grace. Wisdom is Jesus, the embodiment of the Word of God. It is the Holy Spirit. It is an act of salvation.

The priest said:

HOMILY

A little over one year ago, I was privileged to baptize Mr. Clifton Chapman, a 73-year-old man. He is by far the oldest convert to Catholicism that I have ever met. The conversations I've had with him have helped me to deepen my understanding of my own faith, while I have sought to help him. But his story is peculiar.

He has been affluent throughout most of his adulthood, and he has a large family, with grown children that he can be proud of. Though he has sinned, he has not been infamous, and there have been no scandalizing incidents. Yet he confesses that he lived a life full of fear and anxiety before receiving the Word of God.

His fear was a closely guarded secret, but it was perhaps a stronger fear than most people in his condition of relative security tend to feel. Whenever he faced the unexpected, whether it was a minor deviation from routine, or something as significant as a serious medical problem, confronting the unknown caused him to feel deeply troubled.

"A man is an ignorant and pitiable creature," he has told me. For, you see, since his conversion, Clifton has come to a new understanding of the fear which once plagued him. When man is confronted by the vastness of his own ignorance, fear naturally arises. Such a man is truly like the Egyptians under the curse of darkness:

Whether it were a whistling wind, or the melodious voice of birds, among the spreading branches of trees, or a fall of water running down with violence,

Or the mighty noise of stones tumbling down, or the running that could not be seen of beasts playing together, or the roaring voice of wild beasts, or a rebounding echo from the highest mountains: these things made them swoon for fear.

Why was he so terrified even by minor surprises, or trivial challenges to his knowledge and understanding? I say that he anticipated a judgment by which he would be found lacking; he feared a just retribution.

Besides these secret doubts, he also lived in fear of the loss of his reputation. He sometimes believed that friends and colleagues were hoping to see him fail so they could scorn him. He, in his turn, was biting and cruel in his comments when he saw another man fall into disgrace. He guarded against his own humiliation by heaping humiliating comments on others—even those whom we'd expect he would love through ordinary decency. It goes without saying that he was incapable of charity, when he even mocked his own sons when they experienced misfortune.

The event which prompted Mr. Chapman's conversion was rather odd and disturbing. It was an act of violence that he and David, his forty-eight-year-old son, witnessed while walking on the street.

For reasons unknown, three young men attacked and viciously beat another. The Chapmans stopped to observe the attack, only to appreciate it as a spectacle.

After the attackers had brutalized and cursed their victim, they walked off, with little concern. Then Clifton Chapman criticized his son.

"You're a coward, David," he said, "Why didn't you help that guy?"

"What about you?" David replied.

"I'm old," Clifton concluded.

Then they noticed that the victim had raised himself to a seated position, and strangely, though he was bloodied and probably in significant pain, he was smiling almost as if he were content.

They walked away and carried that image with them in their minds. At first the fear didn't touch Clifton, until David asked him, "Why did that young man smile after he was beaten?"

Why indeed?

When he heard this question, Clifton truly quaked with fear. He was troubled for days by the question he couldn't answer: Why had the man smiled? *How* could he smile?

Clifton suffered from nightmares then, as he had previously suffered whenever confronted by the inexplicable. He was once again like the Egyptians in the dark who, even if they could sleep through the darkness and noises, were still plagued in nightmares by this *sudden and unlooked for fear*. Unlooked for because limited human understanding did not even anticipate its possibility.

Though Clifton was unable to answer the question of why

this man smiled, praise God, one of our Catholic friends and a friend to Clifton, a member of this congregation, was able to help him find and understand the answer to the more important "why" question: Why was Clifton afraid?

> For whereas wickedness is fearful, it beareth witness of its condemnation: for a troubled conscience always forecasteth grievous things.

Thanks to his Catholic friend, who knew of his ordeal, Clifton was brought to the Lord, and shown grace. Upon his conversion, he had much to confess—things which are a matter between him and the Lord—and he has now found a wonderful peace, even though his health has been poor and he has experienced some material losses. He is untroubled. He has even had the courage to confess to his wife and family and business associates about some things he has done which brought him shame. But he did not fear to expose his reputation and humble himself. He has sought peace and reconciliation with those close to him, and he is striving to make amends. Now that he strives for righteousness, his fear is banished.

How different is the righteous from the wicked? He has a Lord to call upon. He is shielded by God's wisdom.

> Take hold of arms and shield: and rise up to help me.

> Bring out the sword, and shut up the way against them that persecute me: say to my soul: I am thy salvation.

He has nothing to fear from the coming of the Lord. He calls upon the Lord to abide. Clifton once feared the judgment of his fellow man, but now he is untroubled even while some enemies— those who have been his rivals for years—have shown him open contempt, and have even ridiculed him in his physical infirmity. Though temporarily injured by those who mock him in his suffering—those who *wink with the eyes*—he now has the Word of God.

How precious is God's Word? How valuable is this most true form of wisdom? Recall the prayer of the righteous man in Psalm 34:

Let them blush: and be ashamed together, who rejoice at my evils.
Let them be clothed with confusion and shame, who speak great
things against me.

He calls upon the Lord to punish his enemies by withholding his wisdom from them. What stronger proof is there of the power and value of God's wisdom than that the righteous man has prayed for the ignorance of his enemies?

Their very confusion is its own punishment. Their shame is their guilt. For God to withhold his Word is to withhold his grace. And without his grace, they are bound to fall into their own snares, and fall into a way which is *dark and slippery.*

Yet Clifton is more charitable and righteous than this, for he does not pray for the ignorance of his enemies. He now prays for them to receive God's Word.

But why must the righteous be tried? And how can we receive this wisdom from God that will shield us, defend us, and take away the shame of our own ignorance? Put simply, our trials purify and enlighten us.

As James tells us, our trials benefit us, and furthermore, we can receive wisdom from God if we ask in an unwavering faith.

My brethren, count it all joy, when you shall fall into divers
temptations;

Knowing that the trying of your faith worketh patience.

And patience hath a perfect work; that you may be perfect and
entire, failing nothing.

But if any of you want wisdom, let him ask God who giveth to all
men abundantly, and upbraideth not; and it shall be given him.

But let him ask in faith, nothing wavering. For he that wavereth
is like a wave of the sea, which is moved and carried about by
the wind.

Therefore let not that man think he shall receive any thing of the lord.

A double minded man is inconstant in all his ways.

Clifton has learned the limitations of man's own wisdom, and we all know the fate of him that depends on it:

For the sun rose with a burning heat, and parched the grass, and the flower thereof fell off, and the beauty of the shape thereof perished: so also shall the rich man fade away in his ways.

This is the outlook for a man who has been made rich in the here-and-now but who remains ignorant of the Word of God, and thus withers.

But, finally, what *is* God's wisdom? What *is* his Word? No one can be more clear on this point than John:

In the beginning was the Word, and the Word was with God, and the Word was God.

And how do we come to know God and receive his wisdom?

And the Word was made flesh, and dwelt among us, (and we saw his glory, the glory as it were of the only begotten of the Father,) full of grace and truth.

From John we learn that the Word—the wisdom that keeps us from the terrors and darkness which besiege the wicked and the temporally-wise—is God. And Jesus, *the light of the world*, is the Word made flesh.

The message is crystal clear, yet ignorance clouds the mind if we are *double minded* and *inconstant*.

And the light shineth in the darkness, and the darkness did not comprehend it.

We can receive God's wisdom by asking and receiving in sincerity. Thank God, near the extreme end of his life, after years of the terrors of living without God's grace, Clifton was finally moved to ask in all sincerity. And thus he received.

Jesus, as the embodiment of the Word, and the Holy Spirit which is his Paraclete, bring God's Word unto you. Be unwavering and do not let doubt snare you and hold you within the darkness of frightful ignorance. Only listen, to hear God's Word. Do not let this call go unheard, like *a voice crying out in the wilderness*. Rather, hear the voice, receive God's grace, and spread the Word.

A Rational Faith

When the mass was complete, I rose to leave the cathedral. I intended to arrange a private interview with the Father, but, for the moment, I didn't want to break the spell the homily had woven. I needed time to meditate.

On my way out, I overheard two older ladies gossiping and chatting about the service, and I was confounded by their response.

"What a strange homily," said one to the other. "God bless the new reverend, he tries hard, but he really preaches some strange and boring services."

"I know, tell me about it. He's so abstract, and there's no way to relate what he says to our own lives. A beaten man who smiles? Did he even explain that? Or a man who converts in his seventies? I thank God for that man's sake, but what about us who have been in the church our whole lives? Meanwhile, it's an election year..."

"I know! What a lost opportunity to address some serious social issues. You know, I think nearly seventy percent of our congregation is planning to vote Democrat, regardless of Dawson's position on gay marriages. I'm afraid Reverend Oliver is out of touch with the needs of his congregation."

What astonished me most about this exchange is how it made me feel. I was in a Catholic church to attend a service for the first time in my life, and these ladies were lifelong Catholics, yet I wanted to argue with them and defend the faith from their disparagement. Couldn't they see the irony in their own dismissal of so potent a message?

In the years since then, I have reflected that different people are reached in different ways. That day's sermon really was for me, or someone like me, and it was also for the complacent Catholics who were neglecting to spread God's Word. It could hold meaning for the ones who were forgetting the true message of God's Word, but only if they could see themselves critically enough to relate to the fearful world-wise sinner in need. Ladies like these could not profit from the message that day—they could hardly hear it!—but one day a service with a different tone might get through to them.

Similar considerations helped me also when, later, I struggled in my own reading of the Bible. I couldn't see why the Gospel of Matthew should seem so crude, so artificial—even childish—in its presentation, while the Gospel of John should use more profound and effective presentation of similar or even identical narrative material. Both were inspired by the Holy Spirit in their writing, but they produced different works on similar themes.

Understanding that different people will be reached in different ways, I then came to see how each Gospel serves its purpose. It was later still that I found profundity in what I had failed to appreciate in my first exposure to Matthew. Jesus' divinity is apparent in his detachment and the "artificial"-in-the-eyes-of-our-world presentation. He was here, but he was also not of this earth. He was a play-actor in his own drama, and he admitted this openly at times—like a magician explaining his own tricks throughout the performance while still asking us to be amazed—because his perspective upon the event was (is) infinite, but he could only present a facet of it to the people in that time. Some would be reached in one way, some would be reached in another way, and many would not be reached at all.

But returning to my history, I wanted conversion immediately. I set an appointment to meet Father Gale Oliver on Thursday, I attended daily services, I gave money randomly to whomever I pitied, and I otherwise wasted away the days until our meeting. On the Wednesday night before meeting the reverend, I called my mother from my hotel room.

"I've been out of the hospital for a week," I told her.

"That's wonderful, but where are you? Why didn't you come home? We've been worried."

"I've had some things to think about. I needed my own space, so I'm staying in a hotel."

"Well, we want to see you. Why don't you come back tonight, just for a visit? Your dad will be glad to see you."

"I've found God."

"You what…?"

"I've found God, and I need time to learn and understand."

"But… Oh my God. Look, just come home and let's talk."

"I'd love to see you again, but right now I can't. I'm not even the same person I once was. Look, I'll call you again. I'm not doing anything crazy. I'm not a Hare Krishna or a Muslim or anything. I just want to think about things, and I'll be visiting the Catholic church on a daily basis while I think."

She didn't speak, but her exasperation was demonstrated by the way she breathed.

"I'm sorry. This is something you can't understand right now, but you know I'm independent minded, and I'm a responsible person, so just trust me to work things out, okay?"

"Sure."

"I love you mom."

I ended the call. Years later, I remembered this exchange and realized that I hadn't even spoken to my dad. I hadn't spoken to him for months before either, even though we had lived in the same house and passed each other in the hall and kitchen. On ending my call to my mother, I'd left no message for him either. I'd felt there was nothing to say.

Then Thursday came and I met with Father Oliver. He was very pleased that I had found God in the scripture he had read, and he quite eagerly and clearly answered all my questions related to the Catholic faith. Everything he said was well considered, honestly rendered, and—to my great surprise—sensible! I had lived my whole life expecting that a conversation with a religious person would be full of absurd gibberish or blind and unthinking assertions of faith. But the Father was a true intellectual with a passion and understanding for logic, as much as for the teachings of his religion.

What persuaded me of the truth of Catholicism was its uncompromising pursuit of logically consistent truth. It is a religion that does nothing by half-steps. Fundamental to the faith is that there exists a nature with its own natural laws, and there are also supernatural phenomena which are the exceptions to these laws. That is the very essence of the supernatural. If there were no natural laws, then there would be no miracles.

To put it another way, there could be no miracles if there were no science. If life were truly like a "fairy tale," in which anything can happen at any time, and there were no basis for determining natural laws, then there would be nothing that could be called "supernatural." So-called "miracles," would be natural events.

But, on the other hand, if there were no exceptions to the rigid laws of nature, which are in the realm of science, then there would be no justification for "faith." A merely psychological or symbolic interpretation of religion is an absurdity. Catholic faith is faith in the literal certainty of God as a supernatural agent, and the miraculous occurrence of his incarnation in the flesh as Jesus, his crucifixion, and his resurrection.

Miracles are not metaphorical. They are literal, physical events. That is what makes them miraculous. To deny the supernatural is to deny the Catholic faith. But, if a supernatural event can occur, then this exception points to the agency of God.

Now, there have been hundreds of thousands of people, or more, who have attested to the occurrence of supernatural events. There have been millions who have attested to the miracles of God. By what arrogance had I rejected all of them as liars, simply because my own experience was limited in the early years of my life—when just a little bit of intellectual honesty would have shown me that science has never been able to account for everything, that it has never been a complete system, that the mystery of the mind itself is not accountable to any scientific theory, and it is by this very mind that I am able to perceive and contemplate the mysteries. My mind had been blind to *itself* as a pointing-to-God.

Once I came to understand this, I felt ashamed that it had taken a personal experience of the supernatural to persuade me. As Jesus said to Thomas, the doubter, "*Blessed are they that have not seen, and have believed.*"

Regarding my own experience of the supernatural, Father Oliver was himself somewhat skeptical, or at least guarded, because he told me that he had met many people with true paranormal experiences, but he had also met some who were fooled by something else, something psychological, or other kinds of illusions. There could also be an evil design behind what had occurred, the work of dark spirits. But he assured me that my decision to turn to the church for answers was an inspired choice, and that by doing so I was sure to foil the devil if I would truly embrace the Word of God.

Regarding my bare feet, the Reverend was harsh in his criticism.

"I can see that you are not a poor man, so what sort of game are you playing at?"

"I gave them away to a more needy man."

"Fine. Next time give to charity, but you can still buy yourself some new shoes."

"I felt it was right to give my shoes away. If I bought more, I'd give them away too."

"Why? Whose wisdom is this? Is this your own judgment? Is this pride masked as humility? It's not the wisdom of God. Buy shoes."

"I'm sorry, Father. I want to, but I would feel wrong, as though giving up on a pledge."

"What pledge? To whom did you pledge? You're in no position to pledge anything. It's vanity. Look…"

He paused and braced me with a hard look.

"...your heart seems good, but you're confused. You can't reach God by random experiment or arbitrary whim. It was a whim which you followed, now discard that whim. You're neither a Catholic yet, nor even a Christian, but you're acting like a blessed fool. You won't stand a chance until you receive baptism and then teach your soul the humility to follow Christ. The church will help you. Lacerating your heart while acting senselessly, on the other hand, will just lead you into glorifying your own whims, and it will draw you further away from God."

I nodded to acknowledge that I understood, though I wasn't really sure.

"You got it? Shoes. Put on some shoes."

When I asked him "What's the difference between Catholics and Episcopalians?"—the same question I had asked Father Eckenrode uptown—he answered me with equal force and certainty.

"This."

He had quickly opened a Bible on his desk, and he was pointing to a passage from James:

Thou hast faith, and I have works: shew me thy faith without works; and I will shew thee, by works, my faith.

Thou believest that there is one God. Thou dost well: the devils also believe and tremble.

But wilt though know, O vain man, that faith without works is dead?

"They say they don't believe in interpreting the Bible, they believe only what is written in the Bible itself. Yet this is in the Bible, and they don't believe it. So, what do they believe? They pay God lip service, but they don't *live* the Word of God, and their faith is dead."

This pronouncement was stronger than what I was expecting, and I was already reeling internally, contemplating what the Bible had said about devils also believing in God. I had never thought of that. But I still had an objection:

"But since you support doing good works, in your faith, then why do you discourage me from my charitable acts?"

"I don't discourage charity. Be charitable. Great. But put on some shoes. Is it so complicated? And find faith too. Works without faith won't save you."

CONVERSION

I realized very quickly that I needed to join the church. I had a great sense of urgency, so it upset me when I discovered it would take a minimum of seven months before I could receive my first communion. Yet I was very fortunate that, in response to my pleas and my prayers to heaven, I was accepted into the Rite of Christian Initiation classes at the Church of St. Joseph in late September, somewhat later than the usual starting date. I couldn't imagine having to wait an additional *year* if they hadn't taken me into the program.

The preparatory period was a very difficult time in my life. I had been unemployed for two months before seeing the ghost, and though I had plenty of savings and was conservative with my money, I had intended to get back to work relatively soon. Now, I couldn't even think about such trivia as looking for a job, speaking to friends and family, or engaging the world in any meaningful way. It was difficult for me to do such basic things as switching off a light before bed, or opening a window when the air was too still. I missed many meals simply because I couldn't motivate myself to buy food. I wanted only communion with God. I attended services on several weekdays every week, in addition to Sunday mass, I prayed multiple times daily, and I immersed myself in Bible studies and the reading of catechism.

I moved into a tiny cell-like apartment—basically a pay-by-the-week hotel, or "flophouse"—one of the last remaining in Manhattan's Lower Eastside. I could have afforded better, but for some reason I didn't want better. I was surrounded by drunks, and had trouble accessing the toilet stall sometimes because my neighbor often fell asleep in there after vomiting. I was otherwise satisfied with my minimal living environment.

I visited Long Island only once, had a nice meal with my parents, assured them I was doing well, then drove off in the car I had left parked in their driveway since June and sold it to improve my cash flow situation.

To give myself something meaningful to do, and to start on my road towards becoming a good Catholic, I started volunteering to prepare and distribute food to the poor as part of the soup kitchen in the hall beneath the Church of St. Joseph. It caught me quite by surprise when, one day, I met one of the men from my flophouse as he came in to get his free meal. Only when another volunteer greeted him did I learn his name, James. I said hello to him, and he said "Hi, Buddy." But in our two previous encounters at the flophouse, he had insulted and intimidated me without cause, and called me "faggot." I was very uncomfortable seeing him in this new setting, and I was confused by his almost congenial demeanor.

I normally didn't use the toilet at the hall where we distributed food, but I needed to go, and I wanted a bit of an excuse to get out of sight for a minute. But when I went into the bathroom, James came in after me while I was using the urinal. He stood beside me and started using the other urinal, then turned and said, "So! You piss too, hey?"

I faintly smiled, as though appreciating this as a crude sort of joke. Then he spat right in my face. I was shocked, but remained passive until he walked out and slammed the door… or *half*-slammed it… another man was pushing his way in just behind him. Then I zipped up and wiped the sticky saliva from my face, humiliated.

I was frequently criticized by the pastoral staff and my fellow catechumens for failing to socialize and take an interest in the people and the world around me. I had no charity in my heart. I learned, with time, to fake an interest. I asked the people around me about their families, how they were feeling about their conversion, how their days were going, and though I didn't really listen attentively to their answers, no one seemed to mind as long as I made a token effort. I couldn't really remember names, so I avoided using them even when others addressed me by name.

But my desire to come to God, to be baptized, to receive communion—these were my consuming passions. Discussing scripture was also very interesting to me.

Somehow the time went by, the Easter season arrived, and I received the glorious gifts of baptism, confirmation, and finally the Eucharist! At the altar of St. Patrick's, amid all the celebrants of the mass, for the first time I truly touched Christ and accepted him into my body. Anything I can say about it now would only trivialize it, and every time after that, every single time I received the Eucharist, it was a potent and joyous experience. It's the one deepest regret that has tormented me every moment since I left the church, that I have lost this! Remembering my first communion is too painful when I observe my current state of spiritual desolation.

I screamed out when I received my first communion. This was disconcerting to all around me, and reluctantly forgiven.

I completed the rest of my training as a neophyte, but as you know, this was not enough for me. Though I loved my new life in God, and I felt God's Word as ever-present in my life, I was even less able now to engage the world of the mundane and the material. I was not part of a community. My connection to God, through Jesus and the Holy Spirit, was my only society. The ordinary Catholic laity around me, meanwhile, had little patience for the kinds of theatrics and ecstasies which are more commonly witnessed in heretical churches like the Pentecostals. Thus, I had to practice silence and restraint as I took communion each week.

3.
Dr. Shieling Interprets a Dream

On Dream Interpretation

Though many psychiatrists and analysts have come to discount the value of dream interpretation, and Freud's championing of the practice has fallen into some disrepute within the modern profession, I continue to value dreams as an inroad to the unconscious workings of the patient's mind. The fact that dream interpretation is as much an art as it is a science, or that it is a practice which defies quantification and rigorous structure in its application, simply means that there are few talented interpreters and many untalented ones. It is the untalented interpreters who have damaged the credibility of the practice. But for those of us who do it well, dream interpretation can provide invaluable insight, and the fact that it is somewhat subjective merely means that it can help guide the doctor in understanding his own perspective and the doctor-patient relationship.

Around the time when Bernard had received his first communion, while he was in the period of his Catholic training known as the "mystagogy," he had a memorable dream. Thus I have interrupted his narrative here to relate the dream as he reported it to me, and to discuss what it revealed, because it led to a significant development in my approach to analyzing and treating Bernard.

The Bishop Dream

Bernard dreamed of a Bishop, in an unspecified time and place. The Bishop was a very powerful man, and he had charge of his nephew, whose parents had died. The Bishop loved his nephew as if he were his own son.

The Bishop lived in a castle. He had many enemies, and there was a plot among the priests to assassinate him. It was difficult for them to pull off a murder within his home or within the church, and he avoided going out where he might be vulnerable.

Nearby, there was a site in a country village where it was reputed that miraculous cures could be performed. But the Bishop maintained the belief—a kind of deist heresy—that miracles no longer occurred; either God was entirely passive after having set the course of events in action, or else he acted in only subtle and apparently natural ways.

Unable to get to the Bishop directly, the priests who were his enemies contrived to poison his young nephew with a slow-acting but fatal drug. They expected that the Bishop would at last go out from his castle to seek a miraculous intercession for the sake of the boy. Assassins could then ambush him at the crossing of a stream on the way to the "site of miracles." The Bishop, however, sticking to his principals, did nothing and allowed his beloved nephew to die, despite even the child's own prayers that he would compromise.

As a consequence of his integrity, the Bishop survived, but he lost his power and influence and the faith of his followers, because no one could forgive such a rigid faith that would not compromise with the prayers of a dying child.

A New Approach to Analysis

The obvious interpretation of this dream is that Bernard wished for a world without miracles. In the midst of his conversion, he would have liked to be relieved of the burden of his newfound faith. He would have liked to return to the certainty of atheism and skepticism, not believing in the supernatural events which had thrown his life out of order, which had plunged him into a state of permanent insecurity.

But after Bernard told me about his dream, I continued to think about and meditate on it for the day that followed. I found myself unintentionally thinking about the dream *as though I had dreamed it and it had relevance to myself.* If I had dreamed this dream, then I would have to interpret this as saying that my recent reliance on "miracle cures" proceeded from a death wish. I was unconsciously trying to disprove the existence of miracle cures by pursuing unorthodox treatment that was bound to fail! Then, through my own failure, I could prove the necessity for a return to pure reason and scientifically verifiable method within the practice of psychiatry.

This was a greatly disturbing idea, and it forced me to confront a profound doubt. As a consequence, I resolved to avoid radical experimental therapies in my treatment of Bernard, and I would attempt a more orthodox approach. Yet I was already onto a new heterodoxy, as I then began the practice of *interpreting my dreams as though Bernard had dreamed them, and interpreting his dreams as though I had dreamed them.* There's more of this to come, and you will see where it led me. But for now, let us return to Bernard's telling of the events leading to his becoming a monk.

4.

Layman

Schizoid

I spent another eight months in New York City, feeling entirely inadequate and dissatisfied. I was even less able to integrate into society than before. Though I continued to do charitable acts, including reading to a recently blinded veteran and assisting in a hospice-care facility, I felt that I was only capable of a sham compassion, but in my heart I was unaffected. I couldn't overcome this, despite Father Oliver's assurances that through prayer and sincere devotion I would learn to be compassionate. When this became the leitmotif of my confessions, Father Oliver became almost dismissive of my concern.

"When you made your first confession," he said, "you had so many grave and terrible sins to confess. Remember, you even confessed to abetting the murder of an unborn soul, and God in his infinite mercy absolved you, though by no amount of penance could you ever earn his mercy. It was an act of divine Grace and the intercession of Christ that saved you. But you were not so remorseful when you confessed to that as you seem remorseful now about failing to *feel* compassion. Are you looking for a physical sensation, a fast heartbeat, a thrill of emotion as you hand the bowl of chili to the hungry man? Your problem is excessive doubt. Trust Jesus. Act in good faith, and keep your mind pure. And keep perspective, and keep your attention on what is essential. Confess now to your more serious sins. Your heart must be troubled by something more serious than this, or you wouldn't shiver and blanch in fear. You're not a St. Therese of Lisieux, are you—the little flower?—so that the worst sin you can confess is being mildly impatient and overzealous?"

"Father, help me. The dark cloud of ignorance is upon me. God is so distant. The supernatural terrifies me, as though the fabric of

344

the world could be rent before my eyes at any moment. The world is nothing. I need only the spirit of God."

"Your suffering comes from idleness, an idleness you didn't confess. You lie about, and you indulge in despairing thoughts, inviting doubts and asking the devil in to challenge your faith. Your family is wealthy and you've been idle most of your life, only working as though it were a hobby, not as a necessity, and walking away from responsibilities when they've felt inconvenient. Now that you've given up on material comforts, you still retain your idleness. Get a job and work sincerely. Find a woman for your wife. You're a lay person. Though you've turned away from the carnal sins of your past, you can pursue a love in chastity and find a wife that God approves. Live righteously and faithfully. You are in the world, and your real trouble comes from your unwillingness to engage it."

Though he told me this, I came to the opposite conclusion. I finally admitted to myself that what I truly wanted, and had wanted for some time, was to become a monk and withdraw further from the mundane and the petty. My road to God would not come through *engagement*. Yet I was so foolish, I hadn't even found out what it means to be a monk, or how one can become one.

First Retreat

As soon as I discovered that there was a Cistercian Abbey in upstate New York, I dropped everything and boarded a bus. I brought St. Augustine's *The City of God* as reading material for the bus ride. After forty-two chapters, a bus transfer, and a short nap, I arrived.

The site was beautiful, simple, and pure. I got a thrill imagining that, perhaps, the Abbey of the Genesee could soon be my home. I might even someday die here. But I was in for a huge let-down when I arranged an interview with one of the discerning monks.

I was welcome to stay on a short retreat, to ask as many questions as I liked, and to enjoy a break from the life outside the monastery. But as a recent convert, I would have to wait a minimum of five years before I could even be considered for an application, and the procedure could take another year before I was made a novice. I would have to pass psychological exams, present them with an autobiography, and jump through various other hoops, and could still be rejected. My fanaticism and extreme sense of urgency were of no help to me at all. Why hadn't I asked one of the priests or deacons back in St. Patrick's, or done some kind of research before coming up?

I stayed for four days, and enjoyed some simple meals and the fresh-baked bread of the monks. There was a young married Catholic couple there on retreat (they slept in separate apartments at night), and there was a silent and awkward loner who seemed nervous and twitchy. Finally, there was my own forlorn self. At night I was serenaded by crickets, and my most genuine "monastery experience" was hearing the snoring of the monks in their nearby cells.

On the bus-ride home again, I reflected on the odd thought that I had been given a sort of prison sentence in reverse, sentenced to years in the outside world before I would be allowed to hope for a chance of getting locked away in a monk's cell.

But the monks had assured me that God could love and protect me just as well on the outside, and I'd have better opportunities to demonstrate my faith in my interactions with society and the wider world. Separating myself from the Abbey, even after such a brief taste of monastic life, was a grievous pain. I was heartsick and I called on God's strength to keep me from weeping.

The Carmelites

Two months later—praise the lord!—I actually did my research and found out that in 2015, a Carmelite monastery had been established in Southern Montana, in the Sapphire mountains outside of Philipsburg. It was one of only two Carmelite monasteries in existence (most Carmelites are friars who take a more active role in worldly affairs), and by all reports the abbey was eager in receiving young men with a true vocation into their order.

The Abbey of St. Albert had much in common with the New

Mount Carmel Monastery in Wyoming. But, though St. Albert's was newer, it was failing to attract candidate monks because the conditions of the monastery were poor and there had been several accidental deaths in the first years of its establishment. One wing of a newly constructed building had collapsed in the first year, killing two and injuring eleven, and the next year three monks had drowned while riding in a mini-bus that had been washed off the road during a sudden flash flood and plummeted into a creek at the bottom of a ravine. Meanwhile, donations for the improvement of the monastery were few, and many wondered whether there was any need for a monastery in this region of the country. The choice of the remote location seemed ill conceived, and very few lay people ever came for retreats or to receive the sacrament of penance.

Nonetheless, those who are called by God will come, no matter the difficulty in reaching their destination, and the abbot, Father Joseph White, was faithful, devout, and sincere. So, of course, the monastery did not simply accept all comers; the majority who came were turned away when the monks discerned that they did not have a true vocation.

I made arrangements for my five-day retreat, and disposed of my remaining possessions except for some clothes and cash for traveling. I had no intention of returning to my former life or to New York, regardless of how things went with me in Montana. I paid off my credit cards too, and discarded them along with my ATM/Debit card, though I retained a bank-book and paper documents. I reflected on how foolish I had been to walk into the Abbey of the Genesee with credit cards in my pocket, expecting immediate admission as a monk when I hadn't even cleared my debts! Though perhaps throwing away the ATM card was going a bit overboard.

I flew into Missoula, and I was transported to Philipsburg by limousine van. It was a cheaper but less comfortable option than chartering a plane for local transport.

From Philipsburg, I rode with a delivery driver who was taking a small truck full of tools, concrete mix, and dry foodstuffs up to the abbey. He was supposed to meet me in front of the Philipsburg Brewery at four o'clock, but he was late, so I left a message for him and took the opportunity to walk up to the St. Philip Catholic church. There, I spent twenty minutes in prayer and meditation on the mystery of the Crowning with Thorns. Then the truck arrived and my meditation was interrupted by the honking of a horn.

When I went out, I discovered that the driver, Lance, had reserved the front passenger seat for his girlfriend, whom he was planning to drop off at a campsite in the hills for some undisclosed reason.

"There's no room up front. Climb in the box with the tools."

I was confused at first, but figured out I should get in the back of the truck. When I rolled up the gate and climbed in, I found that he was transporting another young man who was also going on retreat, a man who introduced himself as Del Fleiss.

We left the gate open a few inches at the bottom to admit some light, as there was no electric light and no windows. Del and I sat across from each other on the truck's wooden bed, among the disorganized sacks, boxes, and implements that took up much of the space, and we attempted some small talk as the truck started on its way.

"So, where are you from, Del?"

"Chicago."

"Ah! A big-city boy. Me too. I'm from New York."

"Huh. All right, then."

Time passes.

"Well, have you ever come out west before?" I asked. "Or been so far from the city?"

"No, not really. I mean, I've vacationed in Miami."

"Oh yeah? When?"

"About six years ago."

"I've been there too. Hmmm. I don't feel comfortable thinking about Miami right now, though, you know what I'm saying?"

"No."

"I mean the beaches. You know."

"You mean the girls?"

"Yeah… Listen, how long have you been Catholic?"

"What? What do you mean?"

"I mean… oh, I guess all your life then?"

"Of course. I've always been Catholic."

"Yeah, I know, but I'm a convert."

"Really? I've never met a convert. Why did you convert?"

"Ha ha! What a question. All right, well, I had a pretty terrifying experience, and it made me question my life. With a little searching, I found the church, and with it I found God."

"O.K."

Time passes.

"But look, the thing is, until just now—I mean *right now*—when you mentioned Miami, well… I hadn't even thought of a woman for the last year and a half. Not even a thought! And you had to go and remind me. Temptation on the beach is too much to bear."

"You really haven't thought about women? My God, that's a miracle!"

Del finally sat up with a kind of crazed enthusiasm.

"Is it true?" he demanded. "How?"

"Well, it is a little strange. Every temptation to sin was scared right out of me. My mortality and the peril of my soul became such pressing issues, and my intellectual dissatisfaction about my total ignorance of spiritual matters… they left me nothing to squander on idle thoughts and venality."

"You have just become my personal hero! I can't imagine. I mean, I've been called to God, and I'm committed to serve. But every second of every day my mind is consumed by thoughts of women. It's a painful curse, like a psychic cancer. And to think, it doesn't even trouble you a bit? Inconceivable."

"And you said you've been a Catholic your whole life. So, does that mean you've been a *good* Catholic?"

Now he was hanging his head.

"Oh, lord. Yes!"

He was not happy about this.

"And you have nothing to regret?"

"Yes. I'm pure as the virgin snow, but twice as virginal. And without the snow. Heh heh. I tell you... but I shouldn't say it. But honestly, my most painful regret is having nothing to regret. Uhhh!"

Now he was really upset, and he punched his thigh.

"...If only, just once, I could have confessed to the priest about an *actual* sin. It can't be more embarrassing than confessing to *thinking* about it! And I'd still be forgiven, right? But I know, it's wrong to talk about it... Maybe I could have just gotten it out of my system, you know, maybe sex would be disappointing and I'd be over with sinning, and my mind would be more pure..."

"Nope. Honestly... you're better off not sinning. Seriously. Because it's *not* disappointing."

"You bastard!"

The truck, which was twisting and turning up a steep slope, coming into just the first of the foothills, struck something in the road that shook us up. A pickaxe that was loose went sliding across the dusty floor and out through the space under the back gate, clattering noisily onto the receding blur of pavement. We both got up and started banging on the wall of the box behind the driver's cab, to alert Lance and get him to stop and pick up the fallen tool. But he ignored us, and kept on, so I went and slid the gate all the way closed and we sat back down in the thick darkness, with just the faintest glow perceptible in the spaces around the edges of the gate.

"I think this is probably the last time in my life I'll be able to have such a candid conversation," Del declared.

"Possibly," I admitted. "Well, I'm sure we'll have plenty of candid conversations, maybe, but not about that. Probably not about sex. But it's a topic I've never talked about much anyway."

Time passed. Then I had a bit more to say.

"But, I'm being honest when I say you're better off not sinning.

Seriously, I envy your purity, even though you're naïvely tempted. If you had sinned in act, you'd be more seriously tempted, and you may never have escaped the sinner's life. We've got more serious concerns. Let's not tempt God's divine punishment with our sinful thoughts, just because of a trivial desire of the flesh."

"You're right, of course. But… it's easy for you to say. I just wish I had your cold, cold resolve."

A Little Detour

About half an hour later, the truck pulled to a stop somewhere up in the hills. Lance rolled up the gate a bit, peeked in, and slid us a six pack of cold beer in bottles. Michelob Ultra.

"Drink up boys!"

He disappeared, then peeked in again.

"Don't worry, I'm not drinking myself… much."

His girlfriend laughed, somewhere just out of view.

"But seriously," he continued, "I'm sorry about the light. Really am. I'm gonna get that fixed soon…"

I nodded at him. "Hey, that's all right. You're doing us a favor."

"You're a good sport… I'll be right back."

Lance was gone for about twenty minutes.

Del and I eyed the beer. The bottles were running with condensation, though the air was pretty dry.

"There's no sin in drinking," Del said. "My goodness, some monks even brew the stuff. It's part of their income."

"True. But somehow… well, drinking is another thing I haven't even thought about in a long, long time. And I don't want to show up with beer on my breath… it just seems a little shameful under the circumstances."

"Yeah. I get your point. Maybe it's indiscrete."

We left the beer to sweat and succumb to entropy. We hopped out of the truck to stretch our legs.

We found ourselves in a large dusty lot with just a few cars around, and there was a parked pickup truck with a bunch of goods on display: Styrofoam coolers with beer and ice, packs of toilet paper, magazines, tobacco in pouches, familiar brands of pre-rolled cigarettes, and so on. I assumed this was the local store-on-wheels, supplying folks who lived long term or semi-permanently in a nearby camp. It seemed odd, though.

"Can you imagine a girl like that named Mary?" Del asked.

"What girl?"

"Lance's girl. The one we've been riding with."

"What of it?"

"A girl like that, named for the mother of God."

I paused before speaking. Somehow I felt a different person already, more contemplative, kind of living—or play-acting—the role of a monk, or the way I thought a monk would think about these things. But I was still myself too. No, I was still myself too, not yet a monk.

"Don't judge. We don't know anything about her."

"You really think we don't know?"

I thought about it, and realized that the girl's clothing was pretty revealing, but I hadn't considered it so seriously. He seemed to be jumping to outrageous conclusions.

"Hey, what is it?" I said. "Are you such a city boy that you think you can judge the folks out here, lump them into one or two classes without even speaking a single word to them?"

"It's not about that. I didn't say anything about that. There are more sinful women in the city, I'm sure, but I think we know this girl is no saint."

"She just might be saint. Or may become one. So, anyway, you're calling her a whore, is that right?"

"Where's her husband? Do you think she's married to the driver?"

"Lance?"

"Right, you think she's married to him? You think he's ever going to marry her? Even if she's not up here running wild with other men... or women!"

"Oh my. I was mistaken, Del. Your innocence is nothing to envy with your mind so craven."

"Even if...! Well, do you think we're doing any favor to these people by not telling them about the danger they're in?"

"I'm going back in the truck."

My God, I thought, *am I making a mistake? Will I have to become a hermit? How can I become a member of a divine community when the community includes people like Del? His mind disturbs me more than the innocent minds of the nominal sinners of the secular world.*

But that wasn't true either. I had already developed a horror of sin. A horror, and a pity for the sinner. I had to retreat. Del, though, showed no pity, only a sickening blend of horror and envy.

Though, if I give Del's point of view some consideration, perhaps Lance's Mary was a rather loose woman. I was inclined to refrain from judgment. Though the Vatican has cleared our "Apostle to the Apostles" of the charges of carnal sin, I'm still fascinated by the outmoded medieval version of St. Mary Magdalene, the repentant sinner. She was an archetypal representation of the appealing belief that even the lowliest can be raised to the highest purity.

Del climbed into the truck too. I kicked him in the foot, and we both laughed. Soon enough, Lance hopped in the cab, we closed the gate once more, and he drove us to our destination.

EARTHLY PARADISE

The truck arrived at the monastery, and again we rolled the gate up. Then I saw something I never expected to see. Monks on Horses!

Three monks with tonsured heads were just riding up a path from out of the woods. They were wearing riding chaps but also had short tunics with scapulars. Two of them had taken off their cowboy hats and were holding them in their hands, while the eccentric among them was wearing a high-crowned bowler pulled low over his head, almost down to his protruding ears. They were singing something in Latin, and it didn't sound very sacred.

I soon discovered what a heaven-on-earth this monastery was, and I knew I had to live here for as long as they would keep me. There were sixty monks living together on the compound. They included brewers, metal workers, cooks, gardeners, herdsmen who kept a few goats, all monks did a variety of labor—there was a small library (censored, of course)—and they had a herd of riding horses which they used for occasional recreation. But they also used the horses to raise money from a smattering of very curious tourists who came up for monk-guided riding tours. The novelty of it drew more visitors than ever came for religious retreat. In fact the monks had first mistaken me and Del for a couple of tourists out for a ride and were singing for our entertainment, but we cleared up the mistake immediately.

As a novice named Brother Carlo gave us a brief look around the grounds of the monastery and told us about their life there, the most amazing thing I learned was that the monks had a unique project to create hand-written, -bound and -illuminated manuscripts in a medieval-revival scribal tradition, which they created to-order for wealthy bibliophiles worldwide. They were the one and only source for this service, at least as far as they knew, and the orders for books provided the monastery with enough income for its ongoing development. Frequently, the buyers also gave large voluntary donations which rivaled the sum total of donations that trickled in from American Catholics.

The books they wrote included transcribed Latin and Greek originals, medieval Romance and Germanic texts, and a variety of translated texts rendered into modern English, Spanish, and a couple of other European languages. None of the monks were competent in Slavic languages, and though there was one who was capable of writing Arabic, the Monastery had had to make the decision not to produce manuscripts of the Quran. The abbot had arranged a telephone conference and consulted with several Arabic and Persian Mullahs on the subject, but they all rejected the idea and spoke critically of the Muslims who had made the request. Nonetheless, continuing requests for hand-scribed Qurans came in more frequently than any other text, at least two a week, and they all had to be denied.

There were also frequent prank requests. Well after my first visit to the monastery, I learned about a man who persistently—and apparently in all sincerity—requested and demanded a hand-scribed *Lolita* with illustrations. He would not accept or understand that the monks had moral standards to uphold and had to consider any reflection that could be cast on the church. He eventually was persuaded—after a bitter dispute—to accept that basic copyright law made such a project impossible. This man was a United States Senator.

After our tour, Brother Carlo led us to wait in a guesthouse until the abbot returned. Father Joseph White had gone to see the progress of a new irrigation system the vegetable gardeners were in the process of installing.

When Father Joseph was back, Brother Carlo brought Del and me to join him for tea. Father Joseph greeted us with a warm and firm handshake. He was a large, rugged looking man of about forty. When we sat he poured us out some rosehip tea, heavily sweetened.

"We also grow a lot of mint. I prefer Anise on most days, and drink a lot of it chilled, but we don't produce it ourselves as it doesn't quite suit our climate, so I like to offer our guests a bit of our own local product. Besides the rose, we've got mint and savory."

Del and I nodded our appreciation.

"As farmers, we're not at all self-sufficient, but it's nice to supplement our kitchen with peas, cabbages, radishes and so forth, and we grow plenty of winter wheat and barley for brewing as well."

"I guess I didn't really know what to expect out here, but I find the place so appealing. How's the weather, generally?"

(As for that day, I'd have described the afternoon as mild).

"Mmmm… variable. Day and night see the temperature change pretty dramatically. In the winter, of course, it never gets very warm, but it's tolerable. How was the ride up?"

Del said, "It was fine."

But I said, "It was strange."

"Ha ha!" the abbot laughed, "I'll bet." He sipped his tea silently for a moment. "Anyway, you've both been on retreat before."

"Yes, just once," I replied.

"Three times," said Del.

"But you're new here, and I understand that you believe you have been called. Most men who travel this far come for the very same reason. Well, the brothers have eaten lunch, but we can always pull together some food for our guests on their first day. Some food will be set out for you in the dining area, and soon you can get involved in preparing meals. After today's lunch you can settle in for the afternoon and attend to None prayers privately. At five you can join us for Vespers, and we will get you started on the experience of true monastic living as soon as possible. Praise God and pray in all sincerity that he guide you to your true vocation. Though you must have many questions, and we will have questions for you, now is not the time for that. You've come to a holy place; the wonder of God's creation is here to nourish your soul. And half the day is already gone! Excuse me."

He departed. Brother Carlo then guided us to the dining hall. Along the way, he softly spoke. "He's very dramatic with newcomers. It's just that that is how he tries to meet your expectations." Pause. "I think he's right, too. We all admire him deeply. He's more than a father to us all."

In the dining hall we ate a wonderful green salad, some wheat bread with goat's-milk butter, and a bean stew that seemed to have a bit of meat gravy in it. It all seemed a bit more exotic and nourishing than the ham-and-cheese sandwiches and corn salad I'd prepared for myself while on retreat with the Cistercians. The Cistercians had better bread however.

Del and I quickly settled into the routine of monastic life, even as so much of it was initially strange. I prayed more often and longer than I had ever prayed before, devoting much of my time to the mystery of the Annunciation. I labored vigorously when I was set to work in digging irrigation ditches. I was inwardly ecstatic at daily mass, though I did my best to suppress my urgent passion. Father Joseph White told me he had already been warned in a letter from Father Gale Oliver to expect an occasional disruptive outburst from me, and he was prepared to make allowances.

I was very worried and embarrassed when I had to admit that I had no special linguistic skills, I could only speak English and was baffled by Latin, and I couldn't sing or chant. I was assured, however, that the only thing that mattered was my having a genuine calling. Latin and singing could be learned. Writing and translation were not the only valued skills.

It was only on the third day of my retreat that I received a great shock, and I first awoke to the terror of the place when I received my lunch in the dining hall; it was a raw and bloody pig's foot on a plate.

"Kiss it, Juniper," whispered a voice behind my left ear.

5.
Hunted (Another Dream)

WOLVES AND KNIVES

I, Percival Shieling, dreamed that I was lost and pursued by wolves. I didn't see the wolves, but I knew they were there. It was dark, very slightly breezy, but there was a dull silence in the space between the audible cries of the wolves, which sounded alternatingly close and far—sometimes as close as a breathing animal sleeping just behind my left ear.

With hardly anything to see in a barren landscape—mostly fine sand and clumps of red-green-brown reeds—I also noted a nearby structure: *"The Fragrant Dog Knife Shop."* This brown wooden structure was shadowy and askew. The inverted-V roof, and all exterior walls were set at odd angles that implied it was ready to collapse or even lurch to one side with startling abruptness, though for the moment it was silent and still.

Inside—though I don't recall entering—the knife shop was all twisted and cramped, like a wood-maze mockery of an intestine. There were no knives to be found.

Outside, I was relieved to find I could run faster when my shoes were removed, because a certain damp coldness in the soil propelled me forward and away. The wolves couldn't find me.

Inside, I struck my shoulders against the corners of walls, pursuing hopeless pathways that terminated in dead-ends only eight to ten inches deep. I don't know why I even imagined progress to be possible.

Outside, I was laughing, and I thought about whether to "turn on the lights," though I was afraid that if I did that, I might find myself in a white kitchen, and knives would cut me. I decided, instead, to pursue my skating expedition, riding across the sand on sharp-bladed ice skates.

Inside, I opened a door and I was outside.

Outside, I came to a house and threw myself onto the ground just beside the front door. I started rapidly unlacing my skates, hoping to get out of them as quickly as possible so I could go inside, where I expected to find a vagina. My laces were hopelessly tangled, however.

In the *other* outside, I was again sitting on the sand, passive, near *The Fragrant Dog Knife Shop*, listening to the howling of wolves. I ignored the wolves, and considered deeply how I might assist a patient named Bernard. This patient was a professional basketball player with an oversized nose. His oversized nose was his main psychological malady. It was an illusion. When I say "oversized," I mean about twice the size of a grapefruit.

Back beside the house, several cats and women surrounded me and congratulated me for ice skating, though I wasn't ice skating and I imagined they were mocking me. I was still entangled in the laces, though this seemed more entertaining than troubling.

I was on fire near *The Fragrant Dog Knife Shop*.

I was *not* on fire near *The Fragrant Dog Knife Shop*.

Beside the vagina house, I was pointing to the door, so the women and cats would see me soon emerging. I was only joking, I didn't expect to see myself emerge from the house. But then I *did* emerge.

"This is not a sexual dream," I told my other self, who was still entangled in white laces, seeming more and more absurd and incompetent. "That's a distraction. The real message of the dream is that Bernard is in an inaccessible place within one of these houses, and I'm too hung up in finding myself along the way to consider him. The one who needs help can only find it by embracing Jesus. There's nothing wrong with masturbation."

Sitting on the sand, I was using the blades of the now-removed ice skates to try to cut and chop away the laces that entangled my fingers, hands, knees, etc. But I was nude from the waist down, and I was afraid that I might accidentally strike my erect penis. Perhaps I did.

Wolves, running through the inky breeze, whistled merrily.

INTERPRETATION

Having dreamed this myself, I interpreted the dream as though Bernard had dreamed it. The dream seemed at first to be all about convolution and frustration, but upon further analysis and reflection it then became apparent that the real message was a desire for isolation from the society of women. The intentional strategy of creating an impenetrable maze that excludes outsiders appears to be an escape method devised by the hidden, undiscovered Bernard within. Interestingly, Bernard had conceived an alter-ego for himself, a false ego or disguise, in the character of the psychiatrist (modeled after myself). It is this disguised figure which he cast out into the dangerous wilderness. This allowed his *real* self to be secluded.

Bernard's secret desire really was an escape from sexuality. The dream made it clear to me that Bernard had a psychological preference for masturbation rather than sex with a partner. This reinforced the diagnosis of schizoid personality. He had been sexually active in the period before his religious conversion, but it seems that sex was bothersome to him. He half-believed that many women were actively pursuing him as a sexual partner, that he was unusually attractive to them, and he sought seclusion within a monastery to escape this disturbance.

The recursive and refractive elements of the dream were representative of the elaborate structure of religious faith that he was in the process of constructing in order to justify his retreat from society and the burden of sex.

Of course, mysteries remain, including the meaning of the imagined white kitchen (somehow more dangerous still than the pursuing wolves and the emasculating ice skates), and the reason the knife shop was called *The Fragrant Dog*. I've speculated that the kitchen is an emotional intimacy with a parent figure, and the dog's fragrance is a kind of repulsive sweat/funk that implies a guilt association with self-gratification as a sort of homosexual act inflicted on oneself. But I've reached no conclusion on these particular points.

6.

No Easy Road

Brother Juan Diego

The person responsible for the bloody pig's foot was a novice known as Brother Juan Diego. He was a troublemaker whose presence within the monastery seems almost unaccountable. Though Father Joseph and the Novice Master, Brother Francis, had turned away many candidate monks who they believed did not have a true vocation, they had retained and tolerated this dangerous bully for over two years, though he was willful and cruel and he caused so much difficulty for the other brothers. This latest outrage, however, was too much.

Juan Diego's prank was inspired by what he had somehow learned about me: that I had given away my shoes before joining the church, and I had a compulsion for charity. By this he associated me with the "mad fool" Brother Juniper, and he was oddly compelled to try to humiliate me.

After completing his two year novitiate, Juan Diego had been put on probation for an additional four months as a result of several lapses of discipline. And now this final absurd act resulted in his immediate dismissal and removal from the monastery. He pled, as he had often done when in trouble before, that he was under the influence of an evil spirit, and that he was truly repentant and willing to submit to the authority of his superiors. But it was too late for another "second" chance for him. Father Joseph reassured him that he, Victor Rugamas (no longer entitled "Brother Juan Diego"), would still be able to attain salvation through the Church; he could receive the mass; he could make confession directly to Father Joseph himself if he preferred (and if he remained in the region), and he would be assisted in every possible way to overcome his spiritual troubles if he were sincere in his desire to reform. But there was no place for him in a monastic community among the consecrated monks.

The question of where he got the pig's foot was never quite resolved. Today there may still be a three-legged pig hobbling around somewhere.

A Touch of Madness on the Mountain

And, as much as I came to feel a part of the life of the monastery in only a few days, as much as I came to love the brother monks and the sense of religious community they gave me, as much as my prayers gave me a new and deeper sense of bliss and spiritual fulfillment while I was there, it was soon time for my retreat to end. Too soon, less than a week after my arrival.

In the late afternoon of my last day of retreat, the Novice Master absolutely rejected my request to remain for a three week postulancy and discernment, though my request was quite standard—it was simply a repeat of the written request I'd made upon arrival—and postulancy was the very reason I had travelled from New York. Del, who had arrived the same day as I, was remaining for his postulancy, but I was being turned away. Brother Francis gave no further explanation beyond the insistence that I return to the city and consider one more short retreat some time in autumn. When I told him that I would never return to the city, he met my stubbornness with an inexpressive silence. Father Joseph was not available for consultation.

Cast out, for no clear cause, turned away without ceremony though the monks were known to show such love and compassion to all visitors—all visitors but me!—I was driven wild with rage and despair. All right, many candidates were typically rejected after their postulancy, but I would not even be given the courtesy of a token postulancy? They wouldn't even *pretend* to consider me? I had no luggage to pack; I would willingly give up even the small bag of rags I'd carried around as spare clothing. I skipped Vespers on my last evening so that, while the others were at their prayers, I could run off into the wilderness, alone. They could turn me away if they wanted, but they couldn't force me to return to society. I would become the ultimate hermit, not even bearing one crumb, one tool, or one seed with me to aid in my survival. And knowing nothing about where I was going, I set off to hide in the mountains.

Thus I tempted the Tempter. I pulled my hair and scratched my face with the nails of my hands as I wandered without a trail, aiming only to climb higher and higher, and at first I failed even at that. Darkness rapidly descended upon me, and my brief rise soon also reversed itself into a descent as I crested a hill, then came down through a dense cluster of wood to the edge of a steep gorge. Turning to my right, I found myself mounting once again for a brief span, when I came to a narrow strip of earth cluttered with stones and loose soil where no trees grew. Here, I could see the sky above, and I saw the land rising to greater heights on the other side of the gorge to my left, thanks to a faint tinge of twilight that would soon be gone, and I was barely aided in my sight by the radiance of a moon that was just now peeking out from behind a more distant mountain. But the woods directly ahead of me, and those I had emerged from, were now looming black masses. And before me, on that strangely barren strip of earth, one large white stone among all the gray suddenly rose up. It was not a stone, I soon realized, but in truth it was a wild goat.

I recognized after a few minutes of reflection that I was standing in the dry bed of what would have been a creek in season. I could choose to walk back up its twisted course, off to the right, and return into the shadow of the woods in a direction that would likely take me up behind the monastery I had so recently fled. Or, turning to my left I could follow the stony path to where it plunged over the gorge's edge. While I was thinking, the goat made a little leap and scampered away. Then *Over the edge*, I decided, *it must be*.

"Thou, O Lord, art my hope," I declared.

Where creek bed met gorge, I saw that a series of large boulders jutted out along the slope, washed clean of soil and vegetation, where no doubt they would produce a cascade when the water flowed, but now they served as a sort of oversized staircase to aid my descent. I also saw that the gorge was not exceptionally deep, perhaps only sixty or eighty feet down into the narrow defile, maybe less, it was hard to see for sure, but the bare soil below seemed a different ashen color than the illumined edges of my stone steps. I was fairly sure that I did see the bottom, that I wasn't merely conjuring it up from my imagination in a void of space.

Sitting on each stone in turn, then turning and clambering down, sometimes extending my toes to reach down to the next terrace, and sometimes allowing myself to drop a short distance, I spoke the answer to my own foolish prayer: "Thou shalt not tempt the Lord thy God." Yes, I was being a fool after all. It couldn't be helped, my wrath overwhelmed me in my weakness. My wrath and my pride. Those *damned* monks had turned me away.

I reached the bottom, my body still intact. I was in a place of darkness where the moon was no longer visible to me. I shuffled across loose gravel, stepped into a very shallow and slow flowing stream, with a couple of deeper spots beneath the surface (at one point I sank as deep as my upper thigh), and made my way over to the other side of the gorge where the rise before me was more smooth and less steep than that which I'd left behind. A kind of gully, perpendicular to the main watercourse, cut into the hillside before me and made a scalable slope, almost like a ramp of jagged and slippery stones with weeds among them. I only needed to haul myself over a shallow bank, then incline myself forward and use hands and feet to climb and climb and climb. And there were more shrubs and creeping plants as I came out of the gully, and saplings—I felt a spider—then I was standing upright and grabbing at the branches, then the trunks of mature trees—and then I was off into the woods again and walking up the side of a mountain. The gorge was forgotten.

I managed, in stuttering stages of climbing then resting, to ascend quite a distance. How far? I don't know. But then I felt my strength suddenly drain away from my body, all at once, and I could no longer bear to prick my flesh and stub my toes and scratch my hands in wild groping for a way. I threw myself down on the ground and lay there, to think.

In the place of thoughts, sleep came.

7.
The True Horror of Sin (Dream)

I dreamed of an intense heat. The words *intense* and *blistering* filled my mind. There was a pain to accompany these words: My eye. My left eye was brutally pierced by a fiery red-hot spike, and then new steel implements, razors and hooks, were inserted into the eye and scraped along the flesh that lined the socket. The flesh within was more tender and excruciating in the pain it produced than the eye itself—which seemed to have dissolved—had been. But it wasn't just my eye that was being destroyed. It was the skin of all children, blistering and melting away. It was nuclear war.

Dancing, tortured, scalded children—naked—spun in terror to relieve the intense agony of being cooked on all sides. Their skin was charred and flaky, and bloody flesh was exposed. There was no relief.

I wept and howled with a grief beyond words, and a terror that seemed to fill all space and time was pulling me apart, as I realized that God's own grief had found an expression through the pity that I felt. But I didn't pity those idiot children, nor did I feel any sadness for their mothers and fathers who helplessly watched the suffering of their children on TV (the parents, sick from radiation, were unable to move from their corduroy sofas, and the upholstery was slightly mildewed). No, one hundred thousand lives lost, one hundred thousand dead in agonized suspension were merely a pimple to be popped.

The infinite sadness that I, God, felt, was my great sympathy for the man who had detonated the bomb. Nothing, fundamentally, had changed for his victims, besides a little pain, death, or loss of loved ones. But for the killer himself, eternal grace was lost forever. He had sinned. (I never saw him).

I too, I myself, not God, but I, Bernard, had sinned. My cheeks blushed and my tears flowed. Because I had wanted to stick my head up my high school math teacher's skirt and kiss her.

Unable to Interpret

This dream was very troubling. At first it may seem that this was the kind of dream that psychiatrists were born to analyze. It seems to point unambiguously at a repressed sexual fantasy that traces back to Bernard's adolescence and confusion between a mother/authority figure and an object of erotic desire. But such dreams, which seem to lay their theses bare, are exceedingly rare, and are usually profound in their deception. I felt certain there was a more terrible fantasy buried within this one, and since I was compelled by my new system to interpret the dream as though it were mine and not Bernard's I was soon infected with the terror this dream possessed. Its shame was also my shame.

But what could it mean? The day that Bernard told me this dream, I suffered a sort of depressive episode (though I only gave vent to my feelings after he left my office, of course, when I was alone). I wept and wept, and I got a bottle of bourbon (nurses keep them, sometimes, and sometimes they share) and drank myself into an oblivious state for the first time in years. When I awoke the next day, lying on the floor beneath my desk, I found I had wounded my hand slightly with my stapler.

8.
Novitiate

Ravenous

I awoke when it was still dark, and I didn't know where I was. My body ached terribly, and I felt coated with filth and sweat. I imagined some great mallet had pounded me into the soil during my sleep, and I exerted myself to the limit of my strength just to roll over and stretch out my hands and grasp the detritus. A few live ferns tickled my flesh. I imagined the fragments of rotten leaves I held were so many human souls, condemned. Then I became aware of myself and my circumstances. I had crawled out into the woods in a fit, and I had played a foolish game. My hunger was acute. Though I had thought that I would climb to the mountaintop, cross my legs on a snowy peak, and live without anything to sustain my body for forty days, in imitation of Christ fasting, here I was famished mere hours into my hermitage. Now I stuffed whole fistfuls of rotting vegetation, and whatever insects they contained, into my mouth and chewed vigorously, though my teeth slid and grated without having much effect on the "food" I was attempting to ingest. I forced two swallows of the filth down my throat before spitting out the rest, then shoved my face into the dirt and rubbed it to further humiliate myself.

"Now, go!" I shouted at myself, and lifted myself suddenly erect. I turned downhill and walked, stumbled, fell, rose again, and forced my way back down to the gulley. I would return to the monastery and confess everything, then go back to the city and follow the church's instructions.

Once I had returned to the bottom of the gorge, I recognized that it would be impossible for me to get back to the abbey the way I had come. The face which I had descended at night was too steep and treacherous to climb back up, and the twilight of dawn which was just arriving to enlighten the scene only made the danger more apparent. I chose the easier path downstream, which was still quite rough and difficult, and I managed, through many hours of walking, to follow the course down to lower lands. In the brighter light of mid-morning, I emerged in a place where the gulch widened, the walls faded away, and I pulled myself up onto a grassy embankment in a barely inclined valley floor. A few hundred yards out, I came to a roadside.

After forty minutes of waiting, I flagged down a passing car, and I had myself delivered to the monastery.

Along the way, as we were driving, while the three campers in the car gawked at me in my filthy canvas tunic (I had stolen my working habit from the monastery, but I wore sandals instead of the work-boots that would have spared me a lot of trouble), I observed a helicopter flying rapidly overhead. I wondered whether it was a search and rescue copter out looking for me. It wasn't.

MOURNING

Monks were prostrate on the ground, rubbing dirt on their shaved pates. Prayers were mingled with despairing sobs. Father Jerome, the prior second to Father Joseph, stood with them, his head bowed, his prayers silent. Brother Francis was also standing, but weeping and despondent. There was a police car parked in the flower garden near the front gate.

No one noticed my arrival at first, when I and the campers who had given me a ride got out of the car and slammed our doors. But as I got closer to the small circle of men (about nine or ten of the monks were present in this gathering), Brother Francis saw me and brightened up a bit. He wiped away some of the tears that were bathing his face.

"Thank the Lord and his Blessing! You've returned to us."

Several of the monks lifted their eyes from the dirt, but they were deeply distracted by their sorrow. Brother Francis drew me aside to talk, the campers whispered among themselves, and Father Jerome addressed the gathered monks.

"Please, brothers. Our sadness is profound, but perhaps it is inapt. Let us recall, God shall wipe all tears from their eyes in heaven. Now let's gather with the other brothers in the church and pray together…"

As he continued to admonish the monks, my eyes fell on some strange dark stains in the soil around which the brothers were still sobbing. Brother Francis explained to me a little of what had happened.

"Brother Ignatius has been mortally wounded."—I didn't know this brother—"He's almost certainly dead. The doctors have his body now… Father Joseph administered the extreme unction before they took him. And Del… he should probably survive."

I looked around me again, at the strange sight. It was bright daylight. It seemed it should be night when such news is delivered. But, besides the keening and confusion, everything seemed quite… ordinary. And some of the monks were now sitting, sprawled out a little awkwardly perhaps, and even laughing ironically at their own bewilderment.

Francis continued. "They were attacked by a lion. It came running out of the hills. Then men ran." Brother Francis drew me further away and hurriedly whispered some more of the details, giving in for a moment to the sinful temptation to gossip. "Del fell first, and was wounded around the face and neck. Ignatius tried to help him, but the lion turned on Ignatius, dragged him off and killed him."

"Merciful God!" I exclaimed.

Brother Francis pulled me into the monastery through the gate.

"You must join us in the church. Some of the brothers are still praying for you, thinking you were one of the victims. Some are getting superstitious because of our many misfortunes; it will do them good, and restore their courage, to see you alive and well."

TRUE SERVICE

When Father Joseph returned from the hospital the following day,

I tearfully prayed for forgiveness and asked that he hear my confession. But before he would attend to my selfish needs, he spoke of what he had learned about our Brothers.

"Brother Ignatius died. Your friend Del was severely disfigured and is still in critical condition. We will all visit him in the hospital in turn."

Then he took me to his office and heard my confession. I told him—and God—all about my pride and my anger, my nightmare, and the vulgar ways in which I had offended God by abusing my faith in him.

Father Joseph assured me that he and Francis had both felt that I was sincere in my faith and my calling was genuine. But the time for my enclosure had not yet arrived. I was absolved of my sins, but must do serious penance, and I was advised not to return for at least half a year. God must call me. "Do something charitable with your time," he advised. "Something of a nature that requires true spiritual contact and human sympathy for the recipient. Until you learn charity, you cannot withdraw from society. You wouldn't have sufficient opportunities to learn it here, though a true contemplative... Well... don't jeopardize your soul by retreating only due to cowardice. This is not the place to escape a fear of mortality and suffering."

As I would come to know in the following years, Father Joseph possessed an astounding insight, he was kind and generous, and even in his strictness he was motivated only by true love.

I moved to Billings, to live in the closest thing to a "city" that Montana offers, and to volunteer for the Montana Suicide Prevention Hotline.

After some negotiation, I got a local branch of my bank to issue me a new ATM card and process my withdrawals (thank God I had saved my passport), so I was able to subsist. The priest at St. Pius the X Church recommended me to a Catholic family that was renting out rooms in their home at a reasonably low rate.

The suicide hotline was absolutely the perfect place for me. It was terrible and painful, frustrating, and a challenge to my moral and ethical values. But it taught me to better understand the nature of others' suffering, the diversity of human experience and value, and it also helped me come to terms with my own weakness when attempting to intervene. My job was basically to help people reach their own conclusions. I was trained specifically to avoid passing judgment while offering compassion to those who felt unworthy of compassion, and to those who didn't believe in the compassion of others. As a Catholic, I knew that far more than life and death were at stake in these calls, but I was not permitted to impose my religious faith on the callers, and I concluded very quickly how futile it would have been to try to do so.

The center managers had to be persuaded that I could do this job competently, and they were suspicious of my background, but there was always a shortage of volunteers for the overnight shifts, even from among the psychology students who made up the majority.

I was surprised to discover that Montana has such a high suicide rate. At nearly one suicide per day, considering the small population of the entire state, Montana has the third highest per-capita suicide rate among states in the U.S., even ahead of Nevada (which I had always imagined as the fantasy destination for fools and the dead end for the desperate).

But, to understand the call volume and the demand for volunteers, it's necessary to realize that for every one person who actually kills himself or herself (the majority are men), dozens make serious attempts or threats, and for each of them, there are many dozens of people in an emotional crisis that verges on a suicide attempt. But these callers who are suicidal or close to suicidal represent a small percentage of those who called our center. Most callers had various other crises to deal with and never mentioned suicide. They were seeking mental health services, or substance abuse treatment, or counseling on domestic abuse, or... or... or... Well, the reasons were countless. But we helped them all, or attempted to help them, to the degree that our compassionate listening and our referral to other services could be of assistance. Additionally, we fielded plenty of calls from out of state. Because a suicide crisis is a life-critical emergency, most states require a caller to be placed with a volunteer within thirty seconds or else the call is automatically routed to another server—sometimes a very remote server. While about two-thirds of my calls were in-state, I occasionally fielded calls from as far away as Texas, and I got a surprising number of calls from Minnesota, for whatever reason there may be.

I had hoped to return to the abbey within six-months, but the center wanted volunteers to commit for a year, and that's precisely the time I gave them. I put in a lot of time at the center, including the overnight shifts most nights. In that time, I handled calls from many genuinely suicidal people, and I'm sure that I helped some of them. The few times when I was certain that a caller had chosen to live because of their conversation with me—well, there's nothing to compare to that feeling. I felt almost as though, through them, I had saved myself! But I experienced many lows. Most callers were deeply depressed when they called, the circumstances of their lives were often so bleak I couldn't do justice to their stories if I tried to represent them in a few words now, and though they ended their calls to me on a high note, thankful that I cared, thankful that I'd listened, claiming to have found new strength and new purpose—they didn't improve their lives and they didn't stay encouraged for long.

There are a few who I am sure killed themselves. The police were too late to stop them. One died while I was on the phone with him. Several suicides were reported to me well after the fact. And I can't doubt that several of the others who stopped calling had also committed suicide, or would shortly thereafter, or perhaps some of them who are alive today will still end their lives violently someday.

I actually got a reputation for being remarkably helpful and successful with my callers. I received a few written thank-you notes that were relayed to me by the supervisors. But, for as much as occasional praise helped keep up my morale, I believe my emotional burden was greater than what most other volunteers felt. For me, each caller who ended in suicide was not just another life lost, but an eternally damned soul that I had failed to save. That was when I felt most helpless.

I really felt for these people. I spoke to seniors, and teenagers, some family men, and many loners. People who had lost everyone and everything. People who were in the process of losing everything. People who were, to be frank, too senseless to stop destroying everything of value in their lives. The hell-bent. But, through listening, I came to understand them. As well as I could, I understood them, but I also understood that every human being, in their depth and complexity, contains something arbitrary and incomprehensible, a sort of curse or tempest within them. It may well be a seed of evil. Even when the victim may not be "at fault" for possessing that seed, it's there. For some of those who called me, this thing within was all-consuming.

Some of my callers liked to laugh. They liked it a lot. They may have started a call with a sort of cynical humor, a laughing in the face of death and a mockery of their own helplessness. It may have been ironic at first. But when the call went well, the laughter turned to something more joyful. Just the fun of life and childish joking could lift them out of their depression. There's no rule that says that a one-time high school valedictorian who got raped by her boyfriend's brother and his friends, whose family disbelieved her story and disowned her when she planned to carry the unintended pregnancy to term—though the baby was ultimately stillborn—who got addicted to methamphetamines and whose abusive first-husband turned out to be a pedophile—there's no rule that she can't laugh once in a while. "Did you know that Pope Francis once released a 'dove of peace' in the Vatican, and it got viciously attacked by a seagull? Proves that God has a sense of humor, doesn't it!?"

We got many prank callers, and several truly abusive ones. Some men automatically hung up when they got a male voice on the line, while others would openly comment, "Oh man, how many times do I have to call before I get a chick?" Then they would hang up and try again. I once got the same caller twice in a row this way, but on the second call he decided to confide in me and spent the next twenty minutes talking about his sexual frustrations and fantasies.

"I get excited when I visit public laundromats," he said, "and watch women wash their underpants."

I tried my very best for this man, as I did for every other, but I ended feeling only tainted by his filth. Then I sympathized even more with the female volunteers, who routinely had to tolerate even more profane and vulgar calls—calls which also expressed violent misogyny.

One kind-hearted volunteer, Susie, told me "These disturbed callers... they're expressing something which they can't safely express elsewhere. It's sickening to listen to, but the men live with these thoughts and this bitterness deep inside them every day. I can't really reform them, but sometimes they're even thankful and apologetic in the end. Most importantly, they generally end the call still alive."

Another volunteer, April, countered that abusive men not only angered her, but they left her troubled and conflicted. "Some of the suicidal callers have been victimized by this same kind of guy. The guys who make harassing calls... to vent, to chat, even to masturbate... On some level I don't *want* some of the worse callers to live... but..."—she always reversed herself after expressing something callous—"No, it's *always* better when a caller is inspired to live another day."

We had each had the experience of callers who didn't choose life. So the perverts had to be saved too.

This volunteer hotline was my principal occupation for the year, though I certainly continued to read and study, I prayed, attended church services, and I did additional volunteering to counsel family members of women currently incarcerated in the Montana Women's Prison. The program I participated in sent Catholic woman laity to counsel the woman prisoners directly, while both male and female volunteers were sent to counsel the prisoners' families. But, even in the Catholic families I ment, few had real religious conviction. They were looking for magical intervention, or some practical direct help such as a letter that would help in a parole application, or maybe a charitable hand-out. I felt I was in the uncomfortable position of having to offer false hope of material assistance, while no one was sincerely interested in the very real spiritual assistance I knew the church could offer. The children, meanwhile, had the simplest expectations. They just wanted an assurance that mommy was all right, or she was going to be all right. I gave them this assurance, but I didn't believe it myself.

When the end of my year as a volunteer was approaching, I wondered whether it would be right for me to quit the suicide prevention program. I had made a connection with some of the people at the very bottom of our social hierarchy, the people with the most real need for my sympathy and support. At the same time, I was in a constant emotional turmoil while doing this work, and I felt a sort of hollowness at the end of each day, as though I was at the limit of what I could meaningfully give.

Then, a strange coincidence—or perhaps a meaningful sign— occurred and released me from my service there. I volunteered for the final two nightshifts of my year-long commitment, and picked up an extra four-hour shift on the afternoons that followed. In a total of twenty-eight hours in two days, I fielded all sorts of calls, but not one of them mentioned suicide. I got the usual bored call- ers who wanted to chat about what was on TV, I got the people asking for the phone numbers to call for EBT food assistance, I got threats, and I got complaints of insomnia. But not one person mentioned suicide, the desire to "end" their suffering, not a single person said that they "can't take it anymore," there was just noth- ing even hinting at suicide or death as a way out. Before this, the longest I had ever gone without a suicide-related call was maybe eight hours, and that seemed remarkable. But my co-volunteers were still getting all the suicide calls that they usually got. None of them happened to be routed my way. Without reading too much into this, I concluded that I had done good that year, but other volunteers would be able to continue this good work without me. We had even just brought on two new young volunteers earlier that week, who both seemed bright and motivated. I was free, now, to turn my attention wholly to the service of God.

I sent my parents a postcard from Philipsburg to let them know that all was fine, and that I expected soon to be a Catholic monk. In return, I received a letter to inform me that my father had died.

BACK IN GOOD GRACES

When I returned to St. Albert's, I was taken as a postulant for three weeks, and thereafter I was accepted as a novice. In humility I took the name Brother Juniper when I offered my first vows and received my tonsure. I felt a new purity, and I was very thankful to Father Joseph, who had made such a great difference in my appreciation for the suffering of man, his condition of sin, and the need for God's Word in the world.

My two years as a novice, taken on the whole, were a blissful experience, though there were plenty of troubles to cope with. I learned Latin, calligraphy, chant, and horseback riding, while studying to become a choir monk—pursuing the ultimate goal to be ordained in the regular clergy and qualify to hear confession. But strange accidents continued to happen, including several violent deaths. Two brothers died of carbon-monoxide poisoning after a small fire broke out in the dormitory. Brother Carlo died of a brain hemorrhage after being kicked by a horse.

Del was with us, now known as "Brother Michael," with half of his face intact. The other half looked like a field of pale waxy flesh, somewhat droopy, with a pinched up eye-socket about two-and-a-half inches to the left of where his eye used to be, as though it had drifted outwards to fill the void left by his absent left ear. His mouth was reasonably well constructed, but the muscles only functioned on the right, and his nose too looked only half-natural.

He was generally optimistic, and in good humor most of the time. He took his temporary vows and became a professed monk one year ahead of me, a little over two years after our arrival in the back of the delivery truck.

Further Vows

At the end of my period as a novice, I felt stronger than ever in body, mind, and spirit, and I lived every day celebrating the Word of God. I still puzzled over the great mysteries, and I struggled with petty temptations and doubts, but I was absolutely determined in my desire to live out my life on this mountain in dedication to a religious monastic life. The brothers elected to accept me in my three-year period of temporary profession.

From that day, every time we celebrated Mass, it was as joyful an experience as my first Mass. I felt certain of God's grace. I was willing to face any death that might come to me, or to live and struggle according to God's will.

Shortly thereafter, in the winter, Victor Rugamas returned. I could perceive he was a changed man. Outwardly he was more rough and rugged than he had been. His eyes, though, which had appeared as windows into a void when I first encountered him, now were warm and expressive of a humble sentiment. It seemed, somehow, that he had suffered greatly in his time away from the monastery, but his mind had been purified.

His hair was wet and partially frozen when he arrived for a retreat. He explained to Father Joseph that he hadn't had a shower for several days, so he had washed his face and hair with snow before daring to approach our gate. He didn't explain how he had come up the mountain.

Several of the senior monks who remembered him asked the Father to turn him away after a few meals and a day of rest, but I approached the Father to talk to him privately.

"Father Joseph," I said, "I know I have no special right to speak on this matter."

"Go ahead."

"I think Victor has reformed. I mean, I strongly feel this."

"God be praised. Your enthusiasm is remarkable, advocating for him, but you know we didn't aim to harm him. Some are called and some are not."

"I'm not complaining, Father."

"No. And I'm already inclined to agree with you. I was thinking it would be best to keep him here for a short retreat. Let's say five days. The other brothers are merciful, but I think I've set a bad example for them."

What he said next flattered me in a way that threatened to inflate my pride.

"Brother, you seem to have a charism"—this means talent—"for discerning the spiritual condition of a man."

I was ashamed, and I was tempted to fall to the floor though the Father prevented me.

"I have had experience," I explained, "among men and women of high and low conditions… of moral and immoral characters…"

"You've made your confessions, Brother. But you may be able to help in the guidance of others. We don't have to talk any more of this now. Victor will stay for a while."

Victor completed his retreat. Then, several months later, he came on another retreat; then another time again. After that, Father Joseph strongly persuaded the brother monks to accept Victor as a Novice, going against all precedent. Some brothers were resistant, others supportive of this unique decision, and many were of mixed opinion, but we finally elected to follow the Father's proposal and Victor became, for the second time, Brother Juan Diego.

Brother Juan Diego always wore a look of deep reverence and humility, and never caused any disturbance. He seemed perpetually thrilled that he had received a grace he was undeserving of. In short, he was a true Christian. Sadly, he didn't live much longer, as he soon died of a severe reaction to a bee sting, an allergic condition which he had not disclosed on his application—though perhaps, this being the first time he was ever stung, he may not have known of his vulnerability. I felt assured, though, that he had gone on to Paradise, as had all the men who now lay in our burgeoning cemetery.

More Disturbances

The next to die was Father Jerome, our claustral prior.

I and Brother Michael were coming from delivering some vegetables to the refectory, and as we proceeded out through the inner doors of our compound and approached the monastery's outer gate, we were surprised to find it closed. Then a ring of keys was thrown over the wall. We rushed forward in some alarm, and the scuffling of our feet must have attracted the attention of Father Jerome, as he shouted at us suddenly, "Back inside!"

I caught a glimpse, through a space in the gate, of Father Jerome kneeling on the ground, with two rough-looking men standing over him with guns.

"What do you want, what do you want?" Father Jerome demanded. "This is a sanctuary of the children of God."

As Brother Michael and I hastily retreated, we had just the time to hear, "Let us in. Get up," before pulling the heavy doors of the inner gate shut and barring them. Our monastery was hardly a fortress, and we knew that with a bit of determination the men could pretty easily climb over a couple of walls or batter down our doors, so we rushed to gather the few monks who were currently within the compound. We aimed to shelter ourselves within the church. The men never attempted to force an entry, however. Rather, they fled and took Father Jerome with them.

A police detective came out to speak with our Abbot that evening, to explain the surrounding story and report on the death of Father Jerome. The two gunmen had killed another man earlier in Philipsburg as a result of a traffic dispute, and they raced up into the mountains to evade police pursuit. One of the criminals, Rod Cecil, when taken into custody, testified that Father Jerome, who was tending to some flowers in a garden, saw the speeding vehicle approaching and hastily ran and locked the gate. When they showed their guns, he tossed the keys over the wall. He negotiated with them and offered himself as a hostage to prevent them from doing any other harm to the monastery.

They took him in the car, and drove back down towards the highway, where they immediately fell into a police trap, blockaded on three sides. The criminals wouldn't give in without a fight. They first tried to break through the blockade, then reversed, there was a brief chase, and when the driver ran their car off the road and flipped it into a ditch, Father Jerome lost his life in the crash. The driver was killed in the ensuing shootout.

Rod Cecil, the survivor, gave a full confession from his hospital bed. After recovery from his injuries, he pled guilty to murder and to the capital crime of murder while fugitive, without seeking a deal. He is reported to have converted to Catholicism in prison. As he faces the death penalty, our brothers have prayed for him, and on our behalf Father Joseph has written to the Governor to request a commutation of the death sentence.

Our faith stood strong. Despite what befell Father Jerome, we felt sure of God's mercy and infinite wisdom. And, to us, Father Jerome is a martyr who was sent for our protection. He even caused his own killer, a sinner, to repent and turn to God.

It seems odd, but through the years while I remained at the monastery, there had been a steady increase in the number of Catholics coming on retreat. Initial fears and morbid curiosity started to turn to more sincere compassion and a desire among the faithful to aid us in our times of trouble. Then, in the time after Father Jerome's death, there was a great surge in the number of visitors, which has never fully abated.

In the time since my novitiate had ended, there had already been an increasing number of men, mostly young but some older, who came to apply as postulants. We had just added four new novices, all of whom appeared well suited to join our community, and now our population was beginning to swell again.

There was also a significant increase in donations sent from Catholics around the country. Gossip about the abbey had long suggested there was a curse upon us, but the louder message now was that Catholics were starting to celebrate and support us. The fact that our faith persisted in the face of danger and bitter loss was seen as inspirational.

While we were mourning our loss of dear Father Jerome, we knew—as we always had known upon the loss of any brother—that he would receive God's grace and mercy in eternity. This was our consolation. But when the next act of violence occurred, we were left with no such assurance.

It was summer again, halfway into my third year of temporary profession, when one of our new novices, Brother Guy, committed suicide in his cell. None of us knew why he chose to die. He left no note and had not revealed anything that would cause us to suspect he was depressed. He killed himself by hanging with a belt that he partially jammed between door and frame, held secure by the pressure of the door when it was pressed shut. It had never occurred to any of us that such a thing was even possible.

My charism, which was supposed to be a deep insight into the hearts and minds of others, had not been great enough for me to guess at Brother Guy's suicidal intent, and my volunteer work in suicide prevention had not enabled me to help this poor soul, now forever excluded from God's grace by his damning final act.

The three other novices who were staying with us at this time all chose to leave the monastery. One temporarily professed brother also chose to end his profession and return to secular life, with the blessing of the church. The permanently professed monks (now including Brother Michael) did not have the option to leave, and I, who was merely six months away from permanent profession, would never have dreamt of leaving. I knew my vocation was true.

I had noticed around this time that Brother Michael was looking worried and full of inner conflict. This had gone on for some time. His troubles were apparent on the features of his face, which I felt

I could read well, as I had long ago accepted his disfigurement and didn't fear to look on him as I would on any other of God's creatures. But why was he anxious? Brother Guy's death gave Brother Michael an opportunity to put another mask upon his feelings. Profound sorrow was expected, and that's what he showed.

His Excellency Donald Arnsdorff, Bishop of Helena, came to counsel and comfort us now in our time of grief. Because I was preparing to become a choir monk, through the advice of our Abbot Father Joseph, His Excellency also spoke with me privately about my impending ordination that would allow me to conduct mass and administer the sacraments. "You were surely called to serve God, and I've heard only good things about your devotion, piety, and firm faith. You have come to God through Christ, and may God keep you."

"Amen" was my only reply.

9.
The Dirty Toilet (Daydream)

Dr. Shieling, Entranced, Imagines a Toilet Stall

During a session in which Bernard talked to me in greater depth about the feelings he experienced when Brother Guy committed suicide, I had an uncharacteristic lapse of attention and found myself daydreaming about a terrible toilet. My daydream had a vividness unlike any other daydream I had previously experienced, and I believe that I even entered into a trance-like state. In fact, I may have fallen asleep briefly while Bernard was speaking (a nurse and I had once again had a late night chat with a few sips of whiskey the night before, so I was a little drowsy).

Anyway, in my imagination—or perhaps *vision* is a more suitable description—I saw a small room in a public space which served as a toilet stall. There was no sink or other convenience within; the entire room was maybe one meter square with the toilet filling the space and facing out the door. Unlike most bathrooms, though, the door of this one—painted off-white—was made up mainly of horizontal wooden slats at an oblique angle, like a louvered closet door that ventilates the space and which a person could easily peep through if he were so inclined.

The door opened inwards, quite awkwardly as there was no room for it within the tiny interior space. It could hardly clear the edge of the toilet, and it made no allowance for a space where a human could stand out of the way of its path.

The interior of the stall was lined with square black tiles, and the ceiling was unreasonably low. In the process of entering the stall, one would have to cross over a narrow metal gutter in the floor, which passed in the space between toilet and door. This gutter was slightly flooded with brownish-yellow urine and contained dissolved tobacco from cigarettes that had been tossed into the muck.

The only possible way to enter was to stand on the toilet itself, hunched over to avoid hitting the ceiling with one's head—which one would have to do in full view of anyone who was passing by, or who was actively watching, and one of the many diners who sat at nearby tables was sure to look and wrinkle his nose, offended by the sight and the smell—and then one would have to try to force the door closed past the toilet—and this was rendered more difficult by the fact that the seat of the toilet jutted out slightly further when one was standing on it, thus interfering more with the passage of the door—and finally one could climb down and sit, while maneuvering for enough room to get one's pants down. Obviously one would want to close the door *before* opening one's pants, because of the public location.

In the space behind the door, which would only be revealed after one entered the room and started to close the door, there were bugs. I never quite saw into that space, but I knew that there were bugs there… and I was horrified but obsessed with the idea of having to put my naked legs out into that filthy space.

Cold Reading

In keeping with my newly established program, I tried to interpret this as though Bernard had had the daydream. But I needed Bernard's help to understand it.

I couldn't quite tell him that I was using *my own* daydreams to explore and understand *his* psychology. Bernard had already told me several times, in jest, that I, as a psychiatrist, was more superstitious than he as a monk. So, considering his distrust, I had to resort to more subtle tactics to tease out answers that might satisfy my need to understand.

I had recently, in another case, started to employ cold-reading tactics to learn details and guide conversations without appearing to ask questions, and it was going well, so I decided to apply these techniques with Bernard too.

"When you first heard that Guy had committed suicide, how did you feel?"

"Well, naturally, frightened."

"And fear may have reminded you of something. I perceive that you felt a certain discomfort in your childhood... related to insects, or not insects, but something that is transitory or moving, innocuous but containing a potent fear that only touches you."

"I don't think so. I never feared insects."

"No, I didn't think so, but this touches on the... the fear that one gets that is *like* or *similar to* a child's fear of insects—a fear which you were never susceptible to yourself—but it had another trigger or object... something round... it could be found in a bathroom."

"Well..."

Bernard's pivoting neck and shoulders became a bit more animated.

"I hadn't thought of this for years, so I don't know how you could know about it, but there was a picture in my childhood..."

"Precisely, a picture which was frightening to you."

"Yes, you're exactly right. And..."

"And there was something in this picture that frightened you. Something vaguely round in shape, or having a kind of curvature..."

"Yes, a round moon, exactly as you described it..."

"But to you it was more than a moon."

"Yes! I... this is a deeply buried image, I don't know how you brought it out so suddenly. The moon was indistinct, in a rather rough or impressionistic... black and white... off-white actually... image of an alleyway in London. The scene was foggy."

"And you saw something in the moon."

"...because it wasn't so clear to my child's eye that it was a moon at all. The shape was only vaguely roundish, and it wasn't a full moon... gibbous perhaps, and haloed by the foggy haze, so that when I saw it, it was more like... looking into me..."

"It was an eye to you. A monstrous eye."

"My God, it's like you can see it yourself."

"And this picture hung in a bathroom."

"No. It was in my parents' bedroom."

"I don't think there was a toilet there."

"Ha, ha, of course you're referring to the separate half-bathroom that was just off of my parents' room. They had their own small bathroom."

"And if the lights were off in your parents' room… and the door of the bathroom were open and the light from the bathroom was projected into the room?"

"It would fall on the picture! Yes, in fact I didn't like to go in that bathroom because of the view of the picture. That London scene, with the silhouetted man walking in a lonely alley, and the eye of an enormous monster peering from the sky at him… only later did I realize that it was merely a view of the moon."

"It's not a main factor, but I believe there were sometimes insects in that bathroom."

"Of course, there probably were sometimes. I didn't really think about it."

"No, as I said, that wasn't the main factor, it's simply that it was there, near the true source of your fear… a creepy kind of fear."

"Yes, the picture was certainly creepy. It still has a kind of potency to me when I think about it. Something beyond words. But why did you suddenly bring up this memory?"

"I mentioned it because I believed that this monstrous eye in the sky produced a kind of primitive fear for you, which you felt again in a new form when visualizing Guy after his suicide."

"That's a profound insight, doctor. I'm starting to believe you're onto something after all. Will you… will you find a way to help me?"

"That's what we're trying to do, day by day."

INTERPRETATION

From this conversation, and my reflection on the toilet daydream, I concluded that Bernard's unspoken desire was to *relieve himself* of guilt, which he had defined as sin. The toilet was a kind of confessional, and the insects were the fear of God, which Bernard had transformed into a kind of supernatural fear… something built upon his early childhood image of a terrible eye in the sky. But to enter that stall, to stretch out his legs among the insects, would be to finally confront and submit to this potent supernatural element. He would be purged and then freed from fear once and for all. Thus, his purgatory was a toilet.

Now, let's return to the story of Bernard's monastic life.

10.
Choir Monk

A little more than six years after my first retreat to St. Albert's Abbey, seven and a half years after attending my first service at St. Patrick's Cathedral, I was finally permitted to take my permanent vows, and His Excellency Donald Arnsdorff, Bishop of Helena ordained me as transitional deacon, bringing me one step closer to being a priest.

A mere four months after my deaconate, because our Abbot Father Joseph had advocated for me so energetically and for so long, His Excellency the Bishop returned for my final ordination to the priesthood. Brother Michael, who had already been a deacon for some time, would also be ordained a priest.

On the day of our ordination ceremony, I was the first to receive the laying on of hands.

At that very instant there was an enormous thundering sound and a violent tremor of the earth, as from an earthquake. A terrible wind blasted the monastery, whistling all around, and the roof rattled with the sound of heavy objects being tossed upon it. We all, including the Bishop, felt a great awe and terror, but we persisted in our ceremony. My hands trembled during the anointing, but by then I saw that His Excellency the Bishop was well composed in his bearing, and I drew courage from his strength. Brother Michael went through all the motions as well as he was able.

When we conducted mass and I was—for the first time—able to help distribute communion to my brothers, I perceived that each of them had a more intense desire for the Eucharist than I had seen before. Fear had provoked this new awareness of their need. As for me, I had *always* been aware of the imminence of death, in every communion and every small favor I received from the first day I had been touched by the Holy Spirit. And now, when I was asked to give my blessing to the bishop who had ordained me, it was no mere ceremony; his faith in and dependence upon the power of God were apparent.

With the ritual completed, we all then went out to see what was happening. Our hearts were thundering, though it had otherwise been quiet for some time. Outside, it was calm and the sky was clear, but there were fallen and broken trees and scattered limbs all around. We realized that the noises we'd heard on the roof were probably caused by small branches and debris. But how could there have been such a sudden storm, with hardly a cloud left in the sky soon after, and not a drop of rainwater anywhere?

Some of us guessed "earthquake," while others suspected a miraculous event. It wasn't until the next day that we found out the truth, and we all laughed when we found out it had only been a landslide.

Geologists came out to do a survey, measure things, and do whatever geologists do. News reporters prowled about. When all was concluded, the final story revealed that a 4,000 ton hunk of rock had sheared off from a mountain face and tumbled down, causing a cascade that pulled down an additional 380,000 tons of smaller stones and soil. The fissure that had caused the stone to split had probably formed over a period of several hundred thousand years. Now the stone had come to rest (and permanently planted itself) just beside a rarely used wooded path about 600 yards out behind the monastery.

Soon thereafter, hikers and rock climbers began coming out in greater numbers, especially those who enjoy "bouldering," and the thirty-five foot high stone has come to be called "monk's rock."

Our lives and our buildings were fortunately spared from any harm in the landslide. Our only loss was about eighty percent of our vegetables, plus our herb garden, so we would need to purchase more produce that year, and Father Joseph would have to give up on his rosehip and mint teas. He put in another large order for anise to be delivered up from Philipsburg.

A Discovery

As I went wandering in the hills one day, when I had a little time for private recreation, I approached the field of debris where the landslide had done much of its destruction. I noticed what seemed to be a dark spot several hundred yards up the mountainside. My curiosity attracted me to that spot, and so I climbed, though the way was treacherous and I was compelled to climb over and among heaps of tree trunks, soft soil, cracked stones—every kind of matter all tossed together in a heterogeneous mass.

By the time I reached the "spot," it had grown into a largish hole. I looked in and discovered the entrance to a cave of sorts. The rear of the cave, however, was inaccessible, as it had collapsed. I entered the front of the cave, which was about five feet high and three feet wide. The cave was about eighteen feet deep and it terminated in a wedge where fallen stones and soil prevented any further passage.

The middle of the cave kind of bowed out at the sides, and I recognized that the floor, though quite rough and cratered, had been somewhat smoothed out by tools, so I then realized that this must be all that remained of a mineshaft or manmade shelter. Also, I found that there was a low alcove off to the left side of the cave, and when I crouched down I saw a long rectangular box. I yanked, and tugged, and pulled the box, and it slid out from the alcove. It looked like something that could contain large tools, and it was quite heavy. When I removed the top, which merely rested loosely on the box, I found that it did contain several large iron tools, but there was also a compartment at one end of the box which was overstuffed with stones and crystals. I picked out one large, attractive piece of crystal, about the size of a quail's egg, and came out of the cave again into the direct light of the sun. The crystal had a remarkably attractive deep blue color. It was only then that I discovered that the name of the mountain range, the Sapphire Mountains, was not metaphorical.

I went down to report what I'd found, and to get several of

the brother monks to help bring down the box and salvage any potentially valuable contents. When we returned, we pulled the box just outside the cave, scooped out the gems into a few small sacks, and abandoned the rest.

Among the stones we retrieved, there were some large pieces of a gray and green stone matrix containing multiple blue and violet crystals, there were some elongated prisms, and some large rough gemstones which seemed somewhat rounded and polished. The "quail's egg" fit in this last category.

Father Joseph spoke with a gem specialist from Philipsburg, and then followed up with a call to a bishop in Rome. The Roman bishop connected him with a merchant in Israel, who then referred him to a trustworthy appraiser in New York who handles sapphires as well as diamonds. After we sent a "small" sample to the appraiser, Benjamin Shain, he flew out to meet the abbot in person and inspect the entire collection.

By this time, word had already spread within Montana—presumably the Philipsburg expert spoke to another local—that a great treasure in sapphires had been discovered. But when a few curious treasure seekers came out, the cave had somehow already been closed up and buried again, probably from a sudden shifting of the still loose debris on the mountain. It was never located again.

Mr. Shain informed our abbot that the sapphires we had discovered were entirely unprecedented. He put out inquiries, and everyone he spoke with had the same opinion he held, which was that our story was impossible. This looked like a hoax.

First of all, the sapphires could not have been mined in the mountains. Though, in theory, sapphire crystals *could* reside within schist buried in the mountains, it would be virtually impossible to find them. One would have to pulverize and sift entire mountains to have any reasonable chance of locating any valuable gems. Nobody does this. Sapphires are located deep beneath the surface in lowlands or within streams, where hundreds of thousands or millions of years of water action clean off and isolate the crystals, yet they are still extremely difficult to locate in even the richest sites.

Secondly, the sapphires we found were of a quality and size entirely unknown within Montana or any place on earth outside of Sri Lanka or Burma. The highest quality American sapphires, the Yogo sapphires, are considered extremely valuable if they can produce a cut gem over one carat in weight. The largest cut Yogo is just over ten carats. My "quail's egg" was 720 carats uncut. The other crystals included many gems of the highest quality weighing over 80 carats. Thus, the entire previous sapphire output of the United States was made trivial by the collection of gems we held in a couple of small sacks. Benjamin Shain was not able to give any definite value to the collection, but he did say that altogether their value would certainly be "in the millions."

The appraiser said he could pretty much guarantee that the gems had been transported to the site where I'd found them, and hidden there. By whom, when, or why was impossible to determine. There were no credible reports of such a collection of gems having gone missing anywhere. The gems were uncut and had no history. What purpose the mineshaft on the hillside could have served was also indeterminate.

Father Joseph, consulting with several bishops over the next few months, concluded that the best course of action would be to send the majority of the sapphires to Catholic Charities USA, a large organization whose lawyers would take on the responsibility to determine their rightful ownership. He, however, decided also to have one gem, a crystal apparently polished by natural water action, weighing 135 carats, donated to Wyoming's New Mount Carmel monastery to support the brothers who had established the first foundation for a Carmelite monastic tradition in America. Bishop Arnsdorff expressed his approval, and Mr. Shain was paid with a small piece of schist containing multiple three-to-five-carat stones. He was further contracted as a consultant to Catholic Charities.

We kept nothing of value for ourselves. Our monastery, by this time, was already sufficiently well-funded.

After a couple of years passed, an article in the New York Times reported that there were no supportable claims of ownership, though Catholic Charities USA had made three out-of-court settlements with individuals and families whose ancestors had prospected in the region, two of whom claimed knowledge of a vanishing "secret family treasure." The gemstones I'd found were still being cut, and had supposedly been appraised at a combined value of sixty to eighty million dollars, not including the gemstone at New Mount Carmel, which had separately been appraised at 3.5 million.

Sharing God's Love

Meanwhile, I spent the years, as always, in profound contemplation of spiritual truths and God's will. I found new meaning in my life when I began hearing confession, sometimes from novices, and frequently from Catholics who came on retreat, an event that was becoming increasingly common. The stories of the landslide which occurred at the very moment of my ordination and my subsequent discovery of the buried sapphires contributed to a new wave of curiosity about the activities of our monastery.

By hearing confession, I was at last able to share the fruits of my spiritual investigations, and perhaps even help to keep some of the faithful true to their faith. God would be the one to save them, through his infinite mercy and grace, but I felt a great sense of purpose knowing that I could be used as an instrument in leading them to this salvation. Yet I was also sorely troubled, and I re-experienced some of the frustrations I had felt as a counselor to the suicidal. I was forced to see, once again, how frail humans fell so easily into self-destructive cycles—how they acted perversely and caused themselves such peril.

I felt hope because the sinners turned to God, and he always rewarded their faith with absolution. His love and infinite mercy were a joy to behold and experience. But I felt revulsion when witnessing what went on within the hearts of men, and how they behaved, committing sins both great and small, while they seemed almost incapable of true contrition. They could not reform their ways. I thought then about the pain I must have caused Father Joseph when he had had to hear my own confessions… But why talk of minor affairs… what pain had I given God? And how terribly I must have offended him!

One strange matter to me was how often the people who came to me had questions about sexual sin. They often asked point blank, "Why is the Catholic church so unforgiving of sexual sin?" as though they thought the church were imposing an unreasonable burden or restraint upon them.

To this I could only state the obvious. First, clearly, the church is not "unforgiving." God is infinitely forgiving, but we all recognize the sinful nature of carnal lust. Look at the professional stripper. Isn't she free to decide what to do with her own body? Certainly she is "free" in the sense that we are all *free to commit any act*, good or evil, if we follow only the dictates of our own will. Is she legally free? Not to be a prostitute, perhaps, but certainly she is permitted to put on a show, if we look only to the laws of man. But can she really expect to be free of God's judgment when she acts in defiance of God's own laws?

The worst sinner is the knowing and willing sinner, and God knows there are plenty of those, while the deluded who truly do not know the nature of their sin are to be pitied; if possible, they are to be enlightened and reformed. If they are weak in their will to reform, we must lead them to God's strength which is their surest salvation.

But witness sexual violence. Witness the serial killer, the jealous suicide, the children who go without love while their fathers run into the arms of prostitutes or illicit lovers, or these sex-crazed men who view the shows of "strippers" (who are "only acting on their freedom"). Perhaps these delinquent fathers occasionally return home from their debauchery, at which time the father and mother tear themselves and their children to pieces in their pitiless and selfish contests over who is right, and who's to blame for the failure of the family.

Witness the unwanted pregnancies, the diseases—the physical and mental diseases—the lost jobs, the personal disgraces. Witness the degradation of man and woman. Can "sex workers" and the generally promiscuous deny that their behavior contributes to, reinforces, in fact inevitably results in this sordid and tragic condition within society? And then let us consider how many souls have been turned away from a contemplation of God and his miracles, as they've become obsessed with their animal lust and their slavery to the flesh. What respect, ultimately, do these people have for themselves, for their partners, their families, and for humanity? All of these questions lead to horrible conclusions even before we consider how little respect they show for God's own law.

It's trivial to demonstrate the sinful nature of adultery, and all the perverse acts, promiscuity, and self-abuse which run counter to God's commands and which degrade the soul which is the true life of man. An eternal life, which man neglects in favor of selfish interests in the now. But no demonstration is sufficient to change or even moderate the behavior of the sinner who is only faithful—and only marginally so—for a few minutes in the confessional. Then, upon receiving the security and assurance of God's absolution, he rejects his own salvation, as a dying man with a sick and corrupted body might sometimes reject a healthy transplanted liver which is certainly his last chance for life. But, with our modern medical advances, the rejection of a transplanted organ is the exceptional case, whereas in matters of the spirit, despite the received wisdom of thousands of years, rejecting the law of God is almost the rule!

Every kind of sin was confessed to me. Every sinner was a Catholic. Though I am now no longer rightly a member of the church, I still cannot disclose any of the details of the confessions I heard, which constitute a sacred trust—as I'm sure you can understand. Thus, though the stories of these men and women could more amply illustrate the current crisis in the spiritual state of man, I must now pass them over and return to my own story.

SPECIAL STATUS

I wondered as much as anyone else why I now seemed to possess a sort of special privilege. Why was I administering sacraments to even some of our novices, when it was usual for Father Joseph or Brother Francis to do so in the past? Why were the laity often specifically asking that Brother Juniper hear their sins? Why were some of our brothers seeking me out for conversation on spiritual matters, more so than before? And why had Father Joseph not suggested that I more strictly limit my speech during recreations, as he had done several times for certain other monks when they had become too talkative? Even though I had done nothing to attract or encourage theological questions, I would have expected some greater attempt to enforce discipline, and it was difficult for me on my own to repeatedly turn away the approaches of my brothers who were seeking answers.

I asked Father Joseph's advice.

"Since Father Jerome's death," he said, "there have been only me and Father Damasus to manage most of the monastery's affairs. Brother Francis will soon become a Prior, and I hope to prepare you to take on the role of Novice Master. Your guidance and experience can make a meaningful difference in the formation of new monks. It's true that you are receiving special attention, but you must discipline *yourself* not to become prideful."

"But don't you worry that this privilege might contribute to a sort of... superstition?"

"I understand. You're right that people's interest has been stimulated by whisperings and rumors. I know that some think there have been signs of a special favor of God, or that perhaps you have been singled out for exceptional service. We all know that, through God's love and grace, there have been no harmful accidents since the day of your ordination. Our health, safety, and prosperity seem more secure than ever.

"None of us can know the will of God, and to believe that a miracle has occurred to spare our lives can be just as dangerous as believing we once labored under a curse because we suffered great misfortunes. I'm convinced that every day I live is due to God's grace, as much now as ever before, and I know you feel the same. But can we attribute the recent change in our fortunes to any special sign or signification? Let us be thankful without believing ourselves deserving of any special favor.

"Nonetheless, Brother Juniper, God has graced you with certain talents that you dare not waste. You can learn to guide those who waver in their faith, to lead them back onto the right path… these are tools that God will make use of. It would be uncharitable to decline this work due to your own fear. Pray for humility."

"But," I said, "we are now eighty-four holy men, devoted to the service of God, seeking salvation and seeking divine pardon for the sins of man. Might I, somehow, be disruptive to this?"

"The envious always find an object for their envy." He paused here, and his tone became more grave. "Before you become too enviable, you may well be visited by a new and terrible misfortune. Don't turn away, regardless. God will see you through."

After this conversation, I felt a new sense of purpose. I continued to savor the joy that came when sinners turned to God and received his Word, and I did my best to fight off the doubts that were provoked when the same sinners relapsed into sin. I would not allow myself then to ask the question which I am only now able to articulate: *What really determines the state we shall find ourselves in at the moment of death?*

11.
Seeing God

A Shattering Vision

The experience of my lifetime could be summarized as *long hours and short years*. Through prayer, contemplation, and devotion, I managed to achieve a sort of serenity. The serenity lasted for several years; those years were mere instants.

Though I continued to contribute, through labor and devotion, to the community I shared with my brothers, and though I was promoted to Master of Novices, a good portion of my time was spent in solitary contemplation and prayer. Communion with my God and meditation on the mysteries constituted my treasure—the true source of my joy.

But a day came when I realized this was not enough. An awareness came that it was wrong for me to scribe, to teach... Even God's goodness, the mysteries, the life and acts of Christ, the Blessed Virgin, none should be allowed to distract me any longer... from God himself!

It was my belief that ultimately—after my death—I would confront my God, and I would be brought to account for all the events of my life. My prayers, then, had to prepare me to receive his grace, should he deign to grant it. I lived in the anticipation that death would claim me with a startling suddenness. This did not frighten me. There was no more fear in my heart or mind. If the years fled away quickly, I wouldn't regret it. As for the loss of the world... I had already let go of the world.

I did not want to hurt my father the Abbot, but with my new realization, there was now no choice. I confronted Father Joseph with what I had decided:

"I can no longer be Novice Master. I can hear no more confessions. No more scribbling in books. There is only one life left to me that's been calling me for years. Pure contemplation."

Father Joseph is such a good man! He only smiled at this and told me, "Please, do as you say. Give your thoughts and prayers to God. The rest… the rest shall not concern you."

I went to my cell to *begin* my life, and though I believed what I had read in *The Cloud of Unknowing*, that "In one little time, as little as it is, may heaven be won and lost," I still imagined that more time stood between me and that "one little time."

But as soon as I sat, without allowing me even a hint to prepare myself, a vision came so terrible and shattering that I'm afraid I will never recover. I saw God's face.

How odd that even in the merest moment, I had yet found time for sinful inattention. But I became intensely aware of my mistake just as God filled my sight, my hearing, my mind.

God cannot be comprehended. He is non-temporal. I cannot precisely say that he *was* in the room with me. It would be just as accurate to say he *will have been being* in the room with me. That instant is both infinite and infinitesimal. I *am* with him now. I was *never not* with him, in *that* permanent instant. To think that I have escaped, or that there is or can be an end is absurd. This prison that I'm in now, the prison of my flesh and the prison of these walls—the prison of my permanently blinded eyes which perceive only what *is not* or what *is not essential*—this is the falsehood.

But I also learned not to believe in God in that instant. My atheism condemns me as the most heretical of religious hypocrites.

People wonder, and sometimes ask, "What does God really look like?" I saw him, and see him, and do you think I can answer? Is he a man with a beard? Is he a reflection of myself? A mist? He *is* all of these and none of these; all of these and none of these struck me in the eyes with the searing intensity of a miracle. God's face is fire; he is a bearded man, and oneself, and a light, and a void, and more than anything he is an *unfolding*, and all, and every image one imagines, still and turbulent, paradoxical, all knowing, and he is the fear that dispels all fear, and reveals the truth of all fear. He is the fear *behind* the fear. He is concrete and absolute. But he is *not* death. He is *life* in the true eternal sense.

But I am no longer with him. His life has been denied me.

12.
Distraught

A Plea for Bernard's Salvation

All of the above should be sufficient to summarize the course of Bernard's life from the moment he started to entertain religious thoughts to the moment when a final traumatic experience destroyed his equilibrium.

Shortly after the events described, he was transferred into our program upon referral from St. Patrick Hospital in Missoula. I received a couple of letters from Father Joseph White inquiring about Bernard's health and wellbeing, and Bishop Arnsdorff flew out to visit him on his fourth day with us. Their meeting and conversation were brief. The Bishop emerged from Bernard's room with tears in his eyes. He then requested a few minutes to speak with me privately.

"Brother Juniper has produced a sensation at the abbey," the Bishop said. "The brothers pray for him day and night. They say a miracle has occurred."

"So… what do you believe happened? Has Bernard seen God?"

"What can I say to that question?" He crossed himself and prayed before continuing. "God has revealed himself. Perhaps not as Brother Juniper tells it. Now I feel a trembling in my soul such as I've never felt."

"Why?"

"Just from visiting the St. Albert's. I've heard of their experience. Now, even the walls of the abbey feel as though the Holy Spirit's presence has become tangible. It will become a place of pilgrimage, I'm sure. The brothers say that in the night, when Brother Juniper was in his room, in contemplation, he prayed aloud one word, 'God!' He expressed it in such urgency, the brothers who heard it believed God himself had arrived. They were immediately inspired to a profound stirring of love, and at the same time a deep despondency at the thought of their own sinfulness.

"Even those who had not heard Brother Juniper's cry were swept up by the sensation, and soon the brothers were running from cell to cell. Some fled in panic, and those who went to Brother Juniper's cell found him gripped in a fit or an ecstasy. They didn't know what to call it. To hear their story… I feel such a meekness."

"And what do you think of his being here now?" I asked.

Bishop Arnsdorff sighed heavily.

"It's the church's policy to allow psychiatric medicine to deal with matters of psychiatry… I pray for him and trust in God's grace."

He gripped my hand now.

"I don't know about your own beliefs, Doctor. But I want you to know that you are fighting for more than just this man's mental health. I've been brought closer to God thanks to him. God forbid Brother Juniper should be lost."

"Why should he be lost?" I asked.

"He now refuses the sacraments. He says he considers himself outside of the church and no longer worthy of communion. Though he may have witnessed a miracle, he remains… troubled. This may be his *dark night*. I'm terribly concerned for his spiritual condition just as you must be for the condition of his mind."

13.
To Believe and Not Believe

PARADOXICAL BELIEF

In my discussion with Bernard about his feelings and thoughts since leaving the monastery, I found he had embraced a new system of belief which was the embodiment of contradiction. He insisted that he had truly seen God, yet he had no faith in God's existence. He intellectually maintained the "truth" of God, yet his spiritual and emotional feeling of emptiness left him without faith. He saw himself as sinfully—but helplessly—opposed to the truth, despised by God, an outcast, ignorant and insensate.

I asked him, "How can you claim not to believe in God, when you continue to say 'God is this way,' and 'Wisdom is such-and-such'? You go on, when telling your story, as though you were preaching from current faith. How can you now consider your soul in jeopardy, or consider yourself 'unworthy' of communion, when you no longer believe in God. If you don't believe, then what is there to fear, or to feel yourself excluded from?"

"How could I deny my fear and my un-wisdom in the face of my experience? Yet how can I truly believe after what I have witnessed?"

"But what is that exactly?"

"God."

"That… how is that not proof to you?"

"I can't render it comprehensible or explain it in logical terms because our human logic has been flawed from the beginning. But you must accept that I have been forcefully stripped of my faith. I am bereft. All that remains for me is un-faith. It goes deeper than doubt."

"If doubt is all you have, then why not go all the way and reject belief entirely? Can't you conclude that Catholicism is wrong and there is no God? Why not disbelieve?"

"Get behind me."

"Why not start again? You started with a mystery, and you ended with a mystery, so God cannot have been the answer."

"You're stubborn, Doctor. You seem to blame me for contradicting myself. But self-contradiction is the only truth because it is the only way to accurately depict life. Contrariness, contradiction, paradox, are the essentials of a true understanding. If you can't believe that an object is simultaneously black *and* white, that a certain affirmative statement is both absolutely true and absolutely false, then you can never come to a full understanding."

"Is this really wisdom? How do you reach such conclusions?"

"I am a witness."

"Hmm… Then witness to me. Reveal more to me about what you have seen."

At this, Bernard perked up a bit, and though he could not quite steady himself to look me in the eye, I could see he was trying to gauge my intent.

"Are you asking because you want to know God?"

"I'm asking because I want to know your concept of God."

Bernard took note of my hesitation.

"If a person could attain a truly deep perception, and escape subjective constraints, that person would see something so enormously chaotic and complex, it's very difficult to summarize or to encapsulate in a simple philosophy. Remember, if anything appears paradoxical, in religion, in science, or in any element of our experience, this does not indict God or nature. It is proof of our failure—our inadequacy. In our confusion we see a mirror of ourselves. Yet, to say that is to speak a falsehood! Because nature, in its heart, is ineffable. Perhaps we are the reflection unseen… a reflection of something greater. Is it wonderful? Is it terrible? I don't think that we can honestly say that it is either wonderful or terrible, but wonder and terror are definitely elements of it."

"This 'it' that you're talking about… is it God… is it the Christian God?"

"Yes."

"And you've seen it and been convinced of all you say? Your perception, at least for that moment, was *not* limited? You're not reflecting on your own ignorance now, but telling me... what God really is?"

"Well... to make it simple... yes. Yes, I have seen it exactly as I tell you. This is not my ignorance speaking. To see and acknowledge my own doubt is also a part of the truth."

"Is there anything else that you learned from your experience? Is there something that you're holding back? Maybe something that would better explain why you're suffering so?"

"Yes. There's something more."

"What is it?"

He fell silent.

14.
Convolutions

INTERVIEW CONDITIONS

"Where's the couch?" Many people have asked me this, including colleagues when they were inclined to tease. Only a few of the analysts I know employ couches in their sessions with patients, but they always suggest that *I* should have one. It's a joke. I laugh along, but I find it irksome.

I once asked a colleague in rejoinder, "Where's *your* crystal ball?" But upon reflection, I realized this was exactly what they've all been implying: I'm a mountebank, and I need more props.

But it's never been my style to put on a show or utilize props (except when a patient's particular condition seemed to require a show and props). At most times my office looks like an office, a place to sit and chat. Our sessions resemble interviews, and I like to look at my patients and have them look at me.

With Bernard, though, his condition was such that he usually had to recline, especially during longer sessions, so I finally had a therapy couch brought in, with a firm rail attached on one side for him to grip. Sometimes, when he preferred to sit or lie on the floor, he dropped the rail and rolled over one edge, then lay with his back propped against the couch frame. After a while, we brought in a comfortable rug and large pillows that he could lay on or toss about in, and then we abandoned the couch entirely. In its place, I had two bars firmly bolted to the wall, in-line, horizontal, with a gap between them. He used them as a support that he could grip while pressing his back against the wall or lying prone amid his pillows and blankets. I continued to sit at my desk. This was the condition he was reduced to by the time of our latest discussions.

Despite these unusual arrangements, my sessions with him remained very *interview-like*. Sometimes they transformed into debates as he continued his circular arguments. Thinking it was best at the time, I tried to persuade him towards a complete abandonment of his religious beliefs. I put my hopes in the idea that a return to atheism would be Bernard's saving grace. Yet he persisted in blaming his own spiritual and moral weakness and would not deny God absolutely.

"Reasoning Therapy" Goes Nowhere

"Your arguments don't hold up," I told him. "How is it possible, within one mind—indeed within one breath—to say 'Such and such is true, but I do not believe'? When you testify to the truth of something, don't you simultaneously assert your belief? And, on the other hand, if you say you don't believe, then aren't you essentially declaring a proposition to be false? You're inconsistent, whereas choosing one side or the other of the issue would allow you to resolve the conflict and discover a workable worldview."

"I'm not some new-ageist who claims that choosing to believe something causes it to be true. God's existence does not depend on my belief in him. That's the most foolish of children's fantasies. That is superstition to the extreme."

"You're turning the argument on its head. It's not a question of whether you can make something true by believing it, but whether you should believe something you know isn't so."

"The contradiction is not in my way of thinking."

"Surely, what is true is true; what is false is false."

"Why!?"

"What alternative is there?"

"If you tell me I must choose between A and B… and, because A is logically-flawed, inconsistent, incomplete, I must reject it… Well, what if B is also logically-flawed, inconsistent, and incomplete? What if a world with God is impossible, but a world *without* God is *also* impossible? Yet we see the world. The only option I can find is to reject the claim that 'What is true is true; what is false is false.'"

"I don't see what leads you to this… I mean how this applies. Maybe you've spent too many years rationalizing. Whenever, as a Christian, you run into evidence that contradicts or challenges your faith, you retreat behind the argument that God works in mysterious ways. I.e., Christianity isn't wrong, but only God can see the whole truth, and thus we must have faith to fight our doubts. Which amounts to shutting up your own skepticism and willingly playing the fool. But a secular worldview doesn't work that way."

"Who says it doesn't!? We are routinely discovering the limits of our ability to know and understand. I've studied philosophy and comparative-religion. The way I see it, every investigation runs into a kind of uncertainty or contradiction that is declared an exception. Every honest intellectual recognizes the limits to what he or she knows, and we also run into paradoxical discoveries that we simply can't account for. This isn't limited to theists."

"It's not the same. In science there is more certainty, and we don't depend on faith to shield us from the implications of evidence. It's not right to take the smallest of doubts and inflate it into an exaggerated doubt about everyt…"

"But what if that contradiction, incompleteness, uncertainty, that we routinely run into is not something to explain away; neither is it an anomaly nor a temporary obstacle to our understanding. What if it is the most pertinent datum, the final truth in itself? Truth is self-contrary, the result and cause of a universe of infinite complexity. The impenetrable mystery of God's ways, beyond fathoming, unfolds before our eyes. It can be seen in a drop of water or in the transit of stars within a galaxy over ten billion years."

And so he went on. My efforts to reason with him were becoming increasingly futile. Endless! I cannot relate all the conversations we had at this point, but as interesting as some of his ideas may have been academically, they got us nowhere, and I was unable to wrestle him into choosing one, logically consistent view.

And we remained at this impasse until one day when Bernard had a new dream. And everything went wrong from there.

15.
One Little Time

In my office again, with Bernard in his pillows. Bernard is more blunt than usual, and very worked up about something.

"What's your purpose?" he asked me. "Why are we here?"

"To help you."

"How."

"To treat you. To find a cure."

"Do you believe that? You think you're going to cure me though God wouldn't?"

"The problem is not God."

"Do you believe in God?"

"I..."

"We both know you don't."

"No, I never did. But I don't know why you should be concerned with my belief."

"I had a dream. Do you want to hear it?"

I paused. Then, "Yes."

"I dreamed I was a psychiatrist. I was concerned about a problem patient, someone similar to me—you see the point. You've been identifying with me; you're getting into my head..."

"But...?"

"Don't forget I have a charism. I see your lack of faith, and I understand some of the mind games you play with me."

I frowned at this.

He proceeded. "I was alone in my room. It was a simple cell, mostly white; the walls were roughly painted and some patches were greying... peeling. There was a rough and rickety wooden table in the middle of the room, and that was the only furniture. No chair. The space was small. The ceiling was low. On the table was a leather-bound book with no title. I assumed it was a psychiatry manual. I wanted to find a cure for my patient, but I didn't want to look in the book. I thought that might be... too simple. But I was confused. Frustrated. So I decided to peek in the book. I had a strong suspicion that the answer was there. But in the corner of the room, where two walls joined, there was a space—a kind of crack. Dark. You could hardly notice it. But the darkness shifted, so I knew that it was being shadowed by someone moving on the other side of the wall. I believed someone was looking in through that space, watching me, very curious to see if I would look in the book, and I did not want to be caught looking. Without looking in the book, I could feel my mind disolving. My thoughts were turning into a string of words, and the words made no sense together: *There is an under than when there cannot be other that saw, bobbing, because some did not in the way of...* I couldn't bear it!

Meanwhile, whatever had been obscuring the light from the next room had moved away and I saw that I was unobserved. I quickly opened the book, but turned to the wrong page. The book was the Bible. I read, '*Rise thou that sleepest, and arise from the dead*.' That was not the answer. Without pausing to check that it was safe, I turned to the next page, the psychiatry page, and I found the answer and I understood..."

"What was it?"

"...and I looked up and saw, in the corner, the man who was observing me, with his face blacked out—he was in the room watching. I was caught!"

"What did the page say?"

Bernard was frantic. His passion had been heating up to a boil. "Did you ever think this moment would come so abruptly, Percy!? That you and I would both be damned to Hell because of our inattentiveness?"

"What did the page say!?"

Bernard emitted a fierce, pained moan, and he lapsed into unconsciousness.

BERNARD'S SEIZURE

Bernard had experienced a psychogenic seizure, and he became comatose. We tested Bernard, after thirty-seven hours in his coma, by injecting ice water into his right ear canal (a cold-calorics test). We observed that the twitching in his eyes was most rapid in the direction away from the affected ear, which demonstrated that his coma was of psychogenic origin.

16.
A Re-creation

I was still shaken by what Bernard had said. I was deeply frustrated by Bernard's dream without an ending. But, while he was unconscious, it was impossible for me to get any more information. So, when I went to bed one night, I lay turning about and pondering. What could that book in his dream have said, and why was I so fixated on it? I thought about what I *wanted* it to say. Soon my mind was filled with a string of words, senseless, as sometimes passes through one's mind while drifting off to sleep. The last phrase I can remember is *"saved in a naked instant."*

Then I found myself asleep and then I was in the same room that Bernard had described from his dream. The same walls, the same table, the same book, the same space in the corner of the room, the crack in the wall.

This is wonderful, I thought. *I know I'm dreaming. So, let me walk through this space, step by step, being careful to change nothing, and maybe I will find what I'm looking for.*

I watched the crack in the wall, and saw the shifting darkness. When I believed the observer was absent, I approached the book and opened it. At first, when I looked on the page, I saw only a wavering jumble of words that I couldn't work out. I thought carefully back to what Bernard had said, and then the words arranged themselves: *"Arise thou that sleepest, the dead shall rise…"* or something like that, it didn't really matter, it was the next page I was most interested in. I was tempted to check the crack in the wall, but I didn't, because Bernard hadn't, and I kept my eyes focused on the book. I turned the page, and there it was! I clearly read the answer: *Faith without works is dead.*

Then I was confronted by the observer with the blacked-out face. I had been warned, but I was not prepared for this. I was

seized, perhaps for the first time in my life, with a deep supernatural dread, and I woke up screaming. I trembled all night and felt
a deep hopelessness that I never thought could trouble such a calm
rational mind as my own.

17.
Conclusion

Six days after this, Bernard regained a degree of consciousness, screaming incoherently as he awoke. Then he slept again for a few hours, and awoke once more.

Now his coma has ended, but he is mostly unresponsive. He has since been persistently catatonic, mute, and largely immobile.

On a few occasions, electro-convulsive therapy has been able to bring him out of his stupor, but his typical response, after the drug effects have subsided and his mind is cleared, is to weep and refuse conversation. He looks around the room, seeming very disoriented, but for a short time he is responsive to stimuli. If he is allowed to rise from his bed, he kneels, faces a wall, and repetitively crosses himself. He does not appear to be praying but rather to be engaged in a compulsive ritual which brings him no comfort. It is clear that he knows when he is being spoken to, as he responds by vehemently shaking his head whenever he is requested to speak. He physically resists any effort to lift him or move him away from the wall. He will pull intravenous tubes out unless the nurse pre-emptively removes them and applies bandages.

He says nothing, until several minutes pass, at which time he lies on his side, curled in a fetal position, and complains of "the spinning," as his vertigo returns. Only then will he speak a few words in response to questions, but his speech is vague, ignores the topic of my question, and invariably makes reference to suffering, hopelessness, "a great darkness" or some similarly bleak vision. He is too confused for genuine dialogue. Within the next few hours, he lapses again into a stupor and all awareness is gone.

If he were truly able to express himself and describe his condition, I believe he would say he has died a sort of spiritual death though his body goes on living. Yet he is too demented to form and express such a complex thought. Perhaps I am guilty of projecting here.

Chloe Wright

1.
First Admission

Chloe Wright was a precocious sixteen-year-old high school girl when she was first admitted to my program. Her eyes were a little closer together than one might consider ideal, and her nose was slightly large, but she was otherwise beautiful. Her body was well formed, big-chested, and she could be remarkably seductive, though her manner was as casual as can be. I report these facts because they are an essential part of who she was.

Chloe was referred to me from a psychiatric hospital in Hawai'i, Kahi Mohala Behavioral Health. She had been diagnosed as a psychotic after she created a sensation in her school by eating a live bird in the school's cafeteria. She believed that she was a reincarnation of a 14th-century wooden writing desk. She reported that she could smell colors, and when she was tested, this was determined to be true!

Her doctors believed that she was a very unusual case and that she might especially benefit from participation in my program. When I received their referral, it seemed at first they thought my hospital was a sort of dumping ground for psychiatric freaks. Perhaps they thought that Chloe's conjuring tricks might amuse me. But I have always been interested only in what will benefit my patients. Careful consideration led me to the conclusion that I could help her. Thus, after examining her case files, I accepted Chloe into my program, but it was not because I believed her case would be particularly difficult or intriguing in itself; rather, I believed in the incompetence of the psychiatrist who was treating her. She would benefit from being rescued from his idiocy.

Chloe's father resided in Kansas City, only seven blocks away from my hospital, and he owned and operated a pharmacy downtown. The father's name was Ron Adams. Chloe had no mother.

When I met with Ron he explained to me, first and foremost, that he spoiled Chloe in everything. She could always get whatever she wanted from him. She changed her name, legally, to Wright, because that was her mother's maiden name. As Ron complained, "Never mind the fact that her mother ran away when Chloe was only seven, while I, her father, stuck with her and sacrificed everything to keep her happy; she prefers her mother's name."

Chloe lived in Hawai'i because she and Ron had gone together on vacation for her fourteenth birthday, and she loved it so much she insisted on staying.

"It was ridiculous, I told her," said Ron. "But she absolutely insisted, she threatened, she whined. She told me the boys in Hawai'i were 'much more awesome and wonderful,' and then I *really* didn't want to let her stay. But she told me she would be good, whereas, she said, if I forced her to stay in Kansas City all her life, she would do drugs. 'I'll do drugs!' she said. 'Everyone does drugs, and I'll do it too, 'cause I'm bored to shit!' she said. 'I'll snort a kilo of cocaine every day if you keep me in that shithole with you, and besides, you stink!' This is the kind of language my lovely daughter uses with me. But I'm a bad father. If I were a father, I'd have a backbone, I'd stand up to her. But I can't, because she's my little baby and my princess, and Princess gets what she wants."

He slumped in his chair, making a grand display of his shame and his helplessness. Then he explained how he got her to finish her middle school in Missouri while he "did back flips and jumped through hoops, plus made donations where it was necessary," to get her admitted to Hawai'i Preparatory Academy, a coed boarding school. He bought property in Hinokaa—he justified this to himself as an "investment," though it was expensive and the local property values have since declined—and claimed Hawaiian residency as part of his application to her school. He travelled frequently to visit her, and he made friends with some of the parents of her girl friends in Waimea, so he knew "some trustworthy adults who could watch out for her if she got in trouble."

Ron's whole story, of course, was extremely strange. But I was used to patients—and families of patients—with all kinds of strange stories.

When I asked Ron whether his daughter had ever shown any signs of possible mental problems, maybe even bordering on psychosis, he replied, "Oh yes, of course! She had anorexia or… bulimia. The vomiting one. And she hurt animals sometimes, and she often splashed ink on her face and clothes. 'I'm a desk' she'd say, 'a fucking desk'!

"Sorry for the language, but that's what she'd say."

VERY UNFORTUNATE

After all paperwork was examined carefully, legal records were verified, and her father had signed commission papers as her legal guardian—she was only the third minor to be admitted to our hospital, and the only one to have been transported from such a distance—Chloe was delivered to our hospital and was assigned a room in our secure ward. Her eyes darted about, she trembled constantly, and she looked very disoriented and frightened, but she didn't speak except to mumble incoherently to her father, and then once she barked with a sudden anger at one of the nurses, the largest man on our team. After she was fed—and she put some of the food in her hair—I had her brought into my office for an interview.

"Hello, Chloe," I began. "I know you don't want to talk to me right now. I think I owe it to you to be honest, right from the start, and that is to say I know you're faking your psychosis."

She didn't twitch any more or less than she had been already.

"I expect you might want to keep up the act for a few days, but look… you've been found out. It's not even a particularly convincing sham. I'm surprised at how gullible your earlier doctors must have been."

It took about fifteen or twenty seconds before Chloe stopped shamming and burst out with a laugh.

"Hahaha! All right, I'd heard you were a smart doctor… Congratulations. You've made your first ever fifteen-second diagnosis and cure!"

"I appreciate your honesty, Chloe. Or, well, dishonesty generally, but let's say momentary honesty."

"Hey, listen up and shut your tits, doctor! Just listen."

I listened, but she didn't say anything for a while. So I had to prompt her.

"Okay, I'm listening. Patient."

"Yeah, look, I really ate a fucking bird, all right? And I don't know what you're up to. You're crazier than me. Why did you have me flown all the way here just to… I don't know, act like a chess master or something. Checkmate, crazy person! Ha!"

"Chloe, you're *still* acting. And the reason I brought you here is, well, something is obviously going on with you. I wanted to see what the real problem is."

"So, what you mean is, acting crazy is still crazy, right? Maybe even crazier."

"Well, in a way. I mean, you *did* eat a bird. Why did you do that?"

"Let me begin by getting one thing off my chest. And don't be looking below my neckline, because that's not what I meant. I want you to know that I am the most unfortunate person you have ever met."

"Well… suffering isn't a competition."

"I know, right? But I'm the most unfortunate person you have ever met."

"What's the nature of your misfortune?"

In keeping with the formula established throughout this book, I'll tell you her story in her own words, as follows.

2.
Her Own Story Told: Part 1

The Nature of Her Misfortune

First of all, my father's a lunatic and I just praise God he let me go to that school in Hawai'i because it put enough distance between us that I could start to imagine I was a normal kid. But Hawai'i Prep is a Hell on earth, and the teachers make me vomit.

I learned very quickly how to play nice, and fit in, and be fashionable, which is a pathetic joke because Hawai'i is a place for going to the beach—even though the beaches are so much smaller and more pathetic than you'd think, and you need to get a ride or have a car to get out there—and our school has uniforms, but all the sluts in my school *also* have to spend all their money on fashionable clothes on the weekend? Even though it's a shopping backwater, but you can still spend your ass to buy a bag if you get out to King's Shops. And they just don't shut up about it, but it's cool because it's so easy to learn to speak their language and make friends and manipulate people, and I have a lot of friends. But I don't really *like* them, except for just a couple.

And everyone says I look hot in a swimsuit, which just means they're a bunch of pervs and they should shut up. But that's okay because when I look in the mirror I realize they're right, I do look pretty hot.

Anyway, I had plenty of good reasons for wanting to go to Hawai'i, the main one being to get away from that freak who calls himself my dad. He always acts like he's being *noble* just because he takes care of me, as if that's not the *responsibility* of a father, and he says he spoils me, as if it were some great difficulty for him when in fact he's rich as fuck. What hardship is it? But he makes me feel indebted to him for *everything*. Trivial shit like driving me across town at night *once*, when half the time I have to walk like a homeless person in fucking rags.

There's only one thing I'm indebted to him for, just one thing that maybe really cost him something, and that's the fact that he finally, finally, gave me a chance to get *away from him*, just for a little while, just for a little breathing room in the months when he's not flying into Hawai'i to play the spy and make me more miserable. And I'm going to be hearing about his sacrifice for the rest of my life! When I'm sixty and he's eighty, he'll still be telling me, "Oh Princess, don't you remember when I sent you to school in Hawai'i, and do you know how much that cost me, yadda yadda." Sorry, eighty-nine… eighty-seven… he'll be eighty-nine when I'm sixty. Something like that. I forget his age sometimes, except I always remember he's *old*.

Now, believe me, I'm not stupid. I know you think I'm just acting as spoiled as he says I am, and that I should get some perspective or something… God, I hate that! People say that shit all the time. Or else, like the doctors in Oahu who passed me around and speculated about what kind of sick perversion went on in my house? You're probably thinking my dad's a pervert. Well, he *is* a pervert, but not the kind who would ever touch me! Pervertedly normal is more like it. Straight as can be, doesn't *openly* fuck any guys or any women in the house while I'm around, but who knows what goes on when I'm not. All I know is two things: my mom left because no human can tolerate him for more than a few years without going insane—and they'll only do that if they're held captive—and sometimes his bed and his bed-sheets *reek* of urine. They're soaked with it. I don't know *whose* urine it is. He doesn't normally piss the bed when *I'm* there, but sometimes it happens in the middle of the day when I'm out of the house. And he acts like it isn't true, just ignores it, and leaves it for me to clean up like I'm a maid in my own house. How do you explain that to your normal school friends whose parents have normal problems and normal divorces? And sometimes when I'm cleaning up his filth, I hear the floorboards creak and crack, I mean distinctly, just outside the door. I've run out to catch him, but I've never seen him for sure looking at me, but I have once heard him stumble in his haste to retreat down the stairs when he thought I was coming out. I mean… he's like two steps away from murdering me I think.

So, okay, I totally exploited him to get him to cough up the money to send me to Hawai'i? But I had to. I didn't just tell him I'd do drugs either, like he tells you is the case. I told him I'd put secret cameras in the house and send the video to the police. And he said, all flustered and red-faced "You're sick, Princess, why should you think… oh, you don't think there'd be anything *bad* on the videos… why? I don't believe your nasty threats… oh, oh, oh…" like a total queen, really. But despite his claims of innocence he totally rushed to get me admitted to that shit-hole of a prep school in Hawai'i. Thank God!

Everyone hated me in Kansas City, and that really hurt me, but it turned out to be worse in Hawai'i where most people pretended to really like me. Here's a fact about life that you'd better memorize: That which seems real often is not real, and that which *is* real very often is *fake*. I say shit like that sometimes because it makes me sound smart, but it also happens to be true.

Now, I have a boyfriend. I can't say enough good things about him. Oh Christ [she breaks down and sobs profusely for several minutes]. I feel so bad just to be me… and he's such an innocent creature [more sobs. Eventually she gets back around to talking, though she continues to weep and her voice cracks intermittently].

His name is James Jones. My nickname for him is "Jonestown." It's kind of sick. His nickname for me is "Hiawatha." It comes from a stupid joke. Our history teacher once caught us whispering in class, and heard me calling him "Jonestown." But I guess he thought I'd said "Jamestown?" So he said, "And what's her name, Pocahontas?" I don't know if he was trying to be clever, or just to shame me, but James answered him back, "No sir! Her name is Hiawatha!"

But James is *so* awkward, which is just awesome and cute, and his parents are so weird so I can relate to that, except they're very *normally weird* meaning not creepy, but just embarrassingly uncool.

And wrong. They're just wrong about everything, but they want to be good people.

James is pretty much a rare individual just because he doesn't get baked. He and I are kind of the "survivors" of the school because he doesn't do any kind of drugs, and I haven't been raped. I have a lot of female friends, like I told you, and one of my friends, Carrie and I, we're in a special club for two. We call it the "not yet raped club." Because most of our other friends have been raped, either by friends or family. But they made a really, really big deal out of it when one of the girls in school, a girl I don't like named Cassandra, she got *grabbed and raped* by a total stranger, without any alcohol and without anything to imply it was consensual. So that was reported like it was the first crime to befall any member of our student body, and we all had a moment of silence for the "incident" where she got "assaulted," but even though they avoided openly using the word rape in the public announcement, and even though we had a moment of silence over it, Cassandra could only come back for like four or five days, about a month after the rape, and then she dropped out of school because she was traumatized and couldn't face people. And that's really sad and pathetic, and I feel really horrible actually, because even though I never liked her, I suddenly felt so horrible for *her*, you know? Because what happened is worse than what you'd want for an enemy, but she wasn't that bad, only just *normally bad*, you know?

But I feel like a fucking dick just for talking about this, but the fact is there are a ton of girls who have been *traumatized* in my school, only they don't have to drop out because they've been silently traumatized. Only not *that* silently, because pretty much everyone knows, but it hasn't been in the paper and their parents don't know, and the teachers think we're just snotty kids who don't like to do homework, or a couple of book worms who *only* do homework and ask questions that are harder than anything the teachers ever thought about. They hate that!

So, the thing is, yeah, Carrie and I are in the "not yet raped club,"

which is our way of dealing with and laughing about this stuff...
and Beth "the Jew" Lerner *was* in our club, but we kicked her out
because she was *almost* raped by our other friend Sarah who's a
total dyke but we still love her. Well, it's kind of a joke, really, but
Sarah poked her in the butt when we were swimming out at the
pool, kind of a really hard, full-fingered poke that almost turned
into real penetration, and she screamed so loud we just had to say
"you're out of the club, Beth!" She has come to accept her lowered
status as a result of that "incident," and I think she counts herself
lucky that it wasn't anything more serious than that.

So anyway, I'm almost a virgin in the sense of my not being
violated, but I'm not a *real* virgin. But a lot of kids think I am, and
I don't mind that "purity" image that I've got associated with me in
their minds. But, you know what? There's a lot more to life than
not getting raped, and I'm still damnably miserable. And James
had that kind of "purity" virgin image too because he didn't do
any kind of drugs, but I really improved his image and got him
respect because they all know I'm his girlfriend and that makes a
lot of guys jealous.

Sometimes they call him "Pity Fuck," which is sick and I hate
that, but James is a peaceful guy mostly but he's not *afraid* of
anything, and once he had to ball this kid up because he said the
"Pity Fuck" thing in front of me and that was insulting. And James
smacked him hard in a way that no one expected, and the sucker just
acted astonished like he was just joking and why take it so serious,
so—surprise, surprise—the sucker who everyone thought was a
roughneck was just a coward and James was a little bit of a hero.
But what really got that kid—I forget his name—no, I don't, but
why honor him—what got him was that *I was the one* to call off
James and try to protect his ass. "No, Jamestown, no,"—I changed
it to *Jamestown* after the teacher's mistake, so it was either that or
Jonestown, according to my whim—"James, don't hurt him." And
the sucker tried to act like something cute just to wash away the
humiliation, so he's like "I'm not hurt... But maybe you can take

a little *pity* on me too, huh?" and grabbed his crotch in a vulgar way and looked at me. But then it was a *chair* that came crashing down on his head and no one messed with James for a good long while after that, and no one was going to say anything to any teacher about the true story about Nick's accident—sorry, that's his name—Nick's "skating" accident that got him some stitches and two black eyes. And guess what? Nick doesn't even skate.

So, you probably don't even respect anything I'm saying, but what you don't know is that love is love, and this boy is so good. Like, what *you* have is actually the petty and fake world, and what we know and have experienced is more real because of its profundity. People can't see it.

James is going to achieve things. Most of our classmates are also ambitious, and they have good prospects to go to the best universities if they don't die of syphilis first or fall into a coma from sheer stupidity. But James is a reader and a thinker and he really knows a lot. Also, despite his kind of meek, humble manner, he's actually really confident when it comes to knowledge. He doesn't flaunt it or make anyone feel like less of a person, but if he wanted to he could make anyone doubt his own intelligence, I mean just by comparison.

He doesn't generally do that with me, except that I'm so fascinated and overwhelmed by him sometimes, but he's not trying to hurt me. The only time I thought he showed just a little bit of viciousness to me—and it came as a kind of a shock—was right after I joked with him a bit by insulting his penis, and then even though he said it didn't matter and he didn't care, he had this kind of crestfallen look... it was compounded by the fact that I was being kind of especially abusive towards him around that time for about... well, hours... I just was in a mood... but anyway, I told him then about an art project I was considering where I would get a group of girls to pour some old used motor oil on the pavement in the parking lot, and then we'd chant a poem about how the end of oil will be the end of life on earth, so let's go to the galaxy; the next planet is waiting. I had thought about this a lot, and I told him like I didn't really care and I just wanted to see how stupid he'd think it was, but I knew he'd support me in a non-critical way. But he looked at me like I was *really* a child and said "which galaxy?" But sarcastic. He said it wasn't sarcastic, but it was. And then he *explained* which really pissed me off, because he said that maybe if I said "the stars," because we're already *in* a galaxy, all the stars are in galaxies, and but really I should change the concept completely because it doesn't communicate and it's kind of a common sentiment. Besides, if oil runs out, the earth's population could maybe really diminish but it won't be the *end* of anything because after all, humanity got by without oil for hundreds of thousands of years and only really used it for a century. I really wanted to rip his guts out for that because if I had just thought for a second I would've realized all of that, I'm not stupid, but it was like I'm not capable of *anything* without him showing me the way… which is true.

This is the man in a boy's body who I betrayed and really, really hurt because of a kind of sickness in me that I can't really help. He is like one hundred percent an angel to me, and I just dragged him down hard and his suffering is much more profound than the suffering that weak people feel. He's strong in his suffering. It's all internal, but only I can see how broken he was when he knew that I was beyond his ability to help me… that he would give everything and I would disdain it. And I chewed up that bird because it was the only way to get away from him, a little insanity act, because if I didn't do that, where would he be in ten years? He's going to achieve something, but he could never do that with me as a lead weight about his neck.

But there really wasn't much chewing, I shouldn't exaggerate, and even to say that I *ate* the bird is a lie. I just bit its head off. You would think that would be very difficult psychologically, but it's just about putting your mind into a state where there is no attachment to the now. You can transcend the moment if you regard the decision as identical to the execution. Then you are no longer an agent. There was a lot of blood, of course, and you can believe it made an impression. I can still see those kids and their faces. My God! [She ended laughing].

3.
Surprise

The Truth About Ron Adams

Chloe hadn't been with us for long before I started to develop my initial diagnosis; it would be difficult to fully state her diagnosis in a great degree of detail without turning this book into a highly technical academic study, besides which I was never able to gather as much data as I would have needed to make a less tentative diagnosis. Our program used a very different set of diagnostic criteria than is typically known outside our program, but Chloe seemed roughly to fit the type which I have termed *probabilistic assignment syndrome*, a subclass of *polydimensional sorting personality*. Interested readers are referred to my book *Infrablack, Ultrawhite, and the Flavor Rainbow: A Variety of Extremes*. (As a tangent, though, I must restate the irony of the fact that most psychologists would classify a patient of this type as a so-called "borderline personality." Consider, if every patient either is, or is not of a borderline personality, and the personality is categorically untreatable, then must not the psychologist also exhibit the kind of all-or-nothing thinking that he attributes to his patient? Doctor, diagnose thyself!)

Anyway, I was very suspicious about the veracity of almost everything Chloe told me. I intended to proceed cautiously and continue to gather as much information as possible, including a recheck on some of her admission references. But it was only the third day after her admission to the program when we all confronted a terrible shock, and I would soon regret that I had not done a more thorough background check earlier (or, more specifically, that I had delegated some of this responsibility).

Ron Adams was discovered nude, hiding in a locked supply-closet within the hospital's secure ward. An investigation was launched, Mr. Adams was taken into police custody, and our entire hospital came under close scrutiny that was disruptive to our continuing treatment of other patients. Chloe was also removed and placed into a so-called "safer" environment for a few days. It was not possible to determine exactly how Ron Adams had gotten in, as several hours of security camera footage was deleted by *someone*. A shakeout resulted in the resignation of our security chief, who accepted responsibility for the failure of his department, and the termination of two temp-hire contracts for members of our staff. We can only assume Ron must have bribed somebody to get assistance to sneak him in.

Police investigation quickly concluded that Ron was not Chloe's father, nor was he in any way related to her. He did not own a pharmacy in Kansas City. He was charged with kidnapping, corruption of a minor, and a series of lesser offences related to his break-in at our facility. Chloe's actual parents, Esther and David Wright, were contacted at their home in Waimea, and Chloe was transported back to Hawai'i to be reunited with her family.

Several months later I was informed that rape had been added to the list of Ron's offenses, and that further investigation of our facility would be necessary to determine whether any sex had occurred within the hospital, but the charge was subsequently dropped because Chloe was unwilling to testify to a sexual relationship, and there were no other credible witnesses (psychotics on our ward gave some peculiar, inconsistent, and unreliable testimony in their interviews).

In an odd but minor twist, Ron named one of our nurses as his accomplice for the break-in, but she had an absolutely solid alibi and was cleared, as she had been off for two days earlier in the week and then went to a national training conference for certified clinical nurses in Rockville, Maryland. She was on the plane for the return flight at the time when Ron was discovered.

As can be imagined, great damage was done to our reputation, and we lost the support of several of the donors who contributed annually to our program. We also had quite a mess to sort out, dealing with forged documents that had been submitted and accepted by our staff. One admissions officer, who said she was certain she had spoken with the principal of Chloe's school as part of her background check, turned out never to have contacted the school. The number she had been given to call was registered under the name "Holly Gost," a presumed pseudonym. She called, left a message, and received an immediate callback from... someone. Perhaps Ron himself contrived to impersonate the school principal.

4.
Second Admission

Chloe came back. It was a little less than a year later, and she was now seventeen.

Chloe's parents had had a remarkable change of heart, which is another way of saying that they were manipulated by their daughter. At first they attempted a lawsuit against us, and they harassed the Missouri State Prosecutor's Office to bring criminal charges as though we had been willing participants in the kidnapping. Then, as we were approaching a likely expensive out-of-court settlement, they declared their interest to drop the suit. (In fact, the legal case had a very unusual conclusion, without much precedent, when they intentionally dropped a suit they were almost certain to win, and then we responded by insisting on a settlement anyway, which cost us $180,000. The reasons for this are complex.)

But Chloe had somehow convinced her parents that, though placing her in our program initially was a monumental error, she had quickly determined I was the only doctor in the world who could actually help her. (I was flattered by this excessive praise, though I would not like to admit that I was also manipulated. I prefer to think that I responded as a professional). She also convinced them that their lawsuit was mercenary, and it demonstrated an intent to profit from her suffering.

The dust settled, I met Esther and David, commission papers were signed—identities were triple-checked—and Chloe was readmitted to our secure ward.

5.
Her Own Story, Part 2

CLEARING UP A FEW THINGS

Well… yeah, you probably think I'm just bullshit now. If I told you that 90% of my earlier story was true, would it make any difference? I always feel like a dick when I get caught in a lie, but there are circumstances, you know…

I had to get away. I was trying to get away from *him*, you know, Ron? But somehow I just wound up back in his clutches… he's very manipulative, and a bit too… Hell, I don't want to say smart, because he's *not* that. But just sheer evil bastardy gives him some incredible influence. He plays so weak and slimy, but no one ever suspects him because the world just likes to blind itself to his brand of rottenness. Christ, I feel like vomiting right now.

But, number one, the most important thing was to not hurt James in *that way*. I mean, he already knows how bad I've been so many times before. But his faith in me is so astounding I couldn't dare push him to *really* lose his innocence. I knew it would be better for him to think I've disappeared, even to suspect I was in some kind of trouble, if only he didn't have to know what *kind* of trouble. But for me, there's no disappearing from myself and circumstance. There's just deeper pits of filth.

You know, you're a psychiatrist. You understand that there's safety in abstraction. So I'll just leave you to fill in the blanks. Conjure up monsters in every shadow you see, in every slightly off-white patch in a field of white even, and you *won't* know the terror of it all—not in the slightest—but you can *guess* at the facts. It's not hard, if you're accustomed to hardship and hard tales.

So, anyway, what the fuck? I've got this idea lately that I'm going to be an artist and none of this is going to matter, and maybe it will all make it into a memoir someday. Or maybe it will inspire my art. Like there's going to be a lot of fucking in my art, and a lot of pain expressed. It will be totally lost on the masses. They're fucking jerks anyway.

I just have to find myself a little hole to crawl into, hopefully one with food in it. And I can just intensely, intensely work. I'll spit bird's blood and feathers all over the walls, and piss in my sleep. For fourteen years I'll be a dick with no talent, but in year fifteen I'll be Rembrandt. Can you picture a crazy Rembrandt?

I want to go to New York. I want to *be exposed in a sexual act* in New York, on one of those big TVs they have in Times Square. But if that happens, you'd better tell my mom and dad to close their eyes. They have no idea. Them and my two adorable sisters. Can you believe it, I'm the only case of insanity in my family. They're good people!

Oh, God, and they sent me back to school too. I mean, really? *Pariah*. There is absolutely no such thing as genuine sentiment. My best friends absolutely despise me, and they say they're sorry and that they want me to be happy again. Naïve idiots! They won't talk to me because it's so scary. Just a little token "we really care about you" shit at the beginning, and then dead silence for like nine months.

Except for, oh my God, James, he's so miraculous he doesn't care about anything! He just loves and loves and gives, and forgives despite the pain that's just stabbing him every second. He thinks his love is just going to fix everything, and I want to step on his damned face and say "You idiot! You dumb little doggy. Don't ever let a woman other than me treat you in this way. Why don't you just hate me?" I don't really do that, though. That would be mean.

Sometimes I wish he'd just have sex with someone else once or twice, I don't even care. I'm not jealous. He could even get with Jewie Beth, she's got a hot ass, which I think he likes. I don't know how her ass got that way. Maybe I should start eating more gefilte fish.

Oh, and a lot has happened since the last time I saw you. I met this Japanese so-called "Buddhist" guy. He's thirty-five. He's really just a Japanese-Hawai'ian, not a real Jap, he doesn't even speak Japanese, and his Buddhism is just a total front, like he's getting back to his roots. The white Zen guys are more Buddhist than him. He tries to get me to meditate with him, but then he gets all pervy and weird, like he wants me to meditate with my shirt off so he can look at my tits. And then he talks about satori and tries to get me to smoke weed with him, even though I told him "I don't smoke, I don't drink, I don't do *any* kind of drugs, and you can't put your thing in my mouth when I'm sleeping." By "thing," I mean "cock."

Chiko is a kind of artist, or so he claims, and I met him at a street art festival. They were displaying all kinds of *terrible* art, just really scandalously normal crap. But he was there and looking through a stack of handcrafted paper in one of the booths... with rough edges. And I was there with two girls. They didn't care much about anything, but they loved to crack up whenever I'd go off about how disgusting everything is. And then I got this *feeling*, like I'm being so immature and this is a shameful thing, because if I'm ever going to be an artist I have to find some kind of sincerity, even if it's a positive thing, I don't want to grow up to be a *critic* because they're disgusting. So I said to Holly and Luisa, "Hey, I'm going in this booth for a second, and I'll find something just awful, I'm sure." It was more like a tent, with a kind of canvas flap cover at the front. But I went in there desperately hoping to find something beautiful. And I came in, all breathy and astonished looking, just looking dumb and retarded but pretty, like I sometimes do, and Chiko caught me by surprise. He looked up from his handcrafted paper and said to me "Hello." Right? Normal come on. Then, "If you were a work of art, what kind of paper would you be?" That didn't even make any sense, and I thought what any girl would think: "Faggot, loser, and *no!*"

So then, out I got of there, and I didn't even come out with anything, and my girls asked me what that was about, and I just told them "too boring," and that was that. An hour later, my friends said they had to go home, and then I kind of sashayed back to the festival... kind of a fast sashay for multiple reasons, including the desire to stop the millions of creeps around from staring too long.

And I found Chiko and asked him, "Hey, are you an artist?" And then we had a stupid conversation and started dating.

He reads weird books, and I'm not anti-intellectual. I'm smarter than you think. But he's always tripping, and telling me about how profound "cyclical time" is as a concept. I get it, but it's not profound, and I don't think he even understands the books he's reading. First of all, it's childish. Do you want a simple explanation?

Cyclical time is an idiot's wisdom. The world rotates, end of story. Seriously, end of story!

I don't know why he thinks it's funny when I make fun of him. I tell him, in more detail than I want to get into right now, just exactly how he is wrong in almost everything he thinks and believes. I incisively puncture every element of his faith. But he just laughs. Why does he think I'm being funny? He has no rejoinder, and he knows I'm smarter than him…he! I'm smarter than he.

I don't think he's even an artist. He's just obsessed with paper. He orders paper in special bundles, shipped from far-away places. He fondles paper and sniffs it. It's really a kind of homosexual fetish. I've never seen him *make* anything! But he always has an excuse, he never says anything quite to the point, but he's always involved in some kind of "long term process," and he laughs in half-admission when I chastise him. I've even told him "Hey, inscrutably Asian does *not* mean refusing to answer a direct question just because it's uncomfortable to respond to." Guess what. He doesn't respond.

You might be tempted to say the same things to me, but be forewarned! I draw, and I've drawn all my life, and I do it well. But I don't go posing as an artist just yet, because I'm really only working on the elements. Most of all I just like paper-and-pencil drawings, though I've tried all kinds of media. I can work very well in two dimensions, but I don't like impasto in my own painting, I'm just not very good at it, and I just keep coming back to lines. It's a fault, but come on, I'm young.

What I most like to draw is curved things, mainly non-rep-resentational, but I don't *want* to be an abstract or non-representational artist, it's just what I've been doing lately while working on my form. My biggest fear right now, as an artist, is that people will eventually be interested in my art for the wrong reasons. They won't get it because I don't talk about art well, so I can't explain it. But James gets it. He really, really understands.

In my private time, though, I do sometimes draw pervy things too, and I especially like to draw men and women lining up to suck tits. My tits, if you want to know the truth. But that's exactly why I don't want to produce that kind of work for public consumption, because they absolutely will *not* understand, and it will give the wrong impression of me as an artist. Sometimes I make it into a bird with tits just to disguise my identity.

Now, amid all these important life-considerations, I have to worry about what my parents think of me. I've unfortunately descended, again, into somewhat deceptive behavior. They know I disappear sometimes and I've convinced them that I'm spending time with James, which is just the sickest kind of deception I could think of, but it works. Before my… incident… you know, coming here to see you, they would have thrown a mad fit if they thought I was spending the night with *any* boy, James included. But after, they got the idea that he's my healthy relationship… well, actually, that's true. But he's supposed to be the one who's supporting me through troubled times, and all that. I'm sure they know we have had sex, but very weirdly they think that's a good thing, like that could somehow erase… Well, sometimes I do spend the night over at James's house with him and his mother… his folks are divorced… and we spend a few hours of privacy in the den downstairs, mostly just talking.

But a lot of the time when I'm supposed to be with him, I'm actually somewhere else, and quite often that's with Chiko. His wife is out of town almost always because she is a linguistics professor in the Philippines. As the most ridiculous irony imaginable, she has been doing research for years into the Filipino language as an example of how a bunch of languages resisted Japanese influence.

And she does that at a school called Philippine *Normal* University. I'm not even making that up. She's a white woman, and she knows more Japanese than he does, and while she's using her knowledge, he's dicking around in Hawai'i fantasizing about paper textures and fooling around with a little high-school girl. At least one, I doubt he's got other girls, but there are people in this world who live double lives, and it's not really my business.

Sometimes I run off without anyone, just to see what's going on, maybe talk to strangers. Once I even went about thirty yards into the jungle just off the highway edge, behind some trees, and decided I was going to sleep naked on the ground and see what would happen to me, but the only thing that happened was that bugs bit me and I got dressed and went home in about fifteen minutes. That was probably the best possible way that scenario was going to play out.

I could never ask James to be dishonest for my benefit, so he covers for me when I'm out running around in the best way he knows how: he's honest. He denies I'm with him, when in fact I'm *not* with him, but my parents want to believe I'm with him rather than any worse alternative, so they don't even ask his mom many questions because they think if I'm not *right there* with him, he's hiding me away somewhere. So you see how everyone plays along by lying to themselves all the time, which usually works out perfect. The funny thing is, you don't have to deceive people much. They do it to themselves, so you can't even call me a liar.

But in between all that, there's school. Just boring stuff, I mean I like to learn, but it's the kids who bore me, plus the teachers and the books. They really can't teach me much. I'm just learning to deal with daily humiliation and lowered expectations—that's high school, folks!

But again, sorry. I didn't speak the whole truth. The science teachers sometimes are pretty good. We have some really crazy ones, and I like them. My biology teacher tells the kids he's growing botulin poison in a jar. You'd think—what with fears of terrorism—he'd be smart and shut up about that, but he loves to make kids laugh, and even more he likes to see them squirm… girls especially, or to hear cute girls gasp or fake-shriek. I think he gets off on telling hot girls something crazy like they're going to get cancer if they don't wear gloves, or something. That kind of stuff at least entertains me.

And when I'm *not* the center of attention, listening to kids talk in the cafeteria and hallways is a kind of *comfortable disgust*, because at least it doesn't come with any anxiety, and I just react like "oh my God, philistines!"

Did I tell you there's a girl in my school named Phyllis Steen? I'm not making that up!

6.
Revolving-Door Therapy

Chloe's Escape

Chloe managed to disappear around this point in her narrative. She hadn't yet told me what had gone wrong in Hawai'i the last time, or why she was so urgently pushed into my program again. She also managed to omit telling me anything about the school counselor whom she routinely met with, or her decision not to finish high school, or about the social worker who visited her home unexpectedly—twice—in addition to their scheduled bimonthly appointment in Kona. By Chloe's mother's account, this social worker was suddenly replaced after some anonymous person "blew the whistle" and sent a warning letter to her parents about a comment he made about "feeling attracted" to one of the teens under his care.

Chloe's escape from our hospital was not particularly remarkable. Though we do our best with regards to security, our hospital was never conceived as a prison. When patients specifically request that we allow them to mingle in some of the common areas outside of the secure ward, if they have not shown any tendencies towards self-harm or threatening behavior towards others, we issue them occasional passes as an encouragement for their cooperative participation in therapy. Even though she was never left entirely unsupervised, due to her earlier history, Chloe found a way to turn her mingling into an opportunity for escape when our nurses were attending to a pressing emergency.

Chloe mocked the idea of a cyclical model of time, but I noted that her own life was starting to resemble a cycle. Thus it should come as little surprise that Chloe was admitted to our program for a third time, just a few months later.

Perhaps, before I get to that, I should mention that during the period of her absence, I started having many dreams with her as the protagonist, and I was even starting to identify with her in an extraordinary way. However, by this time I had decided to discontinue dream interpretation as part of my process (see earlier chapters to understand some of the pitfalls of dream interpretation). So I will not examine those dreams here.

7.
Third Admission: Her Version

No Prologue

I will waste no further time, but pause only to state that Chloe was now eighteen years old at the time she returned.

Accounting for Lost Time

You don't have to worry because I called my parents right away when I left you. They wanted me to come home, obviously, or to return to your program. *That* would have been convenient, wouldn't it? But look, I've got a life. But I'm thankful that you are such a kind man, so devoted to your science and to the humanity of your patients, so I really did hope and expect that you would take me back, although I don't deserve it. It's not just because I'm afraid for my life, because to be honest I pissed off a few folks while I was out, but I also genuinely want to make a new start and really get committed to curing myself. I know you're the doctor who can help me make that into a reality.

Yes, the things I do are sometimes dangerous, and may *seem* risqué, a little slutty even. But it's not that at all. If you knew how my heart aches, and how sincere my feelings are… plus, I'm not really into the physical aspects of love. Your image of me is probably *vastly* exaggerated. Have you ever heard of a teenager who never had a love affair? And do *no girls* get themselves into trouble? It's not about sex, that's just how the *older* adult world thinks about it, because their jaded attitude has made them forget about romance, and they immediately think of the horror of it. Oh my God, teenage kinky business! It's so… rude!

Regarding James, my true love, the one who is always waiting for me, I love him so much and so intensely, but the sex is no good, and it never has been. I feel like I have a cunt full of worms after I "sleep" with him. You'd probably have to be a woman to understand that. With others it's not enjoyable either, except that I sometimes have a very brief thrill of fear. Then I come to hate that fear and what it makes me do, but it seems like a fear I can't do without for some reason...

Look, I confess, I've jerked you around by throwing a few ideas into your head, just to see how you would react. I mean, if you can come to terms with the dark side of my *thoughts*, then you won't possibly be offended by my *acts*, which are, all things considered, rather innocent, and appropriate to my emotional age of seven.

Yeah! That's right. I don't have to see into your case files to know what you think of me, and how you imagine me. Should I look into your dreams, too!? Ha, ha. Don't blush. I didn't really know anything.

Well... yeah, okay, you *say* that you never attributed an emotional age of seven to me. Maybe you've forgotten how nasty seven-year-olds are! But, no, you're a psych, right?

But, I just don't know how to straighten things out effectively. I mean, I always have abided by my 90% rule with you, so don't think I've handed you a bunch of lies. Really, it's more than 90%. It's all true, but truth itself is a bit... fuzzy.

Wait, what was I telling you about last time, anyway? Oh, you know, everything was true that time. The only fakery was my personality, as I probably played it up a bit more ditsy than is genuinely me. But you probably want to know what happened to me since I ran away...

Well, first I had to solve the money problem. I'm a responsible adult now, so you realize I'm capable of taking care of myself. I don't fly off on adventures without taking care of practicalities. Now, I had some money, but I had to get my bank card. I'd left it with a friend downtown just before checking into your program last time, because I wasn't quite sure I'd be able to access it when making my escape otherwise. My "friend," like most friends, isn't a real friend. We only met online a couple of times, and when I came into town she met me in the lobby of my parents' hotel room on the night before I was going to check in with you, and I handed over a couple of essentials I wanted her to save for me. But when I got out and got over to her place, I discovered that more than half of the money in my account was now gone, which means she stole more than a thousand dollars.

I really made some errors that set me up for this. I know you can't trust strangers and whatnot, but somehow I think she saw one of the posts that I made about a kind of memory technique I use for remembering long numbers, where you have a different picture of a person or action for a number, and I guess she heard me make a joke once or twice about "fuck a watermelon." Anyway, the clever bitch tried all kinds of combinations of different people and animals fucking watermelons until she discovered my PIN number, which is 279082, a.k.a. "Thor fucking a watermelon."

So she "borrowed" a little money just to pay off some debts she had to other people, but seriously, a thousand dollars in a couple of days? I got angry. She said she'd pay me when she could, and meanwhile I could stay with her for a couple of months so that would be like worth more than the money she'd taken. So, okay, I said that would work for a while, but I had to plot a bit. The thing is, she would never leave the apartment with me in it, so when she had to go out, she made me go out too so she could lock up. I mean, no trust despite the trust I'd shown her. That's fine.

The money I still had was certainly plenty so that I could spare an extra twelve bucks to buy a crowbar, pry a few security bars off her window, smash the glass, and go in and wreck shit including her computer. Besides my own clothes, I got out with enough extra clothes to make up the difference—but her clothes are a bit too loose on me because she's fat—and I got out faster than the police could respond. Then I called up the manager at the sandwich shop where she works and told him that she'd been spitting on the sandwiches. I don't know if that got her fired, but anyway, I moved on.

So, like I told you I telephoned my parents. They said they

had already heard the report that I had escaped from the hospital. Don't worry, I covered for you, I made out that it was all my fault that your program wasn't working, and I didn't say anything about how you were just jerking around writing notes and had no clue about treatment or whatever. Just kidding, don't get mad!

I told my parents very sincerely that I was sorry, I had made a huge mistake again when I manipulated them into sending me out here, and I really, really wanted to come home again if they could just forgive me and fly me back home. I cried a lot, and I was very sincere.

My dad said that he and my mom understood that my problems are very complex and that they want to do everything they can to support me and help me get through difficult times. They were still in shock over my first disappearance and kidnapping. Really, I don't know why, but they just hide behind that event like it was something out of the blue and I was just a normal girl until a criminal predator got his hands on me. Are they blind? So anyway, my dad was going to reserve an air ticket for me right away so I could fly back to Hawai'i. I just needed I.D. Well, actually I had I.D., but not my passport, but I told them that I had nothing except what I'd left behind in the hospital. But they should just wire me the money, and then when I got my I.D., I'd buy my own ticket.

My dad didn't like that idea at all. He had already been sighing in a way that I could tell he was constantly struggling to stay cool under the pressure of what he was feeling. He told me that all I had to do was go back to the hospital, I wouldn't be captured or locked up or anything, I could just ask for my stuff and my passport. He would personally call you up to confirm that I should be released from my commission and freed to return home. There'd be no problem.

Then I confessed to him. "Sorry, dad, I get so confused. You know I do have a little cash that I stashed away but I was afraid to admit it because it was against hospital policy." Also I had my driver's license, and I was scared to go back to the hospital because of all the strange equipment and the rumors about experimental procedures and whatnot. You know, I played up the vulnerable child angle.

You probably are easily deceived yourself. I mean, you probably think of me as a physically well-formed, fully blossomed woman and adult by now. But when I was a kid I was totally a girly-girl obsessed with ponies and pink things, princess dolls and stuffed animals. I mean, that's the big tragedy of it all. Every victim—and every victimizer—was once a child of six. And even now I still feel a little thrill sometimes when I think of those dolls I kept and the magical feeling they gave me… but I just suppress it, you know, because I don't want to be childish.

Anyway, I can let that out a little bit when it's appropriate, especially if it gets me a bit of what I want. Call me a bitch if you want to.

"So now," I said, "I really can fly home without needing to go to the hospital first, but you should wire me the money and let me buy my ticket. It would be a kind of show of faith, which is what I really need at this moment." I totally believed that if they could just show me that faith once more, I would follow through and return home and make a new start. But my dad argued and said it didn't make sense. He could book the ticket, or even he and my mom could fly out to take me back home, or take me on a trip somewhere. There was no reason for me to insist on their sending me money.

Well, I just refused. I told him I'm not coming home at all if he doesn't show enough faith to trust me with the money, and there was no reason I would have to come home anyway. I was just coming because I really wanted to. We got onto other things, rehashed old arguments… Omitted some details because he was afraid of pushing me too far. He acted like he really thought I was going to break, so then I brought up those details just to show him my memory's not so short, I know how fucked up family life is. But I wasn't going to blame him, I just wanted a little compassion and a show of good faith, etcetera. And then he just caved and sent me the money. It was a lot of money too, because flying on next-to-no notice is expensive, and I didn't want to fly economy for nine hours plus the connection into Hilo.

After that, I really thought I would go back to Hawai'i, but then two days later I realized I'd almost forgotten that I'd given my parents a flight number and arrival time and I should be arriving soon. Plus, I'd met this guy who was going to lend me his car for a little cross-country driving expedition. So I called up James and asked him to make my apologies to my parents for not coming. I just really felt pretty guilty to think that they would have to go out to the airport and wait and wait only to find that I wasn't on the plane. So it was better they should hear it directly from James.

James was *cold* when I talked to him. I'd never heard him so cold. I explained to him carefully what he was supposed to do, and how to say it, and I explained that it was necessary that I should find some freedom for a change, just to get my thoughts in order. He should understand that. What he said was "I'll do what you said," and there was no love in the way he said it. It seemed almost angry. But I knew he was just nursing the hurt I'd dealt him.

Freedom

So, you probably wonder what a young girl does when she discovers she has all the freedom in the world, and no responsibility. Well, the first thing I did was drive about an hour out of town, and then I just about stopped. I found myself in a little podunk town called Sedalia. I thought I'd drive around a bit and see some of the local area, but the place had no character and just seemed like every other place. So I found a little crap-ass motel called "Komfort Kort", checked in, and spent the next three days watching TV with my eyes.

I mean, I did nothing. I really almost didn't leave the motel. I might have stayed there forever, except I had a kind of scary run-in with one of the whores on my third night. I was coming in from buying myself some take-out chicken, and this girl was just standing around outside one of the rooms for some reason. Maybe she just got finished blowing a guy or two, I don't know, but there was a lot of moaning in those rooms at night. And she was standing with an *I-don't-know-where-the-hell-I-am* expression. Then she sort of came around and demanded some of my chicken. I mean, you know, first kind of *asking*, as if she had a right to it, and quickly escalating to calling me a bitch and... I don't remember exactly what she said... I had felt pretty weird in that place to begin with, but frankly I didn't have any sense that I belonged anywhere else either, but that confrontation freaked me. I didn't give her any chicken, but I locked myself in the room and made up my mind to leave town the next day. I didn't feel very generous towards that bitch either; I mean I hoped the guys would go extra hard on her that night just as a kind of poetic justice.

The next day, just as I was driving away and got myself a little lost, I made the accidental discovery that they actually had an art museum in town. So, I go in, and the museum has Pop Art? I hate that shit!

"This is my life" I declared. Out loud. I stood surrounded by the most pitiful art and said "this is my life." That really scared me, so I got in my car and got out of there fast.

Then, just when I thought I was making good progress, the scariest thunder and lightning storm came out of absolutely nowhere. The clouds were out of a nightmare. I couldn't drive because the rain was just pure insanity, and I just pulled over into an embankment on the side of the highway, covered my face, and cried. It went on for a long, long time, and all I could think about was James and how he wasn't afraid of anything.

"Bitch," I told myself. I actually poked myself in the open eye. "This is the last time you cry over anything." *I can't let myself be defined by a relationship, and besides I never think of him when it's about him, I only think about him when it's about me... which I regret. I mean, I sincerely and truly regret that. I'm a good person, with a good heart. The mistakes I've made are just mistakes, but that's a part of freedom. You make mistakes, and you learn from them, but that doesn't mean you have to hate your own soul... you have to be the first to forgive yourself. Don't ask a man for a validating-forgiveness. It's better to piss on him first.*

Then I cried a lot more for a long time. Then I got hungry. But I still had to wait-out another thirty minutes of heavy rain. I don't know how I got through that time.

Finally I got on the road again, and eventually I found a Burger King near Warrenton. I like Burger King better than McDonalds.

It was getting dark as I came into the St. Louis area, and I just wanted to pass through. There wasn't any obvious way to get *around* the city. The roads are just insane, all twisted and senseless there, and I remembered that I actually suck at driving. I realized I was going to kill someone other than me if I got in an accident, and I had to slow down as I pulled around one of those twisty off-ramps that just sent me way out of the direction I was going, and yet somehow my right foot just would *not* let up on the gas. It even defied me a little by pushing a little harder. But I knew it was just me, fucking with myself, and so I slammed on the brakes, pulled to the side of the road, and all kinds of cars whipped past honking their horns, but I didn't care. That was it. No more driving.

I didn't know what I was going to do. At that point I was thinking about New York, which was really the way I was headed, specifically with the Met in mind. I mean, I wanted to see all those masterworks and I had an insane envy whenever I saw movies and documentaries that showed even a glimpse of that place.

I was walking in the crepuscule just thinking about Perseus's hand holding the gorgon's head, and all those snakes on the gorgon's head were turning more and more phallic and disgusting in my mind while I wandered next to speeding cars. Some of the cars slowed down a bit to get a look at me even though I was doing *nothing* to attract their attention except walking. One car actually stopped behind me and honked the horn loudly. Some guys called out "hey!" They were sailors! With little white hats. What were they doing there? I ignored them. They cruised alongside me for a little ways, but they were forced to move on by the speeding cars behind them that honked and so forth.

I was worried then that I might get the attention of the police before I could come up with any credible story to account for what I was doing there, or where I was going. So I picked up my pace a bit until I found a way to get off the highway. The road, by the way, smells like heaps and heaps of burnt rubber.

Then I was in the city. This whole tangle of roads was just in the middle of everything. And I went to go in a bar, but I was ejected just as I started to cross the threshold. The guy who pushed me out tried to give me some kind of warning, like he was my uncle, telling me I'd get myself in a lot of trouble walking into a place like that alone. But it seemed like a friendly place inside with young folks just joking around. I don't know what that guy was after.

That's all I can remember from Missouri, I mean the rest is just boring shit, but my first taste of real life without a mom, without a dad, without anyone or anything, was a bit of grit mixed up with a heap of boredom, and I thought that summed up my future.

New York

New York was completely different. I made a few friends, of the false variety, and got along pretty well. I couldn't stay for long because it was expensive. But I really got to see the Met! I went there three times in three days, and I saw so much amazing art, I'm still kind of high thinking about it. Each time I went, I paid a quarter, which means I generously gave a full one-percent of the "recommended donation." I figured for every one of me, there are a hundred suckers who pay the full price, but it would take a hundred of me to pay as much as one sucker... so, mathematically it was like I didn't exist at all.

My first friend was a gay guy named George, and it was probably really good for me that I made friends with a gay guy because, I forgot to tell you, but I took a vow of celibacy before going to New

York. I know you're not going to believe that, but I mainly did it for your sake. I mean, I had a feeling, maybe not fully acknowledged, but I thought about how I would one day be back here, and I really didn't want to have to confess to a lot of sordid details. So I decided on a no-sex diet for a good long while. Maybe forever!

But don't get the idea that I was *completely* innocent in the way I got on with George.

My first meeting with George was something strange that doesn't even sound true, but that's life. I saw him in the park, out on the lawn, wrestling with his shirt off, with two other gay guys, also shirtless, and they all had oil on their muscles and chests. They were struggling and squirming around... they looked like a kind of homo-erotic abattoir. I nearly vomited.

"Oh my God, guys!" I just shouted at them, not really thinking, but I hadn't spoken to anyone recently, so I guess it was a weird loneliness thing that got me to break out of my shell like that. "Get a room!"

George had his face wedged in the hairy armpit of this other *big* guy, and underneath the two, the third guy, who was skinnier, had slipped down and George dropped his knee so it fell painfully on top of that guy's thigh, while the skinny guy looked up with his face kind of sandwiched between their oily bellies. Meanwhile, George twisted his head around and looked at me for a moment with his red face.

"What?! ... Who the hell are you?" he shouted.

"Nobody," I said.

Then I noticed that there were a few other people standing and also watching these guys wrestle, and one guy was standing really close and snapping pictures with a big camera. But otherwise there were a lot of other people in the park just ignoring the scene and carrying on like normal. They wrestled for like another thirty seconds or so, with the skinny guy reaching up his hand between the bigger guy's legs and to the back, to grasp the back of the guy's pants, and with the other hand he pushed the inside of the guy's knee, while George pivoted around and together they knocked the big gorilla guy to the ground, but accidentally the skinny guy got kind of crushed underneath while George straddled the guy's belly; then skinny guy wiggled out and climbed on top and they pinched the big guy's nipples and chest and belly muscles, while the guy with the camera got in and snapped more pictures.

"Hey," I shouted again, though I was kind of being clownish at this point, "don't you guys see that pervert with the camera?"

They all broke out laughing at me at this point, and a couple of the spectators nearby clapped their hands, so I got a little red in the face because I realized I had been stupider than I'd intended. I mean, obviously this was a photo shoot of some sort, and I kind of knew that, but I wasn't used to seeing such spectacles just out in public, and I had just spent hours in the Metropolitan looking at all kinds of art, including these giant wooden Polynesian statues of gods with six-foot phalluses. But I also kind of felt a little clever, like I was a star of sorts because I'd entertained some strangers with my stupid-act, and it went over pretty well.

Short story short, the photographer invited me to join them for coffee after the shoot. He had an assistant nearby, but no other crew, so it was kind of a rinky-dink operation. George and I got on well at the café, the gorilla's name was John, and the skinny guy was also named George, but they called him Smith to avoid confusion. I didn't get to know any of those guys too well, but I did wind up seeing the photographer again later on. He wasn't introduced to me by name at this point, even though I'd told him *my* name, and a bit of my background including the fact that I'd come to New York to be a model. (I hadn't, but it just occurred to me at the time to say that). I didn't even ask the assistant's name, not that he wasn't a nice guy, but he was a bit quiet and seemed like an outsider… all business and probably not gay. He seemed a little sad or uncomfortable too. But the models were all obviously gay, which you could probably guess anyway since they're models, and the photographer, though also mostly quiet, was a little too *interested* to be completely straight. They were all wearing shirts in the café, by the way.

I made plans to meet George again, because he said he just *had* to see me again, because I was so "cute and adorable," and also because he knew I would get murdered if I didn't get a protector to warn me and let me know about the dangers of the city.

I'd told them I was staying with an aunt and uncle, just to sound… well, reasonable… but actually that was the night I was moving out to stay in a super-cheap hostel out in Brooklyn. I had had to wait a few days to get in, since they were fully booked, so I had spent over four hundred bucks in three days on a private room in a hotel, but now I was going to stay in an eight-bunk mixed dormitory for about forty bucks a night. "Mixed" means guys sleep in the same room with you, sometimes they like to come out of the shower still naked and towel off in front of you, and if you happen to be awake at two in the morning you can sometimes hear them masturbating. It's like, when one guy gets started, it's a signal to them all to go, and if a girl shouts out, "What the hell are you doing?" they can all play the game, "It wasn't me, wasn't me," and then giggle, but they've got support of the other guys so they're not too embarrassed about it. It's pretty much better to shut up and pretend you don't know.

Sitting in the common area in that hostel was unbearable, kind of like living in this hospital, so I just didn't do it. I spent as much time out of the place as I could. That meant I visited the Frick and the Guggenheim, and all the other places where I could relax and enjoy art. I visited university galleries as well, and the New Museum. I quickly befriended several different guys, because some of them flirted with me, and others were the sort who just kind of looked and lingered. I knew they were interested, so if I said, "Hi," or asked a question about art, it kind of freaked some of them, but others took up the slack and suddenly everything they'd been waiting to say to *somebody* came out.

An observant girl can learn a lot about people, although a lot of it is disgusting. But there are smart people out there, and some pretty pitiable cases. A lot of people have delusions, and that made me wonder a little about myself too.

For example, I've had guys tell me: "It's time for a new art revolution." "There's nothing to say anymore, but I'm desperate to say it." "I don't really know what I'm doing most of the time." "It's nice to know girls like you really exist in the world." "I hate my mother." "The best art feels like shitting." "I like physicality, and I like a work that expresses physicality." "The same things that were true twenty thousand years ago are true today." "I love Disney movies!" "I'm embarrassed to tell you what I really think, because I have... problems." "Kissing is more intimate than sex." "As long as I have beer, there's nothing wrong with the universe." And "It's so strange when you can really *talk* and have someone understand you, because actually language is the biggest miracle and mystery of human experience."

In addition, there were a lot, a lot, a lot of very *boring* conversations, about brothers and sisters, and politics, and the environment, and just blank empty silences that spoke of ignorance and worthlessness rather than expressing a soul... I can't even bear to think of those mind-numbingly empty utterances that most guys produce, so I'm not going to quote them. Let's move on.

I had a kind of fantasy of becoming a con-artist or something, but I didn't really know how to do it and I wasn't feeling it. It was enough at this point just for me to get on with people. I got invited to parties and shows, and made connections with little circles of friends, mostly university students who accepted me because they were largely lost and trying to find their way too, and I lied sometimes about my own plans so I'd fit into their circles a little better. Everyone trusted me and thought I was, if anything, far too naïve and bound to get exploited. But I just wished I could think of a good way to get the guys to pay me without having sex with them, or maybe I could rob them or something. But I thought I'd have to take it slow until I could find a kind of criminal mentor, or maybe I could learn from books.

George called me up a little over a week after our first meeting, and said I should meet him for lunch at a little Chino-Latino diner in Chelsea. I found my way. Unfortunately, he was the kind of guy who was willing to let *me* pay for lunch. Free meals and drinks were pretty much the only things I was getting out of the straight guys. But I got really honest with George and told him more of my real story. He advised me to definitely get as much as I could get from the guys I *wasn't* having sex with. Those are the suckers who just pay and pay. The guys who you give it to aren't so generous. But George told me how I could get a little bit of money as a life-studies model—not much, just a little, and I'd probably need to get another part-time job just to survive, and I wouldn't survive well. But basically, I could make some quick cash by getting naked and holding poses for a while, while art students and dilettantes practiced their craft.

I tried it once but didn't like it. The models all say that body type doesn't matter; it's very liberating, and the artists don't judge the model; they think only about line, and form, and shade, and highlights. Age, weight, attractiveness, no one cares about that, what matters is professionalism, experience, and the ability to hold a variety of expressive or original poses. That plus personality, because artists want to chat a little and feel comfortable with the experience. But none of that is true once a beautiful, sexy, *young* woman or girl enters the studio, especially someone *new*. Same thing for a beautiful, sexy, young guy, because a lot of artists are into that. Once that happens, there's a tension that different artists deal with in different ways, but there's just a constant electric charge in the air. There's the artists who overcompensate by really trying to *not* care and be ultra-professional and emotionless. You can see them almost muttering to themselves, as though saying internally "so, there's a large shadow falling in this direction, but I just can't get my damn pencil to…" and they go between barely glancing at you and concentrating on their work, to a new phase of looking very closely and minutely at even the most intimate details while projecting "so what, I have to do this, it's my craft," etcetera. At the same time, there are the slow breathers, the almost-shallow-enough-to-be-a-gasp sounds. And there are women who snicker a bit or fume because they can perceive the effect I'm having on the straight men, and there are the women who are also caught up by the excitement of it all, whatever their sexuality, because they know that art is beauty and this is something they've been waiting to capture and express. And then there are the dead ones who really don't give a damn… I don't know, but I've been told such a type exists. And the gay guys seem to fit the pattern of the two different kinds of females, the snickering and smirking males who are emulating the bitter straight female reaction, and the excited ones who are stimulated aesthetically; they're a little hard to tell from the straight guys, so they may be bi.

But when I was standing naked there in front of all of them—there were fourteen or fifteen—I was aware of a presence out in the darkened shadow of the corner behind me… a man who was older than the rest, with thick eyebrows and a moustache, like two black seagulls in flight, framing a reddish nose and a burning stare. Tense as a man facing an execution. He was absorbed in me, and concentrating on my body. He hardly moved, as though he'd forgotten the easel before him and had lost interest in his art. I nearly panicked, and I felt the flesh of my ass and thighs involuntarily tremble, as though in response to his desire. I practiced absolute stillness, and emotional self-restraint. When I was ready to shift pose, I turned about a bit, and saw him watching me, but I couldn't quite bring myself to face him directly, so I ended up exposing my front to him while casting a demure glance over my shoulder towards the other end of the room. By some strange instinct, I cast my left arm across to my right shoulder over which I was looking, so from the rear end it looked naturally as if I were partially covering myself, but actually my arm was over my breasts, so from the front I was fully exposed and he saw the whole damn thing.

When it was almost the end of the first thirty minutes of my session, I suddenly heard a loud, lewd whistle from the doorway.

It was George! He was peeking in, and wearing his robe, coming from another studio down the hall.

"Oh my God!" he shouted at me, seeing me nude for the first time and really embarrassing me... perhaps in revenge for my reaction in the park. "I've got another job for you."

I smiled briefly, then resumed my former expression as the artists hushed George in irritation. Two minutes later, I was ready for a break. I walked around and looked at some of the sketches and complimented them, though they were mostly awkward and crude. A few of the sketch artists *were* genuinely talented, but the rest were just a mess, and as I looked again—this time very directly—into the darkened corner, I saw the man there rise and... vanish. He wasn't there. I made my way towards that corner in my brief little circuit of the room, and it was clear he had never been there. Come to think of it, why would an artist sit in the darkness, out of the light, and why would he be tolerated? But I'd definitely seen *something* rise. Perhaps someone, in rising elsewhere in the room, turned a chair or other reflective surface such that it cast a briefly glimpsed and moving rectangle of light into the shadows, and the rest was all illusion. But why had I been so sure the man was there in the first place, and how had I gotten such a distinct impression of him. No matter. Then I noticed that one young man—a straight man, if I'm any judge—had produced a remarkable and simmeringly erotic portrait of me, perhaps inspired by my own reaction to the perceived threat from the shadows. He shyly apologized for his work, without clearly expressing what there was to be sorry about (it was very good) and told me that I seemed to have a special talent for expression. "Ineffable" he dared to say.

For the rest of the session, after my break was over, I had only that young man in my mind. I modeled for him, to the profit of all. But I tell you, I'll never stand for a portrait or sketch again. It's too potent as an experience, almost supernatural and threatening. A contact with divine essence. But am I a divinity? Cameras are far less personal, and are more suited to my personality.

I did, however, become a regular in the studio as an artist learning to improve my drawing. I tried to keep my response to the models professional, as the rest did, but in a few days I found out that there was a weekly schedule of models, and I preferred to come whenever there was a known beauty, male or female, and especially if there was a new and *unknown* model. I wanted to be a spectator to the magic.

I noticed that the number of paying customers definitely varied based on expectations of who would be modeling. Substitutions produced a little grumbling. Sadly, there weren't many true sensations, except for one young female who embodied a different kind of divine… what can I say… duality of absence and extreme presence. There was an implication that she knew herself as a shadow, or mirrored image of a higher beautiful form. She was really stunning and the electric charge was there. There was her, plus there was George, who was himself rather classically beautiful, and he had a remarkable talent for self-exposure as a form of vulnerability to males. I guess that's why he was so popular and was on his way to more high-class, professional clothes modeling.

The Phone Call

I called up James to tell him about my New York experience, while insisting that he not tell anyone else about it. He didn't believe me at all. I was completely direct and honest with him, but he said it was all bullshit, New York's not like that, "This is a schoolgirl's fantasy of the world of artists." It was ridiculous of him to say that, because I knew exactly what my own life was like.

I told him "There's an infinity of experience in this world, Jonestown. The bold have different experiences from the meek and timid. And weird shit happens, even the kind of weird shit that sounds like a fantasy, that shit happens too. But it's not fantasy; the fact that it's concrete, that makes it all the scarier, more genuinely dangerous, but also full of potential. I haven't gotten myself cut to ribbons, I haven't gotten shat on, I haven't had my whole life fall apart just because I grew up and became a woman and moved away. All those things *can* happen. That's also part of the potential. My life isn't boring, even if it sometimes *is* boring, it's not always. But nothing is as you think it is, until you see it, stare at it, kick it in the balls. I will not be limited."

We had a big fight, and he finally told me some of his frustration about the way I was treating him and the fact that I was so far beyond his ability to control or to help me that he was on the verge of giving everything up. Because I was just destroying myself and my family, the people around me. Also, he said, he knew that I had been stealing money from his mom.

Well, actually, I memorized his mom's credit card number—and also my parents' credit card numbers—before leaving Hawai'i, and I had a bit of a racket where I was buying some stuff to be delivered—mostly expensive art supplies, brushes and paints—which I sold for cash at a cut rate. Plus I'd met a pretty good hacker who turned me on to a site which actually assists in credit card fraud for a fee, so I was able to cash out about four thousand five hundred dollars from just over six or seven thousand dollars in charges before the cards were reported stolen.

"I'm sorry," I told him. "I'm sure my mom and dad will cover your mom's loss because they love me and they want to cover up my mistakes like they always have." And I'm sure that my folks *did* finally pay him, because I sent them a message with a kind of convoluted story about why I had to do what I did and explaining why it was necessary that they prevent me from committing a crime against the innocent. I talked in veiled terms in that message about some of the supposed atrocities that Ron committed. So that straightened that out.

But I made a big, bold, and very mature decision during that phone call. I really didn't think I would ever be capable of such self-awareness and honesty, really.

"James," I said, "You are awesome and perfect, really, but I'm lost to you. Permanently. You're not to think of me anymore. Even though my only hope has always been for a perfect union between me and you, it's impossible because of my sickness. It's impossible. You have to forget me, and… even though I know you'll never really forget me… you have to let me go."

The sweet dope! He couldn't say "yes." He just reacted with a hurt silence, followed by a kind of acknowledging grunt. But I knew his non-verbal acknowledgment would cast me away forever. There was and there will be no going back now.

The Last of New York

I continued my New York adventure, and I even managed to hang on to my *renewed-virginity* per my previous vow. But I knew I wasn't going to make it for long in that town. I wasn't headed for a university degree, and no one was going to pay my way, and I was sure to be a miserable failure as a con-artist. New Yorkers are jaded and sly, and I have no special skills when I play the tease-but-no-sex game. Best I can get is free dinners, entertainment, and drinks (using a fake ID I lined up through some contacts). But I'd already abandoned most of the fat girl's clothes, and most of the vintage stuff that I found that was cute but not chic was becoming a bit too bulky to fit in my storage locker at the hostel. Unless I wanted to crash on sofas among poets and other weirdos—and it would take some careful negotiation to pull that off safely—there weren't many housing options for me beyond the hostel. And even in my casual socializing I did have to fight off the occasional groper. Awkward situations kept preventing any long-term "friends only" situations from working. So it finally made sense to get out of town.

Before I left New York, George reintroduced me to his photographer friend, the older guy whose name I now discovered was Guy. Guy produced some novelty-erotic postcards that were pretty well known and respected within a kind of obscure subculture. His is almost a lost art because hardly anyone sends cards or even collects them anymore, but there is still a subculture of collectors and connoisseurs. There's also a sort of nostalgia-prestige associated with the form. Anyway, George and I posed for a few shots, and I even got nine hundred bucks for one shoot, for a postcard that I just *had* to send to Chiko as a prank goodbye since I'd never said a proper goodbye to him before checking into the hospital.

George got nude and stimulated himself manually, and stuck a roll of toilet tissue over his dick—with the tip protruding, as he's rather large. He stood over me as I sat nude on a tiny little plastic white children's potty, pulling off a piece of paper from the roll with my right hand while, with my left hand to my face, I made a hammy kind of "oh my" expression, looking at the camera. I sent it to Chiko and signed the back "Hugs and Sucks, your little Chloe. OXOX." I just thought, *With his faggot's obsession for paper, he'll never get this image of toilet paper out of his head.* And I wonder if his wife would have been home when the card arrived. That would be hilarious!

Regardless, I had to leave. Even though George tried to help me out, and he put some pressure on me to return to modeling in the life-studies studios because there was a lot of demand among the regular artists to see me again, and he knew a few richer dilettantes who would pay extra for "privates," I declined. I got to know a lot more about George in my final days, when he opened up and told me about his life and childhood, which was surprisingly bland in a way but also terribly sad and pathetic without having anything *too* tragic about it. But I had no worries for him, because I know he's going places and I'm sure he'll be a GQ model someday. He might even hook up with a famous designer. Not a photographer—he says most of the photographers are straight and pretty girl crazy, whereas "Bi Guy" is kind of the exception and very niche, and he doesn't have any growth potential. He's just going to do his hobby cards forever.

A girl in my hostel cornered me one day and said she was leaving town, and because I'd been talking about leaving myself, she suggested I join her. I'd heard her make the same proposition to another girl earlier who turned her down. But she told me she had found a one-room sublet in a private house down in Charlotte, North Carolina, and she needed a roommate to help her afford it. She was pretty straight with me.

"It's two months for one thousand dollars," she told me. "That's one thousand dollars total for the two of us, for two months, not monthly. But honestly I can't afford it, this place has already broke me, so I need a two-hundred-dollar finder's fee. In other words, you pay seven hundred dollars for two months' housing, and I pay three hundred, and we're roommates. You don't have to pay for transportation, I've got that hooked up for the both of us. It's a bigger room than this, and it's not in New York, but fuck New York."

It made sense to me, and I didn't care if it was "fair." That was less than a third of what I was paying at the hostel, and I'd have one roommate instead of seven. I took her up on it, and we left quick.

The Retreat

My new roommate's name was Mallory, and she was pretty cool. We didn't really get on well in the hostel in Brooklyn, but for the four days we were roommates in Charlotte she seemed a lot more relaxed, and I got to know her better.

"I hate being broke," she told me. "I'm educated, middle class, but everything's just falling apart for no good reason at all. I mean I may have made some mistakes in life, but I'm a responsible person and I work when I can."

"What do you do?" I asked. I wasn't that interested, but I figured I could come to understand her a little better if I threw out a few obvious questions.

"Well, I have worked in a couple of convenience stores just for a little money to get by, but I have a media degree. I went up looking for a job in advertising, but they've got interns working for nothing, and the only offers I could get were just unlivable. Meanwhile none of my *most desired* prospects worked out. Now I've got a cousin down here, and I think she might hook me up. She works in a signage shop, and they need someone to help promote sales to other local startup businesses, and places with dilapidated signage.

It's kind of humiliating. I did a journal of self-assessment, and I found out something really meaningful to help guide my forward progress. I'm *not* meant for sales. I just don't sell. I'm supposed to be in creative. But you have to compromise, I guess, sometimes in the beginning. I just don't really have a good relationship with my cousin either. She broke my foot once. It was an accident, but weirdly now I'm looking for work and she acts like I'm putting undue pressure on her and using that accident as leverage. But I didn't even mention it to her, except as a joke."

Mallory would probably have asked about my plans, except I had told her already that I didn't have any plans. She said she'd thought I was a tourist at first, but then she couldn't figure me out and figured I was some kind of drifter. She admitted that something about me scared her too, but she envied me for apparently having no ambition and just learning about life from experience. I don't know what the fuck she was talking about when she said that. It didn't make sense.

Meanwhile, I'd noticed that she was drunk a lot in New York, and I don't know that she was all that serious about finding a job. She didn't even have nice enough clothes for a real interview. She was always laughing like a moron and asking the German guys questions. She didn't seem professional. But once we got out of New York, one-on-one she seemed like a sincere—but rather aimless—individual, not one to hide anything, but not really that self-aware either. Of course, moving south didn't cure her of her nightly drunkenness. I didn't talk to her when she was drunk. That was a different "her" to me.

She told me her mom was partly paralyzed from a stroke even though she wasn't very old, and the family spent a lot to renovate the house to accommodate her mom's inability to walk. But I don't think the family kicked Mallory out. I think she was like me in the sense that she could probably go home anytime, but for some reason she wasn't going to.

Mallory went out at random times, while I mostly stayed in, and then on the fifth day she didn't come back. Ever again. She had paid her share of the two-months' rent, and I'd paid mine, so now I had the room to myself for all the rest of that time. It was like winning the lottery!

I had two other roommates. They were the girls in the other room in the house, Lori and Kate. They worked at a nearby movie theater, not earning much money, while Kate took classes at a community college and Lori read a lot. They were friendly and pretty fun to hang out with. We didn't talk much at first, which was all right, but eventually we talked more when we met in the kitchen, and then they invited me a couple of times to watch free previews of movies in their theater after midnight, which they did every Wednesday and Thursday before opening the films to the public.

Best of all, though, was that I had my little artist's hole. My own room with absolutely nothing to do and no distractions except the few I sought out for myself. So I did a lot of drawing. I worked out a whole series of drawings based on the sketches I had done in the studio of George and that divine girl whose name I've forgotten. Some of them were *really* good. I tried to pair them up a couple of times, but the best drawings were of them as isolated subjects in vague and shaded backgrounds, except there was one that I liked with the two of them observing one another from a little bit of distance. In this picture, I cast the area beyond the forms of their bodies into haphazard and incomplete shadowed areas, while the space between them was brighter, just subtly crossed by a few hints at shadows, and the mostly enlightened space seemed to have a bit of that "charge" I was after.

Lori and Kate came to recognize that they had an artist in residence. They liked my drawings a lot, and I asked them one day to model for me, but they were too shy and seemed a little upset by the suggestion. Then Lori relented a little. She didn't want to do nude, but I could do a facial portrait, or she would even pose in pants and a brassiere, seated on a stool. I didn't like that, so I tried to strike a compromise where she could keep her pants on but pose topless.

She agreed, and I figured she had been sort of leading up to that in her own reluctant way anyway. So I drew something pretty fantastic based on just face and upper torso, but it seemed a little weird and cut off in terms of the framing, so I did another of her whole above the knees including the blue jeans, and that was good. She really liked my initial sketch—which later developed into an even better finished work—so when I proposed she take off her pants and keep her panties on, and I'd just imagine the rest, she agreed, and when I was almost finished she took off the panties too. So I got full nude.

When Kate saw my finished drawings of Lori, she was impressed, so she did full nude for me too, and then did a large variety of poses over the next few days. Then I realized how amazing it was to work with models who had no ambition to be models and who could never have imagined themselves doing such a thing. Real amateurs.

Lori and Kate's boyfriends came around and wanted to see the pictures. I had given each of the girls one of my better works, and the boys wanted to see more. When they saw them they *demanded* I draw more, and they paid me good money to do so. So I picked up a few hundred bucks and became a paid artist. The boys wouldn't pose nude for me when I asked, though, so I dropped it. One offered to let me do a facial portrait. I went ahead and did it, but the fact is he was kind of ugly. I did my best, and like all of my work it was somewhat idealized. He liked the result, so I gave him the picture for free because I never wanted to see it again.

Besides that I just spent a lot of time in my room drawing and sketching various scenes from my imagination, and also working on more abstract works. With a lot of effort I produced a series of three pictures with kind of spaghetti lines turning through three-dimensions and casting kind of... echoes. It's not really conceptual, just a visual effect and I can't describe. Don't think reflections or shadows exactly, though there's a relationship there. It's more that the shape of one form is remotely influenced by another in a complex manner that implies a deeper dimension. Then, I really liked one of the three pictures, so I trashed the other two. I figured they were implied by the one.

My roommates did worry about me a bit, mainly because I wasn't very good at cooking or shopping, so I ate a lot of chicken and biscuits, plus boiled eggs, bags of peanuts, that kind of thing. But I lived. I didn't drink at all, since I only used to do that with men, and I didn't smoke, so what the hell. Should I be a vegan with a heroin needle stuck in my eye so they can applaud me for my healthy habits? I never got fat even if I ate like a pig. But I do have *enough* in just the right places, as I've been told in the past.

Going Commercial

There was a community art fair, way out at Carolina Beach. Amazingly it only cost a hundred bucks to rent a ten-by-ten booth space for a day, and they accommodated a huge number of booths. Of course, that was two-hundred miles away. And the booth "space" didn't include any equipment, meaning no booth. Anyhow, I mailed in my application, paid my fee, and when the day before the festival arrived I took a bus out.

I slept on the bus, which was all for the good, because when I got out there I had no place to stay. Hotels were expensive, all booked up, and the guys at the desk of one place laughed at me when I asked if I could pay cash. "Sure, but you still need a card for the deposit." So hotels were out altogether. But I did find a nice guy at one hotel who let me check my portfolio overnight without a reservation. All my stuff, including pictures, stapler, gator clips and such, was in a nice big leather portfolio that I'd stolen just before my trip.

So then I just had to find a reasonable way to stay awake all night. That was easy enough. There are bars and clubs all over. I don't like drinking, but I first found a restaurant and had a bit to eat—which I paid for. Then I ordered a beer at the restaurant bar. Drank it alone. Big surprise, no interested parties.

Then I went to another place, and as I made my way to the

bar there, I made the stupidest comment of my life. "Oh my god, this music is great!" The music was awful. I don't even know what it was, other than loud.

Then this dufus white guy said, "Yeah, isn't it?" and started buying me drinks.

I drank slow, and soon switched to cola.

"Aw, come on now, why do you want to drink cola?"

"It's a long night ahead."

"Yeah, that's true."

I think that excited him. But I disappointed him soon enough. We blathered about stupid stuff. I didn't say anything too interesting, or anything that might challenge him and show up his inadequacy. We ate up some time, and he started to get the idea that I was just going to sit there all night drinking until he proposed something else.

"Hey, let's go dance, there's a great place for that."

"No, I don't dance."

"Really? But you look like you could move! But I'm just saying."

"Hmmm."

"And I've got some friends, they're hanging out at this other club. They left earlier when we were talking and then messaged me, but I didn't want to rush off…"

"I don't mind."

"No, I'm just saying, why don't you come? We can take it somewhere else, I'm up for anything."

"Hmmm. I'm getting tired."

"Really? Where are you staying?"

"Here, I think. I haven't decided."

"Oh my God, that's crazy! I've heard some lines… but my hotel's not far, you know…"

"No."

"I'm not saying… it's just…"

"No. Thank you. You've been real sweet and all."

"Oh, my god, you're kidding me."

"Not kidding."

"But look, I know, you're really too good a girl and all, I know

469

you're probably... something special. It's just, even if I'm a little drunk and stupid right now, I feel like we could make a connection, you know."

"I really liked the time we spent together chatting. You're a fun guy."

"Oh my..."

He walked off. Message received. But then the guy came back into the bar just half a minute later and shouted.

"Hey, nobody buy that girl a drink, okay! Don't do it!" He turned away, dramatically clutching his hands to his chest. "Heartbreaker!" he cried. And left. And his baseball cap had been on sideways the whole damn time. Idiot.

Chat on the Beach

As soon as that guy left, another guy got up from his seat to join me at the bar. He had a kind of unpremeditated beard.

"I would like to buy you a drink," he declared in a self-effacing dramatic style.

Oh my God, I thought, *he said "would." He must be a philosopher.* It turned out I was right. This guy, Ethan, was a white guy too. *What's wrong with me?* I thought, *I don't warrant a black guy?* There were black guys in there, but not many black women, so you can't tell me that black and white don't mix in Carolina.

Anyway, Ethan was unusually reserved and self-possessed at the same time that he was forward enough to show he was interested in me. I don't know exactly what happened to make him take me so seriously when I was just a girl sitting at the bar by herself after publicly feuding with a drunk moron. But maybe that was just his style, and he always made a show of taking other people seriously because he took himself seriously. We sat there for about half an hour and then went out to the beach, where we lay talking for the rest of the night.

I asked Ethan whether he was planning to go to the art festival the next day.

"No, I'm not really interested in that." Pause. "Are you going?"

"Yeah, I'm an artist, I'm gonna try to sell some stuff."

"Oh." Pause. "What do you think of North Carolina beaches? Did you ever think of us as a beach state?"

"No, but I'm not especially impressed."

"Well, okay, you're from a beach paradise, right?"

"No. There are some pretty beaches in Hawai'i Island, I guess, but we're not Oahu."

"Anyway, you should try Cape Hatteras."

"Why?"

He sat up and propped himself on his elbow, in a stereotyped gesture of incredulity.

"Do you like nature, actually?"

"Not much."

"Oh, come on!"

"What's the value in it? I mean, I've had some fun on beaches, and it's nice relaxing somewhere where you don't have to pay money for a seat. But do you love *nature*? In itself?"

"You have to. Of course. Don't you think… I mean, it's a kind of inherited thinking, but nature is a guide for human behavior. There's wisdom to be gained by observing natural phenomena."

"Fuck that. I've got an idea for you. Go have yourself blindfolded, loaded on a helicopter, and delivered to a randomly selected place in the United States. One of two things will happen, either you'll find yourself in a barren wasteland, inhospitable, where you'll definitely die in like two weeks if no one helps you, or else you'll be in a relative paradise made by people."

"That's sick. Do you really think cities are paradises?"

"No, they're more like hells, but I mean relatively. Listen, what do you eat?"

"Ummm… food."

"Yeah, probably farmed food, right."

"Sure, sure, but farms are just about people using the resources of nature. It's a process that arose from the earth, we only grasped a way to exploit the process."

"So what do you eat, apples? Manna from heaven?"

"I like rice and corn."

"Good, me too. I like corn. Except I call it *Doritos*."

"Ha. Okay."

I ranted for a while more, and then we moved on to other topics. But I'll tell you now, I'm just sick of all this nature worship bullshit. I mean, does this guy even realize that people *invented* rice and apples?

Later I mentioned art and drawing again.

"Would you like to see some of my pictures before I set up my show tomorrow?"

"Uh, thanks, but… I don't really want to get *that* personal right away."

He was seriously reluctant. I was kind of impressed by his tactlessness. Even though, if he wanted to score with me, the natural thing would be to look at the pictures and gush.

"Come on," I said, "they're nudes."

"Really. Well, I'm sure *that's* something new in the art world. But seriously… it's weird to say, but I enjoy getting to know you without cluttering it up with that kind of thing."

"Do you want to know something really interesting about me?"

"Yeah, I do."

"I'm a total slut. Close to a whore, actually."

"Wow. I've never heard a girl say anything like that about herself."

"I guess you don't go to whores much."

"No."

"But you're out of luck because I've recently taken a vow of celibacy."

"Ha hahaha. You crack me up. I mean, you surprise me in every possible way. Now, do you want to know something about me? I'm also a celibate of sorts."

"By choice?"

"Hell, no! Not exactly, but I've been out of circulation. I guess you could say I'm getting over a traumatic break up."

"I don't know anything about that. I don't want to know anything about that."

Eventually morning came. As you can tell, we had some interesting banter of the sort that kind of pushed limits, then retreated, then was honest but had guarded moments too. He was a nice guy, pretty interesting, and I'd probably put him in like the top eight or nine percent of guys, among the ones I would never sleep with. I got him to help in setting up for my show too. He stayed up to like nine-thirty to help me, which was sweet.

The booths to the left, right, and behind me had erected partition walls, so they defined my space for me even though I didn't have any equipment. I had no roof or anything. Ethan and I had scavenged three broken easels that were abandoned at the back of a parking lot. I repaired them with gobs of duck tape, sticks, rods, and unbent wire coat hangers. I also got a bunch of sticks, driftwood, a "found" broomstick—that kind of stuff—and taped that stuff to the frames of the easels to erect a very flimsy and trashy looking extended framework. I spent about forty dollars on umbrellas from a convenience store which I connected to the easels and framework, to create a bit of shade from direct sunlight so the lighting on the pictures would be diffuse and even, to show it to the best effect. I also found some pretty big bits of smooth grey cardboard that someone had discarded from among their packing material, so I used that to create surfaces to clip my pictures to. Then I finally went and retrieved my portfolio, and begged the loan of a stool from the hotel guy who was a total sucker (but not that much of a sucker, because he required an eighty-dollar deposit).

When I put up my pictures with gator clips, Ethan got a kind of stunned expression looking at the work that he'd refused to look at the night before.

"Oh, wow!" he said. "I'm... amazed. These are really good."

"Thanks. You can go now."

"I'm serious, I really like your work. I'm sorry if I didn't want to look earlier, but I was a little afraid that if it wasn't good it would get in the way. I don't like to lie to people. Besides, soul-baring on the first night..."

"I know. But I'm all set up now, so thanks."

"You really want me to go?"

"Yeah, I can handle the rest."

He stood around, a little taken aback.

"Well, since you know I'm a sincere person... let's see each other again."

"I'm not even sticking around here for long. Chats are good. Let's move on."

"Wow! Wow! Alright, you're really remarkable. Thanks for giving me some of your time, and good luck with your show."

"Thanks. Bye."

"Bye."

The Show

There were a lot of people milling about, and like I said, this was a really big festival. Plenty of people came in and looked at my pictures. They were generally surprised by my odd setup, and some were made uncomfortable by the eroticism of some of the pictures. I got some inquiries on the prices, but when I quoted prices between seven hundred and a thousand dollars they looked like they weren't sure if I was serious. Nobody asked for a price on my one noodle-abstract, but I was planning to ask twelve hundred for that.

When things got a bit slow, or when I was bored or I just felt like it, I sometimes shouted "Art!" really loudly, to draw attention. The folks in the neighboring booths laughed and had a good sense of humor about it. Sometimes other artists or their assistants came around to chat a bit, look at the pictures, and pay me some compliments while trying to figure out my age and background. They were friendly enough, and on the few occasions when price was mentioned, they recommended that I come down severely in price. Booth presentation, they said, is a big factor, and annual regulars were more likely to command higher prices because they'd established reputations. They had a good sense of the market value of their works. I politely ignored their advice.

Sometimes, instead of "Art," I shouted "Hotdogs!" That produced more laughs, and it drew the interest of passersby. They came in, saw I didn't have any hotdogs, looked at some nudes, raised their eyebrows a bit, and left.

One guy who had come in and asked about some pictures came back later and offered me $2,400 for a collection of five of my best works. I told him he could have four of them, but I held out my best one, a solo of George. For that one I wanted $800. We haggled, and agreed on $2,900 for the five. So from that one buyer I turned a huge profit from the trip. I tagged those works "sold," and made arrangements for the exchange at the end of the day. It was ridiculous actually, because no one was asking that kind of price for paper-and-pencil drawings. I was glad I'd played hardball.

The rest of the day was mostly the same thing, meaning no more sales, and shouting myself horse while hawking my wares.

But there was one more significant event, perhaps the most significant. Another character came in; he was kind of old and worn looking, a white guy in name but more reddish brown in appearance. He had a scraggly, kinky, brown beard with some white tufts in it, and his style of dress was odd: a wife-beater stretched over his big round belly, with an open green silk shirt on top, coming half off of his left shoulder—which couldn't have been an accidental arrangement—and silver pants. I thought that a fat fairy-bum had just flitted in.

"That is *very* erotic!" he said. Then, with his nose, he indicated that he was referring to the abstract. "Haha ha!"

If that hadn't been the third time I'd heard that joke that day, or some variant of it, then I'd probably have laughed along with him.

"Hey, listen girl. Why do you draw such filthy stuff?"

"Art," I said, "if you'd really like to know, is the only thing divine that mankind has witnessed. It's an emulation of the sacred. Touch art, and you have the spirit of God within your grasp."

He took his greasy palm and pressed it to the surface of my abstract.

"Feels more like spaghetti with clam sauce."

He took his hand off, without smudging the work too drastically, and turned a serious frown on me.

"Listen, girl, where'd you hear that stuff. Are you bringing a New York attitude down here where it don't belong? You'd better forget your artsy bullshit. You might make me feel stupid."

"I'm not from New York, and I don't care how you feel. I'm from Hawai'i."

"Oh yeah. Cool. Well get yourself a grass skirt and put it on. I know a place where they'll pay you good money to dance. Just don't put any panties on underneath."

When he left, I had a good long time to think. I hate to say it, but that guy may have been the wisest guy I met. I mean, he completely showed me up for the fraud I am, and he's the only one who figured it out. I mean, I like art, I really like it, but I'm worshiping a ghost. Art's been dead at least a hundred years, and I was just fooling around like a naïve chump, playing, like a little bit of virtuosity in my execution would make some kind of difference. The charge I felt was really there for me only; the rest of it was just lines on paper as far as other people were concerned. Some people were fooled by a cultural bias that says that art matters, but there were no initiates to the cult of art there. They were just tourists and families looking for some emulation of natural forms to pretty up their living rooms. Even the guy who paid me nearly three thousand bucks—and by the way, I did not neglect to get paid before boarding the bus out of town—well, that guy was a collector. He'd acquired some aesthetic sense somewhere. But he was searching for something that I was only barely able to hint at. It would take me decades to develop something truly worthy of that kind of money or attention. There was no point in my fooling around anymore, particularly because I wasn't going to get that kind of luck, moneywise, for a good long time.

8.
Another Exit; Another Return

Not Interested in a Cure

Chloe had fled from her life back into treatment in my center, claiming sincere remorse and a strong desire to reform her ways. She complained that she wasn't making it on her own, and she believed that someone she had offended was recently stalking her and planning to kill her. And she'd made some kind of amends with her parents when she checked in, all before telling me the details above. But it was her decision to confide in me which was the biggest step in the right direction.

Everything Chloe told me was very revealing and very helpful in my understanding of her psychology. Without necessarily having to distinguish between the truth and potential falsehood of what she told me, I was able to get real insight into her moods, her thoughts, the challenges she faced, and her motives. But most of all I was beginning to truly *believe in* Chloe.

Although I am a professional psychiatrist, I've had my own struggles and existential crises. I can understand how the banalities of life can stand in rude contrast to the child's idealism which we all retain in some buried subconscious layer. To have that child's idealism so close to the surface, though—as Chloe's was—exposes one to many dangers, and makes one prone to the most egregious errors of judgment.

The *perfect Chloe* exists on another plane. It's as though she were pursuing a very natural and logical course according to an ideal map, but it bears no correspondence to the real map of the physical world her body occupies. She constantly collides with corners and rough edges, objects and people, and at the same time, the concerns which consume us on this plane below are completely invisible to her. She's unaware of ethical, moral, even sympathetic boundaries, and as far as safety is concerned, she could well walk right off a cliff.

I was developing some very specific ideas for a treatment plan, but there's no point in laying them out in detail here, because I was never able to make them into a reality. To talk of what *could have been* would be merely speculative. True to form, Chloe showed no interest in pursuing further treatment. As soon as she had given me her update on the latest events of her life, or her version thereof, she was ready to go off and pursue her course once again. I was not able to convince her of the degree to which I truly understood her, and just how much I believed it possible for her to get her life back on a sensible course. Or else, none of that mattered to her.

Chloe, now an adult, could not be restrained from checking out from our hospital whenever she wanted to. She was not bound by any order of commission, she had not signed any legal document that would allow us to keep her against her will, and her parents had no authority. She was also not impressed by threats. She walked away and waved goodbye without bothering to say where she was going.

CHARADES

But of course she returned. Weeping. Distraught. Devastated.

She came into the hospital on a Tuesday, our admissions staff interviewed her, and she was placed into a room and attended by one of our interns. I was not able to meet her myself until Thursday, as I was thoroughly occupied with other cases. Then she was brought into my office for an interview, which ultimately took up most of the rest of my day. Though she had answered several routine questions when she was admitted, she now was completely mute.

Chloe stared at me with an opaque expression. Over the next several hours, she communicated with me entirely in signs. She would not speak, and she sometimes paused for long thoughtful periods; sometimes she retreated from disturbing topics. But she could hear and understand my questions, so by a process of guesswork and prompting her to respond by gestures, I was able to elicit a rather detailed story. She was still careful of what she revealed and what she concealed in her telling. There was a heavy sadness and an air of tragedy throughout the entire exchange. Sometimes she worked her mouth like a gaping fish without forming the outlines of a word.

She "told" me about her continued series of absurd adventures, including a trip to Europe and on to Central Asia, where she travelled with an unnamed man. She only told me that he was a westerner and a "pervert" (between us we developed a sign to indicate this word, since she used it often). She had developed a new fascination for stars, astronomy, and poetry and art devoted to the night sky. She said that she didn't believe in Astrology, yet she did feel that the stars were "significant." She partially repented her previous disavowal of the value and beauty of nature, which she now came to value only in nature's "coldhearted nakedness." She believed that the thousands of years of human fascination with the stars and galaxies had imbued the extra-solar bodies with a mystic significance—that, in effect, humans had "invented" the stars. Not as a physical phenomenon, but as a metaphor whose reference is obscure.

Her fascination with stars was inspired by a visit to the remains of a fifteenth-century observatory somewhere on the Silk Road. She learned more about the stars from some of the late-night conversations she had with a couple of Uzbek students she had sexual relations with.

Should I interrupt here to explain that, *yes I know the reader will find it very hard to believe that so much can be expressed only in signs?* But, yes, it can be. Experiment, you'll see.

Another thing Chloe had learned to appreciate during her travels was the "inhuman, hateful faces of the mountains."

In our "conversation" it came out that Chloe had actually been rather fascinated by stars from her childhood until her early teens, but then had rejected this interest. She had a vague but fond remembrance of an early childhood visit to an observatory not far from her home. But in her later teenage years she became "sickened" (or "nauseated") by how often the stars and destiny were mentioned by her peers, so she had come to view astronomy as a pedestrian interest.

Again, Chloe cried a lot. None of the *deeper secrets* of her past would come out.

Chloe related in a vague sketch—still mimed—how she decided to flee from a man who was "keeping" her, and how she and some German tourists traveled back to Europe… she financed her own way, though she didn't say how she had acquired the money and denied that her recent relationships had had the character of prostitution… and from Germany she departed for a brief trip to Poland, where she went on a concentration camp tour before returning to the United States… specifically, New Jersey.

In New Jersey, Chloe paid a surprise visit to James Jones at Princeton University, where he was now a student of Art History. She showed up on the train, just south of campus, and called him up.

Now she spoke! Her spell of silence was briefly broken:

"We walked around campus… both feeling hopeless. No, I felt that way… he felt light and exhilarated. He had recently met a woman…

"I had told him we were just 'friends.' Now he dared to tell me about mixed feelings—pangs of loss and feelings of hope. Every glance I cast at him was wounding him. Again, I said goodbye.

"What a normal life for him to look forward to. Girlfriends and university, grades and jobs.

"From there, I was transported far into the Pennsylvania countryside, and I had a gun with me. I walked alone in an empty park. I shot at the sky and the tops of trees, and tried to kill invisible birds, black against the black sky. I shot at Uzbekistan in space. The skies were cloudy, and few stars were visible. And it was cold, and I had a nervous feeling that all the bullets I shot would return to bite me. I threw away the pistol, and walked awhile.

"I realized that I had been right: when it comes to space, don't look there; it's dangerous; you could lose your mind.

"I saw a police ranger cruising by with search lights on, looking for something. I flagged him down and reported that my boyfriend had abandoned me in the wilderness. I wanted to go home. The ranger delivered me to a little rural station where I spent part of the night telling stories to the cops, then slept on a bench. They took me to where I could catch a bus..."

Then she stopped talking again.

Eye Contact

As Chloe brought her story to a conclusion by shaking her head and waving her hand dismissively to my final questions—"Did you blame James for abandoning you?" "Did the police threaten you in any way, or search you for drugs, or were you afraid they might hold you until you could better account for yourself?" "Did you meet anyone else on your way here?"—she kept her dark eyes on me while removing her shoes, and her socks, and her pants, and to my terror she removed her underpants too. Then she sat on the floor (only partially visible beyond the edge of my desk until I rose a bit from my seat) and held her legs wide.

We looked into each other's eyes as a stunned and breathless minute passed.

I came around from behind the desk and offered her my hand, to help her rise. I kept my gaze from drifting. I was not concerned with her nakedness, and I hoped to communicate this wordlessly. She got up, then flung herself across my desk. Copious tears flowed. I pulled the small chair closer, and sat still, observing only her face and eyes. She met my glance, then seemed to be lost in the depths.

How can I account for this young woman? I thought. *Some would say she's normal, just a sort of neo-bohemian, irresponsible, criminal even, but not ill. But here I see a deeper, more perplexing insanity than most humans ever see. Is she "not ill" because untreatable by conventional means? "Not ill" because the cause of her troubles remains obscure?*

She saw me again. She would see me periodically; then her eyes would glaze as she saw only her own memories and visions. I held her warm hand, in a gesture of comradeship. Once or twice again, she made fishlike mouth movements, not even approximating words. But not often. Mostly she only wept. At times, I must admit, some boredom crept in, but I maintained my patient composure. We sat in this way until she finally fell asleep. But within that time, I felt that a bond of faith and understanding was formed. These were long, healing moments. A breakthrough in her treatment was imminent.

Trust, and understanding. These are key, always.

While we had been looking into each other's eyes, I had tried to project that I was now taking on a new role in her life, as a kind of surrogate. When I was sure she was fully unconscious, I whispered to her once, "I'm James."

While she slept, I was briefly lost in my own thoughts and sorrows. Then I rose and called in some nurses to dress her and bring her back to her room.

I considered some of the rumors that could arise because we had been alone for so long and the nurses had seen her undressed and unconscious. I was thankful, then, that my office was wired with a CCTV camera. In the last year of our program we had had these cameras installed as a precaution against any possible charges of improper conduct, to avoid criminal liability, and to record the violent outbursts of patients. This video footage should squash any rumors. Just the fact that everyone knew the cameras were present should afford me some protection from unkind gossip, right?

But then a mad thought occurred to me. What if—somehow— the video didn't show reality? What if it showed something that hadn't happened at all? How did this thought pop into my head!? It produced an extreme fear bordering on nausea. I felt I could positively peel my own skin off in the terror that suddenly visited me.

I got up and hurried to requisition the video from security. Privately, I watched the critical minutes in real time, in their entirety. What relief I felt. Just as I had hoped, nothing wrong had happened. There was nothing wrong with those images. Nothing wrong at all.

CONFESSIONAL

The next day, Chloe entered my office, ready to speak. But my office had been transformed. I had had my desk removed, and one corner of my office was screened off from the rest by a huge black lace curtain. The curtain—which I had obtained several months earlier for use in another case—stretched from floor to ceiling, and the pattern—which resembled a dense swirl of leaves being blown about in a gale—had very few spaces in it, thus making it nearly opaque when viewed from the lit side.

I sat in a comfortable chair within the narrow, shadowed space between curtain and wall, seeing only by the light that passed through from the other side. Beside me I had a small side table with a glass of milk, a notepad, and various other necessaries. Outside of my screened-off space, the office lighting scheme was set in *sedative mode*, in which a dim, colored light was reflected off the ceiling. The color was on a subtly shifting three-hertz cycle between indigo-blue and indigo-violet. I was invisible to Chloe, but I was able to see her because the curtain was close to my eyes, and though she was only barely lit, my eyes had become well accustomed to the darkness. In this way I had turned the office into a sort of confessional.

"Doctor?" she said as she entered the room, "Are you back there?"

She hesitated. Then said, "Look, we don't have to play strange games. I'm sorry about yesterday, but today I'm feeling… better. A lot better."

I rapped my knuckles loudly on the table to let her know I was there and I was listening. But I wouldn't speak.

She took a step back and sat in her chair facing me. The nurse had already closed the door. Chloe was still in a strange, confused state of mind, which was quite apparent from her puzzled look. And then, almost miraculously, she responded to my experiment exactly as I'd hoped. She addressed me, but yet not as myself.

"I know I've disappointed you terribly. You've always held onto a fantasy that you could rescue me from myself, but you can't. I can't be you, I can't."

There was a bit more hesitation; then she proceeded.

"You've told me to look at the world with a dispassionate mind. I can't. That's your style, and maybe only you can do that. But for me... passion allows me to see most clearly. The greatest force in the universe is hatred. Your goddamned cure-all love is a myth! Do you think I can be cured!? Cured of what? It's only the peaceful times we live in that have confused you; you know this easy-living business has encouraged us to entertain the most absurd illusions. Only the desperate ones, the ones on the fringe, they are truly aware, and their awareness is visceral, sub-intellectual. Even your self-sacrificial resolve is a lie you tell to yourself, because you don't dare look at the violent passion that boils inside you. But I can't help but see it!"

Chloe rose from her seat to approach the curtain. Quickly, I grabbed the air-horn and blasted her with a brutal "HONK!" so loud it was sure to leave her ears ringing for an hour or more. My own ears were protected by electronic ear-protection plugs that amplified voice but blocked out high decibel and impulse sounds. Chloe was amazed; she stumbled back. She sat.

That air-horn sound has always reminded me of a hoarse, chalky sound and feeling at the back of my throat and within the inner ear and sinuses. I can't quite explain it.

Within a minute or so, Chloe started talking again in her trance-state.

"The day when you are finally dying painfully of cancer, that will be the day when you receive the insight that everyone hides from. Unless, like most people, you use morphine to dull the sensation, and then you can blind yourself forever to the animal nature of man.

"I know, I know, I've lost myself completely in the swirl of life. I've even gone so far as to... to get to you." (She omitted something here, which I naturally assume is reference to a shameful sexual act). "I almost wanted to destroy your manhood.

"So, I know James, you can carry mountains. My god, you

know it all! Most suckers don't see the horror at the bottom of it all. You're without illusion, so how come you're so calm and… logical. Almost immune.

"But don't be so proud, because I'm going to have to face it all alone now. I'm sparing you, I really am, and you're lucky for it."

Chloe stopped speaking as though to James, then turned her head just ten degrees but abruptly, seeming as though returning from a reverie.

"Doctor, could I get some water?"

"Umm. Sure."

I wasn't prepared for this.

"Would you like some milk?" I offered.

"No, why would I want milk?"

"Ok. Hold on."

My phone and intercom system had been removed along with my desk. Complicating matters, a new nurse had recently been appointed to work as a substitute for my secretary until I could find a replacement for the young woman who had recently resigned. And I couldn't remember the nurse's name.

"Nurse!" I called out rather loudly. There was no reply. I fished out my personal phone from my pocket and dialed the front desk to have my call put through to the nurse sitting fifteen yards away. "Hi. Could you bring in some water for the patient? Thanks."

When Chloe had her water and had taken a sip, she asked, "What was I just talking about?"

I sat silently behind my screen. Only, now it seemed a bit silly and ineffectual to play mute. I contemplated using the air-horn again, but then I simply answered.

"You were telling James that you would now have to face the troubles of your life alone."

"Really?"

She had nothing more to say.

"But that's not entirely true, Chloe. I think we're on our way to really being able to help you."

She stood up.

"I just want to go to my room."

I came out from behind my curtain just as she was making for the door.

"That's good, go ahead and rest. Therapy is a process. It will take a while, but trust me. You're doing very well."

Chloe returned to her room, and the next day she began her demands to be released again. She did not engage in any further therapy, and I was not able to persuade her to stay. She left our hospital shortly thereafter.

9.
A Visit and a Conclusion

Only one week later, Chloe came back to see me one final time. She was cheerful, and seemingly full of optimism.

"I just wanted to tell you that I really appreciate what you've done. Actually, my dad insisted I say that. He's in town, he flew in especially to see me. Oh gosh, I've made such a drama for so many people. But really, I'm committed to making some radical and positive changes in my life. My folks have promised to forgive and forget everything, and they're going to help me prepare for college, so I can get back on my feet. You know there's no harm in playing the game, and learning is something I've always valued."

"Huh. Okay. This all sounds really good, but you know… recovery can take time, and you probably will need assistance along the line. Someone needs to give you regular therapy and counseling."

I was a little bewildered by her new character and style.

"Well, of course. Seriously, my dad and I talked about everything. I mean, not *everything*, he told me anything that I wanted to share with him was okay, but anything else is my business and he's not going to pry. He's taken time off from work, and he and I travelled a bit just to get in touch again, remember the positive aspects… I was a little bitchy during our trip. I think I'll always be emotional and moody. But…" Chloe cried a bit. "It's just teenage heartbreak, right?"

"You should bring your father in to meet me. We should discuss the possibility of a longer commitment period, and it has to be something that you will agree to. If you're really serious about getting your life under control, then sacrificing a few months should be no trouble."

"I'm going to get therapy in Hawai'i."

"Okay, okay. Please have your doctor contact me so we can discuss your further treatment and progress."

"I'm leaving tomorrow. But thanks! You've been so awesome!"
She left me. Again.

Final Communication

And then, when she was gone, after I'd made calls to check up on her—Chloe had not returned to Hawai'i with her father after all—when everyone was worried and starting to lose hope that we would ever hear from her again, I received a message. It read:

> *Dear Doctor,*
>
> *A rich, young, handsome, romantic, paralytic voyeur named Alonzo has invited me to stay with him on his ranch in… well, I'd better not share the particulars. And by "young," I mean forty. He has several other young girls down here, but I think he intends to take good care of me, if you take an open-minded view of the matter. I just might jab his eyes out some day, to cure him of his perversion and to purify his soul. But then, I do believe he might marry me, as he has promised to do on several occasions. You might think I'm an idiot, but you can't judge me more harshly than I judge myself. And, to tell the truth, I mainly had to leave for your sake. I admire you too much, and I just nearly fell for the temptation to sink my fangs into you, which would surely ruin you… but then what would become of your patients? You're a noble soul, and you will do great good until our decadent world pulls you apart. Until then, I'd advise that you reject any patient who even vaguely resembles me. If I ever come back to seek your help again, say no. Seriously. I'm crying as I write this, and I blame you for that.*
>
> *Goodbye, my heart.*

There was no signature.

Book Design

Book design and typesetting by the author.

Front-cover image, "American Black Bear" courtesy
The Field Museum Library, Illinois Urban Land-
scapes Project, identifier: Z84222.

Back-cover image photographed and designed by
the author.

Typefaces

Adobe Jenson
ITC Legacy Sans

Also by Paul John Adams

Metarules of the S·M·F
A novel of gang warfare—it's a revolution!
ISBN: 9780692893548

To order books online, visit the author's Amazon
page at: www.amazon.com/author/pja

To see what the author is reading visit:
www.goodreads.com/user/show/4319285

Optional Books: www.optionalbooks.com

www.ingramcontent.com/pod-product-compliance
Lightning Source LLC
Chambersburg PA
CBHW060211030726
47499CB00004B/1007